Wicked Dreams

Fallen Royals
Book 1

S. Massery

To the beginning of my love for fictional bullies
Thank you, Caleb.

Introduction

Hello dear reader!

If you've read me before (especially my Hockey Gods series), you know they run quite dark.

This book contains themes common to dark romance, including bullying, blackmail, stalking, and dubious consent. This story also includes mentions of childhood trauma.

Stay safe out there, friends, and happy reading!

xoxo,
    Sara

P.S. This series was previously published (under the same title) in 2020, but has since been revised.

Chapter 1
Margo

Impossible truth #1: My foster parents decided they didn't want kids anymore.

Maybe I should've suspected that. Their jobs were keeping them so busy: they stayed late at work, they left the house early. They were irritated when they *were* home. I figured the three of us were easy keepers, so to speak. We did our chores and kept quiet.

Impossible truth #2: The social worker found a new home for me.

That's not the impossible part. The impossible part is that it's back in my hometown, just three streets over from where I used to live.

Before Mom got addicted to drugs.

And before Dad got arrested.

Impossible truth #3: I'm going back to private school.

Part of me is elated that I'm returning to familiar territory. But the majority of me is terrified. I'm sure things have changed, that the people I went to elementary school with have changed, but it's going to be... safe.

"Hurry up, now." My social worker stands on the edge of the new home's lawn, waiting for me to get out of the car.

I take a deep breath and open the door, hauling my bag with me. I was lucky enough to get a real backpack. Each other move had my stuff in garbage bags. To be fair, I still have one, which I fetch from the trunk. But the important things are protected by heavy-duty canvas and padding.

"Let's go, Margo." She taps her watch. "We'll make sure you feel settled, and then I need to get to an appointment across town."

Angela McCaw is nice enough. She was assigned to me when I first entered the system, and our meetings have always been brief bordering on rushed. I don't blame her—it took me a while to understand that most of the social workers in New York are overworked and underpaid.

To know she's stacked this introduction with other appointments doesn't surprise me anymore.

I focus on the house, blinking in surprise.

It's giant. Bigger than my old home used to be, that's for sure. My eyes bug out when we walk up to the door. Even that seems expensive, the wood dark and frosted glass cut into it in a long, vertical strip next to the handle.

"What are their names?" My voice comes out scratchy.

I spent the night prior crying, and my throat is on fire.

The abrupt relocation... I grew close to my foster siblings while with my previous family. The three of us thought it would be a permanent thing, because that's what the adults always told us. There was no mention of adoption, of course, but we were guaranteed another four months together. Four months until I turn eighteen, and then I'd be out of the system.

Guaranteed. Joke's on me—I should've known that nothing is guaranteed in this life.

"Robert and Lenora Bryan," she says. "You'd be their first... no, second foster."

I hate those pieces of information but at the same time I grasp at them. Sometimes it feels like the more I know, the worse off I am.

I stop even with her and glance her way. "I don't suppose I should ask what happened to the first."

She purses her lips and rings the doorbell. "She aged out. That's all."

Once you hit eighteen, you're out. Well, that's what they say anyway. I think it's a little more complicated than that. There's housing available for former foster kids—as if the title ever goes away—that have adult supervision, curfews, job or school check-ins. It sounds more claustrophobic than being turned loose on the streets.

The door swings open, and a petite woman stands in front of us. She has dark-brown hair and bright, ocean-blue eyes. Her lips curve up into a smile, and she steps aside.

"Welcome, Margo! It's so nice to meet you." She waves us in.

First impression? She's... *warm*. And while it makes me suspicious, I can't help but smile back.

"Angie." Lenora greets my social worker with a familiarity I do not possess. "Please come in, both of you."

We walk into their large foyer. As soon as the door shuts, I have the urge to yank it open and sprint away.

It's not her. Or the house. *Just nerves.*

"Robert is upstairs," Lenora continues. "Margo, do you want to come with me and I can show you your room? We can go grab him together."

Ms. McCaw follows us up the stairs, clearing her throat every time I pause to study the pictures. Their other foster daughter looks like Lenora. Dark hair with soft bangs, big

3

blue eyes. She's petite, too, framed between Lenora and a taller man. It's more of those pieces of information, just taunting me. I can't help but stop to examine them.

"Margo," Ms. McCaw whispers.

"Sorry, sorry." I force myself faster up the steps.

Lenora glances back, and her face falls. "That's our daughter. She passed away a few years ago."

Shit.

She shows me where I'll be staying, and I drop my backpack on the full-sized bed. It's a nice room, simple enough. I just need to keep reminding myself that I have four months until freedom.

Robert comes out of a room down the hall and grins at us. "Ah, you must be Margo! Lovely. Lenora showed you your room?"

"Yes, sir," I mumble.

They seem like regular rich people, all sweaters and comfortable pants that look more expensive than my entire wardrobe. Their smiles seem genuine, and I pray that there isn't any malice lurking under the surface.

We all sit in their living room.

Ms. McCaw clears her throat again. "Margo turns eighteen in four months, at which point she ages out of the system. You have kindly agreed to enroll her at Emery-Rose Elite School—"

I choke.

"Robert works there," Lenora says, reaching out and patting my hand. "It's a good education, and the tuition was free."

I swallow hard and try to rein in my reaction.

McCaw eyes me. "Well, Margo was originally there on scholarship when she was younger. Is that correct, Margo?"

"The elementary school portion." I shift in my seat.

"They accepted me even though I've been in public schools?"

Nine of them, to be exact. Not just high school—middle and elementary, too.

While my last foster family was good to me, and I was there for two years, there was a period of about five years where I bumped around different families and group homes, and the changing location meant changing schools, too. I tried my best to make it seamless, but jumping into new curriculums every year has pushed me a little behind, I'm sure of it.

Seven years since I entered the system, and I'm almost done.

One more school.

My very first school.

"Congratulations, hon," my social worker coos. "You're going back to Emery-Rose."

I should be happy about this. It's a slice of familiarity, right?

"When do I start?"

"Tomorrow," Robert says. "They only just returned last week, so it's perfect timing. You'll be starting as a senior, although they mentioned you may need some extra credits to graduate with the current seniors. That's no problem, though. We can get you caught up easily enough."

I blow out a breath. I wasn't held back, which means I'm still in the same grade as those elementary kids with whom I started.

How many kids I knew are still there?

Will any remember me?

Those questions—and dozens more—whirl in the back of my mind while Lenora, Robert, and Ms. McCaw continue chatting.

Eventually, Ms. McCaw stands and brushes off her pants. "Margo, call me if you need anything. Same with you, Lenora and Robert."

She hands them her card, and then she's out the door.

We're left in silence that verges on awkward.

"Are you hungry?" Lenora asks. "Tired?"

I nod. "I think I'm going to lie down, if that's okay?"

"Of course, honey. I'll knock when it's time for dinner."

As far as new homes go, the first day is always the worst. It's like learning a new dance, and no one really takes the time to teach you the steps. New schools are the same, except... everyone seems to know I'm the foster kid.

Maybe it's the clothes? Or the attitude? Somehow, they always find out.

It's going to be worse tomorrow.

It's a private school, and some might recognize my name.

There had to have been a story when I vanished. My best friend at the time, Savannah, wrote me exactly one letter a week after I moved schools. It lasted two months, and then they stopped.

She asked me if the rumors about my family were true. Said it was all anyone could talk about. The parents, the kids. Was my mom a coke whore and Dad her dealer?

I didn't even know what a whore was at that age, much less *coke whore*.

I never answered her letters.

Alone at last, I close my door and flop onto the bed.

Strange to be alone. I used to share a room. Group homes were never quiet.

But here...

There are names I could stalk on social media to

prepare myself for tomorrow, but preparation never did me any good.

Instead, my thoughts turn to where my foster sisters, Claire and Hanna, ended up. They were pulled from the home like I was, being split apart without warning.

Hanna, the youngest, went first.

Then Claire.

And me last.

That was the worst. Sitting on the couch with my things stuffed into bags that leaned on my feet, waiting for Ms. McCaw to arrive and take me away.

I fall asleep to that feeling.

When my eyes crack open, it's dark. I feel for my phone and check the time.

It's after midnight?

The Bryans didn't wake me for dinner... Or maybe they tried. I slept hard, the first solid rest I've had in days. There were no dreams, no nightmares. Just... sleep.

Giving them the benefit of the doubt, maybe they knocked and I just didn't wake up for it. It's better than thinking the alternative...

I stand and crack my back, moving around the room. My clothes are still in bags by the door, the backpack containing my phone charger and toiletries right beside it. Ignoring it for now, I shove aside the curtains and open the window.

A cool breeze drifts in, but it's not enough. I slide the screen up, leaning halfway out. The house is brick, but there's nothing to grab on to.

My gaze moves up to the sky, at the smattering of visible stars.

After a long moment, I retreat and close the window, lowering myself to the floor. My phone's glow illuminates the room, the buzz of a text harsh in the silence. The need to check it—for some sort of connection to *anyone*—surges up inside me.

I crawl to the bed and grab my cell, scanning the text.

> **UNKNOWN**
> Rumors say you're back in town.

Who is it? The number is entirely blocked—I can't even see it.

> **ME**
> Who is this?

> We'll be watching you, Margo... Rose Hill isn't how you left it.

I shiver.

What kind of message is that?

They'll be *watching* me?

I slam my phone back on the nightstand facedown. It buzzes again, but I ignore it and crawl into bed. I block out the eerie message and the hunger gnawing at my stomach.

In the morning, things will be different.

But sleep takes a while to come back, and I don't think I've slept two minutes before my alarm goes off.

The sun has risen, although only pale-gray light comes in through the open window. I sit up and fight my immediate yawn. My eyes burn, and I look around the room in a new light.

I need to make this my home, however temporary.

Quickly, I dump the bags of clothes out on the bed and fold them into piles. What needs to be hung—not much, since I only own a few graphic tees and pullovers—are shoved into drawers. In the closet hangs my school uniform.

I pause and reach for the black fabric. The shirts are white button-downs, the collars stiff, but the black skirts are made of a thick, soft material. Gold stitching in both the shirts and the skirts tie everything back to the school.

Robert intercepts me on my way to the bathroom. He's already dressed, slacks and a blue dress shirt. A tie, even, although it's not knotted yet.

"Good morning, Margo! Did you sleep okay?"

I nod, my cheeks heating.

He doesn't bring up that I didn't come down for dinner.

"We've got breakfast downstairs. Lenora put some shoes options by the door downstairs." He smiles encouragingly.

"Thanks." I hurry into the bathroom and lock the door, leaning against it for a single moment.

I'm going to school.

I've been in Rose Hill for less than twenty-four hours and I am now about to start... er, restart... my senior year of high school.

With easy, nimble movements, I brush and braid my dark-brown hair. It's long and thick, and a lot of times a pain in the ass. Once that's done, I turn my attention to my face.

Mascara, concealer to hide the dark circles under my eyes, a shade of pink lip stain on my full lips. I practice smiling in the mirror.

It falls short. I can't keep the tremble out of my hands.

I add a thick swipe of eyeliner. The bolder the better. It feels a bit like a mask, and instead of smiling, I scowl at myself.

Okay.

I get dressed quickly and meet Robert downstairs. He slides a mug of coffee at me, and I smile at him.

"Figured getting up this early is hard enough without caffeine," he says.

9

"Thank you."

He points out the selection of shoes. "She got a few different sizes because we weren't sure..." He rubs the back of his neck. "Hopefully one of these will do."

She got me *four* pairs. Too many. I locate their sizes and try on a pair. It's a perfect fit, and Robert beams.

"We'll get your classes squared away first. Hopefully you'll just miss homeroom, and we'll get one of the kids to give you a tour." He ushers me back into the kitchen. "Easy day, right? Not too scary."

Yeah, right. I don't know what to say to that, so I don't.

We eat cereal in silence.

In the car, a new backpack is waiting for me on the passenger seat. My face heats as Robert explains there's a case of pens and pencils as well as a few notebooks in there. A calculator, too, for math. Things from the required items list.

I thank him, but...

It's a lot.

We listen to Robert's talk radio on the drive.

The high school is a bigger building down the street from the elementary and middle schools, and it looms like a castle at the end of the road. I don't remember paying much attention to it as a kid, as the others are not as grandiose.

My stomach is a ball of nerves.

Robert turns into the driveway, which then branches off into different parking lots. A little sign for visitor parking right in front, faculty parking. Student parking.

We cross into the shadows of one of the two towers, and I automatically shiver. He parks in the faculty lot. As soon as the engine is off, he faces me.

"I figure I'll be giving you rides every morning," Robert tells me. "And we can meet at the car after. If you want to do any sort of sport or after-school activity, that's fine. Lenora or I can arrange how we want to handle the pickup. But don't feel restricted, okay?"

I make a noise of affirmation, and then we're moving. Getting out of the car without delay. I swing the new bag over my shoulder.

I make the mistake of glancing at my phone as we walk up the wide front steps. There's the text from last night still sitting on my lock screen, and I don't even have to open it to read its message.

UNKNOWN

You'll regret coming back.

I shiver.

"Everything okay?"

"Yes."

Getting alarming texts from an anonymous person hours after my arrival? That's a fast way to get kicked out of a good home. When things seem too weird, some foster parents bail.

I don't blame them. I'd bail, too. In fact, I'd love nothing more than to run home and tuck myself back in bed and throw my phone in the trash.

My original home. The one that no longer exists.

Robert shows me to the office and introduces me to one of the guidance counselors, whose name goes in one ear and out the other.

She waves me into the office with a bright smile. "Margo Wolfe? Come with me."

I perch on the chair next to her desk, watching her type.

"You have a lot of different schools on your record," she says in a mild voice. "Why is that?"

"I'm a foster. Some homes didn't work out."

11

"Robert and Lenora are good friends." She's still typing, her nails clacking against the keys. "We were a little worried about them taking in a teenager, but..."

My eye twitches.

"You're going to behave, right?"

I've heard her tone before. A smidge condescending masked by fake lightheartedness. I hate it, and yet I sit perfectly still.

I say, "Yes, ma'am."

She flashes me a smile. "Lovely. Okay, here's your schedule. I had to put you in a lower math class, but perhaps you can find a tutor."

That stings. I used to love math, but the idea of it got harder to grasp until one day I just gave up.

"Thank you."

The bell rings, punctuating my words, and I jump.

"End of homeroom. You're going to be late to first period if you don't hurry. Show this to your teachers, it explains that you're new, et cetera..."

She passes me a pink slip of paper along with the schedule, which is a complex mess of numbers and words. Am I supposed to decipher this on my own? Figure out where to go, how to get there...

My heart beats faster. Why does the idea of being late seem like the absolute worst thing in the world?

"I don't know where to go," I blurt out.

She sighs. "Right. Follow me."

We walk out of her office, and her whole body perks up when her gaze lands on a boy filling out a form. And then I take a good look at him, and something in my chest loosens.

A familiar face.

His gaze snaps to mine, and his name comes out of my memories.

"Caleb Asher," the guidance counselor says. "This is Margo—"

"Wolfe," he finishes. "We've met."

We've met. That's a poor way to cover our history. I can't tell by his tone if he thinks it's a good thing or a bad thing. I would say good, but...

He has a vibe about him, and it immediately raises my hackles.

Caleb Asher.

His gaze travels up and down my body, but he switches it to the guidance counselor when he smiles. All charm, I think, especially as his voice drops lower to say, "I'll take her to class for you, Ms. Ames."

"Thank you, Caleb." She pats his shoulder and spins on her heel without another glance toward me.

If only that wasn't completely normal.

I am in my natural habitat as a complete and utter wallflower.

The clock ticks loudly on the wall, and I face Caleb.

He's examining me again.

"Well?" The word comes out rougher than I wanted, but I don't take it back. I lift my chin, silently daring him to say whatever's on his mind.

The corner of his lip twitches. He suddenly tugs on the papers in my hand, and the slip Ms. Ames gave me comes loose. Not bothering to even read it, he strides out of the room without looking back.

I hurry to follow, practically jogging after his quick steps. When we're out of sight of the office, he pivots toward me.

His sudden closeness has me taking a step back. My shoulder blades hit the lockers.

"Why did you come back, Margo?"

I frown. "I didn't have much of a choice."

What's his problem?

He laughs, leaning down. He doesn't touch me, though. He seems to keep himself perfectly under control, his gaze hardening by the second.

His expression could stop my heart if he wanted.

"You don't stand a chance," he whispers.

I move to edge around him, and his hands slam into the lockers on either side of me. I try not to jump, but I've never been one for violence. It doesn't sit well with me, especially as his smile turns into a sneer.

I'm caged in with nowhere to go.

"Margo Wolfe," he says in my ear. "Haven't you heard? I'm the king now."

He walks away, and I stay frozen against the lockers for a minute. My brain wants to catch up to the present, but all I can picture is the boy I once knew.

This version of him is so far removed, I'm not sure how we got here.

Instead of a charming, sweet friend, I'm left staring at the back of a monster.

One who seems to have scented my blood in the water.

Chapter 2
Margo

L ate. Very, very late.

When I eventually find the correct classroom on the second floor of the huge school, the teacher stops mid-sentence and glares at me.

"Sorry." I pass her the pink paper from the guidance counselor that explains who I am. I found it on the floor after Caleb disappeared.

The teacher, Mrs. Stonewater, scans the note and exhales. "We have a new student. Margo Wolfe."

Someone gasps. I bite my lip as chatter immediately rises around us. The teacher lifts her eyes from the note to look pointedly around the room, and they lapse back into silence.

"Take a seat," she says to me.

My gaze catches on Caleb—the bastard *left* me, and it took me too long to figure out where the hell I was going—and the boys around him. There's an open seat directly in front of Caleb or all the way against the windows. I start to move to the far one, but someone throws their bag on it.

I pause, my face heating.

Slowly, I walk toward Caleb. He raises an eyebrow at me, and I look away. I sink down into the chair in front of him. The weight of his stare is like a laser. He's going to burn a hole through my skull... Either that, or I'm freaking imagining it.

When did he get so beautiful? Dark hair and light gray-blue eyes, muscles packed onto his lean frame. He grew, too. In elementary school, we were the same height. He's got at least six inches on me now.

And hate.

Where did the hate come from?

"Ms. Wolfe?"

I jerk. "Yes?"

The whole class snickers.

"I was asking if you'd had a chance to read through the syllabus."

I slink lower. "No, ma'am."

She pauses at my desk and sets down a textbook. "See me after class."

"Yes, ma'am."

"No, ma'am. Yes, ma'am," the boy next to me parrots under his breath. "Such a fucking saint for a coke-whore's daughter."

More laughter, which the teacher seems fine with ignoring. Her back is to us as she writes on the board, and it seems like I hold more attention in the room than her.

If only the floor could open and swallow me whole.

Coming back was a mistake. I should've insisted on public school. At least that way, the bullies wouldn't know my history. They would've made fun of my secondhand clothes and haircut, but they wouldn't have picked at my past. My parents.

"You planning on snorting up under the bleachers at

lunch?" The guy leans across the aisle toward me. "Like mother, like daughter?"

How have I become an insta-pariah?

I try to ignore him, but he nudges my chair, shaking the whole thing, until I face him. I'm poised to say something—*anything*—but the words lodge in my throat. The vitriol in his glare stops me. He's almost as hateful as Caleb.

Light-brown hair, his nose his most prominent feature. I recognize him.

Ian Fletcher.

One of Caleb's friends from elementary school. Are they still close? They must be if he automatically takes up a stance against me. Pairing that with Caleb's reaction...

"Take a picture," Ian suggests. "It'll last longer than your memory."

I face forward and focus on Mrs. Stonewater. She's talking about the Civil War. I open my textbook and try to find where we are, keeping my head down.

Blend in. That's all I need to do.

I go from class to class, managing to slip in before the bell every time except once. The teacher reads the note from the guidance counselor, and I find a seat toward the back.

And that's how I manage to stay alive until lunchtime.

It takes forever to find my locker, where I drop off my bag and remove the nearly crushed peanut butter and jelly sandwich Robert made for me and a water bottle. I thought I might be okay navigating since I had been to the elementary school, but this building is a whole different beast.

I roll my shoulders, happy to have the weight off my back, and follow the straggling students toward the cafeteria.

Ahead of me, Caleb and his friends are making their

S. Massery

way in the same direction. I automatically slow down, keeping my gaze on them. I hug the lockers and hope they don't see me, while I drink in everything I can about them.

There are four, including Caleb. All muscular and lean. From the back, their heights and hair are the only distinguishing things about them.

I've seen some tough shit in public school, and with foster siblings, but nothing compares to the sheer arrogance that leaks out of these boys.

The feeling that at any minute they can turn around and spot me forces me to move even slower. Even quieter.

Suddenly, an arm is looped through mine, and I'm dragged down a side hall.

"Hey—"

"Quiet." The girl attached to me hurries me down this hallway. Her thick hair is light brown with golden highlights, and her straight-across bangs are slightly overgrown, covering her eyebrows and touching her lashes. She's about my height, maybe an inch shorter, and wears the uniform with the pants option.

Does she think I'm someone else?

"Never go into the cafeteria with a bagged lunch," she murmurs. "Are you insane?"

Um...

Technically, I have a sandwich in a plastic bag and a bottle of water. Robert promised to get more interesting food after work, but they didn't know what I'd like. And this girl is still pulling.

"I—"

"Rhetorical question," she interrupts.

We stop in front of huge, solid oak double doors. She whips out a key and unlocks one. When she yanks it open, a rather grand library comes into view. She ushers me inside, then secures the door behind us.

It's silent in here.

There are stacks of books on both sides, with a wide aisle straight down to an opening in the back with chairs and tables.

One of my foster families had books upon books, and the mom knew just how to stoke a sense of escapism through the stories. They were just a fleeting stop, but she had given me a book before I'd left. I read it a few times, then handed it off to Claire.

We walk down the aisle, and she drops her bag onto one of the tables.

"You're new, right?" she asks. "There are whispers about you."

I stick out my hand. "Margo Wolfe. Entirely undeserving of at least a quarter of the rumors."

She grins and puts her hand in mine. "Riley Appleton. Friends call me Riley."

"Nice to meet you, Riley." I crack a smile in return.

"Aha! We're friends already, I see. Come, come."

She leads me farther into the library, leaving her bag behind. She waves at the librarian tucked away in her office. There are cushioned chairs in the back, and she throws herself down into one. I take another and curl my legs up under me.

"One of the rumors is that you caught Caleb Asher's attention. Is that true?"

I frown. "How'd you hear about that?"

She taps her temple. "I told you. Whispers."

Great.

Her eyes are a startling shade of pale green. She leans

forward and balances her forearms on her knees. I get the impression that she's waiting for the story.

"I knew half of the kids here. I went to school with them until I was ten." I pull out half my sandwich. "Ian Fletcher seems particularly angry about my return."

She snorts. "Yeah, he's a bag of dicks on a good day."

That's a small comfort.

"What about you?"

"Me?" She presses her hand to her chest.

"You're intriguing, too. A bagged lunch—an apparent no-no—and a key to the library? I don't remember you from when we were kids."

She stifles a smile. "You wouldn't. I transferred in when my family moved to Rose Hill a few years ago, but I'm a junior this year."

Ah. I drag my finger along the hem of my skirt. "So you're familiar with everyone. Can you explain Caleb? We used to be friends, but now..." I shrug.

Riley sighs and digs into her lunch. "He's the captain of the hockey team. Everyone wants him—the girls around here would cough up a lung to get a chance to talk to him. You might remember his dad had his own company?"

"Yeah." I never knew the specifics. At ten years old, I didn't really care. I was more concerned about my dolls than grown-up business.

"The company grew super-fast, and his dad sold the managing percent probably around the time that you were here. The family still gets royalties from the company because of that deal. Which means they're *extra* rich. Caleb can do anything, and the school would bend over backward to kiss his ass. Actually, they'd kiss his ass and then name a building after him." She makes a face.

"Fun."

"He and his friends are untouchable. Royalty," she continues. "His closest friends are Liam, Theo, and Eli. That's who he was with when I intercepted you, by the way. Everyone falls at their feet, even the teachers. They will do anything to protect their power—although I like to call it their reign of terror."

"Who are they terrorizing?"

"Me," she half laughs. "Only Eli, though. The rest tend to leave me alone. The hockey boys of Emery-Rose Elite have a dark side."

I grunt. "And now Caleb has his eye on me."

Riley considers that, while I contemplate her. Is there a reason beside the obvious for helping me? Could she really be that nice? At this point, she hasn't shown a hint of using me for information, or for a leg up in the social standing by finding something embarrassing about me. Or personal.

The urges to either pull my cards tight to my chest and freeze her out or immediately make her my best friend war inside me.

"Tell me about you," I say instead. "Siblings? Best friends? Favorite class?"

Between bites, she fills me in. She has an older brother but no best friends. She hasn't found a home with a clique at ERE, but besides being bullied by Eli Black has managed just fine. Favorite class? Math.

I groan at that.

"Show me your schedule," she says, putting her things back in the bag. "I'll get you to class so you aren't late. The bell is going to ring in a few minutes, and it's kind of like a stampede when they open the doors."

"Thanks."

We go out into the hallway. There are a lot more people here. I crane back to check that Riley's still with me and smack into a hard, muscled back. I stumble away, an apology on my lips.

Caleb Asher turns around. My damn heart kicks into gear. I know he doesn't like me based on this morning's treatment, but I don't think my body got the memo.

His eyes go to Riley, who appears beside me. Back to me. "Run along, Appleton."

She gulps, then visibly straightens and pushes her shoulders back. "No. I need to show—"

"I'd be happy to help *our friend* get to class." He scowls at her. "Shoo."

I sigh. "It's okay, Riley. Thanks."

It's not her fault he's proving to be an asshole.

As soon as she's gone, he steps into my personal space and forces me away from his friends. My back touches the wall, and I find myself with nowhere to go.

Again.

"Wolfe."

"Asher."

"How's class?" he asks.

Everyone is pretending I don't exist or coughing mean names behind their fists—but I'd rather swallow my tongue than say that to him. Being a wallflower isn't going to fly at this school, I don't think. Not if the king of hockey is going to make a point of drawing attention to me.

Hockey. What a weird sport. I don't remember him playing when we were kids, but I was so young... It's violent, isn't it? Maybe he grew into the violence, too.

"Classes are going great. It's good to be home," I lie.

"We missed you at lunch."

I snort. "Yeah, okay."

He puts his hand on the back of my neck, his fingers soft for a second before they dig into my skin. I glare at him, but he ignores it. He uses pressure to steer me down the hall, into the throng of students waiting to head for their classes.

It's like everyone has congregated here, with the two sets of double doors closed and probably locked.

In the middle of everyone, he gives me a light shove.

Not expecting it, I lose my balance. My new shoes create an awful squeak on the tile, and momentum sends me to my knees.

Mortification rings through me, while the conversation around us stops.

Caleb leans down. For a sad, sorry second, I think he's going to offer his hand and help me up.

Instead, his lips twist. Disgust coats his features. "This isn't your school."

I'm pretty sure he's amplifying his words on purpose, because now everyone is turned in our direction. His friends join us, circling around. They're sharks, every one of them.

But it's Caleb I have to pay attention to, because he isn't done. "Why don't you go back to the trash family that raised you? Leave the rest of us alone. Oh, I forgot. Your mom's probably high out of her mind in a gutter, and dear old Dad is getting ass-raped on the regular in prison."

His words hit their intended target, and I am ill-prepared to hear them. Each one stabs into me. *Coke-whore's daughter. Dad in prison.* The whispers around us pick up, and if anyone didn't know who I was, or my past—they do now.

It's so different from every other school I attended. Anonymous foster kid, while still bullied, is a hundred times better than this sick feeling in the pit of my stomach.

"Why are you doing this?" I ask him. I'm still on my

fucking knees, unable to move. My legs would've given out anyway.

He leans down, grabbing my arm and hauling me back up. "Why? You don't really know anything, do you?" He sneers. "You're not a wolf. You don't pose any threat at all."

Do not fucking cry.

"Run along now, little lamb."

I bristle, but my eyes are burning. The *flight* instinct rears up, and as soon as he releases my arm, I bolt. My shoulder hits one of his friends, and it's like slamming into a wall. It sends me off-kilter, stumbling away. I get my bearings and push through the crowd.

People are staring, whispering.

The one from class, Ian Fletcher, makes a sheep noise at me.

I move faster, and the farther away from Caleb I get, the easier it is to breathe.

I duck into the nearest bathroom, and tears break loose. I fumble my way into a stall and lock it, leaning on the side wall and burying my face in my hands.

I didn't do anything to deserve this. Hell, all I've done today is walk into a firestorm—one that my departure seven years ago apparently created.

"Margo?"

I blow my nose in tissue and drop it in the toilet. "In here. Hang on."

After a long moment, I straighten and unlock the door.

Riley stands in the middle of the bathroom, her back to the mirrors. Her expression is sympathetic. "Are you okay? That was..."

"A lot?"

"Well..." She sighs. "Maybe he just wanted to send a message. He could leave you alone after this."

I wince. Somehow, I don't think that's possible.

"The golden boys of Emery-Rose are nothing but nasty to their enemies." She leans against the wall. "Sorry to break it to you. I've been the target of Eli's fury for years."

"They can't just get away with it."

"They can and they will." Riley makes a face. "Their families are the richest of the rich. My parents are well-off, and I'm..." She shakes her head. "I'm the lowlife around here."

"You're not." I brush off invisible dust from my skirt. "I'll take that honor, thank you very much."

It gets a laugh from her. Enough that I'm able to mirror it with a small smile.

She hands me a wad of toilet paper, and I take a second to clean up my face. My eyes are bloodshot, eyelids a little puffy, but otherwise, I look normal.

I don't *feel* normal, though.

The bell rings, echoing in the bathroom.

I meet her gaze in the mirror. "Maybe we should skip."

"The rest of the day?" Riley glances around. "On your first day—?"

Ugh.

"Okay, fine. Guess I'll just take the detention for being late."

We exit the bathroom, and she guides me toward my next class. I can't get a grasp on the layout of the school, and after everything, it seems like that's the least of my worries and also one of the biggest.

"If you want, we can meet tomorrow before school," she offers. "Everyone hangs out in the side courtyard since they don't let us in until the first bell."

Gratitude that she didn't cut and run floods through me. "Safety in numbers?"

"Something like that." She double-checks my schedule, then points to one of the open doorways. "There's your room."

For a split second, I envy the way she can shake off everything. It sticks to my skin like glue: the negativity, Caleb's fury. In the class, I hand the teacher my schedule. I don't bother with an excuse about being late.

She clears her throat, motioning for me to take my seat without a word. I'm grateful that no one I know is in this class... until one of Caleb's friends walks in.

The teacher doesn't even stop talking or spare him a glance.

He stops right next to me, staring down, and says, "Nice show, little lamb."

I keep my gaze on the desk and spend the lesson counting down time. I have four months until I turn eighteen, and eight to graduate.

If I can make it that long.

Chapter 3
Margo

Friday's schedule is slightly different. It mirrors my Monday schedule, which I haven't yet experienced, in that it swaps out a science lab third period for a gym class. One of the coaches gets me all set up with a locker in the girls' locker room, and I change along with all the other girls.

I managed a rather quiet Thursday without incident. Caleb missed the first period; Ian called me a few choice names but otherwise didn't bother me—what's the point if there's no ringleader to impress? I also avoided the lunch hall with Riley, which I plan on repeating every day for the rest of the year.

Even Friday's first period is tame. But my luck runs out faster than I hoped regarding Caleb, however, when I spot him marching across the grass in my direction. It's not fair that he looks perfect in a form-fitting t-shirt and shorts. He's tall and broad-shouldered, with a tapered waist and thigh muscles that could crush someone. And his ass...

My body shape is more akin to a bag of marshmallows in comparison.

I'm with the other girls in my gym class, waiting for the coach to tell us what we're doing. Something to do with running, I think.

Unfortunately.

He stops in front of me, making a show of looking me up and down. *Again.* His upper lip curls, and he points at my shoes. "Did they give you these as compensation?"

Huh?

He shakes his head and shoulders past me. I ignore that he flirts with other girls. I ignore that their glares burn the back of my neck and drag a blush to my cheeks.

We run as predicted. It rained overnight, and my new sneakers, courtesy of my foster parents, are uncomfortably wet by the time we make it back to school. Dismissed for the rest of the period, I head straight to my locker to change into my regular shoes and socks.

Except they're gone.

I look everywhere, my stomach knotting. I can't have lost them—my locker was *locked.* That's the whole freaking point.

But the longer I search, the more girls come into the room, and quiet laughter pours out of their hushed conversation. They're watching me search, and they know it's pointless.

Someone took them.

I'd bet anything Caleb is behind it.

When I fill in Riley on what happened, she gets angry on my behalf.

"We'll go shopping tomorrow," she promises. "Fuck him. Honestly."

I agree.

Robert doesn't seem to notice that I'm wearing the wrong shoes on the way home.

Does he hear the rumors about me?

He works in the art department. He teaches four different classes of various difficulty on both painting and film, and he likes to discuss what his students are doing over dinner. Sometimes he even pulls out his phone and flips through pictures of their art.

He's proud. Passionate.

Lenora is the same with her job. She has an office in Rose Hill but occasionally makes the trek into New York City. From what I gather, she manages financial accounts.

I've only spent two nights with them, but I can see how good they are together. They genuinely enjoy hearing about each other's work.

Several times, I've had to take a step back and evaluate how far I've come. I'm back in my hometown after seven years. I'm going to a fancy school that has classes like Renaissance Art History and Film in a Digital Age.

Rose Hill is unlike any other place I've lived.

It's small and tight knit, but only an hour away from New York City.

Three streets over from the Bryans' home, I used to live in the guest house of a mansion with my parents. My dad went to work like a normal person, and Mom was the family's personal chef. I hung out with the other kids, got into the prep school on scholarship, had a solid group of friends.

And then things disintegrated.

What started as a dream childhood turned into a nightmare. One I couldn't wake up from.

Robert doesn't mention the bullying, but he does rest his chin on his fist and says, "Margo..."

I pause with my fork hovering halfway between my plate and mouth.

"Hockey season is starting soon, and I just wanted to let

you know that I volunteer to oversee the spirit committee."
He smiles, proving he knows nothing of what's going on
between Caleb and me. Caleb, the hockey captain. "It just
requires some afternoon meetings, that's all."

I lower my fork. "Oh. Right, okay. I didn't know Emery-
Rose had a spirit committee."

"They run fundraising events, organize the buses for our
sports teams' away games, tackle homecoming and prom, things
like that. Every student has a portion of their tuition funnel into
their budget. But ever since the Eagles won the championship
two years ago, hockey has taken priority. If you're interested in
joining, I can pass your name along to the committee head."

I choke. "Oh, um. Thank you. I'm okay. I've got enough
on my plate..."

Lenora reaches over and pats my hand. "What
happened at school today?"

My lungs stop.

"Anything fun or interesting?" she prompts.

"Um..." I lift one shoulder. "We ran in gym today."

"Oh!" She grins. "Do you like running? I usually
manage a few miles on the treadmill, but I've always wanted
to be the sort who runs outside. Just not in the winter."

I feign a smile but end up going with the truth. Otherwise, I'd end up being roped into morning runs with her,
and that sounds like actual hell. "Running is my least
favorite."

Especially a few miles.

Robert bursts into laughter and quickly covers his
mouth. "Sorry," he says through his fingers. "Sorry, Len, but
the hope in your eyes..."

She waves him off. "No, stop. It's okay, Margo."

My face heats. "I—"

"It's okay," she repeats. "I'll stick to my treadmill, and hopefully your coach will move on to something more interesting soon."

"I did want to ask... do we have plans this weekend?"

Robert and Lenora exchange a glance.

Lenora is the one who says, "No, but we were going to run by you the idea of going to see a movie."

"That sounds great. I was asking because I made a friend, and she wanted to see if I could go to the mall with her."

"Look at that!" Lenora exclaims. "You made a friend? That's so exciting, Margo!"

Oh boy. My face feels like the sun.

"Who is it?" Robert asks.

"Riley Appleton."

Lenora turns to him, and he nods.

"Lovely girl," he tells his wife. "She's a junior, I believe?"

"Yeah."

"Good. Yes, of course."

So... they're not unreasonable. I go back to my meal with a modicum of confidence under my belt. We're going to a movie, Riley and I will wander around the Rose Hill mall, and I'm going to catch up on homework. I can't fail out of Emery-Rose Elite before I've even begun.

Can't and won't.

The sunrise finds me. I've been awake for too long. The shadows have crept across the ceiling until pale sunlight comes in through my window.

I had a terrible nightmare about a darkness that followed me around school.

I roll over and grab my phone, my fingers navigating to the messages from Unknown.

No one has stood out as a likely culprit—no one except Caleb Asher himself. Or one of his friends operating on his orders.

There have been no new messages in the last few days, no threats to worry over. Just the few simple texts warning that I'll regret coming back.

And so far, they're right.

Heaving a sigh, I climb out of bed and collect clean clothes. A shower to wash away the lingering sense of the nightmare and then something to scavenge for breakfast. Once I'm dressed and my makeup is in place, I go downstairs.

Riley is already there.

Sitting at the kitchen table with Robert and Lenora.

I stop short, cocking my head, but she just grins at me.

"Took you long enough," she teases. "I hope you're ready to shop until you drop."

I scoff. There's a plate of toast, another of eggs and bacon. I didn't take *that* long to get ready, but I already feel behind. Coffee, breakfast.

Riley keeps up an easy, steady chatter with my foster parents, and soon enough, we're ready to go.

Robert follows me to the door and calls out softly, "Margo. Would you mind picking up a few paints? And a roll of film? There's a store at the mall, and I've been meaning to go... you'd be saving me a trip."

"Oh, yeah. No problem."

He hands me a piece of paper with the details.

I tuck it into my pocket. It's the least I can do for him.

I follow Riley outside. We pile into her car, and I look around the interior. Leather, with fancy gadgets. A button for heating the seats or cooling them.

"Damn, Riley," I murmur. "You've been hiding your wealth on me."

She snorts. "No more than you've been hiding the Bryans' wealth."

"What's theirs is not mine." I turn up the radio. "It's always been that way."

She's quiet for a moment, contemplating that. It's just a fact for me, but I understand how it would take her aback. My parents shared *their* wealth—the little of it we had. We weren't rich by any means, and I only lived in this neighborhood because of my mom's job.

Going into the foster system, I was made very aware that I was not part of the families I was staying with.

Yes, some came with good intentions. But the business of fostering a kid is that it's temporary. There's an expectation that it will end.

Once I realized that, I held on to it with everything I had. It kept me from getting attached... until the last home. Until Claire and Hanna felt more like home than anything or anyone else had since I was put into the system in the first place.

Then they got ripped away from me, which was the biggest 'fuck you' from life. And I never saw it coming.

Riley clears her throat. "You're right. I shouldn't have said that."

I wave my hand. "Don't worry about it."

She exhales, glancing at me and smiling tentatively. "The mall is the place to be. Forgive me if you already know that. I know you used to live here, but—"

"It was a long time ago," I finish.

Some streets seem familiar, like I used to drive them in a dream. Others... Well, things change, I guess. I'm getting a weird sense of déjà vu.

"The mall is the place to be," I repeat. "Who should we expect to see?"

"The most elite of Emery-Rose Elite." She makes a face. "And us."

Great.

She turns onto the mall driveway. We zip up a steep hill, and suddenly the mall looms in front of us. We circle around it, giving me perspective of the size. I don't remember it from my childhood. Can't remember going as a kid.

Finally, she parks in a space near a side entrance.

"I need a birthday present for my mom," she says. "Something classy. Dad gave me his credit card."

I shake my head. Imagine a world where someone handed me a credit card and said, *Pick something nice out for your mother.* Maybe in another life.

Inside, we're greeted with pop music playing through overhead speakers and a lot more people than I was expecting. I guess I just assumed that malls were kind of a dying thing—but the first thirty seconds of being in one is absolutely proving me wrong.

"Wow."

There are some people I automatically recognize from school.

I duck my head, pulling Riley to the side. "I'm not ready for this."

"You totally got this," she says. "Head high, yeah?"

"I've got the urge to turn invisible."

She shakes her head. "This is your public debut. There

are no golden boys here looking down on you—just mean girls and their boyfriends."

I snort. "I think that's worse."

"Arguably. But we can't let that stop us, otherwise we'd never leave our houses. Let's go check out the makeup—I loved that lip stain you wore the first day."

Right. That lip stain helped stop me from chewing on my lips, which tends to be one of my responses to anxiety. The urge to trap my lower lip between my teeth comes over me again. It seems like people are staring, but that *has* to be my nerves.

Paranoia, even.

I follow Riley from store to store, although I'm hesitant to spend the money Robert gave me. It feels almost too precious, like I need to stash it away in case something bad happens. In the next four months... or beyond. Once I'm out, I don't really know where I'm going to go.

Will I even have a chance to finish out the school year at Emery-Rose?

Will I even want to?

In the end, I walk out of the shoe store with new boots in a bag and tennis shoes laced on my feet. My old pair goes directly in the trash.

That's one thing I had to splurge on. Riley practically insisted, bouncing on her heels next to me when I caved and brought the two pairs up to the register.

"Ready to eat?" she asks.

"Only if we can get froyo after."

For the first time, I feel light. I make a mental note to call Claire and Hanna, to make sure they're okay. It's been a week, and I don't even know where they might've been placed.

"Do you ever think of seeing your dad?" Riley asks.

We grab food and find an empty table.

"No."

She raises an eyebrow. "Okay, that was a snappy answer. So, you've obviously thought about it."

I lift one shoulder. Mom's been MIA for years, and I've known exactly where Dad is... until he gets released. And then I'm assuming he'll be in the wind, too. It's not exactly an easy subject. When I was younger, he refused to let me visit him. And then I stopped trying. The message was obvious: he didn't want me anywhere near him.

Abandoned by not one but *two* parents.

"I don't want to talk about this," I tell her. "Sorry."

Her expression is sympathetic for a fleeting moment. Her gaze moves over my shoulder, the sympathy quickly shifting to wariness. "Incoming."

It might be my imagination, but I swear the temperature in the room drops by ten degrees.

I twist in my seat, following her line of sight to the escalator. Four gorgeous boys lean on the railings, in various poses, on the way down. Liam, Eli, and Theo are joking around... but Caleb's already found me.

Somehow.

His dark hair is wild. His black sweatshirt has the Emery-Rose Elite emblem on the front in gold, and his jeans are doing almost too much work clinging to his legs and ass. He seems, by all accounts, the picture of relaxed and confident.

His eyes tell a different story. They bore into mine, and I'm surprised at how much it hurts. The vitriol is apparent from here. It was apparent close up, too, but this is different. He's projecting it across to me, and there's some question in there, too.

A silent, how dare you show your face here?

A question I cannot answer.

I turn back around, focusing on my food, and hold my breath. Earlier, I just wanted to be invisible. But I'm not sure how to accomplish that when I seem to already have a target painted on my back. I wait for him to approach and make some threat. To feel his fingers on the back of my neck or sliding into my hair.

Am I so depraved that I can already picture it?

After a long moment of absolutely nothing happening, not even a hitched breath from Riley, I glance back.

I zero in on Caleb again. They've moved away from the elevator and to a table across the food court. His attention is focused on a seated, pretty blonde girl. He lifts her out of her seat and steals it, then lowers her onto his lap.

My heart spasms.

More than just knowing he wants another girl on his lap —here comes another wave of familiarity. Recognition.

I face Riley, my mouth drying. "Is that—"

"Savannah Dunley." Riley sounds pained. Maybe because Eli glares at her, and Caleb now completely ignores my existence.

"She and I—"

"Used to be friends? I guess that was one of the rumors that was true." She gives me a half-smile, shoving a bite of food in her mouth.

I'm confused.

"Her and Caleb?"

"They used to date." She covers her mouth with her hand as she chews. "It was a quick thing. Kind of unmonumental, if you ask me."

That's so great. They used to date, but it was *unmonu-*

37

mental? What the hell does that mean? Especially when he has her perched on his lap right now.

"I haven't seen her since I've been back." I make a face. "I kind of thought she must've transferred or something."

"I heard she was gone last week." Riley shrugs. "Her family goes on random trips. She'll probably be back on Monday spinning stories of swimming with dolphins or having a private tour of the Taj Mahal."

"That's..." I wrinkle my nose. "Lavish."

"She's one of the lucky ones." Riley sighs. "Trust me, if my parents could donate a building to the school, I'm sure they'd let me go for weeks at a time, too. She does half of her coursework online. Just watch, she'll be here maybe four days of the five, every other week. And she's not the only one who gets special treatment."

"Why doesn't Caleb do that?" I can't help but twist around and watch them again. "It'd certainly make our lives easier."

He's talking in Savannah's ear. She's dressed exactly how I would imagine her to be. As a kid, her outfits were chosen by her parents. And now that she's seventeen— maybe eighteen at this rate—she seems to have inherited their style. A pink cardigan over a white-collar shirt, a pleated skirt, and tights. White high-top tennis shoes. Her makeup is flawless, cheeks painted a pale shade of pink.

She puts her hand on his chest, her lips parting as if she's surprised by what he's saying.

Her eyes flash to me, hatred so blinding that I drop my fork. It clatters across the tile, and the noise draws eyes. Not for the first time, I get the urge to melt into the floor.

"Fuck," I mutter, diving for my lost utensil. I reach for it, but once it's in my grasp I just... pause. Take a breath.

I shouldn't care that Savannah now seems to hate my

guts. It could've just been a misunderstanding, or she was directing her ire at Caleb's words and just happened to look at me.

Who's to say she even recognized me?

"Margo," Riley murmurs. She nudges my leg with her foot, narrowly missing my face.

Point taken, though. I can't hide down here forever.

When I sit up, Caleb is at the head of our table. Closer to me than Riley, leaning forward and looming over me.

I have to crane my head back, he's so close. He doesn't touch me, just stares. I can't decide if it's better or worse.

"What?" I finally ask.

He grabs my wrist, squeezing so tight my bones grind together. "This is how you hold on to something, butterfingers. Go ahead. Try to break free."

I tug on my arm, but his fingers hold fast.

"This isn't funny."

"We're in agreement," he replies.

I stand and yank, but he doesn't let go. He jerks me forward, off balance, and then backward. He twists my arm behind my back easily, folding me like a piece of paper. A twinge of pain travels up my arm, and I bend to relieve it. Bend and bend and bend until I'm staring at the floor and his shoes.

"Caleb—"

"Beg."

My stomach knots, and I glare up at him. "Are you serious?"

"You want it to stop? You want me to let you go? It's clear you can't do it on your own."

I shake my head. Helplessness crawls along my skin. My face is level with his groin, and a sudden shot of fear bleeds through me.

We're in a crowded mall—but what if this was happening in private?

As it is, no one tries to stop him.

"Please," I whisper. "Please let me go."

He drops my wrist, stepping back and grunting in disgust. Something flashes in his eyes—like he's angrier that I've given in to him. And yeah, maybe I should've stayed strong. Maybe I should fight the bully next time and make an even bigger scene.

I straighten slowly, smoothing my shirt and ignoring the pulse in my wrist.

The whole food court is staring at us.

They're not going to reprimand him, though. He's Caleb Asher, heir to a Rose Hill fortune. If his business up and moved out of the county, how many jobs would be lost? How many people would that devastate?

Just another thing I learned in my first week at Emery-Rose Elite.

Caleb is royalty, and it gives him certain privileges I could never hope of holding. One is that no one says a word to him about his treatment of me as he winds through the tables. He heads back to his friends like nothing happened.

I glare at his back, hoping he can feel it. If he does, he's unfazed. His shoulders remain even, his back straight. When he sits back down, he leans into Savannah and kisses her.

Their lips part, and his tongue plunges into her mouth. They aren't so much kissing as... he's invading her. She's trying to keep up, but this is so much more of a show than true intimacy.

He must get off on that shit. Or he's doing it to drive another nail into my heart, because my whole body feels like I'm drowning. At the same moment I'm glad he's out of reach, I don't want him to touch anyone else.

Why do I care?

If he kissed me like that, I'd punch him. I haven't actually had a boyfriend, but I've read enough romance books to know that kissing someone like you're conquering them isn't showing them you care.

It's just a performance, and I'm sick of being his captive audience.

When it doesn't stop, I frown. "We need to leave."

She sighs. "Figured you'd say that."

"I just need to get the paint for Robert, and then we should go."

We do that, and I practically drag Riley to her car.

"I don't think I like the mall," I tell her.

She laughs but nods, too. She picked up a few things, including a little crafting set for her mom in the art supply store. Bags dangle from her wrist. The car beeps, the trunk clicking as it opens. We put our stuff inside, and I exhale.

Caleb is probably still lording over the food court, but I can't stop looking over my shoulder. While my wrist has a few red splotches, my pride hurts worse.

"Hey, Applebottom."

Riley turns instinctively, her face shuttering when she sees Eli.

"Where you running off to?" he asks her.

He's more sly than Caleb. A bit on the leaner side, a hair shorter. His hair is light brown, almost blond, and hangs over his forehead. The tips just barely brush his eyelids. He rakes a hand through it, displacing the strands for a moment. They fall right back in place, and he smirks at her.

Not me. He doesn't give a shit about me.

"Just leave us alone," I say to him.

He smirks. Hands in the pockets of his jeans, he's the picture of ease. But something about him seems almost predatory, and Riley is definitely his intended target.

He's handsome, too. Maybe not as much as Caleb—or I have a one-track brain—but still enough to get himself in trouble. Hot guys are always in trouble and slip out of it just as easily.

His dark-brown eyes stay focused on Riley. "Come talk to me."

Riley eyes him, her teeth worrying at her lower lip. She's holding on to my arm, and for a moment it seems like she's going to tuck herself harder against my body. Forcing him to leave or pry her away.

He lifts his chin, the picture of bored indifference. "Just you. I don't give a shit about your friend, and Asher isn't going to scare her while we're gone."

I scowl at him, but surprise radiates through me when Riley releases my arm.

"I'll be okay." She nods, more likely attempting to convince herself than him, and follows Eli around the corner of the building. She doesn't even leave me her keys.

I lean against the car and wait, and ten minutes pass before Riley comes storming back toward me. Her expression is fierce, but her hair is messed up... and it might be my imagination, but her lips seem swollen.

"You okay?" I raise my eyebrows when she gets close enough.

She grunts. "Perfectly fine."

Uh-huh.

She studiously ignores my gaze and unlocks the car. She climbs in, and I follow suit. The car rumbles to life, but she doesn't put it in drive. We sit in silence for a moment, and I roll my eyes.

"What happened?" I ask.

"Nothing." She frowns. "I'm all good. He's just an asshole."

I'm not buying her act, but I don't think I can press her any more without risking the friendship. So I settle on saying softly, "And we know just how to deal with them, don't we?"

Chapter 4
Margo

Robert suggests I switch into one of his classes. Since I'm still in a smooth-everything-over mode, I readily agree. I don't necessarily think I'd be good at art, but painting is better than doing homework in a study hall.

Monday morning, bright and early, he slides a wrapped box across the kitchen island.

"This is for you." His voice is as warm as the coffee I've been sipping on.

It takes me a long moment to reach for it. Care went into folding the edges of the brown paper around the box. My name is written on the top in Robert's block-style print.

I unwrap it slowly, savoring the pull and release of tape. I can count on one hand how many presents I've gotten from people other than my social worker's obligatory Christmas present. When the wrapping falls away, I can't stop the wide smile from spreading.

It's the set of paints I had bought for him the other day, plus brushes.

"Everything you'll need," he explains.

"You were planning on me saying yes." Why are my eyes burning? I blink rapidly and try not to think about the sentimentality of the gift.

He holds up his hands in surrender. "Guilty as charged. Art can be therapeutic and relaxing."

"Even if I suck at it?" I ask.

"Yeah, even if you suck at it. But honestly, I don't think you will."

At school, Robert ushers me into the building instead of leaving me to wait for Riley in the courtyard. On one hand, I'm sorry to miss her, but on the other, I breathe a little easier knowing I won't run into Savannah quite yet.

Her glare is burned into my brain, and I can only imagine what nonsense she's been holding against me since I left. It seems a few people have a warped view of that year. Her. Caleb...

Robert talks to my guidance counselor. She switches me out of a study hall that was slowly boring me to death and into his painting class. When I have my new schedule printed and in hand, we're released from her office.

"Thank you," I tell him.

"I'm happy to have you," he says. "See you at the end of the day."

With time still remaining before the homeroom bell, I enter the courtyard and stick to the edges. Caleb and his crew are throwing around a football, taking up a huge space. I spot Savannah and her new friends in the corner. Some of the cheerleaders are smoking, cigarettes dangling from their fingers. My eyes almost bug out at the sight of it.

She's a *cool girl*. The one who rebels in the name of fashion. Short skirt, long legs, uniform shirt unbuttoned one too low. A hot-pink lace bra peeks out of her shirt. I imagine she has guys drooling over her, but all she can focus on is Caleb.

I have a niggling suspicion that she's the mysterious texter. The texter who has blissfully remained silent for the past week. I don't know if she would warn me away to my face. Would that ruin her cool-girl façade?

Underneath those layers, does the girl I was best friends with as a kid even still exist?

They haven't seen me, which is fine by me. I sit on a bench and pull out homework due at the end of the week. Someone else sits on the other end, but they don't get too close.

The bell rings with no sign of Riley, and I take a deep breath. I put my phone and pen in my bag, and my textbook slides off my lap. It hits the gravel. I reach, but a polished shoe steps on its spine before I can touch it.

"Hey—" I stop when I see who the shoe belongs to.

Caleb. There's darkness in his eyes, and I want to crawl away from him. How many times do I have to remind myself that he isn't the boy I knew? That something changed him for the worse, leaving this *monster* in his place?

"Thought I told you to leave."

I grimace. "Did you?"

I tug at my book, but it's useless. He leans his weight on it, crushing the spine.

Maybe he'll do that to you, Margo. If you don't listen to him.

I bolt to my feet, finding myself inches away from him.

"What's your problem?" I demand. "Why are you such an asshole?"

His laugh goes straight through my chest and decimates me from the inside out. His hand winds around the back of my neck, keeping me in place. But it isn't like I have anywhere else to go, with the bench right behind me and him at my front. I'm trapped whether he touches me or not.

Logic, however, doesn't stop the thrill that zips down my spine at the heat of his palm on my nape.

"Go run to Savannah," I goad. "Take whatever your problem is out on her."

His eyes flash.

"I have, little lamb. I broke her, and she still follows me like a wind-up doll." He tilts his head. "I have a feeling if I broke you, you wouldn't do that."

"What?" He wants to *break* me?

"Let's play a game." He leans down, until we're eye to eye. "First one to fold loses."

"Caleb—"

He pulls me forward by my neck, slamming his lips to mine. I fight him for a second. I struggle against the unyielding pressure of his lips on mine, but he captures my wrists behind my back with his free hand.

Hate radiates through me. He's *kissing* me, but it's all anger and fire. It's hot and stupid. Honestly? I didn't know kissing could feel this way. Desire and loathing rush through me in opposite directions—one to an unfamiliar pulse between my legs and the other straight to my head.

His lips slide against mine, soft and warm, and all I can picture is scratching his eyeballs out. Or tearing his clothes off.

What the hell is wrong with me?

His fingernails dig into the back of my neck, then relax.

He was the boy I used to love. I was ten and smitten. When we were torn apart, the thought of him was all that kept me afloat in the turbulent first few years of foster care. I wanted to get back to Rose Hill to see him, but it seemed like I could never get close enough. I'm strong enough to admit that I used to think about what grown-up Caleb would look like. What he would sound like. Sometimes I'd dream about him tracing my jaw, wrapping his arms around me and never letting go. Innocent touches for a preteen.

In my imagination, it was never anything like this bitter agony.

Here, now, he's someone else. Someone meaner, angrier.

I just want my old friend back.

An irrational thought strikes me: *He's still in there.* My friend is hiding inside this boy who loathes me—I just need to remind him who I am.

For an instant, I give in to the kiss. How could I not, with thoughts like these running through my brain?

My body softens, letting him mold me. It's a relief for him to take over, for his lips to part mine. I wait for his tongue to sweep into my mouth, for the rest of the symphony to strike up in my mind. Him winning is bliss and sugar, and I'm drunk on it in less than a second.

And then he's gone.

He releases me, and I sway. My eyes flutter open in time to spot his wince, but it's quickly replaced by a smirk.

Back to cold, although he was affected by that kiss, too. You can't tell me he wasn't.

His expression is distant when he says, "You lose, Margo. You know what that means?"

I clench my fist to hide my trembling. Of course I lost a game I had no chance of winning. It was rigged against me before he moved closer. Although I have a sneaking suspicion he lost, too. He just won't admit it.

Caleb has given me a handful of punishments in the

span of a week. Even kissing Savannah on Saturday was some sort of payback. Why would this be any different?

"It's going to cost you," he continues.

Instead of telling me the price of my supposed failure, though, he steps away. My knees bang together, and I fall hard back to the bench. He strides away with his shoulders straight, bag slung over one shoulder. He's the portrayal of perfection, and I am a wreck in comparison.

That was my first kiss.

He claimed my mouth like I'm no better than an object he's writing his name on. The problem is—I'm not a puppet who will dance when he jerks my strings. I'm not soft—my childhood has seen to that. I will not bend to him.

And I will certainly not break.

I just need to remind myself of my strength when he steps into my space. There's a flutter in my chest, although I can't pinpoint if it's nerves or excitement. Just being back in Rose Hill is a novelty.

After a long moment of trying to rein in my thoughts, I lift my textbook and brush off the dirt from his shoe. I stuff it and my notebook into my bag, skipping homeroom and heading straight for my first class. I'd be late to homeroom if I went now, and I don't want to be the center of attention. For five minutes, I get to be alone in the hallway.

Silence prevails. I lean against a locker and blow out a slow breath.

Caleb Asher has turned this into a game—but what kind? From pushing me down to pressing buttons I barely knew existed, like kissing Savannah, or twisting my arm behind my back, it's clear I am Public Enemy Number One.

But why?

My phone buzzes in my pocket.

UNKNOWN

Do you regret coming back yet?

Rumor has it, Caleb is out for your blood.

Fuck off.

I put my phone on silent, my mood officially soured. My lips still tingle from where Caleb touched them, and I can't help but press my finger to them. Can't help but replay that scene again, as twisted as it is.

The softening. The wince. The flutter.

The sneer.

I rub the back of my hand along my mouth, suddenly wanting to remove any trace of him. Disgust twists my stomach.

The bell rings, and I straighten up off the lockers.

In a matter of moments, the hallways are flooded with students. They stream out of the classroom I need to enter, the chatter loud and jarring. I am so apart from it, it's almost like I'm invisible. Standing against the wall, while my peers pass me by without a second glance.

It's oddly unsettling. But rather this than stares and whispers, which I'm sure will be Caleb's eventual intention.

No one witnessed the kiss this morning. The courtyard was empty except for us.

Was that intentional?

He'd rather kiss Savannah in a crowded mall food court.

Finally, the room empties. I slip inside, crossing it and taking a seat. It's the same seat I had before, because I don't want to rock the boat and choose something new.

If there's one thing I've learned across so many different schools: kids are all the same. Once they've claimed something—say, a seat in a class—they'd be loath to give it up.

The royalty comes in after everyone else. Caleb, obviously, but Ian—the lackey who picked on me the first day—is with him, along with a few girls I don't recognize. They take their time moving through the students, greeting everyone, and finally sprawl out in their chairs, laughing with each other.

Mrs. Stonewater stands from her desk and closes the door with a purpose. "We're going to start a history project that will carry us through the semester." She passes out papers and explains the details of the project.

It sounds boring, honestly. History is one of my least favorite subjects.

Someone raises their hand. "Can we work with a partner?"

"Yes."

"Do we get to pick?" another asks.

Caleb's gaze burns into the back of my neck. I don't have to turn around to feel it, and I pick at my nails to keep from squirming.

Our teacher's cold gaze shifts around the room, and she seems to be deciding something. "I'll allow you to submit three names to me at the end of class, and I'll be making final decision on the partners by the end of the week. Moving on..."

"Better see my name on your paper, little lamb," Caleb whispers. "We're inevitable."

This time, I can't hide my shudder. It's stupid that I can still taste him. I drag the back of my hand across my lips again, and he kicks the back of my chair. I repeat the motion, and he kicks harder.

Why? Because he doesn't want me to be as disgusted with him as he as with me?

I'm beginning to understand this resentment he's harboring. My own is growing.

"Stop," I hiss.

"Make me."

"Mr. Asher," Mrs. Stonewater snaps. "Are you paying attention?"

"Trying to, ma'am. Wolfe here is quite distracting."

The students snicker.

"Margo?"

Twenty-five pairs of eyes land on me, and I hunch lower in my seat.

"Sorry, ma'am."

The students' attention slowly drifts back to the teacher. We write out who we'd like to be partners with on papers that she collects at the end of her lecture, and I hate the way I only have Caleb's name to put down.

There's no one else in class I know. Familiar faces, like Ian Fletcher, I wouldn't touch with a ten-foot pole. The girls seem to be all in agreement about hating me on sight, taking the lead from Caleb's treatment.

The bell finally rings, and I book it out of the room. I leave Caleb and his judgment behind, dodging between people until I'm safely at my next class.

Rinse and repeat.

On the way to lunch, I manage to catch a glimpse of Caleb and his friends by the stairwell. It's the main route to the cafeteria, and the way they're taking their time raises my hackles.

They're not waiting for me, right?

Instead of finding out, I take a hall on my left. I hurry, because with every second it grows emptier. I take a right, then go up a half flight of stairs. I haven't been over here yet, and the next door I push through exits into a stairwell with rounded sides.

The steps go up and down in a spiral.

One of the towers, then?

Curiosity gets the better of me. I tighten my grip on the strap of my bag and go up. And up and up and up.

Finally, the stairs end at an open doorway. I step through, only a little surprised to find an empty classroom. The blackboard on a stand—not attached to the curved wall —has been wiped clean, and a small collection of desks face it.

I go to the window and look out. This one faces the second of the two front towers. Another window shows the front lawn and beyond, the houses speckled between the mature trees, the curving roads barely visible. In the far, far distance is New York City. The skyscrapers are just little sharp lines against the horizon.

"Contemplating jumping?"

I whirl around.

Caleb leans in the doorway, his arms crossed.

"What are you doing up here?" I ask.

He smirks. "I saw you trying to dodge us. Didn't expect you to come up here, though..."

His perfect lips quirk as he waits for my reply. His stare is too intense, and I find myself pivoting slightly to face the window again.

Off to the left is where I used to live... in the house behind his.

"Funny how things change," he murmurs, suddenly right behind me.

I stiffen, bracing for his touch. It comes a second later, his fingers brushing my nape as he moves my hair over one shoulder. A chill travels down my spine, goosebumps rising in reaction.

"What changed?" I grip the windowsill; I'm going to lose my balance if I don't. My knees don't seem steady around him, no matter what I do.

He leans in. Down. His lips coast against the top of my ear. "Everything except you."

My heart squeezes. I close my eyes, but it doesn't matter. He leaves me standing there with my heartbeat thundering in my ears.

Chapter 5
Margo

"I'm so sorry I missed this morning." Riley grips both my hands. "I overslept, and then my brother needed a ride, and my mom had to call and get permission for me to come in at second period. Are you mad?"

We are just inside the library doors. I'm late to lunch, but Riley was waiting for me in the hallway. After Caleb left, I took a minute to sort my mind and then hurried down.

But I don't know why I would be mad at her.

"Mad? Why?" I ask.

"For leaving you to fend for yourself." She makes a face, her lips twisting. "Was it not as bad as I assumed? Your dad —er, Robert—brought you in early, right? The courtyard can be vicious, and I worried."

I nod and keep my expression light. No need to further concern her. "We came in early and switched around my schedule a bit. I'm taking a painting class of his now. But other than that, it was fine."

She makes a noise in the back of her throat. Disbelief? But before I can ask, she continues, "Painting sounds like a cool elective, but I don't know anyone in that class. Maybe you'll

55

meet a cute, emotional artistic boy who will take you out for coffee with paint on his fingers. His idea of romance will be asking if he can paint you like one of his French girls—"

"Fat chance of that." I snort. "Have you noticed no one will talk to me? I'm invisible unless Caleb draws attention."

My invisibility doesn't bother me. I like that I can stand outside my first period class, and no one sends pointed glares. I like that the whispers that followed me around for the first week have abated.

"Still," Riley murmurs. "I feel guilty. No way around that."

"I'm fine," I reassure her. "I can handle Caleb."

We take our lunch to our chairs and spread out our options. We've gotten used to trading items, because Riley's dad likes her to be healthy, and Robert hasn't figured out my favorites yet.

Lenora and I went grocery shopping on Sunday, which was an adventure in and of itself. I don't think I've ever been in a fancy grocery store until that moment. Organic was the name of the game, even if I couldn't figure out *why*. Like, what made these apples any different from those? Except for paying two dollars more... She let me pick whatever I would want to have in the house: breakfast and snacks for school, lunch and dinner options.

It was just another piece of settling into a new home.

"Salt and vinegar chips?" I hold out the blue bag.

"Yum."

"Gross." I laugh and toss them at her.

"Trade you for... the carrots?"

"Deal."

She sighs. "By the way, Caleb and Eli are only low-level insufferable right now. But hockey season is starting up next week, and we'll be reminded of how much they *actually* rule the school. When they skate out and do their warm-ups..."

I wave my hand in front of her dreamy gaze. She focuses back on me with a start.

"Lost you there for a second." I laugh.

"You just wait," she says on a sigh. "You'll feel it, too."

"Feel... what?

"The carnal energy. No girl gets through unscathed."

I laugh it off, but my stomach twists. "It's that bad?"

"Every girl loses their mind. Football is big in the south. But here, hockey rules."

Interesting. Not to say I have no interest in the game, but... I don't know anything about hockey. The closest I got to sports was a foster dad taking us to his biological kid's high school basketball game one year. Even that, I could barely follow.

"We could go to a game," she offers. "It's a good intro-duction to the craziness, and no one would fault us for attending."

"You want to go to a hockey game?" I repeat.

She bounces on her seat. "Listen, it's just something you have to experience."

I narrow my eyes. But really, the idea of going to a hockey game sounds kind of fun.

She blushes. "And hey, I'm sure we can get into the party after, even if Caleb will be holding court with his friends."

I stare at her. "Riley Appleton, who are you? Hockey games and parties?"

Her blush deepens. "I've never had a friend to take, and going alone is a total buzzkill. And then there's the whole courage thing, so... please say you'll go with me? Please, Margo? You can sleep over my house—"

"I'm not allowed to do sleepovers without a lot of paperwork. Foster rule."

She heaves a sigh, her face falling.

"But..." I throw her a bone, even if anxiety is slowly winding around my lungs. "Maybe Lenora and Robert will let you stay at their house?"

She claps. "Yay! You talk to them, and I'll find out who's hosting the party next weekend. I'd bet it's at Theo's house. Word is, he has a giant swimming pool with a slide, and sometimes they jump in from the second-floor balcony. Cool, right?"

Totally... *not.*

"Besides, we've got some time. The game isn't this weekend but the following. Plenty of opportunity to ask your foster parents!"

"What could possibly go wrong?" My voice is faint.

I try to shake off the apprehension for Riley's sake, although it's damn hard. As long as Caleb doesn't find out I plan on going, it should be fine. We gather our wrappers and toss them in the trash, making our way to the front of the library.

Out in the hall, students are waiting to get into the academic wing.

My gaze finds Caleb in the center of the crowd without trying. I swear, he always has a beacon of light on him. How else can I pick him out so effortlessly?

And just as fast, he spots me. His beautiful lips tip down, down, down, until they threaten to slide right off his face.

His two other friends, Liam and Theo, are throwing around a football. Eli is in the middle of them trying to intercept it. But Caleb stands still, hands in his pockets and completely unbothered.

Except for the way he watches me.

"Why's he staring at you?" Riley whispers.

"Great question." I wet my lips. "Maybe we can just go a different way?"

"The other doors are locked," she mumbles. "And I don't have a key for those."

Of course not.

"Caleb!" Savannah brushes past me, headed straight for him.

She walks right up to him and touches his chest. He glances at her, but his gaze switches back to me. There's a new gleam in them, one that gives me pause. He touches Savannah's shoulder, but not in a friendly way. He pushes her aside and sweeps past her, still zeroed in on me.

I don't love where this is going.

"Oh dear." Riley gulps.

He stops right in front of me, impossibly tall. I crane my head back to meet his burning gaze. Something has him angry, but I have no idea what it could be. I just saw him an hour ago in the tower, and...

"Where do you go?" he demands.

Huh? I tilt my head, trying to make sense of his question. "When?"

"For lunch," he spits. "Do you hide out in the bathrooms?"

We're gaining more and more attention by the second.

But instead of cowing, I straighten. His interrogation pisses me off.

"I'm sorry, Caleb, am I supposed to report to you?" I plant my hands on my hips.

His eyes flick down, lingering on the opening of my

shirt for a heartbeat before his eyes trail upward. His movements are slow and steady, everything in complete control.

In opposition, my heart races.

"You should," he says. "Haven't you heard?"

"Heard what?"

"That I'm the fucking king of this castle. My word is law."

"You're ridiculous," I snap.

He grins. Not in a good way—in an unhinged way. I don't love that look and have the distinct feeling that I misstepped. It's like calling a girl crazy and suddenly being proven right. That she is, indeed, crazy.

Is Caleb about to go full psycho on me? Surrounded by people?

"Ridiculous," he echoes.

"Yes."

"You think *I'm* ridiculous?" His voice gets louder.

Riley inches away from me, and I can't even blame her for it.

"How?"

He takes a step closer, invading my space. His expression... I don't know who else realizes their school royalty is insane, but I see it. I try not to show any fear, even as it snatches at me the way wind tears at leaves in a hurricane. Endlessly, without remorse for the damage it causes.

His face is carefully blank, all for show, but his eyes can't hide his inner storm.

He's angry, unimaginably *pissed*, and it's directed at me. His fury, his fire... I'm on the receiving end of all of it. It's easy to see that when we're inches apart.

He grasps my chin, twisting my head to the side.

"Look at your friend," he whispers in my ear.

She's at the edge of the crowd and won't meet my eyes.

60

Her gaze is glued to her feet, but everyone else is staring at us.

"She's the smart one, Margo."

I flinch when he says my name. Am I so conditioned to *little lamb*—a nickname, by the way, I should rage at—that it's my actual name that gives me pause? I'm the only one who can hear him this close, and I'm sure he likes it that way. I'm sure he likes to keep me off-balance.

"Let go of me," I demand.

"You're not having fun?" He pouts and drops his hand from my chin. Except immediately, he snags my wrist instead. His palm is hot enough to brand itself on my skin. He reels me in closer, his voice pitched low. "You know the rules. First one to flinch loses."

"I'm not playing games with you." I half expect him to kiss me again, which would be absolutely ridiculous. He wouldn't do that in front of all these people. There's too much at stake. He's made it his mission to bury me, and that can't happen if he *kisses* me.

His lips quirk. "What makes you think we stopped?"

His fingers slide down my hand, falling off completely. I stand totally still, caught between wanting to argue more and simply wishing he'd walk away.

He does the latter, returning to his three friends. They'd paused their game to watch us, but they slap his hand in greeting, or congratulations for a job well done.

Caleb gestures to Savannah, and a stone plummets into my stomach. She's wearing the same uniform as me, but she could be a model. The button-down dress shirt is form-fitting, tucked into her short skirt. Her long legs are tan and smooth, extending out from under the skirt to the white socks covering her ankles. Her blonde hair is curled.

I shouldn't be surprised when he kisses her again.

This time it's savage, open-mouthed. She presses her whole body into him, her hands fisting his shirt at his waist. Their tongues fight, but it's a one-sided battle. Caleb is in charge.

That should be you, a voice whispers. No—it shouldn't. Not like that. But it *was* me, not too long ago, folding like a cheap accordion against him.

Instead of jealousy or anger, the emotion swarming me is *disgust*. His mind games shouldn't fucking matter, and yet... I can't stop staring at their mouths. So long, I barely register that his gaze is locked on me.

I cringe.

He shudders, more in tune to me than the girl he's locking lips with. I don't know if anyone can tell. But... I am not flinching.

I'm not losing this game.

And I don't. Time slows to a crawl. He bites and sucks at her lip, the obscenity of it burning my eyes. His friends hoot and holler.

Caleb separates from her just as the bell rings.

The river of students flows around them, and shoulders bang into me on the way past. They don't get the same treatment—the berth around both of them is wide. I lose sight of them for an instant, and when the path is restored, Caleb watches me. Savannah, on the other hand, gazes at him like he just impregnated her.

It hurts. I'm not quite sure *why* it hurts, because everything else he's done to me has been so much worse.

Savannah scowls, his lack of attention apparent. She follows his line of sight, surprised to see me standing in front of her, and then... *triumphant*.

Chapter 6
Caleb

Class passes slowly. My mind drifts, not comprehending the lecture the teacher gives at the front of the room. I paste on a bored expression and hope he doesn't ask questions.

Two girls try to pass me notes, but Theo intercepts and reads them. He scrawls crude little stick-figure drawings of people fucking doggy-style or in a sixty-nine position. He flashes them at me before flicking them back to the girls.

I don't catch how they take it. I don't really fucking care either.

My attention is on *Margo*. Filled with the sight of her, her sweet, innocent reactions when I do something obscene. Like kissing Savannah, which was risky at best.

That's twice now that I've used Margo's ex-best friend in retaliation, and an uncomfortable feeling worms down my spine. Savannah is known to get attached—especially when it comes to things she wants but can't have.

Nothing I can't handle, but something to be mindful about.

The second-to-last bell rings, and I unfold myself from the desk with a slow exhale.

Hockey practice has been kicking our asses lately. Coach Marzden just wants us to be ready for our first game. With a whole slew of new teammates, and us stepping up into the senior positions, it's been an adjustment. Nothing we can't handle, of course. I run a well-oiled first line.

Last year, at the end of the season, I was made captain. There was nothing better—except perhaps winning the championship title. Something we have our sights set on again this year.

My ribs are bruised from an ill-timed block the other night, hitting just above my padding. They're sore, but everything should be fine by the time we hit the ice to play against Lion's Head next weekend.

Theo follows me out the door. We go in the same direction, our classrooms for the next period in the south tower. We don't speak, but that's always been the way of things. He's quiet and stoic, only lightening up when we drag it out of him. It usually takes strong-arming or ribbing him incessantly to peel away his brooding mood.

His classroom is at the base of the tower, and mine is at the top. Four stories up. I march up the spiral steps without complaint, although my ribs make sure to ache at every step.

I've done my best to keep this part of my life low-key. It's not that I'm embarrassed about this class, it's just that I don't like to advertise it. I'd hate to get a bad rep for being soft—or worse, *artsy*—when I've done so much to protect my charming asshole vibe.

Finally at the top, I enter the room. I take a deep breath, shifting the strap of my bag on my shoulder. Up here, the scent of paint and paper is soothing. There's faint classical music playing from the desk in the corner.

Mr. Bryan walks around the empty easels and stools. They're arranged in a circle, all pointing inward. We've been working on various small projects, learning the different mediums, and sometimes our art class takes a break from *doing* to learn about the history of it.

The days that I walk in and the easels are stacked against the wall aren't my favorite, but I put up with it for the rest. Mr. Bryan and I have an understanding. He seems to see me without any of the strings that the other teachers regard.

Mainly, my last name.

The legacy of it, plus the business I stand to inherit sooner or later. My career has been laid out for me since I was young. I'm going to finish at Emery-Rose Elite at the top of my class, go to an Ivy League college—preferably Harvard, but maybe Yale or Brown—and then go work under my uncle. Learn the ropes.

With that kind of power amassing, it's understandable why teachers—and so-called peers, instructed by their parents—walk around me as if on eggshells. Or worse, try to get close to me for disingenuous reasons.

Mr. Bryan isn't like that. He treats me like everyone else, which at first I loathed, but now have a grudging respect for. I took my first class with him my sopho-more year. While I've been drawing since I was twelve, only recently has he convinced me to try other mediums.

"You might be surprised," he said, winking.

How could I resist that curiosity?

Now, I've come to realize that it's like therapy. Who needs to talk when I can mess with paint for an hour and soothe some of the wild anger inside me? It's either that or beat people to a pulp on the regular. Since my aggression can usually be handled on the ice, we breathe a bit easier during the season.

Hockey, too, fills a void. It's something I naturally excel at, and I am addicted to the rush of the game. It's strictly at odds with my artistic side.

I know, I know. I'm a complex human.

The classroom slowly fills, picking their regular spots. No one pays attention to me.

Art students, I've learned, don't give a shit about the popular kids. It's a relief not to be considered a fucking royal here, in the brightly lit classroom, surrounded by other disinterested students. It's like the art department has a mind of its own.

And then Margo Wolfe walks in.

My blood boils before I even comprehend why. Her dark hair is long and silky, pulled over one shoulder. There are little twists in some of the locks, like she's been nervously twirling it. Her plump pink lips are scored by her teeth.

The habit is a sign of worry, and it's one of her weaknesses. My uncle broke any bad habits from me before I even entered high school. But watching her chew her lower lip and scan the room, big brown eyes wide, the urge to slam her against the wall grows stronger.

My heartbeat rages in my ears the longer she doesn't see me. She really is like a lost lamb, standing waiting for a predator to devour her.

Me. I'm her biggest predator.

I'm half hidden by my easel, but it's impossible to consider that she can't feel my stare.

Mr. Bryan makes his way in her direction, but he's stopped by another student with a question. Margo's gaze falls to her feet and stays there.

Look at me, I want to yell. And if she still didn't, I'd go up and wrap my hands around her pretty throat until she had no choice.

My dick hardens. I shift, but I can't take my eyes away from her. This type of response from my body is... unusual, to say the least. I'm always in control of myself—until I'm not. But that comes with anger, not lust.

At the very least, if anyone glances back, they won't be staring at my pants. It's the face that's the moneymaker, at least in a school uniform. Naked... whole different story.

Look at me.

She jerks around like I had spoken out loud, her eyes big as saucers.

I hate that she became beautiful.

She was a pretty child, a head of dark curls and big brown eyes, but she's prettier without the baby fat. And the haunted glint in her eyes? It'd be better if I knew I was the one who put it there.

Right now, there's too much uncertainty. Too many gaps in time for me to be confident in my involvement in her life.

"Go sit, Margo," Mr. Bryan says, giving her a little push.

How dare he touch her?

I glower at him, but it's lost when she finally moves. Her steps are quick and short, more of a skitter than walk, and she picks the farthest easel from me.

That won't do. I gather my things and move to the seat next to her. "What am I? Chopped liver?"

Her expression blanks.

Before she can come up with something to say, Mr. Bryan claps.

"Welcome back," Mr. Bryan says to the class. "Let's start on a fresh canvas today, one of the smaller ones."

He nods to one of the kids, a fragile-looking boy who's flown under the radar for the most part. Tim? Tom? The kid picks up a stack of six-inch-by-six-inch canvases and passes them around.

"Quick warmup," Mr. Bryan says. "Let's use one color paint, and I want you to depict the mood you're feeling. Ten minutes, then we'll move on."

I open my paint set and squirt black onto my palette. I ignore Margo and dip a thin brush into it, getting to work. It's easy to sweep the black across the canvas, to project all of my locked-up feelings onto it.

As I said, this is *way* better than talk therapy. Even though I'm not watching Margo, I'm channeling my feelings toward her into this six-by-six frame.

And when I'm done?

Well, it's a self-portrait, obviously.

A black monster escaping from the closet, its lower half a vortex of black smoke. The teeth are the best: white against its black face. White eyes.

Mr. Bryan never looks at these. Not when we're around, at any rate.

I scrawl my initials at the bottom and put it off to the side to dry. Margo does the same, setting aside her square canvas. I can't see it, but I do catch a glimpse of baby-blue paint on her brush. She wipes it clean and sets it down, fiddling with the hem of her shirt.

"Excellent," Mr. Bryan calls. "How did that feel?"

Someone else answers. He has a particular skill of knowing exactly how to tune in and listen, and he nods emphatically at everything the girl says.

"Good. Now, we're going to start our semester-long project. I know a lot of you are intimidated by oil paints." There are a few snickers and gasps around the room. "Well, don't be. Oil paints are persnickety things, but once you've mastered it... Beauty. And endless possibilities." His voice is too fucking dreamy to be talking about oil paints.

Although an image flashes in my mind. Margo, covered in paint. Naked, of course. Maybe even tied down...

Hmm. Now that's not a bad idea.

"A lot like life," Margo says.

I snap to attention.

"Fuck no." It comes out automatically. Pretty sure I would've disagreed with her no matter what she said.

She bristles, and I smirk in her direction.

Mr. Bryan ignores us and continues. "We'll be pairing up and doing portraits. I expect you to see past the person's exterior and bring out their best qualities."

"Portraits?" Tim or Tom groans. "Like..."

I think he joined this class to work on his comic drawings, but the little shit would never admit such a thing.

"Like da Vinci," Mr. Bryan answers, "or Picasso."

"Wildly different examples," another student says.

"And I expect you to explore your options before settling on a technique," Mr. Bryan responds. "You'll turn in one painting on the last day of class. It'll be your entire grade."

Margo groans. "Is this based at all on skill?"

"Afraid you aren't up to par?" I goad under my breath.

"Yes and no," Mr. Bryan answers her. "Whether you start working on that final piece today or a week before it's due is up to you. Take time to improve upon skills or learn about your partner..." He shrugs. "Turn to the person beside you and introduce yourself. You're going to get quite familiar with their face. I'd suggest starting with getting to know them, and if you feel comfortable, start with a sketch."

That same kid goes around with bigger canvases, setting

them on our easels quickly before returning to his chair. There's a flurry of movement and chatter rising, everyone pairing up, but I remain still.

Margo turns in the opposite direction, but her neighbor has already paired with someone.

I clear my throat, pulling my lips up in the best imitation of a true smile. "Buckle up, buttercup. We're going to get quite familiar."

She swallows, and my pants tighten again. *Damn her*.

This is pure revenge—I'd do well to remember that. Toying with her, baiting her along...

She stares at me, the fear flashing across her eyes. She acts strong one minute and cowers the next. I don't know what's going on in her head. There used to be a time when we could practically communicate without words, when I could read her slight expression changes and she could read mine.

I fear we're well beyond that now.

"Please don't make my life hell in this class," she whispers.

I lean closer to her, not sure I heard her correctly. She should know better than to ask for favors. It makes me want to give her the opposite. To twist the knife just to watch the betrayal flicker across her innocent face.

We could do this all year. She'll ask and I'll deny.

Just like she denied me of my dreams seven years ago. I know that sounds dramatic, but the truth of it burns inside me. The old fury that I used to keep locked away stirs in my chest. It demands justice. Repentance. *Vengeance*.

I've held on to this anger since I was young enough to pinpoint blame. Over the years, I've fantasized about how to make her pay. Or at the very least, how to make things *right*. But it seems like the only path forward is through pain.

I lean back on my stool, kicking out one leg. Around the room, people are maneuvering their easels to get a clear line of view of their partner. Margo doesn't move. I just stare at her, trying to resist the urge to drag her out of the room and show her what *hell* is like.

Instead, I ask, "Why?"

"B-because." She looks away. Toward the teacher.

I scowl at her. "What does Mr. Bryan have to do with anything?"

She turns bright red. It's fascinating, really. The color crawls up her neck, over her jaw, and devours her face.

"I asked you a question, little lamb."

"Is this part of the game?" Her perfect brows furrow.

"Yes." Everything is part of this game. And it's a game because it forces me to not take her too seriously. Not like when we were kids—

Don't think about that.

For the longest time, I ached for my friend. But then I learned the truth, and it was like my whole childhood warped. Imagine learning that you're colorblind, and here are these glasses to give you a new perspective.

That's what happened to me.

Softening to Margo would be going back to a gray world.

She eyes me, the corner of her lip tilting up. "You're too curious, Caleb. I think that means you lose."

I lose? I blink in shock, then laugh. It's been a while since someone has surprised me. But that's the thing about Margo: she's full of fucking *surprises*.

She doesn't say anything, and her lips press together.

"Mr. Bryan." I draw him closer. "Margo isn't feeling well. I think I should escort her to the nurse."

He comes over and puts his hand on her shoulder.

She doesn't flinch.

She doesn't even *twitch*.

My eyebrows hike up, and my gaze goes from his hand to his face and back to her. I will her to pull away, but she does no such thing.

He leans down. "You okay, hon?"

"Just woozy," she lies. "I think the past week is catching up to me."

He nods, sympathetic.

Hon?

I want to strangle him.

"Caleb will take you to the nurse. Let me know if you decide to go home, I'll write a slip."

She nods and stands. I jump to my feet, too, waiting for his hand to leave her shoulder. When it does, I take her arm. I grip just above the elbow and lead her out of the room.

My breathing is steady. Years of perfecting my nonchalant attitude has prepared me for this moment. I try not to squeeze too hard, not wanting to scare her away just yet.

Instead of going to the nurse, we go down the spiral steps and across the top hall. Its windows look out toward the front lawn. She doesn't say a word until we're in an empty classroom two floors away. It's a science lab, the rows of benches set out with equipment for the next class.

But for now, we're alone.

I lock the door and face her. She's just now realizing there's no nurse here, and the first flicker of fear comes back.

I clench my fists in an effort not to do something stupid, like throttle her. He was touching her, and she didn't give a fuck. To think, I actually used to like Mr. Bryan.

Not any-fucking-more.

Leaning against the door, I spit out, "I didn't think you'd have the guts to bone a teacher."

She blanches. "Excuse me?"

"You and Mr. Bryan. I can see why you wouldn't want me to *make your life hell*. So many secrets to hide," I muse.

She snorts and turns, like she plans on going to the window or something. She likes to do that. She did it when I found her in the other tower, and now she's trying to retreat again. I move forward, ignoring the tug of pain across my ribs. I slide my fingers through her hair, burrowing until I reach her hot skin. I grip the back of her neck and pull her back toward me.

She swings around, much more pliable than expected, and hits my chest with hers. Her little grunt does dangerous things to my body. Surprise is on my side, though. I capture her wrist with my free hand and pin it to the small of her back.

"Tell me, how good of a lay is he?"

She's struggling against my hold, but my grip is iron.

"Does he have a giant dick? Cuddle you after—"

"He's my foster dad," she snarls. "Let go of me."

"No," I snap, just so I have a second to process. Then, "Foster dad."

The words sound weird on my tongue.

I know her dad. And her mom. That she has another family... I mean, I know she's had a myriad of other families, a lot of which were absolute shit. Does she call him Mr. Bryan in his home? And his wife? She can't be on a first-name basis with them... or worse, call them her parents.

Foster dad.

Huh.

"Caleb. Let go."

While I consider her words, she's still putting up a struggle. Her free hand has wedged between us, shoving at

73

my chest. But her squirming is only igniting a new sensation inside me. One that's been dormant for too long.

Don't get me wrong—I've fucked around. But this is different... this is electricity.

I walk her backward, until the tall workbench stops us. It hits just under where I hold her wrist captive. I release it and trail my hand up, over the side of her breast. I pause there. The urge to maul her when she's helpless...

It's not the time or place to give in to my baser urges. If it was, I don't think I'd stop at just touching her breast over her shirt. I'd want to touch her skin, see her nipples stiffen under my gaze, taste her...

I force my hand higher, up the front of her neck. Her pulse beats against my palm, and my fingers dig lightly into her jaw. "You afraid, baby?"

"Don't call me that." She tips her head away from me.

"I think you secretly like it."

"Is this because I said you lost?" She wriggles again.

God, I cannot stand her.

I shove my hips forward, making my unfortunate situation in my pants very clear.

Her eyes widen, and she goes perfectly still.

"Remember one thing about me." I put my face right in front of hers.

Her breath, each ragged exhale, touches my lips. My thoughts go back to the game, to the only way I won't lose my mind over her. The game with no prizes, no end in sight. Just Margo and I, locked in combat.

"I'll do anything to win."

Chapter 7
Margo

My head is spinning when I walk out of the classroom. Caleb follows close behind me, a menacing shadow I can't shake.

He said he'd do anything to win—but my heartbeat stutters, and the fear crawls up and down my throat. I can't speak. And I have plenty of things to say—or ask—but I won't give him the satisfaction.

He stole my first kiss. And then to feel his erection against my belly...

You're not supposed to show fear to the enemy. Yet underneath it all, Caleb wasn't always the enemy. He was a boy who I liked. A friend. We were closer than even Savannah and I, running wild together as kids.

I just don't understand how things got so twisted between us.

I don't know that I expected the warmest of welcomes, but I did think it would be better than this. It's been over a week, and I still can hardly believe that he looks at me with such vitriol. No boy has shown me such hatred...

And I don't know what I did to deserve it.

If I deserve it at all.

"Come with me." He's gruff, but he doesn't touch me. Not since he dropped his hand from my throat and stepped back entirely. Every emotion on display—most of which were not positive—suddenly disappeared behind a cold mask.

I follow him without a word, although I can't help but touch my heated skin. I wouldn't be surprised if there was a handprint seared there. Our route is twisting, down a level, across, then another staircase.

Finally, we reach the nurse's station. It's right by the front office where Robert signed me up for classes. Right by where I first saw Caleb and he pushed me against the wall.

The nurse sits at a desk in her room, and she looks up at our entrance.

"Hi, Ms. Peters. How are you?"

Why am I not surprised that Caleb can be charming when he wants to be?

"Margo isn't feeling well. Mr. Bryan said it would be all right if I brought her home, but I just wanted to check in with you." His voice lowers. "I'm afraid she threw up a few minutes ago."

The nurse's attention swings in my direction, and she tuts at me. She doesn't do more than glance, because apparently Caleb's word is law around here—even for the staff.

She scribbles a note and passes it to him. "I'll let him know, thank you."

Just like that?

His hand touches the small of my back, guiding me outside. He hands the slip to the teacher sitting by the door, who then waves us through.

I open and close my mouth, but then we're outside. No one stops us, and...

"You aren't serious," I say slowly. "I can't leave school. I'm not even sick—"

"Can't a guy bring a girl home?"

"Not when the girl is me and the guy is you."

He snorts, unlocking his car as we approach it. It's a sleek Audi. Matte black. He opens the passenger door and waves his hand for me to get in. I lean down and peer inside like someone might be waiting in the backseat.

The leather interior is black with lime-green accents, the screen on the dash already glowing with the car's logo. It just seems excessive. All of it. If I was rich, would I go for this sort of car?

It's an attention-seeker, through and through. The matte paint puts his vehicle at odds with everything else on the road, but he seems perfectly comfortable standing beside it.

Me? There may as well be a spotlight following me around.

With a long sigh, I climb in. He closes my door and circles around, taking the driver's seat. The car starts with a push of a button.

"Well?" He eyes me.

I glance at him. "What?"

"Where do you want to go?"

"Back to school." I motion toward the doors we just exited.

"You're a shit liar, baby. We're missing out on the last twenty minutes of the day, not skipping the whole thing. Don't blow it." His gaze turns contemplative. "Or do. After all, it'll just make things more... interesting."

Baby. Is it better than the patronizing little lamb, or worse? It implies a familiarity that has long since eroded.

But I also immediately objected to it—could that be why he's sticking with it? Twice in one day.

I cannot be afraid of him. Even with the posturing and the games, even not truly knowing his intentions. My head is spinning with everything that's happened in the last week —at least that much is true—but suddenly, I don't feel like he's going to kill me.

When some of the fear falls away, I can breathe a little easier.

Four months. I just need four more months, and then I can go wherever the hell I want. I don't have to finish at Emery-Rose. Hell, I could get my GED and move to Japan, if I wanted.

Slight issue of money, but whatever.

I face him, my eyebrow lifting.

What's the worst he can do?

And he knows it, judging from his expression.

"Tell me," he says. Dark and deadly. There's no crowd to witness his posturing, which leaves us with whatever monster chews him up from the inside.

There has to be something to knock him off-balance. Something that will give me the upper hand, if only for a moment.

I settle on, "Take me to your house."

He tenses but otherwise doesn't react. His blue eyes burn into my face for a long moment, then he finally nods. He backs out of the space without a word.

Now, *I'm* the one disappointed. It rings through me in a minor key, with too much dissonance to handle. How does he manage to make me feel so much with just a change of his mood?

"Now you're playing the game," he murmurs.

He guns it out of the parking lot. I gasp, clutching at my

seat belt as we fly down streets we used to run through. It's surreal, in a way. It's a dream turned nightmare.

"What if I don't want to play your game? I just want to end it."

My grip tightens on the strap across my chest. He drives like a madman, but his car handles his speed well. It's low to the ground and hugs the sharp curves. My arm bumps the window, and I grimace.

He ignores it, and soon enough—faster than anticipated —we're turning into a neighborhood of mansions.

Listen. I know Caleb is rich. I knew it when I was ten years old, too. It's hard to hide the fact that we lived in the *guest house* behind his, down the sloping lawn. Perfectly cut grass, manicured gardens, and a pool separated the back patio of the giant house his family lived in and the small two-bedroom one my parents and I did.

We didn't always live there. I remember a cramped apartment in the city...

He pulls onto the long driveway. The gravel crunches under his car's tires. It's a circular driveway, coming down off the main road and passing by the front of the house before reconnecting. There's a garage off to the side, and another narrower driveway that bypasses the garage and goes down to the guest house.

He parks right in front of the main house. Wide steps lead up to a wraparound porch, the wood-and-glass double doors foreboding. He twists to face me and grins.

It's the smile that belongs to a madman, leaking darkness like an oil spill.

"Sorry, baby. You don't get a choice."

I blink, at a loss before it registers that he's replying to my earlier statement about wanting to end the game. Or at the very least, not play.

No choice in the matter?

Great.

Without further ado, Caleb climbs out of the car. I take a deep breath and mirror his movements, following him up the steps onto the covered porch. He unlocks the door and opens it, gesturing for me to go in front of him.

This place...

Memories sucker punch me. Chasing him around, eating dinner in the summer on this porch. There used to be outdoor furniture down a bit, cushioned rocking chairs and side tables that we would sit at, listening to his mom read us chapter books.

My mother kissing the top of my head as she set down plates beside us.

All that, and I'm not even *in* yet.

My stomach twists. "I changed my mind."

I back away, right into him.

"Oh no, you don't." He grips my arms and propels me forward, straight into the house. "You asked for this."

"Caleb, stop."

"Who said we could stop?"

I dig my heels in, but he doesn't relent. It's either walk or topple over, and I don't think Caleb would mind either option. I finally take a step, then another, into the house that hosts too many memories to bear.

But the farther in we go, the more confused I get. Room after room, the furniture pieces are covered in white sheets and dust. The air is still and almost stale.

A chill rattles my bones, and I fight against the urge to rip myself free of Caleb's hold and sprint out of the house.

No one has been here in a very, very long time.

"What happened?" I manage.

He squeezes my arms.

"Caleb."

"I'm not sure a little lamb could be so direct." He talks above my head to the empty house. We enter the kitchen, and he stops suddenly. Releases me to stumble ahead a few paces and stare at the huge expanse of counters and appliances.

This is where my mother worked. She was their private chef, after all. She's the reason we ended up in Rose Hill, although the particular details of the job allude me. I was young, and it didn't really matter to me at that age.

We didn't eat with the Ashers—they weren't running a charity, Mom often told Dad—but I was allowed in when Caleb was home, or when she was preparing meals for their family. I sat at the kitchen bar many times, doing my homework while she worked.

Everything has changed.

My eyes burn, and I blink rapidly to try and keep tears from forming.

"I don't want to be here anymore." I turn back to him when I have a handle on my emotions.

He regards me, and nothing in his expression is nice or understanding.

I move to slip past him, and he catches me around the waist. I grip his wrist, but my fight is half-hearted. This place, and the horror of it being so abandoned, sucks at me.

He drags me toward the counter and lifts me onto it. He parts my legs and steps in close, effectively trapping me there.

His eyes are level with my throat at this angle, but he raises his chin to meet my gaze. Everything in me is screaming to get out. Being trapped by him only heightens it, until my skin crawls and I grip the edge of the counter with all my strength.

"Caleb, please," I whisper.

"Please?" He watches me. "Since when does *please* work?"

Please don't tell them, Margo.

His voice echoes out of the recesses of my mind, so loud that I flinch.

"One day I'm going to fuck you on this counter." His voice is low.

My body is a live wire, I just can't tell if it's the good kind or bad. One spark, and I'll set this whole house on fire. One touch, and Caleb and I will go up in flames. His words are brazen, crass... but I'm leaning toward him instead of away.

"You're going to enjoy it," he continues. "Even knowing what happened here. Because all you'll be able to think about is my dick in your pussy, spreading you wide. Hitting every. Fucking. Nerve."

One of his hands comes up and palms my breast. It's like he finally gave in to the earlier urge, and now he squeezes. Feels every bit of its weight in his palm. His tongue flicks out, wetting his lips, and he undoes the buttons of my shirt. He starts at the bottom, working his way up.

"Stop." I hate how everything inside me is alive in a way that it hasn't been in a really fucking long time. So much hate, I don't want him to touch me ever again.

Have I been numb before this?

Floating in oblivion?

Frozen?

He's barely touching me now, just his fingertips grazing my stomach as each button slips free and the shirt parts more and more.

"Admit you're attracted to me," he breathes, "and I'll stop."

I bite my lip. It's dumb, really, because I don't even believe that he's telling me the truth. Before, he said I had no choice but to play his game. Now he's dangling freedom as a carrot, and a tiny, terrified part of me screams to say whatever I need to in order to escape. To claim my sanity back, because he's slowly walking us to the cliff's edge.

Once I fall, there will be no going back.

"Admit you like it, and I'll stop," he repeats.

He focuses on my bra, tugging my shirt open wider. Just the top button is left connected. My chest rises and falls quickly with my rapid breaths. He hasn't touched me, and I'm already spiraling.

First kiss, now this?

Trailing a finger over the swell of my breast, raising goosebumps on my skin, he hooks his nail in the top of the cup. He digs in and pulls it down without hesitation. It exposes my breast, nipple pebbling under his attention.

What the fuck is wrong with me?

All I need to do is say stop.

Stop.

But I don't. I'm too curious, too fascinated, to put an end to this.

He leans down and touches his lips to the flesh just above my nipple. And then he bites, sucking hard, and my whole body stiffens. My back arches, lifting my chest to him by accident. His mouth brings pleasure and pain wrapped together. Building until I can't take it anymore.

"S-stop." I push at his head, and my skin pulls before he releases his teeth's hold.

For a split second, I imagine he will ignore me and continue. He'll push me past where I think the line in the sand should be.

But then he lifts his head, his wet lips so close to mine

we're only a moment away from kissing. His blue eyes laser in on mine, taking in whatever emotions are written on my face, and steps back.

He smirks. "Afraid?"

"Of you?"

His eyes gleam, and he looks down. "I know you're afraid of me. I don't need to ask. Are you wet?"

I choke on my gasp. Being *wet*—God, it sounds so dumb of me to admit that I've never really experimented in that department. It's kind of hard when I've had almost zero privacy. Sharing a room with foster siblings doesn't really cultivate an explore-your-anatomy environment.

So, while I know what he's talking about, and have tentatively made myself feel good at points in the past, hearing him say it so brashly...

"Yes or no, baby," he says. "If you don't answer, I can easily find out."

I just shake my head, my eyes big.

His eyebrow rises, calling me out.

Waiting for an answer I cannot—or will not—give him. Am I wet? Maybe. He was just sucking on my breast, and the tingling sensation between my legs is still present. I didn't notice it, but now that he's directed my attention down there...

I shove at his chest, but he uses the contact to catch both of my hands. He maneuvers them into one of his, and his other hand slides up the inside of my thigh. My breath hitches when his fingers dip under the edge of my panties. He pauses, meeting my gaze, then strokes one finger down the center of me. It's sudden and vicious, not at all gentle like my own hesitant wandering.

He does it again, more fingers dragging from the top of my pussy down to my slit. Pressing in just a little, then withdrawing. Back up and over my clit. I try not to react, but I can barely catch my breath.

When he withdraws, he holds up two glistening fingers. "Soaked."

"You can't just—"

"Take what I want? Or get away with this?" He rolls his eyes and licks one finger. "I almost wish you were right. We stood in a hallway full of students, and no one batted an eye at your misery. Want to know why?"

He slowly licks one finger, then holds out the other to me.

I gape—but that was the point, wasn't it? He pushes his finger into my mouth, swiping across my tongue. The flavor is barely there, but like salt and musk, and my stomach turns.

"Suck," he orders. "And I'll take you home. Promise."

My eyes burn, but I keep my mouth open. He waits for only a moment for my lips to close around his finger, then sighs. He removes it and licks it clean himself. His lips close around his middle finger, and that uncomfortable desire makes itself known again.

"Mmm," he murmurs, releasing his digit with a *pop*. "You taste like..."

"Like what?"

He smirks. "Like sin, baby."

My mouth drops open again, but I'm in no danger of him shoving fingers down my throat. He seems more interested in leaving this haunted house, pivoting and striding toward the front door with sudden urgency.

I hop off the counter and follow him on shaky legs. Exhaustion settles over me, cold and thick. It's good that we're leaving, that I don't have to return to school. It's out for the day anyway, and I can't imagine facing anyone who might've seen me leave with him.

He climbs in his car. Again, I follow.

Except the passenger door is locked.

He rolls down the window, shooting me a wink. "I said I'd give you a ride home if you sucked. You missed your chance."

"You can't be serious."

But he is, because the window rolls back up, and he hits the gas so suddenly I have to leap away from the car. He reaches the end of the long driveway and turns, heading away from the school. The sound of his engine reaches me long after he's gone.

Only then do my knees give out. My tears evolve into huge, hiccuping sobs.

From a first kiss to... *this*.

I regret ever being excited about coming back to Rose Hill. Not with a monster as the school's leader.

Chapter 8
Margo

I get home fifteen minutes before Robert. Luckily, he had a few after school meetings that delayed him, and Lenora is working late in the city, too.

He comes in and kicks off his shoes by the door and finds me curled up in the living room. Staying down here was difficult when all I wanted was to retreat to my room. But I need to make an effort with my foster parents.

If I don't, they may as well get rid of me.

"Feeling better?" Robert asks. "You looked pale in class."

I nod, my fingers digging into the blanket covering my legs. "I was a bit dizzy."

They have a big open-concept house. The kitchen is separated from the dining room and living room by a large island, and the other spaces are sectioned off by artfully placed furniture. I'd bet Lenora designed it. If she did, her style is impressive. She knows how to fill a home without overwhelming it.

But it just means that when Robert heads to the kitchen, I can still keep an eye on him—and vice versa.

"It's probably been overwhelming," he sympathizes. "Did you have anything to eat?"

I hesitate. I haven't thought about food—it was far from the front of my mind as I walked home, and then I didn't want to get in trouble for eating something I shouldn't have. I can't really say that, though, without it sounding like a guilt trip.

"I didn't."

I push the blanket off and move to one of the kitchen stools. It's counter height, the island flat with a sink in the center. He pulls a soda from the fridge and holds it out to me. I take it carefully, cracking it open, while he does the same with a beer.

"Lenora will be home soon, and I like to have dinner ready. Want to help me cook?"

I freeze. "Me?"

After I became a ward of the state, I learned to cook to survive. I can make rice and chicken, ground beef and pasta. I know how to thin out a can of soup to make it last an extra three days... But that was always about not starving. There was no enjoyment in it.

"I could teach you," he offers. "If you had any interest."

I swallow. "Yeah," I manage in a hoarse voice, "that'd be... that'd be great."

"Okay, first thing's first." He goes into the pantry and returns with two aprons. He slings one over his head and ties it at the small of his back.

I mirror him, but the ties are long enough to wrap around my waist and knot in the front. It's very clearly Lenora's, and a twinge of guilt at borrowing something without asking almost makes me take it off.

But Robert gave it to me to use... surely it's okay?

"You look pale again." He picks up my soda can and

offers it to me. "The sugar will help until we can get some sustenance in you."

I manage a smile.

He points to the fridge and gives me a list of items to retrieve. While I do that, he pulls out pans and a pot, gleaming knives, a cutting board.

"Have you chopped onions before?"

I shake my head.

"Okay." He takes the huge knife and shows me how to do it. "If your eyes water, it's totally normal. I have that effect on people."

I laugh.

Laugh. Then stop just as fast.

The corner of his lip turns up, and he leaves me to it. I'm mindful of the safety tips he just advised, because the last thing we need is a trip to urgent care for cutting my finger off.

And sure enough, my eyes burn and water. Tears drip down my cheeks by the time I'm done. My face is hot, and I wipe at it with the back of my hand as soon as I set the knife down.

"You good?"

"Yeah," I sniff.

"Let's bring those onions over here, we're going to caramelize them."

I bring the board over and use the knife to slide the tiny pieces into the pan.

He takes both from me and hands me a wooden spoon. "Just move it around constantly so nothing burns."

With that, I man the stove, and he chops something else.

I don't even know what we're making, and I think we're past the point of asking.

It isn't until we have a simmering, meat red sauce in

front of me, with a pot of pasta boiling on the diagonal burner, that the Italian-ness of it hits me. And also, splatters of sauce hit me—well, the apron. Little speckles that are nearly orange. I changed into a sweatshirt when I got home, and I'm grateful I don't have to worry about staining the white uniform shirt.

We've made spaghetti.

"A time-old classic," Robert says.

The front door opens, and Lenora's sing-song voice floats ahead of her entrance.

"It smells amazing in here!" She comes into the kitchen. "Oh, Margo, you're cooking!"

My face burns, but I don't know what to say. Sorry for using your apron? I hope I didn't accidentally poison the tomato sauce?

She doesn't wait for a reply, though, and comes over and hugs me.

It takes me a minute to unlock my muscles and hug her back. Touching is a weird thing in foster care. It gets to the point that you can't really trust anyone, especially once you're a teenager.

I survived all of that.

She rubs my back in small circles, and I lean my cheek on her shoulder. I close my eyes, absorbing her warmth. But then it's over.

"I'm sorry," she says. "I should've asked—"

"It was just what I needed," I say.

"Margo came home early from school," Robert says. "She wasn't feeling well."

Lenora tuts and touches my forehead with the back of her hand. It's so... well... *motherly*, that my eyes burn for the fifteenth time this afternoon. And, unfortunately, it's the kindness of the small gesture that breaks the dam.

Or maybe it was the onions.

Either way, I can't stop the flood of tears. My face crumples.

"Oh, Margo," Lenora whispers. "It's okay, honey."

She hugs me again, tighter, and I try to remember how to breathe. And then Robert is joining in, chuckling to himself.

"I felt left out," he whispers above our heads.

I laugh, too, and Lenora follows.

When I've collected myself, I slowly step out of their embrace.

"You're home," Lenora says firmly. "I believe that, and I hope you do, too."

I don't see it, and it's not that I don't like them. I actually really, really do.

It's just that I don't believe in happily ever afters for me. Not anymore.

Lenora makes a salad while Robert makes garlic bread, and I sit and watch them move in sync around the kitchen. She talks about her co-workers—one's in her second trimester, and another just got engaged—and articles she read. Robert details anecdotes about nameless students, including one that tripped and dumped dirty paint water across his floor.

I don't have much to contribute, but the longer I sit and watch them, the more I realize... that's what I want in a relationship. The comfort, the ease. The laughter.

We finish dinner at the kitchen table, and we all clean up. Lenora collects the leftovers, Robert rinses the plates, and I stow them in the dishwasher. We're done in no time.

There's no moment for awkwardness. Robert guides me into the living room and hands me the remote, saying to pick a movie for us to watch. Lenora disappears upstairs to change out of her work clothes.

I fiddle with the hem of my sweatshirt with one hand, pulling on a loose thread while scrolling the movie channels. I finally land on one I'd been wanting to watch and glance over to catch Robert's approving nod.

When Lenora joins us, she sits beside me on the couch.

And it's *nice*. I know I've been here a week already. I know I should be more comfortable, but tonight is the first we've had a chance to do this. The other nights were simple dinners, no big fuss or production, and I retreated to my room as soon as they were over.

When the movie ends, I stretch and yawn. I beg off to bed, and they both wish me goodnight. With a glass of water in hand, I trot upstairs and step into my room.

I close the door and rest my forehead on it in the darkness.

My heart is full, and my smile is quick to appear. It was a good night. One that I now have to strong-arm into a box, because this cannot be my new normal.

If I believe that, then being proven wrong will break me.

A long, slow exhale later, all those happy feelings are bundled up in the back of my mind. I don't want to let go of the effervescence just yet. I keep a piece of it—like Lenora's cheerful greeting—front and center.

Finally under control, I cross the room and set my glass down. It's still dark, with just the streetlamps and moonlight coming through the front window. The fluttering curtain catches my attention, as does the chilled wind that sweeps in.

I didn't leave my window open.

The lamp on my desk clicks on. I whirl toward the light and gasp. I slap my hand over my mouth.

Caleb leans against the wall. One hand in his pocket, the other hanging loose. He's the picture of smug arrogance. His dark hair is mussed, like he's been running his fingers through it, and the ends are damp. I can't help but take in his olive-green long-sleeved Henley shirt, the way it fits snugly to his body. His jeans are light-washed and ripped, and his tennis shoes are white and pristine.

I can't manage to keep a pair from scuffing in my first week of owning them—but I think that comes down to the fact that I wear my new shoes into the ground. I don't get the luxury of only wearing a certain pair sometimes.

"You could take a picture," he drawls. "It would last longer."

I scowl. "Get out."

He smirks and nudges my pajama pants from where I left them this morning. "Have you been dreaming of me?"

"Only nightmares." I square my shoulders and smile sweetly. "That's what you like to be, right? The monster chasing me?"

He tilts his head and pushes off the wall. The bed is still between us, and it might take him a minute to get to the door. It's closer to me than him. But do I really want to burst out and let Lenora and Robert know—

Caleb *knows* Robert.

"Any excuse you make about me being here will sound like a horny girl's lie," Caleb says in a low voice. He peels off his shirt. "Especially if they find me naked and you out of sorts."

"Shut up," I hiss. "Did you come in the window?"

He inclines his chin. His jaw is sharp enough to cut glass, and he knows just how to move to accentuate that feature. I swallow sharply.

I go to the door, ready to throw it open and demand that

he leave anyway. I mean, fuck it, right? There's a slim chance...

He meets me there, keeping it closed with one hand over my head. His other goes to my hip, slowly rotating me until my back is flush to the wall.

"I think you like the idea of me in your room." His gaze drops to my sweatshirt. It's from The Wrecks merch line, although I was able to snag it secondhand. I fucking love that band, even though I'd never be able to afford one of their concerts.

"You and your fucking mind games." I shake my head. "Isn't tormenting me in school enough?"

He's solemn when he answers, "No."

"No?"

"It's not enough. Don't think it ever will be."

I let my head fall back. His eyes are dark. "Why?"

His lips ghost along the shell of my ear. "Because you fucking deserve it."

I laugh. "I deserve torment?"

He shakes his head. "You didn't just get that, little lamb. You're getting all of it. My whole self utterly focused on your sweet reactions. The fear, the excitement, the disgust. You fold when I want you to... but sometimes you stand up straight and face me."

My legs tremble. "What does that mean?"

"It means..." He's got his jeans undone, his dick in his hand. He's silhouetted by the lamp behind him, but I don't need a spotlight to see him pump his length in his fist.

Oh God.

The wall keeps me upright while he slowly jacks himself off. His thumb rolls over the top of his dick, smearing the clear pre-cum, and his grip twists as he gets to the base.

Over and over.

It's weirdly mesmerizing.

Something is seriously wrong with you, Margo.

"It means I think of your mouth when I do this," he finally continues. "So get on your knees and make my fantasy come true."

I scoff.

"You want me to leave you alone. That's the whole point. Drool on my dick, baby, and show me that you're nothing special." He lifts his eyebrow. "Show me that your mouth isn't something I should fantasize about."

Twisted logic.

And yet.

There are probably a million other girls who can give him blow jobs. A hundred at Emery-Rose, at least, who would willingly drop down and take him in their mouths.

And they'd almost surely do it better than me. I've never done it before.

Considering that, and his offer...

"I give you a bad blow job and you're just going to forget about me?"

He bares his teeth. "Guaranteed."

Butterflies take over my chest. I don't want to cave... but I really would love nothing more than for Caleb to leave me alone.

Would you really?

Okay, well, I don't know.

My body is already in motion before my mind makes itself up.

I don't think the very act of being on your knees in front of a guy is talked about enough. It puts me so much lower than him; his intimidation factor automatically goes up a notch. It's nothing he's doing—he's intimidating enough in his own right—but now, he looms so high above me. He could lift his knee and smash me in the nose, or...

Anything, I guess.

So the quicker I pull this off, the faster I can get out of this position.

I pull his hand off his dick, and he grunts in surprise. It bobs in front of me, not just longer than expected—I don't really know what I was expecting, honestly—but thicker, too. I wrap my hand around it, my fingers barely overlapping, and mimic his movement.

He exhales, letting me do that for a moment. But then he grabs my wrist, stopping me, and tuts.

"Blow jobs require your mouth," he says.

I narrow my eyes, but his lips just quirk.

His one hand is still on the wall, bracing himself over me.

I open my mouth and inch forward. The first taste is a tentative lick, a swipe of my tongue across the head. The tip of my tongue catches on his slit, and the flavor of his pre-cum is surprising. Better than when he made me taste my own arousal, but barely.

I lick again and put my hand back on his dick. At the base. I use my grip to guide it into my mouth. An inch, then out.

Drooling on it.

Right.

The wetter the better, someone once said. Another foster kid at a group home. Talking about sex was a currency all its own there. I didn't have anything to contribute, but I tried to listen.

Some of those tricks they always talked about come back. Twisting my hand, taking him deeper as I let my saliva run down his shaft. I drag my hand up and catch the wetness, coating the rest of his length.

I try again, taking him deeper, and remember the key point of blowing a guy is to suck.

So I do, and he lets out a grunt above me.

My tongue swirls around his length when I come back up. I've only taken half of him in my mouth, but I don't know that I can take much more. He's already nearing the back of my throat when I dip down.

On the way out, I flick my tongue against the underside of the mushroom head. His hips jerk, and only my hand keeps him from thrusting deeper. Until he grabs my wrist and removes my hand, and his fingers slide into my hair.

Is that a control thing?

I ignore it and keep going. Down, suck, swirl. Flick.

Suddenly, his fingers tighten on my scalp, and he uses my downward momentum to keep pushing. His hips slide forward, and his dick hits the back of my throat.

Deeper.

I gag, my body tensing, and as soon as I relax, he slides in farther. I choke on him, my eyes pricking with tears. He pulls out, his grip firm, and I suck in a ragged breath. And then he's filling my mouth again.

My hands find his thighs, gripping through his jeans as his hips rock forward.

He fucks my face. I guess there's no other way to describe it.

I look up at him, catch his expression. His gaze is locked on my mouth. I am caught, gagging and choking every time he plunges too far.

"Relax," he finally orders. "Relax your throat."

I try. The other option is for him to treat me like a door

he's knocking down with a battering ram. And surprisingly, he's able to get through.

I just don't expect my air to be cut off.

"Fuck, that's tight." His fingers move along my hair, almost like a caress.

A caress if he was delusional and I was dead.

He withdraws and does it again.

This isn't me giving him a blow job—he's fucking my face. He finally hits deep enough that my nose touches his pelvis. His skin there is smooth. The pubic hair he should have has been shaved away.

And he keeps me there, his hold on the back of my head unyielding, until white spots flicker in front of my eyes and my grasp on his thighs loosens.

Only then does he continue. On and on, his movements getting jerkier and more frantic. I barely remember to suck, my cheeks hollowing, when he gives me room to breathe. My nostrils flare, greedily gulping down air when I get a chance.

Suddenly, he pauses. Pulls out entirely. A strand of my saliva connects my lower lip to his cock.

A second later, someone knocks on my door. "Just saying goodnight, Margo," Lenora calls. "Sleep well."

Caleb's eyebrow rises at my silence.

I lick my lips. I'm not sure my voice will even work, but I call back a throaty, "Goodnight."

He brushes his thumb over my lower lip, forcing my mouth open again, and... well... resumes.

It's clinical on my side. I don't much think about his fierce expression, or how his grip went soft in my hair for a split second. It's back to tight, pulling at my scalp, directing my face and head in a way that suits him.

My mind clicks over into some sort of numb analysis.

What I'm doing—not much—and what he's doing. He's taken over, which shouldn't surprise me. It doesn't surprise me.

Nothing surprises me right now.

Except when he finally stops, sitting heavy on my tongue, and it... erupts.

I'm not prepared for his cum to fill my mouth. I choke on it, even when he pushes back deeper. I can't escape it, not when it hits the back of my throat. I either suffocate or swallow, and instinct kicks in. My bruised throat works around him.

He pulls out of my mouth, and I sag backward. I wipe his cum from my lips with the back of my hand. I can't even register the taste—besides *not great*. Who likes this kind of thing?

Not me.

He turns away, leaving me to pant for breath on the floor by the door. After a long minute, I hoist myself up and go for the water. I chug half of it, then force myself to set it down.

My scalp aches where he tugged my hair. My throat hurts from the sheer force...

It took him a long time to come. That must mean I'm not good, right? Like, a great blow job would've had him coming way faster.

Pleased with my terrible attempt, I sit on my bed with a leg folded under me.

"Well," I say softly, "I'm sorry to disappoint—"

His laugh kills the words on my lips. When he faces me, I get a better look at his chest.

It's all muscle, which is so unfair. His abdomen flexes, and he eyes me with renewed interest.

"Disappoint?" he echoes. "I think I've been waiting my

whole life to ravage your mouth like that. How am I supposed to let you go now?"

Well... that's not good.

Chapter 9
Margo

CALEB

> When you wear that skirt, I'm tempted to haul you into a supply closet and taste you again. But this time, with my face between your legs instead of my fingers.

The text is waiting for me when I check my phone at lunch. It's only one day after Caleb's, um, *visit*.

I resolve to wear pants for the rest of the week. It's getting colder out, especially in the mornings. It wouldn't be a leap to make an argument against the skirts hanging in my closet.

Besides the text, he's been completely ignoring me.

Acting like nothing happened.

It was enough this morning that I did a double take. He didn't do anything crazy to me in the courtyard before school, even though Riley and I were prepared. Savannah preened nearby, but he stuck close with his three friends.

Maybe it's not just me he's ignoring, but everyone else?

Riley and I decided to venture into the lunchroom. Another oddity of the week. We find a table in a back corner, and someone else from one of Riley's classes joins us. They're not really *with* us, although they look nice enough. They introduced themselves as Jacq. Even in the uniform—pants and a loose-fitting shirt—their style is instantly clear. Buzzed, bleach-blonde hair, oversized, pink-framed glasses, and glitter highlighter spread across the tops of their cheeks. I'd imagine outside of the uniform their wardrobe is even more impressive.

"You used to be friends with that?" Riley points with her spoon toward Savannah.

She sits with her cheerleader friends at a table in the center of the room, taking up as much space and noise as possible. Today's a game day, which means the football players are wearing their jerseys and the cheerleaders are in their uniforms. They stand out against the monotonous sea of white shirts.

"Um, yeah, when I was like nine."

Jacq laughs. "Bad choice, dude."

Riley nods. "I've got to agree. You had poor taste as a nine-year-old."

"Well, I was friends with Caleb, too."

"Like, *friends*-friends? Or, you went to the same school and kind of knew each other—"

"Definitely friends-friends. I don't want to talk about that." I can't get into the whole complex thing right now. Not when we're surrounded by enemies.

Enemies who are also called classmates.

Jacq makes a face, but Riley must suddenly be reminded of an earlier conversation. This morning, I whispered to her what happened.

I couldn't keep it to myself. I mean, I don't know what

the fuck to do. I gave him a terrible blow job, and he decides it's the best he's had?

Okay, he didn't quite say it that way.

But it wasn't bad enough to warn him off...

And what was Riley's first question, you ask? *Did you use teeth?*

I should've.

"Have you come up with a plan?" she asks now.

"A plan for a diabolical mind-fuck of Caleb Asher? Yes, yes I have." I make them wait a minute before I say, "I need to find a boyfriend."

Silence.

Shock.

"What? Who?"

Jacq laughs again, but quieter. To themselves.

I shrug. "I'm not too picky. I just need someone to hold my hand and maybe kiss me... Why are you looking at me like that?"

"Who's kissing you?" Caleb asks from directly behind me.

I nearly jump out of my skin. But I guess that explains Riley's weird expression.

Jacq suddenly grabs their stuff and moves down to the far end of the table, which we can totally blame on Caleb's negative energy.

Caleb drops down beside me, like this isn't unusual or weird. I survived all morning. Even our first class together, nothing. The back of my neck didn't burn with his usual glare.

But now? He drapes his arm over my shoulders and winks at Riley.

"Earth to Margo." He taps my temple. "Anyone home?"

I grimace and try to inch away from him. I should know by now that it's useless.

"We almost made it a full day," I say to Riley, sighing heavily.

"Aw, you noticed." Caleb smirks. "I'm flattered. Have you met Savannah?"

I pause and meet his gaze. He seems... Well, not angry, which is a change in and of itself. But maybe mischievous?

My chest tightens, and my stomach does a somersault. "You're not serious."

"I'm *dead* serious. Excuse us, Appleton."

He lifts me out of my seat like I weigh nothing. I dig my heels in, but it's even worse than at his house. Here, my feet just slide across the polished tile, until I finally give in and stumble forward.

He guides me to the table where Savannah reigns over the other cheerleaders. I've noticed that she doesn't sit with the hockey guys. The team groups together at one long table, and there are no other girls there.

Wonder if that's an unspoken rule?

"Savannah, sweetie." Caleb draws *all* of the eyes. Every last one. "You were out last week, you must've missed the news: our old friend Margo has returned."

Like she didn't see me for the first part of the week?

Savannah faces us, her body stiff. Her expression is carefully blank, but flickering under the surface is intense rage. And judging by the way Caleb leans into my side, he sees it, too.

He's not stupid. He knows what he's doing.

"Savannah," Caleb prompts.

"Welcome back," Savannah answers in a voice that— well, it's downright frozen. And insincere.

If I ever wanted to stab someone with a pencil more than Caleb, it'd be her.

"I'm sure you'd love to catch up with Margo, right?" he continues.

I shake my head, but his fingers dig into my arm. A silent warning that kills my voice.

"Of course." She feigns a frown and eyes the packed table. "Oh, but there's no room at our table. Maybe next time, Margo, okay?"

Caleb sighs, and I have to remind myself that this is an act. However sincere he appears—he's *lying*. He seems to have perfected the art of war while I've been gone.

He sighs again and says, "Ah, you're right. It's okay. Margo can come sit with me." He jerks his chin toward the boys-only hockey table.

Savannah pales.

"No." She glances around the table. "Stephanie, move over."

"There's no—"

"Move."

The girl, who could be a freshman, stares at Savannah and tries to stop her chin from wobbling. It doesn't work, and Savannah's mean-girl act clearly gets the best of the underclassman. She gets up and runs out of the cafeteria, chased by laughter.

Caleb is feeding me to the sharks.

"I hate you," I say under my breath.

He just hums over a broad smile.

"Sit." Savannah points at the empty seat at the end of the table. "God knows you didn't earn it."

I wait for Caleb to let go of me.

He watches Savannah, his head cocked. "Savannah,

sweetie, how are you supposed to welcome Margo when she's so far away?"

Silence.

Savannah's face pinkens, and the color slowly deepens into a red flush. She nods to the girls across from her, who all dutifully slide down a seat. Leaving the one directly across from Savannah open.

Caleb releases me one finger at a time. After a long moment of me standing beside him untethered, he gives me a push. I stumble forward, toward the empty chair.

"I'm so glad you two are getting reacquainted," he says. "See you later."

"See you," Savannah replies, even though Caleb's eyes don't leave mine.

I don't answer, just sit between two girls. A hush falls over the table as Caleb leaves, and I almost stand and bolt.

"Don't you dare," Savannah snaps. She reaches across the table and grabs my wrist. "You get up and then what?"

I snatch my wrist away and lean back. "Who, exactly, do you think you are?"

Ex-friend or not, I don't want her touching me.

She shakes out her wheat-blonde hair. "Me? I'm not the one who stomped in here thinking she could slip right back into her old role—"

"And what role is that, exactly?" I put my elbows on the table. "I was never mean to you. I didn't try to step on anyone's toes—"

"Oh, bullshit, Margo." She flips her hair over her shoulder, taking a moment to compose herself.

I press my lips together. The eyes of most of our classmates are on us right now. Whether or not they can hear our conversation is anyone's guess, but the rumors will be flying in no time.

Across the room, Riley and Jacq watch with sympathetic expressions. They still didn't manage to stop Caleb from putting me in this mess, though.

"You want to know what your role is, Margo? You want to steal Caleb away from me!"

I laugh.

It's ridiculous.

"I don't want him." My volume is inching up, matching her escalating crazy. "I don't want anything to do with him. But that doesn't negate the fact that *I had him first.*"

She gasps.

Okay, everyone gasps.

And then her eyes narrow. "You fucked him over, Margo, and then you left."

I didn't have a choice. And I certainly don't have a retort.

I get up from the table. "You know what, Sav? You have nothing to worry about. You can have him."

I walk away, and a little voice in my head chants, *Liar, liar, liar.*

Riley follows me into the hallway, her eyes wide. She loops her arm through mine, and we leave without a word. It isn't until we reach the locked doors that will admit us into the academic wings that we both blow out slow breaths.

We're the first ones here, although some students loiter farther down the hall.

"*That* is why we avoid the cafeteria," she says. "Agreed?"

I bump my fist against hers. "Agreed. Yikes."

She barks out a laugh. "*Yikes* is right. I don't think that could've got more awkward."

Slowly, the hallway fills. And by the time the bell rings and the doors open, we barely have room to move.

Riley keeps ahold of my hand and elbows someone out of her space, and we make it to the hallway that has both of our lockers in it. Someone slams their shoulder into mine, knocking me into the lockers. I yelp, but the cheerleader—clearly the culprit—doesn't even glance at me as she passes.

A second later, another one snags my fallen bookbag with her foot, kicking it across the floor. Papers and books go flying.

Riley gasps. "What the hell? Are you okay?"

I force myself to laugh, even when a lump forms in my throat. I should've automatically expected retaliation. I wasn't born yesterday.

We dart between students to grab my scattered things. By the time Riley and I have gathered everything, the hallway is deserted.

"Shit. We're going to be late." She glances at her watch.

"Go," I tell her. "I... Honestly, I'd rather just—I should've expected her to do something. Didn't think it would happen this quick, though."

She squints at me. "What happened?"

"I didn't do anything." I sigh. "I've told you everything I know. I would've mentioned if I had a vendetta against Savannah or... Ah, fuck."

Caleb and his crew saunter down the hall in our direction. Theo and Liam are in front, arguing about something. Their heads are turned in, toward each other, and they pass us without pausing.

I blow out the slightest breath.

Eli catches Riley's arm mid-step, pulling her along with him. She lets out a squeak, but he doesn't relent. She throws me an apologetic look, right before they round a corner and disappear from sight.

And Caleb has stopped beside me.

"You enjoyed that, didn't you?" He raises one eyebrow. "The showdown?"

"No."

He leans in like a co-conspirator. "You're not going to thank me?"

"We both know all you did was open a can of worms for me." I stuff the last of my papers in my bag. "Before, it was just you. Now it's you and *them*, and then it'll be everyone else, too. People love to gang up on the weak one."

He straightens, his eyes wide. "Excuse me?"

"You didn't *want* the cheerleaders to hate me?"

"I wanted you to stand up to Sav. And prove that you're not the fucking weak one."

Once I start laughing, it's hard to stop. *Oh, the nerve of this boy.* "That's not how this works. What do you mean I'm not the weak one? You've spent the last few weeks proving—"

"If you were weak, you'd be bowing at my feet every time I passed you." He touches my cheek, once, fleeting. "But you don't. Which makes it all the more interesting. I don't really give a fuck. Not about your social standing, and not about her. You're interesting. She was... but now she isn't." He lifts one shoulder. "This isn't personal."

Oh, how I hate him.

I give him my best glare, but it ricochets off his armor.

"You do give a fuck," I say quietly, going in another direction. "About me."

"About your mouth, certainly." He smirks. "Tell me... how wet were you after I left?"

I open and close my mouth. I am *not* going down that road with him—no way. But he doesn't seem to care at my lack of an answer. He knows something I don't, judging by his smug expression.

S. Massery

"What?" I demand.

"Nothing."

"And how did you get my number?"

He grins. "Ah, you *did* get my text. I got it from your friend."

"Riley?"

We're still just standing in the middle of the empty hall. He seems to register it at the same time I do, because we both jump into motion. I keep glancing at him, waiting for his answer, but it doesn't come. And when I lag, he reaches for me. His fingers slide under my hair, to the back of my neck.

I shiver, but I don't fight him off.

After Savannah, and arguing...

Maybe I should keep fighting or pushing for answers. Or ask if Riley really gave him my number, knowing what she knows.

We reach my classroom door, and he stops just before it.

"What are you doing?"

Quick as a snake, he uses his body to back me against the wall. From where we stand, no one in the classroom can see us. The window in the door is useless, and it happens too fast for me to avoid it.

One minute... walking. The next, pressed to the wall, a hair's breadth from touching him. It's a wonder I don't get freaking whiplash.

"Answer my question," he demands.

I focus on his throat instead of his eyes. I can't even remember the question. Instead of admitting that, though, I remain silent.

His hand trails up my arm, the column of my throat, and captures my chin between his fingers. He jerks my head

110

up and down, then side to side. "Yes or no. You should've learned that in kindergarten."

"If I didn't, it was because you were too damn busy distracting me—"

His fingers tighten, and I suppress a yelp of pain.

He leans in close. "What did you say?"

"We used to be friends," I say to his ear. It's all I can bear to look at. And once this word vomit starts, I don't think I'll be able to stop. "You used to be nice. I was taken from my family, and you turned into—"

"Taken away?" he asks, his voice incredulous. "Is that what you call it?"

I meet his stare. "What would you call it?"

"I'd say you threw a goddamn grenade into our lives, Margo. And you never thought about the casualties."

He releases me, stepping back like I'm on fire. I can't even move as he takes three long strides to the classroom door—*my classroom door*—and yanks it open. He disappears inside, and it clicks closed softly behind him.

Now he's in another of my classes?

And he thinks... No, of course he blames me.

I sink to the floor, wrapping my arms around my legs. But I was ten years old. Had I known the ripple effect that was going to be set off, I wouldn't have—

Please don't, his voice whispers in my ear. The younger version of him.

I hang my head, the answer for his anger finally in front of me.

It's my fault. It's always been my fault.

Chapter 10
Caleb

I transferred into this math class this morning. Liam told me she was in it with him, and I couldn't resist. Not after last night.

Damn girl has a magic mouth.

How many guys has she blown?

And why do I want to kill all of them?

But anyway—this math class is pretty much the same as the one I was in, but I just wanted to fix my schedule to get maximum Margo time. She's always thrown when I show up, seeming caught between scared and excited.

Isn't that funny? She thinks she can wreck my family and then be happy to see me.

The teacher is a balding man in his seventies. I don't know him personally—haven't had the pleasure of taking a class of his—but he scans the slip from my guidance counselor and gruffly waves me into the room.

Late or not, I suppose it doesn't matter.

I pick the chair next to Liam's, and we bump fists. There's rustling of paper as my classmates pull out notebooks and folders, pencils, textbooks. I don't even have a bag with me, just a single notebook and pen.

People who do math with pencils just don't know how to commit.

Mr. McGuire drops off a textbook at my desk. He ambles to the front of the room just in time for Margo to enter. Her face is redder than when I left, her eyes bloodshot. Her makeup—which is always too intense, in my opinion—has smeared some under her eyes.

Oh, no. Did I make the poor little lamb cry?

I lean back in my chair, kicking out my legs. My feet extend under the chair in front of me. The open desk that I'd bet she's going to take.

Liam eyes me, his brows pulling down, but I ignore him.

Mr. McGuire gives her a bit of a hard time for being late without a pass, and I catch the word *restroom*. Little lamb knows how to lie, then.

That's expected.

She looks around the room, and her gaze settles on me. I meet it with a raised eyebrow. A silent, *Well?* She takes the seat in front of me, and I lift my foot until my toe touches the bottom of her seat.

I kick it gently. Just a tiny thump, and she jolts.

She's got to be turned on by me. By that BJ last night, sure, but also... I'm pretty confident I can smell her arousal whenever I get close enough. She's just too prim and proper to say anything.

And the worst thing is that she's wearing pants. It's definitely because of that text I sent this morning about the skirt... but that's just because I'm an asshole, and I jacked myself off to the memory of her mouth as soon as I got into bed that night.

Fortunately for me, her uniform pants hug her ass and create an entirely new picture.

She was mostly sitting when I found her in the mall food court. Her jeans didn't accentuate *anything*, and I didn't exactly stand behind her.

Anyway, all that to say, I'm not mad about the pants.

There will be time later to talk her into skirts. Or, if she doesn't acquiesce on her own, to blackmail her into it.

A cheerleader next to her, in front of Liam, shoots her a look and leans away. Her nose wrinkles, as if Margo smells, and I chuckle.

I was actually starting to like her for a second there. A spark of the old Margo had come through, and the innocent child in me had risen to her call.

For a while, we were happy, carefree kids. Inseparable, even.

Imagine that, knowing how far we've come.

Mr. McGuire starts explaining a new formula. We did this same exact thing the week prior, so I zone out and spend the rest of class staring at the back of her head.

What's going on in that little brain of hers? What will the next bomb she'll drop be?

A game. Playing games with her is almost as fun as hockey. Kiss her and see when she'll give in to me. Kiss her enemy and wait for her flinch. Fuck her where—

"Dude." Liam jostles my arm. "Class is over."

I shake my head, banishing thoughts. Margo is gone, as is half the class. Even Mr. McGuire has packed up and left the room, leaving Liam and I alone.

"Why are you looking at me like that?" I get up, taking the textbook with me.

"Because..."

I raise my eyebrow. "Spit it out, why don't you."

He groans. "Don't punch me for this shit, okay? But what's your issue?"

"With Margo?"

He throws up his hands. "You're on a first-name basis with her? That's fucked up, man. You won't even tell us why you hate her so much."

Irrational possessiveness overtakes me. The fact that he wants to know about Margo? *Bad.* He shouldn't even be looking at her, much less saying her name.

Wait. He didn't say her name.

But he implied it.

I glower at him. All my secrets surrounding Margo are locked up tight. There is no risk of them slipping out—but I might deck my best friend.

Liam and I are the fighters of our group. We're the two with the most friction and the most likely to end up playing a game of testosterone chicken. We're also too reckless to get out of the way when we should... which means we crash more often than not.

Our other two friends, Eli and Theo, balance us out.

But seeing as they're not here, and I'm itching for a fight, I throw back my shoulders. "I don't need to tell you *why*."

"You can't fight every battle on your own."

"What?" I square up to him in the hallway.

Even though it's packed and we're between periods, students automatically veer around us without making contact.

Liam and I are an even match. Coach sometimes puts us on opposite teams for practice to keep things fair. Although since we play on the same line, we do practice *together*. Scrimmages or not.

I'm a center, Liam is a left wing. Eli is our right wing,

and Theo plays left defense. When we're all on the same page—together with Ian, Theo's partner on defense—it's magic.

But right now, I want to throttle him.

He's almost the same height as me—an inch shorter, if that. Around the same build. If not for the wildly different features, people might think we're related. His hair light, mine dark. His skin golden to my paler complexion. Hazel eyes contrasting my blue.

Minus the fact that I play hockey better than him, we could be carbon copies.

"Get out of my fucking face, asshole." He shoves me.

I rock back a few steps and put some distance between us. He shakes out his arms, reading me well. I've been needing an outlet for ages now. Even since before Margo showed up, I've been bottling my emotions. At hockey practice, I've been restrained. With her, I've showed control.

Now, it's all about to explode outward.

I crack my neck and grin. "It's been a while since we've done this."

His smile is just as unhinged. "Ready to get your ass beat? Bring it."

I lunge for him and land the first punch. His head snaps back at the impact, absorbing the blow with a sneer. Blood drips from his nose, over his top lip. His tongue flicks out, tasting it, and a switch flips inside him.

Game on.

Classmates make space for us, some jeering while girls down the hall scream. My blood pumps hotter, faster.

Liam and I dance around each other, maneuvering for the best angle. He strikes fast, his fist coming out of nowhere. His knuckles glance off my cheekbone, and pain spikes through my face.

More.

I dive for him, a tackle better made for a football player than me, and we go down. We roll, trading punches, until I end up on top. Hands grasp at the back of my shirt. I almost shrug them off, but their grip tightens. I'm lifted bodily off of Liam and slammed face-first into a locker.

Fuck.

Ow.

Only one person in the school is strong enough to do that.

"Sorry, Coach," I say against the metal, ignoring the bite of pain where Liam hit me.

Coach's grip on my neck doesn't soften. "You think a sorry will cover this mess? In my office before practice. *Both of you.*"

And then he's gone. The crowd parts for him, most students jumping out of the way to avoid his ire. He's as much of a legend as the rest of us, honestly. He went to Emery-Rose when he was in high school and captained the hockey team for three years. He led them to two championship titles.

The main takeaway from his accolades: he's not someone to disappoint or piss off, and we singlehandedly did both.

The disgust in his voice spears through me.

I push myself off the locker and offer my hand to Liam. He takes it, and I haul him up. We both look in the direction Coach left.

"Damn," Liam mutters. "He's going to take it out on us with drills, isn't he?"

I sigh. "I don't even want to fucking think about it."

He brushes under his nose, smearing blood, and then glances at me. "I got you good. Split lip."

I laugh, touching it. "Better than my eyes swollen shut. Have fun with that at practice."

He grimaces. "Fuck you."

We part ways, me headed for my third class of the day with Margo Wolfe, and him who fucking knows where.

And I feel exponentially better—and worse.

Chapter 11
Margo

"You got into a fight?" I blurt out.

Caleb settles on the stool beside me, his easel already loaded with his year-end project canvas. It's blank—I checked when he didn't immediately come in. We haven't worked on it in the past few days, and Robert mentioned that we'd be dedicating one day a week to it.

He looks like shit, though. There's a drop of blood on the collar of his crisp white shirt. His lip is bleeding—or was, I guess, since it seems to have stopped—and there's a blooming red mark across his cheekbone.

The rumor mill was fast at work, and Riley already sent me a video of it. Him and *Liam*, his best friend. Why on earth they fought is anyone's guess. The person who videoed it didn't start until after it was well underway.

And now he's here, his posture straight, his gaze on the canvas.

Boys are idiots.

"Should I add that to my painting?" I ask dryly.

He shrugs again, avoiding my eye.

I turn back to my canvas. It's also blank, but not for lack

of trying. I've got paints on my palette, my brushes laid out. The turpentine to clean the oil paint in a mason jar on a side table. Everything is ready, and all I need to do is that first wash of color.

I just need to start.

Robert—er, Mr. Bryan—is circling around the room, and he stops behind me.

"Interesting," he says. "Is that how you see Caleb?"

I glance up at him. "Can I just paint the whole thing black?"

Caleb grunts. "Real original."

"You wanted a window into his soul," I tell Robert. "And his soul is—"

"Okay." He holds up his hand. "I'm sure there's more to Mr. Asher than what meets the eye. You're our only pair that hasn't even *started*. Why is that?"

"I have her figured out," Caleb says. "It's just a matter of finding the right way to portray it."

I hum. "Pretty sure he's blowing smoke out of his—"

"All right," Robert interrupts. "Come on, Margo. Caleb. Get to work."

He leaves us, and I focus back on Caleb. Not him, per se, but the shape of his head. I use my pencil to sketch out a rough outline. When I'm satisfied with the shape, I dip my brush in the orange-brown paint, then turpentine. I use broad strokes to cover the canvas, and the color is thin enough to still see my pencil markings.

Caleb sits back, a clean brush in his grasp. He fiddles with it, his gaze steady on my face.

"You're unnerving," I say.

"You don't look like a soul-sucking demon when you're concentrating." He leans forward and braces his elbow on his knee. "You stick your tongue out a little, like this."

The tip of his tongue peeks out of his lips.

I frown. "No, I don't."

"Okay, fine." He sits back with a smile.

So fucking smug.

"I'm going to add the bruises." Not that I even have his face figured out... or where to start.

The other day, we worked on mapping faces. You know, drawing the circle and then the curved lines through it, essentially figuring out where to put the nose and eyes and lips proportionally. It was difficult at first, but actually more like math than anything else.

I got the hang of it pretty fast after that.

Robert circles back around, pausing at Caleb's shoulder. He waits. The pause is pointed. Enough for the hotshot hockey star to heave a sigh and get his brush coated in the same orange-brown color. A lot of turpentine, which is meant to thin out the paint in this way. It makes it nearly translucent on the canvas.

Layering is the name of the game.

My little warm-up canvas sits on the table next to my mason jar. I painted a flower because he asked us to capture something pretty. And seeing as how there isn't a lot of beauty in my life, recently—thank you, Caleb Asher—I went with some figment of my imagination.

"So, Margo." Caleb eyes me, dropping his brush again as soon as Robert has moved on.

Should I be calling him Mr. Bryan when I'm here?

"So, Caleb," I parrot. Unlike him, I keep going. I layer on more color, deepening where shadows are meant to be.

"You're coming to my game."

I freeze. "What? No."

It's a really bad lie.

"Riley's going." He smirks. "She told Eli she would. And she's bringing her new best friend along, isn't she?"

I clear my throat. "It would be supportive of me to go."

He snorts. "For the team? Or her?"

"Her, obviously." I wrinkle my nose. Maybe I can add a double chin to this painting of Caleb. It's a whole lot of nothing right about now.

"I'll drive you."

I shake my head. "I'm going with *Riley*, as you just deduced—"

"Riley's going with Eli."

"You're bossy." My palms are sweating.

"You're a pain in the ass."

"Aren't you playing?" I clean my brush and set it down. "You have to be there early, don't you?"

He rolls his eyes. "You'll be fine."

"What about Savannah?"

"What about her?"

I really do not like him. "You're just going to kiss her again, aren't you? Embarrass me in some way—"

His smile grows. "By all means, keep giving me ideas."

I groan and turn back to the canvas. Robert is across the room, demonstrating to a few students a different way to hold their palettes.

"I'll pick you up at four," Caleb whispers.

"No, you won't."

He tuts. "Arguing will do you no good, baby."

Why does he keep calling me that?

I can feel his smile, even when I'm not looking at him. It's because I didn't protest or keep arguing. He knows that I know I lost.

Just another piece of this sick game we must play. He's

bullheaded about things. He'll push and push and push until I give in... and then what?

We don't speak for the rest of class—clearly, I'm no good to him once he gets what he wants—and he leaves as soon as the last bell rings.

Luckily, there are two days before the first hockey game of the year. That's plenty of time to get Caleb to change his mind. Or convince Riley to skip altogether...

I'm the last person to clean her station. And Caleb's, too, since he hightailed it out of here without doing a damn thing.

When I'm done, I stop at Robert's desk. He's all done, too, sitting with his leather briefcase closed on top of the desk. He's typing on his phone and belatedly looks up at me.

"I'm not sure I'm getting the hang of this painting thing," I blurt out. "And being paired with Caleb..."

Robert sighs. "We've known Caleb's family for years. He may come off strong, but he's a good guy. I wouldn't let you be paired up with him if I didn't truly believe that."

Of course he's already won them over. I haven't even had a chance to make a case. And yet, this has been years in the making, and the unfortunate luck of my foster placement.

"He wants me to go to the game," I say. "The hockey game."

He brightens. "That's fantastic, honey."

Snakes writhe in my belly. I can't answer and ruin his delight, just as he thinks I'm making more friends. Becoming social. Whatever his and Lenora's expectations are for me... I am going to disappoint them.

There's no way around it.

He and I walk to his car together.

"What time is he picking you up?" Robert asks. "The game is Friday night, right?"

"You're on board with him taking me, even though he got into a fight?"

"Boys do that. Especially over girls." He lifts a shoulder. "He shows good judgment other than the occasional tussle."

Jesus.

If he knew what Caleb did in my room, I doubt he'd be so blasé.

Or...

I don't know. Perhaps he's not as invested as I'm making him out to be. Like, if I bring home a drug dealer boyfriend, they might welcome him the same as they would Caleb or a science geek.

I ponder that, plus Robert's words. Boys fight—*especially over girls*.

It wasn't over me, though. It happened right after class with me, but they didn't even talk. And I haven't spoken to Liam at all. He's acted like I was invisible this whole time—which is fine by me.

But if we're in the spirit of making Caleb angry... angry enough to fight and get suspended from the hockey team... Maybe that's the angle I need to take. Get on his nerves by going after one of his friends.

Not Eli, of course. He seems to have something going on with Riley, even if she hardly knows. He's usually cold toward her, but suddenly he's offering to take her to the game? Unless Caleb asked him to do it to separate Riley and me.

Anyway. Theo is scary. Of the four, I'd go so far as to say he's the most sinister of them. He barely speaks, never so much as looks at me. It's like there's a firestorm in his chest, and he's just waiting for the perfect person to unleash it on. Inner demons, who?

I shiver at the thought.

That leaves Liam—the one Caleb got into a fight with, as a matter of fact.

Perfect. Unless Liam was bad-mouthing me, then I risk supreme embarrassment by going to him.

How much do I want to piss off Caleb?

All the way.

Resolved, I form a plan in my mind.

Friday night, I'm going to the hockey game. Riley will get us into the after-party, which I think she said might be held at Theo's house. All I must do is corner Liam and lay out my plan of pissing off Caleb, and if he likes to push his buttons, maybe he'll agree.

Or maybe I'm screwing myself over with this plan...

I guess I'll find out.

Chapter 12
Caleb

Coach Marzden bag skates us—which essentially means we do sprints until we collapse, and then we get thirty seconds to pick ourselves back up and do it again or we'll be there all night.

His gaze is hard and cutting. With every lap, every blow of the whistle, my anger shreds.

It doesn't go away, of course. That would be asking too much. But Liam and I keep exchanging glances with our other teammates, accepting the blame.

It would be more cowardly to pretend we weren't to blame.

Time seems to slow to a crawl, and I rip my mask off long enough to puke up the water I drank earlier. My legs are numb, but my lungs are on fire. I can't seem to take in a deep enough breath to satisfy it, and that kind of pain only comes with extreme physical exertion.

My stomach cramps again, just as the whistle goes off, and I jam my helmet on. I take off after my teammates. I have to trust that my legs can still move, that my skates can dig into the ice with enough force to propel me forward.

Down to the goal line. Turn. Back.

I'm far from the last, but I'm not doing stellar either.

Ian dry heaves in the corner, one hand braced on the wall.

"Have you had enough?" Coach roars.

"Yes, Coach," we manage, a collective not nearly as loud as we were at the start of practice.

"You're in this predicament because of two players." He strides onto the ice. He hooks his fingers in the cage of Liam's helmet, using it to drag him alongside him. He shoves my left winger at me. "Because they decided to fight *each other* two days before our game."

I stand straighter. "Sorry, Coach."

"It won't happen again," Liam adds.

"It better not," Coach growls. "Because I will not stand for this. If I catch any of you stepping a *toe* out of line, you're out for six games, minimum. I don't care what that does to our season. I'm serious. Clear?"

"Clear," we all echo.

Six games for fighting would be bullshit—but now isn't the time to argue. I keep quiet until he releases us, and I wait to be the last player off the ice. I pat everyone's back or legs with my stick.

They grumble, but they won't hold it against me for long.

Eli waits for me down the hall, outside the locker room. His eyebrow rises, and I scowl. He and I have a shorthand way of speaking, and right now he's asking me, *What the fuck?*

The answer? I don't know.

I shouldn't have gone after Liam like that. In the hallway, no less.

S. Massery

Margo just... she gets under my skin. I keep needling her, hoping to have the same result, but I don't think I do.

She tolerates my bullshit. When I do something truly wicked, the flash of fear satiates the beast inside me... but it's not enough. Liam got into my business about Margo, making it seem like I shouldn't even be talking to her, and I snapped.

The thought of him coming between us...

"You look like you're ready for another round," Eli comments. "Whatever you're thinking, I suggest you stop until we're off school grounds."

I grunt.

What I need is a cold shower and a handful of Tylenol. After finding just that, I walk out with Eli Black. My best friend since we were eleven. Ever since we discovered a mutual love of hockey—specifically the Colorado Titans, our absolute fucking idols—we've been inseparable.

Actually, that's how we looped Liam and Theo into our friend group, too. Playing hockey as squirts, proclaiming our love for certain players... Theo used to declare he just wants to make enough money to buy the team. It's ambitious, sure. But ambition is what's going to get us far in life.

"You and Liam haven't fought in a while," Eli comments.

"Yeah, well."

"This about Margo?"

My shoulders stiffen. I'm too tired to fight—Coach ensured that—but it doesn't mean I'd just roll over and let him say her name.

Jesus.

"Okay, okay." Eli holds up his hands. "I see why you punched Liam."

Exactly.

We part ways in the parking lot. Eli to his truck, me to my Audi. It starts with a purr, everything fine-tuned to perfection, and I blow out a breath.

I could go home...

Or I could sneak into Margo's room again.

So that's exactly where I go, parked outside the Bryans' home. Gotta say, I didn't expect her to be taken in by them, of all people. It's just... unexpected. My family has known the Bryans for quite some time. Lenora works in the city and frequently comes into contact with my uncle. Same circles and all that. And obviously Robert Bryan brings his wife to the Emery-Rose Elite functions.

Charity and fundraising functions, among other things.

They also happen to live in Liam's childhood home.

I kill the engine and stare up at Margo's window. Liam and I used to practice scaling the trellis, but it was usually to sneak out. Using that skill to get *into* Margo's room was kismet.

It's still early, and her window is dark. I settle in to wait, although part of me wants to go up now and hide in her closet. It was so sweet when she jumped, completely unaware that I shared the same space as her the other night.

My phone rings, killing that idea.

My aunt's name flashes on my phone and watch. With a grimace, I accept the call.

"Hello, Aunt," I greet her.

"Caleb." Her voice is light. "Are we seeing you tonight?"

Forced light.

Is my uncle hovering over her shoulder?

"I'm with Theo," I lie. "We're doing some skill work Coach wanted us to perfect."

"Ah. Okay, well, I just wanted to remind you that we're coming to your game on Friday."

My chest tightens. "Okay."

Players gets season tickets every year for family, and my uncle has already been whispering in Marzden's ear about better seats. Or a suite, because God forbid he interact with *normal* people.

The added bonus of my aunt and uncle attending my games?

Endless beratement.

My mood sours, and I find my attention drifting back to Margo's window. The light is on, now, which kills my plan of sneaking in before she got up there. She moves past the window, which is open to allow the cool night air in.

My aunt's voice continues in my ear, talking about some dinner plans with who the fuck knows. My uncle must've drifted away, because she sounds more relaxed. Even though I'm ignoring her. She just talks *so much* about nothing at all. It's exhausting.

What's it like in her mind?

Mine is sometimes so quiet, I may as well be meditating. Other times, it races and screams. Right now, I'm somewhere in the middle. Considering my options as I would consider a chessboard.

She pauses, waiting for a response.

"Theo's mom is calling us. I'll talk to you later?" I lean to the side to get a better glimpse of Margo through her window. The curtains block the details of her body, but her silhouette is clear. My mouth waters.

"Yes, yes, of course. We'll see you tomorrow!"

She hangs up before I can get to it, which is impressive. My thumb was poised above the red *end* button.

I settle in to wait, and an idea strikes me.

> What are you wearing?

I stare at my phone until Margo's little typing dots pop up on the screen.

MARGO
> Completely unsexy pajamas.

> I'm going to need proof of that.

> No.

I grit my teeth. No is not a word I hear very often.

> Why didn't you wear a skirt today?

The typing dots appear.
Disappear.
Reappear.

MARGO
> Because I don't want you tasting me, and I'm not going to give you any ideas.

> Baby, you should've seen yourself in those pants today. Your ass is tight enough to bounce a quarter off of.

> Please stop.

> I do like it when you beg...

I toss my phone on the passenger seat, smiling to myself. Mainly because I don't need to see her response to know I'm under her skin.

Please stop. Those sweet words would sound better coming out of her mouth.

Her light goes out. I give it another hour—passing the

time by watching Lion's Head hockey videos and doing some of the assigned math homework—then climb out of the car. I shut my door gently, the lights flashing as it automatically locks.

Scaling the trellis this time is as easy as the last. I have a folded knife in my pocket just in case her window is locked, but she left it open.

I peer in. Her body is buried under blankets in the middle of the bed. I carefully pop the screen out and set it in her room, push the window open farther, and slip inside.

My feet make the barest of noises when I land, and I take the time to toe off my shoes. Then shed my sweatshirt. My eyes adjust to the darkness, and I move to the edge of her bed. Her eyes are closed, her lips parted.

I wish I could fall asleep so easily.

I reach for her, brushing my fingertips along her jaw. When she doesn't wake, I move lower. I drag the blankets down, exposing her threadbare t-shirt and shorts. Her legs are slim and pale. I touch them, too. Her skin is too soft.

Too alluring.

With pressure on her knee, she rolls onto her back.

My cock rises. It stiffens against my jeans with a mind of its own. Well, we are of similar mind—we want Margo.

I can wait to fuck her, but I need to taste her.

She shifts, her arm covering her chest. Her head turns, face almost completely in the pillow, and I chuckle.

It's endearing when it shouldn't be.

Carefully, *slowly*, I tug her sleep shorts down. I keep expecting her to wake up. It's an eventuality I am planning for, and I really don't want to miss her expression when she registers that I'm back.

This time, though, I have another thought.

Leaving her like that, I jump back and go to her closet.

Obviously she has skirts—but after the first week, she stopped wearing them. Smiling to myself, I pull the pocketknife and flick it open. Without hesitation, I cut through her pants. One leg off on one, a rip through the apex on another. It would be fun to see her try and wear these *now*.

That'll teach her to disobey me.

Satisfied, I return to the bed. I crawl up between her legs, pushing her thighs wider.

My face is right in front of her pussy, and I need to introduce myself. Her puffy lips, the clit hidden in its hood, the arousal seeping from her slit.

I lean forward and run my tongue through it, getting a burst of flavor. I've gone down on girls before, but not like this.

Not with them being asleep, without asking...

But the more I inhale her scent, the more I want to devour her.

I take my time, licking her as if she were a decadent dessert. I ignore her clit until I can't take it—she has to wake up.

And as soon as I suck the little bud into my mouth, she does.

Chapter 13
Margo

I dream of running down the street, chasing some ghost just out of my line of sight. The franticness is real, though. My heart might burst trying to catch up.

Something rises out of the asphalt and catches my ankles. I scream as I fall forward, but I don't hit the ground. I go through it, tumbling across the open sky. It's brilliant blue all around me, and a bed of flowers catches me.

I slowly push myself up on my hands and knees. Long-stemmed flowers wave in the gentle breeze around me. My hair is caught up in the wind, too. I stand and come face-to-face with Caleb.

He smirks at me.

Something brushes between my legs.

"Are you doing that?" I ask him.

His smile widens. "Are you dreaming about me, baby?"

My stance shifts, and I glance down between my legs. There's nothing there, but—

Oh God.

"What are you doing?"

"Eating you out," he replies. "You taste like my new favorite meal."

The dream burns out around me, and suddenly I'm gasping awake in the darkness. My heart pounds, and there's a rushing noise in my ears. It takes a minute for the room to come into focus, and—

Oh God. Again. Except I'm awake.

I rise on my elbows and lock eyes with Caleb.

Maybe I'm still dreaming? Because he's between my legs... and then his tongue moves again, and I whimper. He doesn't say anything, even when I reach out and run my fingers through his hair.

What the hell is happening?

I collapse back, unable to look at him. I grip the bedsheets, and when he sucks on my clit, my hips automatically move. He focuses on that one little spot, alternating between sucking and licking, even scraping his teeth along it.

It shoves me over the edge.

I arch and twist, the brilliant pleasure whiting out my vision for a moment. My legs tense, squeezing his head, and it's only when I sag, the energy flooding out of me, that he lifts his head.

"Delicious," he murmurs. "Did you dream of me?"

I force my eyes to open. "What?"

"You moaned before you woke up."

My face heats. I should be madder than I am, but the overwhelming feeling is disorientation.

I'm still not convinced I'm awake.

He moves backwards, then stands and circles the bed. He takes my wrists and pulls, lifting me into a sitting position. His hands go to my ankles, swinging them over the edge of the bed.

And in a matter of seconds, I'm standing in front of him. With no panties or shorts on... just a t-shirt I've had for a long time. He's blocking the path to my closet. Unsure, I cover my chest with one arm.

My outfit isn't the only embarrassing thing. There are clothes on my floor, my hair is probably a wild mess—

I tuck my hair behind my ear to minimize the damage. "What are you doing here?"

He raises a shoulder.

Great non-answer. Maybe he just wants sexual things? I exhale.

"We're sneaking out," he declares in a low voice.

Excuse me?

His gaze goes to the window, then back to me. His lips curve into a sneer. "Unless you're afraid."

I *am* afraid—but I also don't want to admit that.

Can't.

So that's how I find myself dressed in sweatpants and an oversized hoodie he tossed at me, climbing down the trellis after him. It was a stretch to even reach it in the first place. It involved reaching my leg out of the window and feeling for it with my toe. Then repeating with my hand, then my other leg.

Caleb jumps to the ground below me. I move faster, the fear of being left behind striking through me.

I don't know what happens.

One minute I'm lowering myself down, the next, my grip has slipped and I'm falling.

"*Oof.*"

I don't hit the grass—

Caleb catches me.

He looks down at me, his brows furrowing, then shakes his head.

"You should be more careful." He sounds *cross*.

"You should come up with less dangerous activities."

His expression lights up. "But those are the only ones worth doing."

Abruptly, he drops my feet to the ground. I stumble away from him, straightening the sweatshirt. Belatedly, it occurs to me that this is *his* sweatshirt.

It even smells faintly of him.

Not that I remember what he smells like...

"Come on." He heads toward his car. With his hand on the passenger door handle, he asks, "Want to drive?"

I purse my lips. "No."

"Why not? Afraid you wouldn't be able to handle her?"

"It's not that." I narrow my eyes when he doesn't move.

He rolls his and opens the door for me. He circles around and starts the car with a press of a button. In no time, we're zipping down the street.

"Tell me." His palm lands on my thigh. He finger-walks his hand higher, a devilish smile on his face.

"Stop." The coiling heat in my stomach shifts lower.

"Do you mean that?"

I shiver.

"Are you suddenly shy, baby? I just had my face buried between your legs, and you're scared of my fingers?"

His eyes are dark. They always seem to be dark when he does wicked things to me. My abdomen is tense, my stomach knotting. I cover his hand with mine, not to be nice —just to get his wandering to halt.

"I can't drive," I blurt out.

He pauses. "Really."

"What, do you think a foster parent would've taught me?"

He withdraws with a scowl.

S. Massery

Slowly, I relax into the leather seat. His expression is contemplative. Maybe he's going to ask—sooner or later, everyone asks.

What's it like?

Don't people want you?

Why hasn't someone adopted you?

So caught up in past questions, I fail to notice where he's taking me.

Honestly, I kind of assumed we were going back to his house. His empty, abandoned house... in the middle of the night...

But we're far from there. The sign at the entrance of a park has been updated, but the name carries a flash of recognition.

It's the same one my parents used to take me to for picnics. It's also...

I close my eyes, fighting the roll of my stomach. He would absolutely leave me here if I puked in his car.

It's where Dad was arrested.

"Why?"

He shuts off the car. "To relive the past."

"But not all of it. Just the hard parts."

"Yes." He gets out and circles around, opening my door.

He's smart: I would've just stayed here.

He grabs my hands and takes me out by force. "Show me. Walk me through it, because no one else has been able to. And I wasn't here, after all."

I shudder.

"You weren't," I agree. "It was..."

The worst day of my life.

Mom was already gone, and Dad must've wanted peace and quiet before the next step. Before the other shoe dropped on our family.

138

I stride forward, and Caleb's hand slides from my arm. It's like there's a ten-year-old Margo guiding me to the exact spot. We were sitting on a bench overlooking the pond. The running path was behind us. The sound of footsteps hitting the dirt wasn't out of place in my memory.

Even in the dark, with Caleb's phone's flashlight bobbing behind me, there's no way I could get lost.

I sit on the bench. The pond has shriveled since the last time I saw it. The soft sound of crickets fills the air, along with an occasional frog. The wind rustles the dying fronds at the edges of the small pond.

Caleb sits next to me, his hands in his pockets.

Watching me. Examining me.

I haven't been here since that day, and if I let down my guard, echoes of the past surround us. I can almost hear my dad again. *I haven't heard his voice in six years.*

"Speak," Caleb finally orders. "You were here?"

I take a deep breath. "We didn't notice the detective."

He nods, an encouragement to keep going.

"She came around from his side—where you're sitting. She said..." I don't know what she told us. I shake my head and backtrack. "Dad gave me a handful of seeds for the ducks, and they talked while I was throwing them at the water."

"How kind," he says. His tone is sarcastic.

He doesn't like my father.

I don't know that I like him much either. But at the time, I loved him with my whole heart. How could I not have? He was my *dad*.

I continue. "When I was done, I turned around and he was in handcuffs. He didn't struggle until that lady motioned for him to be taken away. As soon as they tried to separate us, he fought. It took two... maybe three officers to force him to go."

That was horrible. I stood frozen, the empty paper cup in my hands. I wanted to scream and chase after him, but I was stuck. Every muscle locked up.

Someone else approached me. A woman. Not the first lady—this one had kinder eyes. She squatted next to me and introduced herself. When she offered her hand, I took it. And that, really, was the beginning of the end.

She was the emergency social worker brought on scene to take custody of me. From there, I was transferred into Ms. McCaw's caseload.

"Why'd he bring you here of all places?"

"It was our spot." There are no fowl in the mostly dead pond now. No ducks to scare away. Frogs, sure. They keep croaking and making themselves known. I pick up a rock and lob it at the water, and everything goes silent.

Caleb frowns. "Your home was—"

"No," I interrupt. "That house was never *our home*. It was yours. Always."

He lifts one eyebrow.

"Every inch of that property was yours." I stare out at the water. It's different but the same—kind of like us. Or maybe just me. I've been wilting and dying with neglect for years with no recourse. "We vanished like smoke. Did you even realize we were gone?"

"Did I *realize*?" His jaw tics. "How could I not realize, Margo? You ruined my life."

I jump to my feet, fighting against a cringe. Fighting against *guilt*. He thinks I hurt his life so badly? He got to stay here—

"Run and hide like you always do," he bites out.

Running sounds like a great plan. Maybe I shouldn't,

but I can't stand here and take his beratement. I pivot and burst into a sprint, running back over the hill toward where Caleb parked his car.

He catches me like he always does. His arms bind around my chest, and he stops short of flinging me to the grass. As soon as his arms drop, I put space between us.

This is crazy.

Why the *fuck* did I get in his car?

"You cannot run from me." He points in my face. "You can't hide. And you will fucking pay for what you've done."

My lip trembles. How do I focus on the hate when the most prominent feeling is terror?

"I don't know what I did," I tell him. "How am I supposed to make that right? If I don't *know*—"

One hand covers my mouth, the other lands on my shoulder. His gaze is wilder than I've ever seen it. "Shut up. Shut up, shut up, shut *up,* you lying whore." He shakes me for good measure, a jostle of my body against his.

Shut up, you lying whore. Those words—I've heard them, but not at me. And not out of Caleb's mouth.

"Like father, like son?" I say against his palm.

He glowers. "Don't you dare speak about my father."

I won't speak at all with the way he's gripping my face.

"I was almost starting to like you again," he mutters. "And then—" There's an awful glint in his eyes. He's dangerous. Based on past behaviors, maybe worse than a demon.

He's the fucking Devil.

Shoving him away, I sprint up the running path. I don't have a phone, and the moon is covered in clouds. I'm flying blind, but I trust my memory. I make it to the curve in the path. My tennis shoes slide a bit, but I push onward.

Fear holds my body in a vise: squeezing, squeezing, squeezing.

His footsteps pound the ground behind me.

He's taller than me, he's in shape. It comes as no surprise when his fingers catch my hair. I ignore it and pour on another dose of speed, but it's too late. He tackles me from behind.

He doesn't cushion our landing either. I don't have time to protect myself, except to bring my arms in like tucked wings. We hit the ground hard on our shoulders, sliding and rolling down an embankment, and I immediately propel us sideways. We're a wild tangle of limbs, but every instinct in me screams to *fight*.

Fight, flight, or freeze?

Right now, I'm choosing the first. I flail and catch him in the mouth. My knee lands dangerously close to his groin. He grunts in my ear.

One of his legs pins mine. I drag my nails down his throat, and his wild gaze crashes into mine. He catches my wrists and pins them above my head. Fury burns through me. A wild banshee screech leaves my lips, surprising both of us.

But I'm immobile—and as soon as that's confirmed, triumph glints in his gaze.

The last thing I expect him to do is kiss me.

But he does. Hard.

Another mind game.

Second kiss ever, and I want to scream into his mouth.

His lips slide across mine, rough and insistent. Our lips part, our teeth clash. Doesn't matter. *Fuck, I'm kissing him back.* But he still doesn't stop. That's not losing the game, I suppose. It's some other sacrifice I'd have to make.

I bite his lower lip. The sharp metallic flavor of blood

touches my tongue, but he doesn't stop. His tongue surges into my mouth, easily claiming all of my space. All of my oxygen.

I hate you, I say on repeat in my mind, if only to try to remind myself that I'm not this person. I'm not the person who falls for the bully. I'm not the girl who falls to her knees when the handsome boy pays attention to her.

If I want to win his games, I need to remember that.

If I lose, I could lose myself, too.

"Kiss me," he growls against my lips.

It's my only reprieve, then he's back on me.

Damn it, the kiss brings out feelings my body doesn't know how to handle. His hand slides down my side, into my sweatpants. His fingers follow the same path his tongue did earlier, stroking in just the right places. I want to curse him out, but my mouth is a little busy at the moment.

His lips leave mine and drag down my throat. "I used to dream of this."

Neck kisses? A whole new deal.

I moan. It's surreal, and for a moment I've left my body, watching us on the damp grass.

Who is that on the ground, making sounds she's only heard in movies? Feeling things she doesn't have a right to feel?

A burning ache spreads through me, chased by a spark of something extraordinary. I shift. I curl my fingers into fists. His pace between my legs slows, his fingers inching along my throbbing skin.

"Should I leave you like this?" he asks. "Spread out, begging for me?"

He rises on his elbow, staring down at me while his fingers move on the most sensitive part of me.

How did I go from sleeping in my own bed, *alone*, to this?

"Finish the job or bring me home," I say on an exhale.

He pouts, and his finger dips back into me. *Inside* me, where it has no business being. And yet my muscles clench at his digit on their own, and his knowing smile fucks me up.

Not in a good way.

"I guess I'll take you home, then, little lamb."

Chapter 14
Margo

When Caleb walks into first period on Thursday morning, he meets my death glare.

His eyebrows hike, and then his gaze drops to my legs.

Bare legs.

Ugh.

He didn't just wake me up with oral last night—he destroyed my uniform pants. The skirt is fine, I guess, minus the fact that it hits me mid-thigh and feels way too revealing. And I didn't have any stockings or pantyhose to conceal my legs...

It'll be on the list of things I need to ask Lenora about.

Another would be period products. That should be coming any day now, and I ran out last month. Doesn't help that I've changed homes and schools since then.

Lenora has been working late. I didn't see her yesterday until right before I headed upstairs to bed. She hugged me and Robert, apologized for being absent, then went to hunt down the plate Robert had saved for her.

I didn't see her this morning either. Robert didn't

comment on my skirt. He was probably the one to bring the options from Emery-Rose home, after all. Half his students wear skirts.

The morning air had a bite to it, which made standing out in the courtyard even worse. Goosebumps prickled my flesh, and I practically hid behind Riley and Jacq. No need for Savannah and her squad of evil cheerleaders to spot me. Or Caleb.

Anyway, now we're in the same class, and Caleb's gaze heats the back of my neck.

"I like it when you wear your hair up," he says in my ear.

I jump at his closeness. "Why?"

He trails a finger along my nape, and I shiver.

"Because of that," he whispers.

He slides back into his seat just as Mrs. Stonewater closes the door.

Luckily, the rest of the day passes without incident. Riley and I hole up in the library for lunch, and we wait until the bell has rung and the main stampede of students have passed before we venture out.

Caleb comes in late to art class, and he mutters something to Robert before taking his seat beside me.

I shoot him a questioning look, then catch myself.

I should not be *inquisitive* about anything Caleb is doing. Curiosity is just attention that he doesn't need. Trust me, his head—and ego—don't need any help.

He ignores me.

I tug at the bottom of my skirt absently, wishing it was a few inches longer, and his lips twitch.

But Robert—Mr. Bryan in this setting—has begun the lesson about shading techniques. There's no room in this small classroom for side chats because the sound travels so easily. Anyway, it's a good excuse to stay silent.

We follow along with my foster dad's lesson, and then he sets us loose to practice shading. He has a table in the center of the room with a variety of objects on it—square blocks, solid-colored marbles, a bowling pin—and a standing lamp directed at it.

"Depending on where you are in the room, the shadows are going to hit differently."

I adjust my position and dip my brush into the blue paint.

When the class ends, Caleb waits for me to pack up my stuff. He, per usual, has almost nothing. He has a near-empty bag slung over his shoulder that he stowed his set of brushes in, but otherwise, his hands are in his pockets, and he watches me.

"You normally bolt out of here," I say.

He smiles. "Not today. You're coming with me."

Again, with the orders.

My foster dad shrugs. "If you're okay with it, I'm okay with it."

Great.

The whole I-know-his-family conversation pops into the forefront of my mind. I can't say what I think—which is that Caleb is crazy and there's no way I'm getting back in the car with him. I can barely think it without fear of him reading my mind and punishing me for it.

Excuses about homework die on my tongue, and I sigh. Nod.

Robert squints at me, but Caleb already has his hand on the small of my back. He wastes no time propelling me out of the room and down the long, curving staircase. All the way down and out the door closest to the student parking lot.

Across the lawn, the cheerleaders are beginning their practice. They mainly perform at the football games, but weirdly enough, they sometimes show up for hockey. And since hockey is the main sport at Emery-Rose Elite, it's obvious that they care more about them than stinky, hulking football players.

Well, maybe hockey guys also stink?

I don't know.

I glance over at him. "What are you scheming?"

"What are you afraid of?" he replies.

I wonder if me giving in was a bad thing. If he'd only like me for the chase.

Wait—no. Shoot. I don't want him to *like* me. But the same question applies, doesn't it? Is he only fascinated with me because of the fight I put up? And if so, does giving in make it better or worse for me?

"Margo."

I've grown accustomed to him calling me anything but my name.

"I'm afraid..." I press my lips together. "Of my dreams."

He snorts. "Of the boogeyman coming out of your closet?"

"There are things I don't understand," I say. "My mother—"

He glances at me sharply. "She was a drug-addicted slut."

A muscle in his jaw tics, but he doesn't take it out on me. He just urges me toward the passenger seat, then circles around for his side. The interior is somehow cool, even in direct sun, and I set my bag at my feet. Caleb tosses his in the back.

"Tell me how you really feel," I mumble.

We haven't talked about my mother. Why would we? She's obviously a sore subject. But since we're opening that can of worms, the least I can do is hear him out.

Unless it's all slander, then I can pretend we're going to agree to disagree.

"You shouldn't talk about her," he says. "Shouldn't think about her."

He twists toward me. I suck in a breath, but he's just putting his hand on the back of my seat to back out of his parking space. It puts his head too close to mine. Is this sudden bout of dizziness normal?

We get out onto the road, zooming back toward the Bryans' neighborhood and our childhood one. Who knows where we're actually going with Caleb at the wheel? We could end up at that forsaken park or...

"I can't help who I dream about—" We speed around a corner, and I shut my mouth. Close my eyes, too, but I can only handle not seeing for a moment. "Please stop."

"Stop? Stop what?"

I'm going to throw up.

We're gaining speed. It's a sunny day on one of Rose Hill's many back roads. We're nowhere near other cars, other life. Hell, we could hit a ditch flipped over, and it might be an hour before someone finds us.

Why did we go this way?

"I'm afraid of *you*," I blurt out. "When you get that look in your eye. When you do mean things. When you hurt me."

He shakes his head and slams on the brakes. The tires squeal, smoking as the car stops on a dime. He meets my gaze. "I don't do anything you don't deserve."

I laugh in disbelief. "I didn't deserve you kissing Savannah. I don't deserve these games."

He inhales deeply. Under his armor, he's human, too. I can't forget that. We sit in the middle of the road in silence, both of us catching our breath. I loosen my grip on the edge of the seat, smoothing my palms down my bare legs.

After a long moment, he continues at a normal speed.

We take a few turns, suddenly headed back toward the Bryans' house. Or... his. The neighborhoods are right next to each other, so it's a guessing game at this point.

Still.

In the end, we arrive at his house. He parks in front, either expecting or not caring about the two other vehicles parked in the circular drive. He hops out and disappears into the house.

Per usual, I'm left to follow him.

The last time I was here... bad shit happened. *And* he left me to walk back to the Bryans'. If he does that again, I'm never going to get in another vehicle with him.

After a long moment of consideration, I grab my bag and get out of the car.

Entering the house takes another spoonful of courage, but then I'm in, with the door swinging shut behind me.

Liam and Theo are in the front room, leaning over a chessboard. The furniture is still covered in sheets. Everything has a ghost-like quality to it, and I'm not convinced anyone *actually* lives here. Not the downstairs anyway.

But why would Caleb be living in a shut-down house?

They don't acknowledge me, even though I watch their game from the room's threshold.

The sound of voices from farther back in the house float toward me, and I head down the hall.

Eli and Caleb are in the kitchen.

"She's arrived," Eli announces.

I frown. "What's going on?"

Eli pops the cap off a beer bottle and offers it to me. Caleb is at the sink, hands braced on the counter. There's a window there that looks out onto the back patio, and his expression is distant.

When I silently decline the beer, Eli takes a long swallow.

"We're planning a party," he says. "A real rager."

Parties. I think I hate those. The public schools I went to had parties, but they were loud and obnoxious. The cops were almost always called, which is a disaster if you're in the foster system and they catch you. Those had cheap liquor and a half-keg that everyone was "taxed" for—someone's way of recouping their money. People drank out of red off-brand cups.

I'm curious how the rich kids really party. Do they use actual Solo cups? Or maybe they drink their mixed drinks out of actual glassware? And they probably splurge on a full keg, possibly two. Alcohol that doesn't taste like gasoline, and mixers to boot.

Imagine.

"A party for what?"

"Why does anyone plan a party?" Eli asks.

"For after the Fall Ball," Caleb answers, turning away from the window.

I pause. "Is that a school dance?"

Eli's gaze sharpens. "I don't know if *dance* is the correct way to describe the horribly rhyming Fall Ball, but it's something like that. Are you into school dances, Margo?"

"No."

"Everyone goes to Fall Ball," Caleb mutters.

"Not me." I cross my arms.

S. Massery

I haven't yet put into motion my plan to ask Liam to be my fake boyfriend. I was planning on doing that tomorrow, but now there's talk of this *Fall Ball*. What a terrible name. But, as the name suggests, it's probably held in the autumn. And since we've swept into October without a mention of it...

Eli snickers. "Not sure I've ever seen you rejected, Asher. Maybe she'd rather go with someone else—"

My eyes widen.

Caleb shoves Eli, so hard and fast I almost don't register it. Eli hits the counter, snarling. Caleb's expression is impassive, but the muscle along his jaw is jumping as he clenches his teeth. They square off, although I'm not sure either wants to escalate it.

Or maybe not. I have no idea when it comes to guys and their testosterone.

I back out of the kitchen—a guilty relief—and into a strong pair of hands.

Theo scowls down at me. *Shocker.*

Liam pushes between Eli and Caleb before the tension can boil over. "What's this about?"

Caleb glares at Eli, while the latter glares at *me*. Because I said I wouldn't go to this dance? Or because he insinuated I'd go with someone other than Caleb?

I mean... that's my plan, right? My new plan. Forget boyfriend—I just need someone to take to this stupid thing.

"You're an idiot," Eli declares to Caleb.

The change in his mood doesn't go unnoticed, although I don't understand it.

His expression is vicious, his gaze lasered in on his best friend. All his features are sharp, from his nose and cheekbones to the lines of his jaw, to the heated gleam in his eyes.

152

"You should just leave your history with her in the past. She and her family—"

Crunch. Caleb's fist smashes into Eli's nose, narrowly avoiding Liam.

I leap back, hitting Theo's chest. Eli stumbles, touching his nose, and lunges at Caleb. Caleb, who still has marks on his face from Liam. I scream when they collide, and Caleb's head whips around.

Eli takes advantage of the distraction. He hits Caleb hard in the stomach, doubling him over.

Theo shoves me to the side and dives forward, along with Liam. They wrangle Eli and Caleb and force them apart.

My hand is glued to my mouth. It's one thing to hear about the violence or see it on video. It's another for it to happen right in front of me. Or even... it's not because of me, is it?

No... it is.

"Goddamn it." Theo has Caleb against the far counter, one hand on his chest. With his other, he points at me. "You. *Leave.*"

You know what? I'm totally on board with that plan.

I take two quick steps backward, unable to even look at Caleb. When no one stops me, when he doesn't tell Theo to fuck off, I spin on my heel and run.

The house is so familiar, I don't even think about where I'm going. I cut through the dining room, which leads to a parlor that was once a den for Caleb's father to host his friends. And partially a library.

All the books are still on the shelves, but the furniture is piled up in a far corner. I pass through it and out the side door. It deposits me behind the garage, on a concrete side-walk that runs down toward the guest house.

I go in that direction. My lungs are tight by the time I get there, and I gasp for breath. My fingers brush the doorknob. Shock filters through me when it easily turns under my hand.

I take a second to pray that no one lives here, and then I'm pushing inside.

Into the house I spent half of my childhood.

It's just as I remember it, plus a thick layer of dust. The kitchen is pale yellow with one of those retro green refrigerators at the end of the counter. A worn and scratched round table with four chairs set by a window. Magnetic block letters are on the fridge, all jumbled. A drawing—one of mine—clipped to it, too.

There's a cup by the sink.

Mesmerized, I pick it up. It sticks a bit, leaving a ring on the vinyl.

I can't remember who left it here. Whose cup it was. The liquid—water if I had to guess—had long since evaporated.

It's been seven years, after all.

"Put that down," Caleb hisses from the doorway. He marches across the room, kicking up dust, and wrenches the plastic cup from my grip.

My fingers are frozen.

He slams the cup back down in its spot and grabs my arm just above my elbow. When he drags me out of the room, something wild fractures in my chest. I shove him and manage to get loose.

He can't tear me out of here.

This was—

I used to—

You said it wasn't your home. Just a house, nothing

more. But that was a lie. My family was happy here, weren't we?

I race down the hallway and open a door. I stop dead in the doorway, my brain glitching.

My things.

My bed and toys and clothes and drawings on the wall.

Oh my God.

It's a time capsule. The whole place is. It's stuck in the past, probably the exact moment we were all dragged out of here. The social worker didn't let me come back. One of my drawers is open, and a flashing image of some stranger rooting through my clothes blindsides me.

I can't breathe. Everything inside me is twisting, shredding.

Why is it all the same? Why hasn't this place been cleared out or burned to the fucking ground? For the hate he's shown me, the loathing he so clearly feels, he should've destroyed it.

My palm flattens to my chest. My heart races, and I take another step forward. Toward the bed. We made it that morning, my dad and me. We painstakingly organized all the stuffed animals in a row along the wall side of it, my favorites in the middle.

Caleb grabs me from behind. He picks me up off my feet and carries me out.

I scream and thrash, but it doesn't matter. Not when my heel connects with his shin, or when I throw my head back and barely miss his face. My voice is shrill, the sound endless. It's disconnected from me, though. Not my high-pitched noise.

Once we're outside, he pushes me against the house. He claps his hand over my mouth, his fingers digging into my cheeks.

I scratch at his arms and kick out. It just makes him pin me down harder. His hips pressed to mine, our torsos aligned.

His breathing is out of control, even his hair is messier than before, but his eyes suck me in.

"Stop," he says. "Just stop."

The noise ringing in my ears slowly fades. I suck in gulps of air through my nose. Slowly, he releases my face.

"Breathe, baby."

My heartbeat is going to jump out of my throat, but I focus on his lips. He makes a show of inhaling and exhaling dramatically, enough for me to follow along.

My vision blurs.

Did I do something wrong?

"You didn't—no one—"

"We left it," he says. "No one's gone in there since they took you away."

"Caleb." I don't know why it sounds like I'm pleading with him. I'm still gripping his wrists. His forearms are scratched...

My mother shaking me hard enough to snap my head back.

I flinch at the jarring thought. "Those are my things. My childhood."

All of my memories of my parents are in that house.

He cups my cheek. "You don't go in there. It isn't yours to take."

It *is* mine.

My life unraveled, and all I want is to roll it back up again. Now Caleb is the gatekeeper to my past.

My present.

Hell, maybe my future—but not if I have anything to do with it.

"Please," I whisper. I'm less than air, floating away. His hand on my cheek, hotter than fire, is the only thing keeping me grounded.

But *please* is the wrong word to say.

His gaze hardens. His fingers dig into my skin, as if he'd like nothing less than to claw my heart out. He leans in close, close enough that I could move forward just a bit and kiss him if I wanted to. Or bite him.

Or claw his eyes out.

His gaze goes from my lips to my eyes and back, the burning fury at odds with how soft his hand still is on my face. For the briefest moments, I had my friend. But he's quickly reverting back to the bully.

His posture straightens, shoulders back. The arrogant asshole transforms right before my eyes, and one word decrees my death sentence: "No."

Chapter 15
Margo

When I was seven, we moved into the Ashers' guest house. It didn't occur to me what it was at that point—I just thought it was cool that there was another house so close. We shared a driveway, and my mom happened to work right across the lawn in their home.

It didn't make sense until I overheard my parents talking about Mom's employers: *the Ashers*. We weren't here by accident. This house didn't magically become ours.

My mom pulled me out of my new room one day, maybe a week or two after moving in, and brought me across the grass to the Asher house.

She introduced me to Caleb. A boy with short, dark hair and huge, piercing blue eyes. He was in a school uniform, and his mom was there, too. She was waiting with him in the kitchen, trying to stop him from disappearing farther into his huge house.

He stopped fidgeting when we walked in.

Our moms smiled at each other, while Caleb and I just stared.

The next day, my mom presented me with a similar uniform—in dress form, though—and drove me to my new school. Caleb was in my kindergarten class, although he didn't really look twice at me.

He was as odd as an alien. He ran around with boys twice his size and didn't flinch. I made friends with some girls and stuck close to them. We played with dolls and dressed up, hanging out in their big rooms in their giant homes. Their closets were almost bigger than my entire room.

A month later, I left the house with my mom to find Caleb playing alone in the backyard.

Her finger pressed into my spine. She did it when I slouched. I snapped my back straight, if only to relieve the pressure.

"Go say hello," she murmured.

I forced a smile and crossed the lawn to where he was playing with a firetruck.

"Hello, Caleb."

He narrowed his eyes at me.

"My mom said I should come talk to you."

"I don't want to talk to a dumb girl."

I strode forward and smacked his shoulder. "I'm not dumb."

Strange as it was, Caleb and I became fast friends after that. The way to a boy's heart is through physical violence, apparently. He still hung out with his friends at school, and I stayed with Amelie and Savannah. On the playground, if their ball sometimes rolled in our direction, I'd be the one to climb to my feet and toss it back to him.

He'd give me a weird, appraising look and mutter a grudging thank you.

He also sat with me on the bus. After the first time

driving me to school and registering me, Mom turned me over to their transportation system. Even rich kids have terrible buses, though.

I hadn't realized how awful it was until he sat next to me.

Everything got better because of it.

We carried on that way until we were eight. At that point, our friendship got a little more immediate. I ate the occasional dinner with his family—prepared and served by my mother. He helped me with my history homework, and I helped him with math.

"I'll only be friends with you if we play dress-up," I declared one day. We were sitting in the yard by the pool, tossing grass into the water.

Caleb sighed, loud and dramatic. "Guess I don't really have a choice then, huh?"

He followed me to his room.

I pointed to the door. "You need a suit."

"Why?"

"Because I said so!" I chucked a shoe at him for good measure, but it soared wide. If he threw it back, he'd probably nail me in the chest. His aim was a *lot* better than mine.

He grunted and left the room, and I put on the special dress I had snuck out of the house.

When he came back, he was wearing one of his father's suit jackets over his school uniform. It's giant on him, the sleeves extending well past his fingertips.

Still.

He stopped dead. "What is this?"

I smoothed the old white fabric with my hands. I'd been a flower girl only a few months ago. My dad's cousin got married, and I was apparently the only one eligible to walk down the aisle and throw flowers. The dress was lacy and frilly, with a full skirt and short sleeves.

"What does it look like?" I asked him.

He squinted at me, the tip of his tongue sliding out of his mouth with his concentration.

"We're getting married?"

I grinned, but was he going to go through with it? He'd either be in or out—with Caleb, you never knew. I figured this was a good way to solve my dilemma of how much he actually liked me.

You know: *friend*-like or *marriage*-like.

He straightened his tie and came closer. "I didn't get you a ring."

I shook my head and reached into my pocket.

"Got it covered," I said, showing him the two woven friendship bracelets in my hand.

I'd made one that was equal parts gold and blue, and the other was blue with a single cluster of gold thread. I struggled to make something so small it would fit around my finger, so I gave up and made bracelets.

"We're married until these fall off."

That was how those types of bracelets worked: keep them on until they fall off or it's bad luck. For*ever*.

"Okay," he agreed. He pushed the sleeves up on the suit jacket, exposing his hands. "But..."

Oh, no. He was about to back out. Or change the deal.

"What?" I held my breath.

"Do we have to kiss? To seal the deal?"

My eyebrows furrowed. I hadn't thought that far ahead.

He grinned and walked closer. The suit sleeves were falling back down, but he shoved them up to his elbows. "We could, you know."

"Kiss?"

"Adults do it."

My heart raced. "Do they?"

Mom and Dad didn't really kiss in front of me. They barely touched. *Do Caleb's parents kiss in front of him?* I'd seen it on movies, but I thought it was just that: fiction.

I knew the definition of fiction at age eight. I wasn't dumb.

Some things just weren't real: Santa, parents who really loved each other, and my future with Caleb. It was a fact I had already accepted before I came up with this idea. Before I decided to test what kind of *like* he had for me.

He picked up both bracelets. My dad had helped me singe the strings on each end so they wouldn't unravel, but they were open and ready for tying. He seemed to debate for a moment, then held up the one with more gold.

"I want this one. It reminds me of you."

He tied the mostly blue one around my wrist. He left it loose enough that I could've inched it over my hand, but I didn't. I slid it farther up, until it got stuck on my forearm. I couldn't lose it so quickly.

"Now me." He pushed his claimed bracelet at me.

I tied it with clumsy fingers, as loose as he had made mine. Who knew when these things would fall off? I suddenly wished I had made them out of steel.

"Kiss me," he demanded. "Make it official."

I leaned in, my hand on his wrist and my gaze on his mouth.

Our lips touched, just the barest of brushes. So brief that I don't think it counted. We both pulled back and stared at each other for a moment.

Then Caleb lifted my hand. "Wow. So this is what marriage feels like."

I waited. And then it hit me.

The *bond*. We'd be linked, him and me, by our wrists and our lips, forever. I wasn't mad about it. I was selfishly glad that he was mine.

Mine and no one else's. I'd fight them, and he would come back to me. Because: marriage. Even if Mom and Dad's marriage sucked, and Caleb's parents' marriage was rocky, sometimes fiction and real life could be the same.

We'd be the happy couple when we got into our older years. Twenties, thirties, forties. Hell, he'd probably love me through gray hair and wrinkles. I knew it, and judging from the look in his eye, he knew it, too.

And then, two years later, our lives imploded.

Chapter 16
Caleb

I meet the guys at Liam's place. They evacuated my house shortly after I dragged Margo out. I slink into the kitchen and grab a beer, then go find them in Liam's game room.

"That was fun," Theo grunts from his chair.

It's directed at me, I know. He keeps his eyes on the racing game they're playing.

I drop into the chair next to him. It's best that, for now, I stay the hell away from Liam. And Eli. They've both given me bruises... after fights that I started. How fucked up is that?

We're supposed to be in the trenches together, and I'm making it all about me.

They raise their eyebrows at me.

All I can do is scowl at them and say, "I don't want to talk about it."

Margo has gotten under *my* skin. It was supposed to be the other way around, damn it.

Liam shrugs. "Fine."

"I just said—"

"He didn't ask you a fucking question, man," Eli snaps. "If you want to be an asshole and sulk in the corner, fine. We'll leave you the fuck alone."

My lips flatten. I pick up the extra control and opt into Theo's next game. Video games won't release the tension I feel. The anger swirls like a fucking hurricane in my chest.

After about ten minutes, I say, "You never knew her."

They exchange glances.

"She left right before you transferred in." My words are directed at Eli.

His family moved here when we were eleven. I was an angry son of a bitch then, but no worse than I am now. Eh, no, probably less angry then.

It's grown in the years since.

"Okay," Eli says. "We do know this part of the story. The whole school's been talking about it."

I've kept this under wraps for a reason. It's personal shit. But I've got to say something to stop their squawking. "Yeah, but you don't know *my* side. We weren't just acquaintances. She didn't just live with her family in our guest house. She *was* family. She was my best friend."

"And then all the drama with her family?" That comes from Liam.

"Something like that." I jerk the controller, smashing Theo's character out of the way.

I don't feel anything when I win—except for Theo's elbow jabbed into my ribs.

"So why do you hate her?"

I drop the controller on the counter and lean back, taking a long swallow of beer. I'll need six more of these before I share any more secrets about her. And how she's still needling me after all these years.

"It's a long story." I stand. "I'm going. See you guys tomorrow."

Tomorrow is game day, which means... I really shouldn't sneak into Margo's room tonight. I need sleep. The thought sours my mood further. Although, the probability of her window being locked is high after I dropped her off. She didn't speak to me the entire ride back, as short as it was.

Ridiculous.

I say hello to Liam's mom on my way out, hurrying down the long driveway to my car. I parked behind Eli's truck. We always pull halfway off the gravel to allow for his mom's car to pass by. She gets home from work in the evenings exhausted.

Stone Ridge is the town next to Rose Hill. Same county but different schools. Actually, Stone Ridge High is the catch-all public school. The other two towns—Rose Hill and Beacon—have private schools.

Rival schools.

Lion's Head has been the biggest pain in Emery-Rose Elite's ass since sports were added to both schools. And of course, both seemed to level up in competitiveness over the course of a few decades. It helps that the teams play each other so often, and the proximity creates a certain friction between the towns.

Liam's family moved here from Rose Hill after some financial difficulty, although he was able to get a hockey scholarship and remain at ERE.

Luckily for us.

I crank the music in my car on the drive to my uncle's house. I need to see them before tomorrow's game, or he'll end up embarrassing me in some way or another.

I haven't been here in almost a week, which probably means the floodgates are going to open on me. Things I could be doing better. How he talked to my coach about my game. Talk of sending me to Lion's Head to be closer to *them*, how it's a better team.

They're not a better team.

And no one is as good as Coach Marzden.

The route I take winds me back through Rose Hill and the looming spires of Emery-Rose Elite. It's silent now, so far after hours.

Too soon, I'm pulling past the gate of my uncle's estate in Beacon. His property is much more sprawling than my childhood home. He owns acres and acres of land, half of which is maintained woods. Then there are gardens, a pool, a tennis court. A separate garage for their many vehicles. A boathouse.

There's a vehicle parked beside my uncle's silver Porsche that doesn't belong. I narrow my eyes at it as I park beside it, and exhale when Savannah meets my gaze from her driver's seat.

Her face is a mess of puffy eyelids and streaked mascara. Her chin is wobbling.

I don't give a fuck about that—she can't just show up. I get out of my car and circle around to hers, yanking her door open.

"What are you doing here?"

She climbs out, barely flinching at my tone. She throws her arms around my waist, and I raise my hands away from her body. I don't want to touch her more than I have to—and why would I want to, if Margo isn't here to witness it?

That's not part of the plan.

I don't like anyone's hands on me. Except Margo.

"Amelie is coming back," she sniffs. "Two months early!"

"And that's a... bad thing?"

Best I can recall, she and Amelie have been good friends since day one. Margo used to be in their mix, too. The fact that Savannah openly turned on Margo has been nothing short of delicious to watch unfold. Poor girl carried a torch for Margo for about a year, until the bullies beat her down. Eleven-year-olds are ruthless.

It's hard being the friend of a coke-whore's daughter.

"No," Savannah cries, using my shirt as a face wipe. She nuzzles her head into my chest. "It's great, it's just, she's coming back early..."

Revulsion sweeps through me. First, that she's *nuzzling* me. Second, that her tears are staining my shirt when all I want to do is go inside and get yelled at by my uncle.

I'm giving *myself* whiplash.

In their friend group—the popular girls—Amelie is in charge. She's the captain of the cheerleading squad. The queen bee. She's studying abroad this semester... well, I suppose she *was*. But something has drawn her back home.

In her absence, Savannah stepped into her role almost *too* flawlessly. She doesn't need to be reminded that there are consequences for every action. This one is clear as day.

And along with revulsion, my irritation spikes.

"You're just upset that she's going to knock you off the top of the pyramid?"

She pulls back, staring up at my face. She nods emphatically. "Yes, yes, that's it. But I thought if... maybe you and I..."

I push her off of me. Enough is enough. "You came here to proposition me. To use me against your best friend?"

Devious little creature.

"Well..."

I glower at her, and she cowers. I don't usually let anyone but Margo and my friends see the demons under my skin, but I let them out for her. *She needs to know to be afraid of me.*

"Bad idea, Sav."

"We—"

I stalk forward. Satisfaction spreads through me when she takes a quick step backward, then another one.

"We, what?" I bark. "We fucked once. I kissed you to make Margo jealous. You spread rumors about us dating that no one believed, not even your friends. How did that work out for you?"

She turns pale. "I'm sorry—"

"Get off your high horse," I snap. "Amelie is coming back, and you'll go back to being second..." I lift my eyebrow. "Well, now *third* best."

She gasps. "What?"

"Amelie and Margo were friends, too. And while she didn't defend Margo... she doesn't hate her as much as you do." *Probably because we only bullied you about being friends with her.* Of the two of them, Amelie is the traitorous snitch. She didn't have to publicly declare herself against Margo. She went behind everyone's backs and said so to my face.

But I don't say that.

Savannah lets out a ragged breath. "I'm such an idiot," she moans.

Well, *duh*.

She scrambles around me and practically dives into her car. She backs out fast, yanking the wheel around. Her hasty exit should give me some satisfaction, but I'm left with a damp shirt and a twisting sensation of being watched.

My gaze turns to the mansion's windows, ticking across all of the first-floor ones, then the second floor. There's no movement, no rustling curtains. No aunt spying on me to later report to my mother or uncle.

How will Margo react to the news that her ex-friend is back?

Will there be fireworks when the two collide...?

Probably. Especially since Amelie still thinks we're dating.

Part of me hopes the little lamb will drop the innocent act and draw first blood. She could easily assert her dominance over either girl, and the rest of the popular kids who follow either of them would fold.

My dick stiffens at the thought of Margo going after Amelie.

Wild fantasy. I doubt either girl would play fair in that fight. There would be hair pulling, maybe even blood drawn. Bruised skin. I'd press each bruise left on Margo, then kiss her flushed skin until she forgot about her anger.

Amelie is a means to an end... Margo *is* the end.

Chapter 17
Margo

I t was only a matter of time before Caleb's attention moved on to something a little more... stable. He said it himself, I was only a game.

Savannah was a tool to mess with me.

Which is why, when Amelie Page, former best friend, arrives before school, my heart sinks. She flicks her golden hair behind her shoulder, smiling at the circle of people around her.

She has an arm looped around Caleb's. He stands beside her with his hands in his pockets, completely unbothered by the girl hanging on him.

Seriously. Why is she touching him?

Riley joins me at the edge of the courtyard, keeping her voice low to explain, "Amelie was studying in France as an exchange student."

Shame seeps into my skin. It's a cold, vile feeling, and I almost turn away from them. I don't need to see Caleb with *another* ex-friend. Did he just go around collecting them after I left? I'm transfixed on her hand. The possessive way she touches him.

S. Massery

Everyone is watching her. A bad feeling twists my stomach. Savannah might've been holding the top spot, but Amelie owns it. It's clear to see how much influence she has, just by standing with Caleb.

It's all well and good—okay, it's not, but it's survivable—until I catch her eye.

She breaks away from Caleb and approaches me. "Margo! Welcome home."

Uh-oh.

"I should say that to you," I answer. "Back early?"

She waves me off. "Those things happen. Lots going on back here, I was missed. How shocked I was to learn that you had returned! Have you been reintroduced? You've seen Sav..." She turns to her friend across the way, and her perfectly sculpted eyebrow rises. "Oh, that isn't a happy face on our dear friend."

Savannah looks like she's bitten into a lemon.

Doesn't seem to matter, though. Amelie leads me over to her with a hand locked on my wrist. She throws her free arm around Savannah's shoulders, cinching Sav to her side.

"Our friend is back," Amelie says. "We're welcoming her with open arms."

That's a decree from a queen if I've ever heard one.

Savannah gives me a polite smile that hides daggers. *Uh-huh.* Very convincing.

"And you remember Caleb." Amelie drags me over to him. "My boyfriend."

Everything stops moving.

I stare at her, unable to even look at him. "What?"

"Darling, we've been dating since last year." She flips her hair back and leans in close. "Sure, you may have had him first... not in the traditional sense, obviously. And Sav got her pound of flesh. But he's *not* yours anymore."

I swallow. "Interesting. I wouldn't have expected—"

She smiles. "The bell is about to ring. You know the way?"

"To—"

She drops my arm.

"Let's go, Caleb." Her tone is different. Brisk, having lost that sugary sweetness directed at me. "We're going to be late."

The bell rings, and I flinch. Was that whole interaction fake?

He takes her away. The courtyard empties in seconds.

Long ago, I thought Caleb and I would have a happy ever after. Clearly... I was so wrong.

Riley stops beside me. We're the only two left. Everyone else followed *her*.

"That was the most cunning and brutal thing I've ever witnessed."

I swallow shards of glass. Pretty sure my insides are all hollowed out. "Yeah."

"Do you want to skip?"

I shake my head. "I really wish we had classes together. I can't skip. I should go in there with my head held high..."

I've dealt with mean girls before, remember? At every school, there's one who thinks they can take the new girl down a peg. The way to deal with them is to show how unaffected you can be.

And that means not skipping.

"Okay. I'll check on you after our first class and we'll see how you feel."

I successfully avoid Amelie and Caleb together for the rest of the day. Caleb is kind of unavoidable—he's in three of my classes.

First period, he tries to talk to me. Opens his mouth to

speak and everything. But I take someone else's seat across the room and death-glare at them when they try to say anything.

Crisis averted.

Lunch is spent with Riley, who again asks if I want to skip. But Robert, who dropped me off this morning, would absolutely notice my absence.

Sixth period, I sit in front of Liam. It's not the best solution, because I can see Caleb out of the corner of my eye the entire class. As soon as Mr. McGuire releases us, I bolt... to Robert's classroom.

"You can't avoid me forever." Caleb is positioned across from me, our easels angled to give us a view of each other.

"I can," I retort.

He scoffs.

My canvas is a mess. I've begun applying the shading technique, sketching out the parts of Caleb's face in shadow and highlights.

It holds only the vaguest passing for human.

Halfway through, Robert calls for us to set aside those canvases. We clean our brushes and wrap the palettes, then face him for the next lesson. Which, in this case, is watercolors. He demonstrates how to blend colors into a smooth gradient, then turns us loose. We sit at actual desks, usually shoved in one corner, because watercolors require the paper to be horizontal.

I take the opportunity to sit far from Caleb.

My two colors aren't working.

I chew on my lip and try again. Then again.

"You okay?" Robert asks.

I jerk my head up.

The room is empty except for us.

"The bell rang a few minutes ago. Did you even hear it?"

I stare at my paper. Heat crawls across my cheeks. "Sorry. I've had a bad day."

He drags a chair over and sits next to me. He points to one of my groupings, where I'd managed to make green fade into blue. "You did this one right. You can see the blue and the green, but there's also the middle space where it becomes a new color entirely."

"I got lucky on that one."

He shakes his head. "No, it just takes practice. Like this?" He taps his pencil next to the orange-into-pink one. "We don't see the two separate colors. May I?"

"Sure."

He cleans my brush in my cup of water and dips it in the pink. He pulls the brush down, the pink section almost the same size as my little ombré square. He repeats the process for the orange, everything bigger... and suddenly I can see it.

"I was close." I sigh. So close and yet... not it at all.

"Sometimes it's hard to see the big picture when you're so zoomed in." He glances at me. "A lot can be said about taking a step back."

"Like impressionism."

He laughs. "Yeah, like that. Or relationships. How you see people, and how they see you."

"Do you ever think you and Lenora are too... muddled?"

"Not often. I used to try to only see the good in her, but it doesn't work like that. You have to accept every part of someone." He taps my colors again. "Just like this. The colors are nice on their own, but if you only focus on the pretty parts, are they still beautiful?"

"I don't think someone will accept all of my flaws." I

175

keep my attention on the paper, not ready to see whatever is going to come across Robert's face next. They've been nice —more than nice, really. It feels like I've been welcomed into a complete family.

But maybe I've only been paying attention to the good pieces to convince myself that I belong.

"Someone will," he says firmly. "And not just in a romantic sense. Lenora and I are lucky to have you, too. I'm sure Riley would say the same."

"Maybe." God, it's hot in here.

Does Caleb see only my flaws? Robert's philosophy of seeing the good *and* the bad could go the other way, too. If we only focus on the negative traits, are they entirely bad?

Robert pats my shoulder. "Let's go home, kiddo. Are you still going to the hockey game with Riley?"

I wince at the reminder. "Yeah, I guess so."

Caleb didn't even bring it up. Is he still going to show up and take me to the game?

The school is a ghost town by the time we leave the classroom. We walk in easy silence back to his car, and I cast one look back toward the field where the teams have started practicing. Including the cheerleaders.

Atop of the pyramid is Amelie, smiling like a conqueror. On the second level, seeming pained with Amelie's knee in her back, is Savannah.

Interesting.

Only last week, she was the one on top. I give her credit where it's due: she's got talent for it. Except, clearly, Amelie is better. Brighter. Hell, she radiates joy even when she's not trying.

I take a mental step back. Maybe she *is* trying, and that's her secret.

And maybe...

"Margo?"

I stop, and my head snaps forward. I was about an inch from walking right into Robert's car. "Oops."

He frowns. "Have you thought about trying out for a sport?"

"I don't know what I'd go for." The idea of bonding with a team, involved in a sport where people rely on me... that is too much.

Three and a half more months. That's how long I have to last here... I'll figure out the rest later.

"It could give you a sense of community." Robert watches me over the roof of the vehicle.

"I'll think about it," I promise.

And I do. Half-heartedly, I consider how it would feel to let down an entire team. By the time we get home, I've made up my mind that I'm not going to do anything. Between painting and Riley, and... I don't know, *Caleb*... I've got enough going on.

Lenora's car is already in the driveway. We park beside it and head in. Immediately, the scent of garlic reaches us. My mouth waters.

"We're home, Len," Robert calls. "Your cooking smells wonderful!"

She rounds the corner wearing a bright-red apron. "I'm glad you're back! You're just in time."

"For what?" It's barely three o'clock. Caleb will be picking me up for the game in two hours.

"For you to help me." She pulls something from behind her back, holding it out to me.

"Is that... my own apron?"

It's light blue, with embroidered butterflies across the chest.

"Yes, it has your name on it and everything." She taps

the stitched *Margo* on the top left, nestled between the butterflies. "Come on, before I burn everything."

My throat closes.

No one has ever gotten me anything like this, and I'm not sure I'm processing it.

I drop my bag and follow her into the kitchen, where there are a million bowls. Okay, more like six, but *still*.

"This is..." I gulp.

"Overwhelming?"

She helps me put the apron on. The loop over my head, the strings wrapping behind me and tying in the front. She leaves me to knot it, then stands back with a big smile.

"It's your color," she declares. "Okay, so we take this one veggie at a time. I'll show you how to chop an onion without crying and then we'll move on to easier stuff."

"There's a way to cut an onion without crying?" I shoot a glance at Robert. Where was this tip when I had tears and snot running down my face?

He holds up his hands in surrender. "Oops."

Lenora chuckles. She shows me the proper way. Not surprisingly, she's as good of a teacher as Robert. Maybe that's why they're happy together? Or why they don't get muddled?

She seasons chicken while the oven preheats. We work in silence for a few minutes. Besides the onions—bigger chopped pieces—we have squared yams, half-moons of zucchini and yellow squash, and broccoli.

"What are we making?"

"We're going to cut up some chicken and bake all of this together with some salt and pepper," she says. "I'll get the chicken going. Here's the dish."

She sets a glass dish next to my cutting board. I slide the cut veggies into it, then move on to the broccoli. She demonstrated how to cut it without getting the little bits of green everywhere, and I toss them in.

Lenora cuts the chicken and adds it. She drizzles the garlic-infused olive oil over everything and gives it a toss with her tongs. We cover the whole mixture with a bit of salt and pepper, and then we're done.

"That was easy."

"And it's almost guaranteed to taste good." She washes her hands. "I'll put it in the oven. Rob mentioned you're going to the hockey game tonight?"

I pause. "Yeah. Is that okay?"

"Absolutely! It's part of the reason why I wanted to prep so early."

"Caleb is coming to get me at four."

She tilts her head. "Caleb Asher? Isn't he on the team?"

I lift my shoulder. "Yeah, but he wanted to drive me. I don't know."

"Okay. No worries, honey, I just wanted to make sure."

By the time the dish comes out of the oven, my stomach is making obnoxious sounds.

"I didn't think I'd be able to do something like this," I admit to her.

"I wouldn't have been able to do it without your help. My mother once told me to have at least *one* meal you're good at. That you can make for potluck parties or holidays. If you have more than one, that's fine. This might not be that dish for me, but it is an easy go-to."

I mirror her smile. "It's a great one."

"If you want to choose a meal to perfect in your own way, we can pick up the ingredients and make it next week," she offers.

Making plans for the future? Butterflies burst to life in my chest.

179

Plan-making is not something I take for granted.

Robert comes in, eyeing the table. "My mouth has been watering for the last half hour," he admonishes. "And now that it's ready, you don't even call me?"

Lenora chuckles, kissing his cheek. "We were just about to, dear. Wash your hands."

"Yes, ma'am."

We all sit, hesitating for a split second before diving into the food. I put a bite in my mouth and groan.

"Food made with love." Lenora sighs. "Always tastes good to the stomach and the soul."

Chapter 18
Margo

There are a few messages waiting for me after dinner. I returned to my room to get ready, but now I sit heavily on my bed. One message is from Caleb, another from Riley, and another from that unknown number. My stomach swoops, and I click that one first.

What can I say? Maybe I'm a little masochistic.

I scan the text with my heart in my throat.

UNKNOWN

Don't get too comfortable, drug princess.
Once a stray, always a stray.

I hadn't heard from this mystery texter in a while. I thought—wrongly—that they had gotten bored. I mean, Caleb seems to outwardly hate me, Amelie made it clear I'm not welcome, and Savannah went out of her way to give me a rough time. Along with the cheerleaders following her lead.

Go away.

> You wish it would be that easy, don't you?

I switch over to Riley's text.

RILEY
> Eli is grabbing me. Guess we're both going to be there early. Not weird at all, right?

> LOL

> Right.

Then, finally, Caleb.

CALEB
> Be there in five.

As I'm typing a reply, the doorbell rings.
Uh-oh.
"I've got it," Robert calls from downstairs.

Before I can warn him, he's swinging the door open and admitting Caleb Asher inside. I rush down the steps and skid to a halt on the landing.

He's not wearing anything particularly interesting—an Emery-Rose Elite sweatshirt, jeans, white tennis shoes. His hair is all messy and falling into his eyes.

And he *smiles* at me.

"Thank you for letting me take Margo to my game," he says to Robert.

"We appreciate you getting her out and about," my foster father says.

Ugh.

Caleb's gaze flicks to me, still stuck on the steps, and he smirks.

After dinner, and before checking my messages, I cleaned up my makeup and brushed my hair out. I'm wearing *his* sweatshirt, the one I ended up going home in after the night in the park, and black jeans. His name is embroidered in gold on the sleeve.

Maybe that will cause problems with Amelie?

He doesn't tell me to take it off and give it back, though. In fact, he's made absolutely no mention of Amelie whatsoever. Or that he has a girlfriend. He hasn't refuted it yet either.

Don't expect that of him.

Does Robert know that Caleb is dating the most popular girl in school? Is any of this raising a freaking red flag for him?

Probably not... if only because Caleb knows exactly how to charm people.

"Ready, Margo?"

I meet Caleb's stare and slowly nod. I go down the remaining steps and stop in front of him. I'm ready to get him out of this house and away from my foster parents. I'm ready to pretend to know what the fuck is going on in the sport of ice hockey...

Robert gives me some money for concessions, Lenora takes a picture of us just because, and then we're out the door. We don't speak until we're in Caleb's Audi, the engine purring.

"You're wearing my sweatshirt." His voice is husky.

I frown. "I... yeah. I'll take it off."

His hand lands on my arm, pausing my movements. "No."

Oh.

I sit back. "Do I need a ticket?"

"I have one for you."

"Where do I sit?"

"You have a good seat." He glances my way. "Next to

Riley, in fact."

I narrow my eyes. "Did you stick me in the nosebleeds?"

"It's a high school arena, baby. There are no nosebleeds."

That's fair.

"How does the game work?"

He glances over at me, his eyebrows rising. "What?"

I motion to... well, him.

"How does the game of *hockey* work?"

I scoff. "You should've asked if I knew anything about it before you invited me."

"Jesus, Margo."

"What? I mean, I get the concept. Get the puck in the net. Hit people."

He laughs. "Yeah, that about covers it."

Lovely. I cross my arms, but the true extent of my lack of knowledge only becomes apparent when Riley and I are sitting in the arena, five rows back from the glass—*there's glass that goes all the way around the ice?*—and I can barely follow a thing.

The players zip around, the refs randomly blow the whistle. They restart. Sometimes someone goes in the box to our left.

Riley has to stifle her laughter.

"I just don't get it," I say for the thousandth time. "Why do they keep stopping?"

"That was offsides," she says.

Great. That's helpful.

I lean forward in my seat. So far, I've been able to track Caleb around the rink a few times. He's number twenty-four, with *Asher* in block print across his back. When he's on the ice, Eli and Liam are also with him.

Which makes it marginally easier, because every time Riley spots Eli, she elbows me.

I'm going to have bruised ribs.

The arena is a mix of black-and-gold-clad students and parents and purple-and-white fans rooting for Lion's Head.

The word *rivalry* has been tossed around.

But for the first period—of which there are three—it seems relatively... maybe calm is the wrong word.

Civil?

It all explodes in the second period. One of the Lion's Head guys crashes into Liam, and they *both* career into the Emery-Rose goalie. The three of them slide into the net in a tangle of limbs, sending the whole goal flying.

Caleb and Theo are there in an instant, wrenching the Lion's Head player up. Instead of letting go, though, Theo holds on tight.

It becomes a free-for-all. It seems like all the players already on the ice, sans the goalies, jump into the fray.

The referees break everything up. Caleb emerges with blood on his lip, the split from earlier in the week opened up. He spits pink saliva on the ice and glances in my direction.

"Did he just wink at you?" Riley asks.

I laugh it off. But, yeah, he totally did.

This sport is *violent*... and I think I like it.

I'm clueless, completely lost, but I want more of it.

He skates by the glass, his mouth guard popped out of his mouth. He chews on a corner of it, then easily maneuvers it back into place.

That shouldn't be hot... but it is.

The score is 1-1, and my anticipation climbs as Emery-Rose seems to put on an aggressive offense. At least, I'm assuming that's what happens. They spend a good amount of time in front of the Lion's Head goalie.

When the horn blows at the end of the period, the game is still tied.

I swivel in my seat. We're surrounded by Emery-Rose students and parents. One section over, Amelie holds court. Savannah is one row lower than her, with two cheerleaders on either side.

"Usually the football games happen on the same night," Riley says. "Which means they won't normally be here."

Amelie's head turns sharply, and she stares right at me.

"She probably didn't like her boyfriend winking at someone else." I force a smile at her, then get up. "I'm going to get something to eat."

Riley joins me.

We climb the steps and exit into the hall, where there's a few vendors still open. One sells Emery-Rose Elite clothing—jerseys, t-shirts, hoodies—and another has food. The line is kind of long, but we stand at the end without complaint.

"Margo!"

I wince inwardly, then turn to face Amelie.

And Savannah.

And sixteen other girls.

Exaggeration? Only slightly.

"Hi," I greet them.

"Are you enjoying the game?" Amelie touches the corner of her pink-painted lip. "You haven't seen them play before, right?"

"First hockey game," I admit.

"So nice," Amelie coos. "I'm surprised, though."

I eye her.

When I don't reply, Savannah jumps in. "Why is that, Ames?"

"Well," Amelie says slowly. "If I knew the captain of the hockey team hated me so much... I wouldn't want to be a distraction."

My throat closes.

"A distraction," Savannah echoes.

"It's bad business for hockey players. They're superstitious, you know? If you go to a game and he sees you, what's he going to think when they lose?" Amelie sighs. "Listen, Margo, I'm just trying to protect you."

"No, you're not." Riley snorts. "Come on, Margo."

She hooks her arm through mine and drags me away.

But... jeez. Amelie leaves me off-kilter. The feeling doesn't abate through the rest of the second intermission, or when the third period begins. My heart slams against my rib cage, and I sit as still as possible.

Because if she *is* right, I don't want to draw his attention.

I have it, though.

He skates past our section after a whistle is blown, and his blue eyes find me easily. He points in my direction.

He has a girlfriend who he's ignoring.

He drove me here.

"If he didn't want you to go, he would've left it alone," Riley assures me. "We would've ended up here, but he literally brought you."

I guess so.

There's a fight in the third period—Theo and some Lion's Head player. They lock on to each other, ripping away their helmets and trading punches. The refs break it up fast... Riley mutters that fighting isn't really a thing in high school hockey. But the crowd is on its feet, everyone cheering and screaming.

Because the enjoyment of violence is universal.

Five minutes later—with only two minutes to go—Caleb gets the puck. He's all alone when he pours on a burst of speed toward the other goalie. I jump to my feet, clutching at Riley's arm, just in time for him to send the puck sailing past the goalie and into the net.

He scored.

2-1, with two minutes to go.

"Holy shit!" I throw my arms in the air. "That was awesome."

The next two minutes are stressful—but the Emery-Rose goalie holds firm.

And our team wins it.

CALEB

Meet me at my car.

I show Riley the text on my lock screen, and she nods. We follow the line of people out into the hall, then toward the stairwells that will put us on the street. Once on the sidewalk, in the cool night air, Riley loops her arm in mine and steers me toward the side parking lot. Not the main one where most of the driving crowd has parked.

We round the corner and come face-to-face with Amelie and Savannah.

My grip on Riley tightens.

"We were just talking about you," Savannah says to me.

"Shocker."

Riley steers me around them, half dragging to get me moving faster.

"He's *my* boyfriend," Amelie calls after me. "You need to leave him alone."

I dig my heels in, stopping my friend, and face her. "He treats you like garbage. Maybe you should dump him."

"Maybe it's more complicated than that." Her eyes flash.

I shrug. "I'm not in charge of him, Amelie. And you're not in charge of me."

The laugh that bursts out of her is cold. "No? Try me, Wolfe. We'll see how far you get."

The threat rolls right off my shoulders. Who *am* I? A month ago, I would've absolutely backed off... but if Caleb isn't, then I'm not.

If my head was screwed on straight, I'd be shoving Caleb back into her arms.

But he's mine. A girlfriend isn't going to change that. His antics toward me aren't either.

He's always fucking been mine.

Chapter 19
Caleb

I love hockey.

But I'd give anything to be next to Margo, experiencing the game for the first time.

That thought plagues me on the way back to her house. My hand on her thigh, my fingers caressing her through the denim. She doesn't stop me or pepper me with questions. Her gaze is heavy-lidded, and she glances at me questioningly when I pull to the curb.

It's a *will I see you later?* look.

Yes, baby. You absolutely will.

If the Bryans weren't expecting her home after, I would take her back to my house and show her how winning a game makes me feel.

I reveal the game winning puck from my pocket and hold it out.

"For me?"

Fuck me, her voice rasps. My dick leaps to attention.

I nod. "Keep it."

She smiles... and then gets out of the car. I watch her ass

sway as she walks up the front steps. The porch light gives her a halo for a moment, and then she's in.

I make a show of driving away, just in case Lenora or Robert are watching from a window.

But make no mistake. I'll be back.

Chapter 20
Margo

My bed dips, and my eyes fly open.

A shadow looms above me.

I open my mouth to scream, but all that comes out is a hoarse wheeze before a hand clamps over the lower half of my face. Strong fingers dig into my skin.

"Easy, baby," Caleb whispers.

When I relax, he removes his hand from my lips and raises an eyebrow.

"You came back?"

"Am I unwelcome?" He smirks.

"Y-yes," I sputter. I try to sit up, but he's lying on top of my comforter. It pins me in place. "Get out."

He seems to contemplate it for a second, then rolls his eyes. "No. You gave me a look when I dropped you off. I thought we were finally on the same page."

"Yeah, right..." Okay, fine. I did give him a look, but it was more of a *I hope you don't sneak in through my window tonight* expression. Clearly our wires got a little crossed.

Then there was the whole *he's mine* thought process. As soon as I got inside, I realized... how fucking dumb am I?

Do I want Amelie or anyone else touching him?

No. Especially not in front of me. Or behind my back. Or in any innocent or nefarious capacity.

Do I want him touching *me*?

No.

Well, except for when I woke up with his head between my legs... that was nice.

Nice. I just described waking up to *that*, and the subsequential orgasm, as *nice*.

I'm losing it.

He hops off the bed and sheds his clothes. Sweatshirt, t-shirt, jeans. Even his socks come off. He pulls back the edge of my comforter and slides underneath clad only in his boxers.

"What are you doing?" I shift to give him room... although I'm not really sure I want him to settle in. I mean, Lenora and Robert are right down the hall.

He moves down so we're face-to-face. He puts his elbow on my pillow, propping up his head. "I was thinking about something after I dropped you off. You never apologized."

I eye him. "Why would I apologize?"

"For going into my guest house without permission."

I rise up on my elbow, too, narrowing my eyes. "Excuse me, Mr. High and Mighty—"

His free hand shoots out, grabbing my throat and forcing me flat on my back. He leans over me, the picture of calm. "Do not test me."

"It was *my*—"

His fingers tighten, and I automatically stop talking.

Clearly, when I said I was losing it, I should've said *we* were losing it. He's lost his fucking marbles, too, judging by his dark expression. He stares down at me with a promise—or threat—to unleash all his demons on me.

All I need to do is continue down the denial road.

"I'm sorry," I squeak.

He loosens his hold, but his face is still a calm mask. I don't trust it one bit.

His hand moves over my collarbone and down the center of my chest. "You're not wearing a bra."

"It's the middle of the night," I breathe. "What kind of girls have you been hanging out with who sleep in underwire?"

His finger brushes over one of my nipples, and it pebbles under his touch. My lips part, but the question of where he's going dies on my lips when he smirks.

"Wouldn't you like to know?"

I grab his wrist, stopping his hand from moving farther south. "I would, actually."

His gaze crashes into mine. "Currently? None."

"None," I repeat. "No one. Not a single girl?"

He goes for the hem of my shirt. I try to fight him, but suddenly he's hovering over me. He takes my arms and holds them above my head.

"Don't move," he orders.

My breath comes in sharp pants. "W-what are you going to—"

"Quiet, baby. It's just you, okay?"

I press my lips together.

His fingers return to the hem of my nightshirt. He raises it slowly, revealing my stomach, my rib cage, my breasts. He massages one breast in his hand, fingers rolling and pinching my nipple. It's aching pain and pleasure. My back arches off the bed. He pushes me down again. His palm burns up against my stomach.

Why am I letting him touch me like this?

Because no one ever has.

My heart skips when his hot mouth touches my other breast, clamping on my nipple.

Holy shit. Every nerve is on fire, begging to be touched, but I can't speak.

His tongue swirls on my skin. It's the only warning I get before he bites me. Hard.

I yelp, my hands coming down and shoving at his head. He chuckles against my skin and allows me to push him off. Sitting back and kneeling next to my body, he shoves my blankets off of me. In a quick move, he grabs the waistband of my shorts and yanks them down, taking my panties with it.

"Caleb." I sit up fast. My back hits my headboard, and I put my hand between my legs. Mainly to hide myself from him. My t-shirt slides back down, concealing my breasts.

I'm burning with shame and a tiny bit too much desire for this situation. He drops my shorts but keeps my white lace panties in one hand.

"If looks could kill." He appraises me. "Do you not want me to touch you, little lamb?"

Well...

He sees my indecision plain as day. And he makes the choice for me. "Give me your hands."

We watch each other in the dark. This is another test, isn't it? Another fucking game. But this one... I guess it feels a bit safe, here in my bedroom. I offer my arms, and he loops my panties around each wrist. He moves to the headboard and ties it to one of the bars.

The position has my head back on the pillow. My heart lurches, but all he does is lean down and trail kisses down my jaw, my throat. "Will you scream? Wake up your foster parents?"

There's something inexplicably aggravating about how

helpless I feel. The more he touches me, the more I want to touch him back.

It's just me, he said.

"No." I swallow. "I wouldn't scream. Not now. And certainly not—"

He thrusts a finger into me without warning. I hadn't even realized his hand had drifted, so focused on his expression. But the feeling is unlike anything else, and my mouth opens and shuts uselessly.

His other hand goes to my throat, caressing the spot where I'm sure he can feel my pulse leaping out of my skin. His eyes gleam with a challenge as he slowly withdraws and pumps it back in. Again and again until my legs shake.

He hasn't touched anything else.

I tug on the restraint, and he kisses the corner of my lips.

"Don't ask me to fuck you," he whispers. "Because when I do, you *will* be screaming my name."

He latches on to my nipple, sucking hard before his teeth scrape my skin.

I buck, fighting the feeling. He withdraws his finger from my pussy, and two push back in. It stretches me, and I groan. His thumb brushes my clit.

"Do that again."

His laugh rumbles in his chest.

His slow assault continues. Each move brings me closer to the edge, although he seems content to take his time. He tastes my breast, my sternum. My other nipple, biting and sucking the flesh above it. That plus what he's doing between my legs... My core pulses around his fingers.

He takes everything.

So when the orgasm finally crests, he releases my nipple and watches me. My face flames—and the flush takes over my body. He finally releases my pussy, and I sag against the bed.

The glint in his gaze conveys that we haven't even started yet. Not truly.

He lifts his fingers; they're glistening in the faint moonlight. He puts them on my lips.

"Suck."

We've done this before.

I open my mouth to tell him to fuck off, but he takes the opening. He pushes his fingers into my mouth, and the taste of *me* takes over my senses. Tentatively, I touch my tongue to his fingers. He presses down on my tongue, and saliva fills my mouth.

His gaze is fastened on my lips.

I bite his fingers.

He jerks them out of my mouth and scowls. "Didn't take you as one into blood play."

"I could be into a whole range of things you know nothing about."

"Is that a promise?" He undoes my panties from the headboard and carefully unwinds them from my wrists.

"Maybe," I reply.

He rolls onto his back. He drags his boxers down, exposing his dick. It springs to attention, stiff and straight.

"Um..."

"Straddle my chest," he orders.

"Why?"

"So I can lick your pussy while you choke on my cock."

Oh, fuck. My face heats, and I shake my head—then stop. Because I *just* said I might be into a whole range of things... but I'm not going to know either. Not unless I try.

So I do what he says. I get up on my knees and swing

one leg over, facing his dick. It's a totally different angle this way, instead of on my knees while he stands above me.

I gather my hair and pull it over one shoulder, then lower myself.

I spit on him, and it twitches. I wrap my fingers around it and stroke it a few times, then... well, I just go for it. I take him deep, and he groans. He waits until I've found some semblance of a rhythm, a pattern, and then absolutely obliterates it by licking straight up my center.

"Keep going." He nips at my ass cheek.

I lurch. His hands on my hips keep me in place, then drag me back harder against his face.

If I thought *I* wasn't holding back... surely he's just trying to outdo me. His tongue plunges into me, then moves to my sensitive clit. Everything throbs in time with his ministrations, and I try to keep up. I twist my hand around the base of his dick, then reach down and cup his balls.

He moans. His hips jack, forcing himself deeper into my mouth. He hits the back of my throat. He continues to fuck my face until his balls lift up toward his body. I only feel it because of my fingers on them, and it's the warning I need.

He comes in my mouth.

Across my tongue, down my throat. I swallow hard, sucking until there's nothing left. And then I focus on the sensation between my legs and the pleasure spiraling through me.

I press my forehead to his stomach and struggle to keep my composure—and to keep quiet. I come with a low groan, twisting the sheets up in my fists. And when I finally gain my sanity back, I pitch sideways off of him.

I take deep breaths, then roll out of bed and hurry into the bathroom. My chest is tight, restricting my lungs, and my heartbeat hammers so loud in my ears I can't think straight.

How am I supposed to react to the way he always sneaks in and does wicked things to me?

Not to mention—he said I was the only one.

Do I believe him?

I just need to wait until he gets dressed and climbs back out the window. Which shouldn't take him too long, right?

Wrong.

By the time I've cleaned myself up, washed my face, and re-brushed my teeth—because, *ew*, cum breath—I've wasted a good ten minutes. And my heart rate is back to normal. The anxiety holding me hostage has loosened its grip.

It's late, but tomorrow is Saturday. I can sleep in... and then deal with the consequences later.

I leave the light on to see the damage Caleb caused to my bed and open the door. The warm glow spills across the room, slanting over my bed, and highlighting Caleb.

He's lying on bed.

Still.

I glare at him, but he's not even looking at me. He's fixed the sheets and blankets, put his boxers back into place, and is curled on his side. His eyes are closed.

There's an empty spot next to him.

"What are you doing?" I whisper-yell.

He frowns at my tone. "What are *you* doing?"

"Waiting for you to leave."

"Huh." He pats the space next to him. "I've been waiting for you to join me."

"That's my bed."

"I'm in the right place, then."

I narrow my eyes.

"No funny business," he promises. "Come on."

"There's no talking you out of leaving?"

"I like some quality skin-to-skin action after sex."

"That wasn't sex."

"It's oral *sex*, baby." He glances over. "You going to deny me?"

"Maybe I should." I cross my arms. "Didn't you once say that? The more I ask, the more you'll deny."

An idea takes hold.

I drop to my knees, so fast the impact travels up into my hips.

Caleb sits up slowly.

I lock my fingers together, as if to pray, and raise them. "Oh, please, Caleb. Please stay with me tonight."

His gaze is thunderous, but I hold his eye contact.

"Get in bed, Margo." A slow smile curls his lips. "Unless you're still hungry. Then you can stay right there and I'll fuck your face. Nice and slow."

"Will you leave, then?"

"Do you want me to?"

"I just begged for the opposite..."

He shakes his head and unfolds his body from the mattress. My muscles tremble when he comes closer, but I don't stand. My knees would probably give out anyway.

Nerves or anxiety or whatever.

He slides his fingers into my hair, feeling the silky strands. After a minute of stroking, he tangles them in my hair and tugs sharply.

My head falls backward, going with the pressure.

"You don't fold when I threaten to shove my cock so deep down your throat you'll be unable to breathe," he murmurs. "And you don't say anything about me touching you. Or hurting you."

"I'm just letting you work out your trauma," I say on an exhale.

His grip tightens. "Fuck you."

"You keep threatening that, but nothing happens."

"You're a virgin, aren't you? Sweet little lamb, holding on to that innocence with a white-knuckled grip. You talk a big game, you know that?"

"I learned from the best."

"Your coke-whore mother?" he guesses. "Or your father?"

I nut-punch him.

I didn't think it would actually work—I mean, I grew up around a lot of children, many of whom came to the group homes with bad habits. One girl would nut-punch the adult men if she didn't get her way, and eventually started doing it to the boys who irritated her or stole her toys.

She didn't last long... But I was always fascinated with how they folded.

Just like Caleb, folding in front of me.

I shove him away, my hair sliding through his fingers, and rush to the window. I shove it all the way open, letting in a blast of cold October night air. He should take the hint and get out.

I climb into bed, completely ignoring his mutterings, and yank the blankets up to my ears.

He'll get the message.

He'll leave.

Wrong again.

The blankets lift behind me, and a hot body presses to my back. I stiffen, even when the blankets settle around us, and his arm drapes over my hip.

His slow chuckle vibrates in his chest. "I love how you think you can get rid of me with a little pain."

S. Massery

"Well, a girl can dream."

"Dream about me." He smooths my hair out of the way, shifting me closer. "Go to sleep."

And the most surprising part: I do sleep.

Caleb curled around me wards off the bad dreams, and I wake up once, in the middle of the night, to find that I'd flipped around in my sleep. My cheek is plastered to his chest, head tucked under his chin, and I'm wrapped around him like an octopus.

As much as it disturbs me, I let his quiet *shush* drag me back under.

In the morning, he's gone.

Chapter 21
Margo

"Are you going to spill, or what?"

"Spill about..."

"Everything, Margo. I think it's time we talked about your secrets."

I scowl. "Your bribery isn't going to work."

Riley rolls her eyes and reaches into her backseat, revealing a bag from the coffee shop. It's Saturday morning, approximately two hours after I discovered Caleb had left sometime around dawn.

The fact that he left shouldn't have surprised me. It's not like I have a semblance of privacy. As a foster kid, the lack thereof kind of comes with the territory. But him leaving has left me off balance.

Unsettled?

It's not so much that he came over and made *me* come. Or that he drove me to the game. Or said there was only me. All things I'm latching on to in an attempt to reconcile this Caleb with the ten-year-old boy I loved.

No, it's that he still does terrible things to me.

And God help me, but they're almost forgivable.

S. Massery

Two orgasms and I change my mind about him. *That* caused some panic. A full-fledged panic attack, actually, when I was in the shower. I gasped and scratched at my hickey-covered chest, trying to remember how to breathe, while warm water poured down on my back.

Once I was dry, I sent Riley an SOS. She showed up not long after, armed with a smile and an excuse for Robert and Lenora.

I open the coffee shop bag and eye the muffin.

"Okay, the bribery might work," I say.

"Knew it." Riley grins.

We're on our way to school, which is hosting a farmers' market in the parking lot. Apparently, the board of Emery-Rose Elite allows vendors to set up there once a month, and they donate most of the table fee profits back into Rose Hill.

Good visibility for the vendors, good publicity for the school.

"Out with it." She taps her nail on one of the paper cups between us. "And this coffee is yours."

See? Bribery totally works.

I shift. "I knew Amelie and Savannah in elementary school. And Caleb, of course."

"Right. You knew more than just them, I'd reckon."

"Well, yeah. But they're the important ones. Amelie said she's dating Caleb. That he's her boyfriend. He never mentioned her, though." I gnaw on my bottom lip. "He snuck into my room last night."

She gasps. "Excuse me?"

"He's..." *Wicked.*

"That's devious," she says. "To be one way at school and another after? What is he trying to do? Confuse the hell out of you?"

"I guess. The bullying is over the top, too. Sooner or later, Robert is going to notice."

She winces as we park in the faculty lot. "Eh, teachers don't hear *everything*—"

"But they hear enough."

Across the parking lot, Caleb and his friends walk toward the farmers' market that's spread across the student parking lot. There are rows and rows of stands, tents covering the different tables all different colors. It's bigger than I would've imagined.

He's absorbed in a conversation with Eli. As we watch, Amelie trots over and throws herself at him, a move he narrowly dodges. I'll give him credit: he makes it seem like a happy accident.

He says something, and she rears back, distain flashing across her face.

"Wonder what that's about?" I ask. "And why are they here?"

She shakes her head. "They must be bored. And he was just... with you?"

Dread climbs up my throat. "Yeah."

After we finish the muffins, I take a large gulp of my coffee.

"We don't have to stay long," she tells me. "Just say the word, and we'll go. Hell, we can go right now."

I wave her off. "I want to see it."

We head toward the stands, but my attention is drawn to an approaching person. Not one of our usual cohorts—which, admittedly, just contains me, Riley, and occasionally Jacq.

Ian Fletcher.

"What does he want?" I ask under my breath.

Riley finds who I'm looking at. "Oh no."

"Hey," Ian calls.

I swear, everyone within earshot stops what they're doing and stares.

"What're you going to do now that your fifteen minutes of fame are over?" he continues.

My palms sweat.

Ian keeps coming. "You gonna move on to someone else?"

"Go away, Fletcher," Riley snaps.

The louder he talks, the more attention he draws. Until students drift in our direction, forming a wide circle around us.

He scoffs, ignoring her and keeping his glare pinned on me. "Keep your whore cunt away from me and my friends. God knows you've caused enough damage."

I lift my chin. "Lucky us, my *cunt* wants nothing to do with you. Or your friends."

He pretends to be hurt for a second. It falls away easily, and his expression is just... blank. Frozen. "I've been wondering what'd you do to make your coke-whore mom run away. But then I realized! It's just a fucking personality defect."

—please don't go—

My ten-year-old voice rings in my ear.

Funny how that's the button to push that makes me crack.

Ian's laugh follows me when I bolt. I shove past people and pass the farmers' market. Riley calls my name, but it's easier to just leave everything behind. I run across the soccer field and up a path into the woods.

I keep going until my ribs ache and the laughter stops chasing me.

Panting, I lean against a tree.

206

"That was quite a show. Although, to be fair, I only saw it through my phone."

I jerk around, pressing my hand to my chest.

Theo stands down the path from me, in the opposite direction of where I came. He walked into the market with Caleb, but he must've peeled away. To come out here...

He stubs out a cigarette against a tree and tosses it into the woods, winking at me. "Our little secret, yeah?"

"How did you see it on your phone?"

He flashes his screen at me. Ian's tinny voice comes out of the speaker. "Live streaming on social media is all the rage for embarrassing moments."

Great.

"What do you want?" I dab at my face with my sleeve. The tears didn't fall long enough to make my mascara run or puff up my eyelids.

"What do I want?" He pauses. "I'd love to know why Ian got such a visceral reaction out of you. God knows Caleb's been trying to do the same for weeks."

I shrug and look away. "He just touched a nerve."

"Your mom."

There's a gleam in his eye that I don't like.

I straighten and face him. "If you run back and tell Caleb that's my secret weakness, I will destroy you."

He laughs. *Laughs.* "I've always wanted to hear what it would sound like to be threatened by a toddler."

I turn away from him. "I came out here to be alone. Not..."

"Not accosted by your bully's best friend?"

I snort.

"I was just heading back. I should've offered you a hit before I tossed the joint." He comes up beside me, offering his arm. "Besides, isn't this just what you need?"

I squint at him. *Of course it wasn't a cigarette.* A star hockey player wouldn't ruin his body with nicotine and tobacco. Instead, he's getting high in the woods behind the school. On a Saturday.

"Liam was going to make this offer, but I'm happy I beat him to it," he says.

I straighten. "What?"

"We walk in there together, pretend to have a newfound interest in each other... It'll get the cheerleaders off my back, and Caleb will put you on yours." He grins. "Win-win."

I swallow. Do I want to play that game?

I did before. I was going to corner Liam and ask. And here's Theo, offering the very thing I schemed about. I should do it, just to rub in Caleb's face the fact that he's dating Amelie.

He's mine, but he's not until he breaks up with her.

"It's a useful trick. Old-school play." He keeps his arm offered, seeming to know that I'm having an internal debate about it.

"Why are you being nice?"

He scowls. "Who said anything about *nice*? Liam isn't the only one who enjoys getting on Caleb's nerves."

I haven't heard him say more than one sentence to me, and now we're having a full-blown conversation. About... Caleb. The one person I'd rather not talk about.

"Just admit that the idea of him and Amelie is driving you nuts," he says softly. "And let's do something about it."

I raise my eyebrows. "Are you into her?"

"Me?"

"Why else would you want to get on his nerves, if not about Amelie? Or do you hate her?"

"I don't hate Amelie," he answers. "And I'm not into her. But..."

But, what? The way he stops has me grinding my teeth in frustration. I don't like not knowing things, and this seems like a juicy secret.

"We're not here to discuss this," he finishes.

The wall he usually hides behind is back. The time to decide is now.

I take his arm. "If this goes badly—it was all your idea."

He winks. "Whatever you say, sweetheart."

This is not going to end well.

He glances at his watch as we walk across the soccer field. "Not necessarily the best timing. But good enough for me."

There are a lot of people at this farmers' market. More than I thought would show up on a Saturday morning. There's a food truck parked in the corner with a long line, and almost all the vendors are packed.

The silence comes in waves. First the people closest to us, and then the screeching halt of the rest of the crowd rolls down like dominoes. He leads me down the first row of vendors, glancing in them with a casualness I try to embody.

"Pretend you like me," he says through his teeth.

Clearly, I'm failing.

I swallow my apprehension and inch closer, smiling up at him. "You look like you swallowed a box of staples."

He laughs. *Loudly*.

And somehow, he manages to ignore everyone else around us. We turn a corner, to the picnic tables the smokers usually occupy at lunch and after school. There are no smokers there today—just Caleb, with Amelie perched beside him. Eli. Liam. And Ian fucking Fletcher.

I really hate that guy.

My grip on Theo's arm tightens, and he pats my fingers. It's not really comforting, but he doesn't seem bothered.

They notice us one at a time.

Liam's eyebrows skyrocket.

Eli does a double take.

Amelie is talking, fiddling with Caleb's sleeve. She spots us, and her jaw drops.

Then Caleb, but I can't even look at him.

Murmurs break out around us.

"You know," Theo whispers, tipping his head toward mine, "you're really putting a wrench in the middle of my friend group."

"Did I walk into a trap?" He's quite a bit taller than Caleb. "Is your plan to say, 'Ha, ha, I tricked Margo?'"

He smiles. "Not at all."

And then Caleb is on us, shoving Theo away from me. The force of it must surprise Theo, because he staggers backward. I get the impression that Theo isn't one easily moved. He releases me, though, so I don't get dragged with him.

Theo's face transforms into a mask of anger, and he lunges forward. I don't even think he's *that* mad at Caleb—they just want an excuse to hit each other.

Someone pulls me out of the way.

I glance back, surprised at the firm grip that tows me around the market, back toward the cars.

Amelie?

Her full, painted lips are pressed into a flat line, and she doesn't relent until we're well away from the idiots fighting.

"What was that for?" I yank my arm out of her manicured hands.

"What are you doing?" She glares daggers at me.

"Me? I'm just standing with Theo and *your boyfriend*

210

goes nuts." *This is what you wanted*, I remind myself. "Maybe you should've dragged him out here to ask *him* why he's so bothered—"

"Oh, drop the act, Margo." She looks away. "We all know that he only sees you."

Her mean-girl bravado is not all it's cracked up to be.

"I don't want him to only see me."

I'm lying. I'm *so* lying.

It's why I agreed to walk in on Theo's arm in the first place, right? To urge Caleb toward breaking up with her. If I'm throwing a wrench in their friend group, it isn't without help.

Amelie shakes her head. "It's sad, you know?"

I tilt my head.

"That he would pick *you* over... Well, over everyone. You're not worth it, Margo."

Ouch.

She continues. "He didn't fight for you. Remember that when he's promising you the world. Shit gets real, and he gets lost."

We both turn toward a commotion at the end of the closest row, and I step away from her. It's not safe standing next to a viper—never has been, never will be.

But I either believe her or I trust my gut.

What happens if they're telling me the same thing?

Caleb strides toward me, ignoring the teacher who's following him. I expect him to go for Amelie. After all, they're dating. Maybe he'll shove her up against the lockers and kiss her right in front of me, just to drive the knife in deeper.

He touched me. He's done wicked things to my body. To my mind.

And yet.

He didn't fight for you. Remember that.

I watch Amelie as he gets closer. She doesn't seem afraid... just resigned.

And then he puts his arm around my waist and pulls me along with him. I squeak, suddenly moving, but he just snarls under his breath.

I cast a glance behind me. Amelie leans on the hood of a car, her head tipped back.

Then it's too late. He unlocks his and yanks the door open, shoving me inside. I start to scramble out—*this is kidnapping*—but he blocks my way and leans in.

Ooh, he's furious.

"Stay."

I roll my eyes but fold myself back in the car. He slams the door and circles it as Riley rushes up to his vehicle.

"She's not feeling well," he tells her. "I'm taking her home."

"Yeah, right." Riley scowls. "You okay, Margo?"

I give her a thumbs-up. There's a slim possibility of ending up dead in a ditch, I suppose... But I trust that Caleb won't be that irrational.

He guns it out of the parking lot. His anger takes up most of the oxygen, but the longer it remains, the madder I get.

He finally turns off the road at an overlook, and I leap out. He follows me, watching like a lion waiting to fucking pounce. I have electricity in my veins, energy that has to come out.

"Not cool." I rub my arms.

"Not *cool*?" He scowls at me. "What the fuck, Margo?"

I stare at him. "What the *fuck*? Like I'm supposed to just sit on the sidelines and watch you date my ex-friend?

Talk about hypocrisy! Let me live my life if you won't make room in yours for me."

"You can't *live* with Theo." He paces in front of me. His hands rake through his hair, tugging at the strands. "I can't do this. I can't—"

"Oh, fuck you, Caleb." *Can't do it.* He's getting on my ever-loving last nerve. I kick at the ground, gravel scattering ahead of me. "Can't do *what*?"

He stalks toward me. "How did you crawl under my skin so easily?"

I back away, but he keeps coming.

"I'll swear to God, Margo, I have the urge to kill whoever touches you. I don't give a flying fuck if they're a friend, because all that matters is how I can possess you. My touch. My words. You're mine."

He said it. He said I'm his—but does he mean it when he doesn't show it? My brain is stuck on that fact.

My dad used to say: People will show you who they really are. *Believe them.*

What has Caleb done for me? All his actions are against me.

I shove him away from me, my temper flaring. The asshole barely moves.

"You're right, Caleb. You can be the big, bad control freak while you kiss your girlfriend a-and *cheat* on her. I'm not a puppet whose strings you can jerk around."

His face is dark, and he stops abruptly in front of me. His expression is... *pained.* That's the only way I can describe it. Pained or devastated.

He cups my cheek. His thumb strokes across my lips. "I don't want to pull your strings, baby. I want to cut them."

The air leaves my lungs in a rush.

His hand falls away from me, and he goes back to the car, the conversation apparently over.

The slight fear of him leaving me here, like he left me at his house, gnaws at me. I get in the car before he can bark at me, and we're once again entombed in silence.

Finally, I glance over at him. "You can't just..."

I stop, frustrated with myself. With *him*. What is he trying to do, isolate me?

Yes, that's probably exactly what he wants.

"I'm not an island that you can fortify," I murmur. "I'm a person."

He glowers at me. "You might think so, little lamb, but you're *mine*. No one else's. Stop fucking testing me."

I don't have anything to say to that.

Stop fucking testing me. Sure—as soon as he loses the girlfriend. Eh, even then... maybe not. Still, he might throw me out of the car if I argue, and weariness tugs at my bones. He drives me back to the Bryans' house, shadowing me up to the front door like a hulking bodyguard.

I slip inside without a word.

He might've won this battle, but he won't win the war.

Chapter 22
Margo

CALEB

Meet me in the locker room at lunch.

I've been ignoring him. He's been ignoring Amelie. It's only been a week, but...

Rumors have been swirling that she's been duped —and dumped. She sulks behind a wall of cheerleaders, who all send hateful glares in my direction. They've extended the same courtesy to Riley, even though my quiet friend walks around like a shadow half of the time.

The girl's got some serious talent staying under the radar, that's for sure.

And Caleb? Theo? They've all been acting like nothing is wrong. Theo sends an occasional wink my way, and Caleb snarls at him under his breath.

He's worse than a feral dog.

CALEB

Answer me.

> Your read receipts are on, little lamb. Don't make me hunt you down...

> Or do. You're my favorite sport.

> You're with Amelie.

I think. Honestly, maybe he *did* dump her.

> That didn't stop us the other night.

He has no boundaries.

Did I make him that way?

I bite my lip as I type out a reply under my desk. Sure, this could absolutely backfire on me. He could become worse than he already is. How, I don't know, but I'm sure he would think of something.

He's managed to get under my skin, and as much as I try to scrub him free, he isn't leaving. Hell, I don't think he ever left.

And he accused me of the same thing.

> It should've. What do you want in the locker room?

There's a long pause. Class will be ending in about ten minutes, and we'll break for lunch. Then two more classes, and I'll be able to go hide at home until tomorrow. And then we'll just do that a hundred more times until I graduate.

Or less, seeing as how I turn eighteen in just over three months.

Not that anyone is counting...

I focus on my fifth period English teacher, Ms. Devereux. She's attempting to talk us through an analysis of a short story we just read, but it's kind of going over my head.

I slouch lower in my chair. This is one of the only classes I have without Caleb or any of his friends, and I pretend to be studying the story again while I collect myself. My phone buzzes against my leg, sending another pitter-patter of nerves through me. My heart pounds so loud it's the only thing I can hear.

I take a deep breath, then check my phone.

CALEB

Thinking of your mouth

[IMAGE]

Oh God.

It's a dick pic.

I squirm in my seat, trying to ignore the sensations traveling between my legs. Why does the sight of his cock turn me on? Why is he sending me a picture of it? Is that real time?

He's thinking of my mouth?

My mouth turns him on?

When the bell rings, I stow my bag, shoot a text to Riley that I'm running an errand, and make my way across the sprawling building to the athletic wing. I locate the boys' locker room and hesitate outside it.

He said in.

So...

The door swings inward under my fingertips, and I walk inside.

It's a mirrored layout to the girls' down the hall, with rows of smaller lockers on one side and shower stalls on the other. Farther back are the bathrooms and sinks.

Caleb sits on a bench in the second row. He straddles it, his phone face-up between his knees. His gaze lifts, going from my shoes to my bare legs, all the way up to the skirt—I've somehow managed to avoid questions from Lenora and Robert about the pants—and my tucked-in shirt.

He leans back, exposing the top of his unbuttoned pants.

"I keep thinking about you." His voice is husky. "Namely, that noise you make when you gag on my cock."

I gulp.

He rises. "There's a football game tonight."

My brow furrows. "Okay?"

"We don't have a game until Sunday afternoon. Come with me."

I shake my head. "No, I'm good. I don't like football."

He raises an eyebrow. "You said the same about hockey, but..."

Yeah, I was proven wrong.

"I don't want to be stared at."

"You won't."

"Amelie will make fun of me."

"She won't," he promises. His gaze turns calculating. "Do I need to give you something in return?"

There must be a song about making deals with devils... but I can't think of any.

"I want to see my old house again," I blurt out.

He goes still.

Well, minus his dick. That just seems to be stiffening, until it's tenting his pants. They're unbuttoned, but the zipper is hanging on.

"Remind me of that noise you make," he murmurs, "and we'll have a deal."

Seems like he's getting more out of it than me. Attendance at a football game—*yuck*—and a blow job?

And yet...

I want to get back in that house. I want to unravel all the mysteries of what happened and what was left behind.

The most infuriating part is that I don't remember the key moments. I remember flashes, little pieces that don't make sense, and my father being arrested at the park. But other than that, there's nothing coherent.

Being there could settle my memories.

I go to my knees in front of him, and he braces a hand on the locker. The other on the back of my head.

Immediately, he takes control. He doesn't go easy, and I fight between closing my teeth on him and relaxing my throat so it doesn't hurt as bad. The first time he pushes past the ring of muscles protecting my throat, he cuts off my breath.

I dig my nails into his thighs, but he only withdraws when my grip loosens. My head swims. As soon as I get air, I inhale a ragged breath. It's almost enough.

He fucks my face until saliva drips from the corners of my lips and tears roll down my cheeks. I give him the satisfaction—I'm assuming—of gagging around his length.

"Unbutton your shirt," he grunts.

I don't question it, releasing his legs to fumble with my uniform shirt. It hangs open, exposing my nude-colored bra. Just when I think he's going to come in my mouth, he pulls out at the last minute. His hand takes over, pumping once, twice.

He comes on my chest. My throat.

It misses my face and hair, with the majority across my breasts. It's warmer than I thought it would be.

S. Massery

After the initial shock fades, horror takes over. I look down at myself, then up at Caleb.

He's grinning like the Devil.

And then the flash of his camera goes off in my face.

Chapter 23
Margo

I slide into the kitchen, where Lenora is making dinner. "Um, is it okay if I go to the football game?"

She glances up at me. "Are you going with Riley?"

The doorbell rings, and I curse under my breath.

"I got it," Robert calls. A minute later, he says, "Ah, Caleb. Good to see you."

Lenora raises her eyebrows at me.

I make a face.

Caleb comes into the kitchen behind Robert.

"Found your friend," Robert says to me. "Were you expecting him?"

"No," I say, at the same time that Caleb answers, "Yes."

I glare at him. "He asked if I would go to the game, and I was just asking Lenora..."

"Sorry, Mrs. Bryan." Caleb steps closer to me. He's ever the school supporter; his hoodie is the gold-and-black colors of our school, plus the addition of a black shell jacket over it. To me, he says, "It's a bit chilly, you might want to wear something warmer..."

My cheeks burn. "Right. *If* I can go—"

"Of course," Lenora blurts out. "We don't want to restrict your social experience, especially now as you're making more—"

"Thanks!" I lean away from Caleb, shooting Lenora a look that I hope translates to, *Please don't embarrass me.*

She smiles sheepishly.

It's such a startling mom-daughter thing to do, I almost pause. But I shake it off and race back to my room. I change from my uniform skirt into fishnet tights, then black jeans with big rips in the legs that show off the fishnet. I pair it with Caleb's sweatshirt that he never took back, and belatedly realize we're going to match.

You're dressed to support the football team. Of course we're going to match. Us and five hundred other people.

After the locker room incident at lunch, which I was able to clean up with a lot of paper towels and cold water, I almost showered as soon as I got home.

But then I got talking to Robert at the base of the stairs, and by the time I remembered to ask them about going to the football game, Caleb was arriving.

I touch up my makeup and yank on my boots. When I get downstairs, I find Caleb and Robert discussing hockey. They both look over at me.

"Ready?" Caleb asks.

I bite my lip and nod. This screams of being a trap, or a nasty trick, but anticipation swirls through me. I'm going to the game because he's giving me something I want.

No, need.

I'm going to get to see my home again, and it'll be more than just a glance.

He puts his hand on the small of my back, propelling me out of the house toward his car. "I like that you wear my sweatshirt. But I can't help but consider that you're up to something."

I lift one shoulder. "Not sure what you mean?"

I get in the passenger seat and close the door in his face. I'm not up to anything except wanting to go see where my life splintered into pieces.

My life and my memory.

He doesn't confirm where we're going, but soon enough he's pulling into the driveway of his house, then aiming for the narrow path beside the garage. He stops in front of the house we lived in, exactly where my father used to park.

My stomach cramps. Nausea-inducing snakes in my belly won't settle.

We approach the door that I burst through in a mad rush last time. Slower now. More in control. Except, I can *almost* smell my mother's cooking.

There's grime on the windows, weeds and vines crawling up the siding. I hadn't noticed it before, but now its state is clear.

It has been abandoned.

Just like me.

Even sitting in Caleb's family's backyard, a stone's throw away from their back door, my old home has turned into a graveyard of memories.

He unlocks the door to my old childhood home and then steps aside. "The past isn't a happy place. Why don't you want to leave it buried?"

He's been tormenting me because of *this*. Because of a past that only he seems to understand. It doesn't make sense —shouldn't he want me to remember?

"Why don't *you*?" I counter.

He exhales and shoves the door open. "After you."

Stepping inside now hurts worse than before.

Before was shock. Spikes of pain. Relief that I remembered things the way they were.

Now it's total annihilation.

I stop just across the threshold. Ghosts are here, bringing an icy chill with them. I can't do this.

You must face your fear.

I glance over my shoulder at Caleb, but his expression is unreadable.

I'm on my own.

There's dust collecting over every inch of the space. The wine-red rug under the kitchen table with four chairs crowded around it, one of which has a loose leg. Dad used to stuff a folded newspaper under it when company came over.

Company being Caleb, of course. Sometimes Savannah.

The cup is in the exact same spot by the sink. I move through the kitchen. Caleb follows me like a second shadow, past the living room on our right and into the narrow hallway. Mom got a grippy material to put under the rug when I was eight, after I slid headlong into the wall with the rug bunched around my feet.

That was a game of chase that ended poorly, but I never blamed Caleb. The bump on my forehead made him feel guilty enough.

The first door on the left is the bathroom, and my bedroom the next door down. Between them, on the right, is the door to my parents' bedroom. I hesitate, brushing my fingers against the painted wood.

"It's not going to bite," Caleb whispers.

Yes, it will. The memories will sink their teeth into me and never let me go.

I take a deep breath and push the door open anyway. What I see steals the air from my lungs.

It's a wreck. Vandalized.

There's a broken lamp on the floor next to the bed, cracked into three pieces. The lightbulb is smashed. Clothes... *everywhere*. It's like a hurricane went through the room.

I take a step back, bumping into Caleb.

"What happened?" My voice is steady, even if the rest of my body wobbles.

He doesn't answer.

I turn. "Caleb, what happened?"

"This wasn't part of the deal," he says. "You wanted to come in here. You're asking questions you should already know the answer to."

I... should?

He takes a step back. "Move on."

I shut the door.

After a second, I continue into my old room, where I had run the other day. The door swings open with the barest touch.

I walk in and inhale the odor of stale air.

When I was twelve, I had nightmares about being locked in here. In the dream, I beat my fists against the door until they were bloody and bruised. After Caleb follows me in, moving a bit slower than I'd prefer, I close the door.

I don't expect to find anything.

Hell, it was just a dream I had when I was twelve.

And thirteen.

And fourteen.

Ms. McCaw, my social worker, set me up with a therapist. The foster families I was with were terrified of the screaming that happened while I was asleep. And with the therapist, I convinced myself it was just a dream blown out of proportion.

But...

There are smudges of blood on the white door, at my chest level. Scratches, too.

I point at it. "What the hell happened?"

He watches me like I'm crazy. "You did that."

I shake my head and sink down onto the bed. It's either sit voluntarily or collapse—and then my visit would be cut short.

"That's wrong," I whisper.

I drag the pad of my finger over one of my nails. I couldn't have scratched at the wood hard enough to leave those marks. I would've ripped my nails out. Whatever happened when I was ten... there's no trace of it on my skin now.

He trails a finger over my dresser. He lifts something from it and tucks it away before I can get a good look.

At my raised eyebrows, he just rolls his eyes. "Just something of mine that you stole."

"Why has no one come back here?"

He yanks the door open and points. "Time's up. If you want me to explain exactly what happened... that's another beast entirely. You'll owe me more than a sloppy blow job."

"So you do know."

His nod is short and jerky. "I know pieces."

"I know pieces, too."

His expression is pitying. "Apparently not."

This is a puzzle I'm trying to solve blind. But why am I so fucking blind? What happened that was bad enough for my brain to block it out?

Am I ever going to get it back?

Or, better yet, will I survive if it does come back?

A weight settles on my chest, and even though the door is open, those scratches are ingrained in my mind. The dreams of frantic pounding, screaming, breaking nails against paint. Confusion and anger.

"I can't breathe." I press my palm to my chest. "I think I'm h-having a p-panic attack."

Caleb suddenly kneels in front of me. His face swims in my vision, concern drawing his brows together.

Or I'm delusional, and he's just clinically fascinated.

"Hey. It's okay." His palms are hot on my cold skin.

I'm gasping for air at this point. My heart is pounding out of my chest.

"Margo." Caleb's voice breaks through the fog. Barely. "Look at me."

I can't really see anything except for the floor between my knees.

He tugs my hand away from my head—*when did I grab my head?*—and pinches my chin, forcing me to meet his eyes. "Breathe."

A whole damn waterfall of grief and confusion is thundering down on me. It's the realization that my nightmares have been real. Caleb will never be nice, or tell me the truth, unless I give him something in return. My parents are gone.

He lifts me suddenly, cradling me to his chest, and starts walking. I suck in short gasps as the hallway melds into a living room, then a kitchen, and then suddenly we're outside. The sun beats down on us, but it doesn't touch the ice frosting over my skin.

He sets me down on the hood of his car, and with no hesitation, he cups my face with both of his hands and presses his lips to mine.

I can't respond—shock, the panic—until he nips my lower lip. The pain wakes me up.

I gasp against his mouth. He kisses me harder, licking

along the seam of my lips until I open for him. My horror falls away. The panic ebbs. I wrap myself around him, my legs around his hips, my hands on his shoulders.

God, what kind of demon is he?

Finally, he pulls back. His hands stay on my face, his fingers fanned from my ears to my jaw. It's a nice act, except for the smirk—which seems to grow wider while my face bursts into flames.

Can I manage to have one normal interaction?

No.

On the other hand, he's perfectly composed, the bastard. My body aches like I just ran a marathon.

He pats my thighs, winking at me. "You want to stay here?"

My legs are still locked around his hips. I grimace and release him, then slide off the hood of his car. "We're going to be late."

To a stupid game I don't even care about. But right now, it seems like a great excuse to get out of here.

"You don't want to be late," he repeats.

"I was hoping to slip in undetected..."

He grins. "There's no such thing as undetected when you're with me."

"Oh, come on."

He raises an eyebrow. "You think people wouldn't notice me walk in to one of the biggest football games of the year? They love it when the other athletes support the football team."

"Time out." I make a T with my hands. "Biggest game of the year?"

He unlocks his car. "Well, yeah. It's against Lion's Head. Emery-Rose's biggest rival... number one in the division... You don't pay attention, do you?"

I huff. "I've been too busy being mocked and tripped at school for people to talk to me."

"Eh. Well, a lot of people are going to be there."

I swallow.

"Get in, little lamb." He opens the passenger door for me.

I guess there's no avoiding this.

Once we're on our way, I ask, "Is Amelie going to kill me for walking in with you?"

His grip tightens on the wheel. "Are you jealous? You threw in my face that I was cheating on her with you."

"You can't be serious."

"Either you're jealous or you're not." He glances at me. "But I hope you are."

I groan. "I just don't want to be involved in your mess."

He turns into the school parking lot, killing the engine in a spot right up front. It seems to have been left open just for him, because the rest of the parking lot is completely full. He twists toward me, meeting my gaze. "You want me to break up with her."

"You haven't." I shake my head. "Of course you haven't."

"Not yet." He grins. "I had to get your thoughts on the matter. And your thoughts are... that you're jealous?"

"She's literally going to murder me for even talking to you. You-you've been avoiding her for days!" I smack my forehead. "I hate you."

He taps my temple with one finger. "I do love a good mind fuck. Just admit that you're jealous, and I won't 'accidentally' leave you to the wolves."

"Did you just air quote at me?" I glower at him.

"Say you're jealous and I'll break up with her."

I climb out of the car. Amelie and I used to be friends,

but now we're the furthest thing from it. Hell, I'd go so far as to claim we're enemies—if only because of Caleb Asher.

He stops in front of me. The football field is around the corner, just out of sight. Yet the smell of a food truck, the sound of hundreds of people, drifts toward us.

"Well?"

I clench my teeth and force out, "Yeah, I am."

"Good girl." He beams at me.

That does something interesting to my insides.

"Are you going to?" I demand.

He winks. "Let's find out."

Chapter 24
Margo

"Caleb Asher, what the fuck?"

I crane my head back as Amelie storms toward us. He's had his arm around my shoulder for the last twenty minutes—about the time I started shivering in my sweatshirt. His sweatshirt, I guess. Technically. But since he's warm, I don't mind the closeness.

That's the only reason. Pinky promise.

We haven't looked at each other in twenty minutes either.

At Amelie's shrill voice, his fingers tighten on my shoulder. Can he sense my desire to escape?

We survived until halftime. Granted, we showed up halfway into the first quarter, and the game's been exciting enough to keep the crowd entertained. Meaning: they haven't really noticed us yet. My plan of not drawing Amelie's ire has, so far, worked. Sure, his presence turned heads, and people keep glancing over at us, but Amelie and her gang? So far, no.

That's about to end.

Caleb pivots us toward his girlfriend. I try to step back, and he gives me a stern look.

"What the hell, Caleb?" she yells, still yards away.

People turn toward us, and murmurs break out.

"Got a problem, Amelie?" he drawls.

He's the freaking perfect picture of calm. His face betrays nothing, but he likes causing chaos. He's most certainly enjoying this... however this is going to go.

Where did the sweet boy I knew as a child go?

Keep asking yourself that, Margo. He'd no sooner answer that question than solve the rest of my puzzle. As much as I slide the pieces around, they just... don't fit together.

This Caleb thrives on darkness. Maybe I didn't realize it before, but I can see it like a rising tide inside him. He's ready to shatter Amelie's world, and he's thrilled for it.

"Do I have a problem?" she repeats. "Yes, I have a fucking problem."

"You're an attention-seeking slut." He shrugs as her face turns red. His grip stays ironclad on my shoulder, keeping me right there next to him. "I should've realized you were only after my reputation."

"How dare you? We're *dating,* and you show up with *her?*"

"Gee, Amelie, maybe you should break up with me." He steps forward, towing me with him.

Her gaze cuts to mine, but all I can do is stare at her. It's either that or drop my gaze to my shoes, and she's said enough wretched things about me to deserve the stare-down.

"I'm not sure why you care so much," he continues. "It isn't like you haven't been sleeping around with Ian Fletcher."

He releases me, and I stumble away from him. He's focused on the annihilation of Amelie Page—no Margo Wolfe presence required.

When he's mad at me, he gets physical. His hands on my skin. His tongue in my mouth. Every inch of him was built to punish me. And for that reason, I can't bear the idea of him touching her—even if it's out of anger.

It takes a moment for his words to sink in. She's been sleeping around on him.

I cover my mouth, holding back my laugh. Oh, the fucking irony.

Excluding the fact that Ian Fletcher is the *worst* human being in Rose Hill, I'm fairly certain that Caleb doesn't give a fuck about who Amelie's been sleeping with. Hell, besides the annoyance flashing across his face, she could drop dead at his feet and he wouldn't even stoop down to check her pulse.

She scowls at him, fear fluttering across her features. "Who told you that?"

He laughs. There's a circle around us, people eager to see what will happen with the king and queen of Emery-Rose.

Ex-queen? Does their breakup signal the end of an era, or will she continue to rule separately?

I back away until I hit someone.

Eli murmurs in my ear, "He'll hunt you down if you aren't in his line of sight when he's done."

I grimace.

Riley grabs my other arm. "You came with Caleb? I thought you said you didn't want..."

"You're ridiculous," Caleb proclaims, once more drawing our attention. "And I'm sick of you, Amelie. If you're not going to say it, I will. Happily. *We're done.*"

Her mouth gapes open and shut like a fish desperate for oxygen, but she doesn't have a witty comeback. No retort. She stands there for a long moment, then slowly turns and strides away.

The crowd parts for her, then fills in the gaps. Still watching and waiting...

Caleb searches for me. Eli releases me quickly, giving me a light shove between my shoulder blades. I stumble to a stop before Caleb and tilt my head to the side.

"That's one way to do things," I tell him.

There's a gleam in his eye that wasn't there before. My stomach flips.

"Just the beginning." He puts his arm back around my shoulder, hugging me into his side, and we walk toward the stands. "One more thing."

Caleb whistles, clear and sharp. It takes me a moment longer to spot Theo and Liam, who detach themselves from a group and come down to the ground.

"Yo." Liam grins at us. "You two a thing now?"

"Yes," Caleb clips out.

I stare at him, leaning away. "What?"

"I don't really care to hear your protests right now. And that means one thing." He points at Theo. "You. Don't you fucking touch her."

Theo salutes Caleb. "Yes, sir."

Caleb grunts.

The dismissal is as clear as they're going to get, and once again we're left alone.

My skin itches.

"I don't know what dating you is supposed to feel like," I admit. "And I don't remember agreeing to it either."

He smiles, and we follow the path Liam and Theo made up the bleacher steps. We'd been sitting off to the side, but now the king retakes his throne. We walk right up the center aisle, and people make room for us.

I didn't understand it until now. The way people treat him—he's freaking *royalty* at this school. And I'm seeing it in action, but I'm still mystified by it. Even as a younger kid asks if he needs anything, and Caleb actually says yes.

Minutes later, the kid returns with a bag of popcorn and two sodas.

"Hey, Asher." A guy in purple and black comes toward us, lifting his hand.

Caleb grins, reaching out and bumping his knuckles against the new guy's. "What's up, Bonner? I heard a rumor you're not playing this year?"

He chuckles. "I had to have surgery on my knee at the beginning of the summer. Coach wouldn't let me play."

Caleb shakes his head. "Sorry to hear that."

Bonner shrugs. His gaze sweeps up and down my body. "I don't think we've met. Matt Bonner."

"Margo Wolfe," Caleb drawls. "And don't fucking look at her like that."

Bonner laughs again, scratching at the back of his neck. "Hey, Asher. No disrespect. You got yourself a beautiful—"

"I'm *right here*," I snap.

A muscle in Caleb's jaw jumps. He glares at Matt, the niceties ending abruptly, until Matt nods and stuffs his hands in his pockets. When he retreats to the Lion's Head side of the bleachers, Caleb finally focuses on me.

I wait.

"I'm not apologizing for that," he says.

"I didn't ask you to." I find myself leaning closer to him. "I don't like people staring at me."

"You don't like *men* staring at you," he clarifies.

"I'll pass on all types of attention."

235

He rolls his eyes. "You better get used to it."

After that, we lapse back into silence. Besides the uncomfortable quiet around us, and the glances in my direction, it's easy to block it out and enjoy the second half of the game.

That is, until Theo catches sight of someone.

"Shit," Caleb growls. He looks back at Eli, who's two rows up.

They've both straightened in their seats.

"Who is he—"

Theo lurches down the bleachers. He strides straight toward the Lion's Head side.

Caleb's hand twitches against my shoulder.

"Are you going to stop him? He seems ready to murder someone."

"Not this time," Caleb answers.

Eli hasn't moved either.

I wince when Theo grabs a girl from the sidelines, her camera falling to the ground. He gets in her face, his face a smooth mask of fury. And then he shoves her back toward her friends and stalks away.

"Well, that could've gone worse," Eli calls.

Caleb chuckles.

Liam just groans.

"How could that have gone worse?" I whisper. I watch the girl get lifted to her feet.

He tilts his head toward me. "Sometimes we're driven to do crazy things."

Speaking of crazy things...

I meet his gaze. "What happens next?"

"With what?"

"Us."

He smirks. "You're admitting to an us, then?"

I shift. "Seems inevitable."

"We are." He grabs my hand and brings it to his mouth. He kisses my knuckles, then sets it back on my lap. But he doesn't let go.

Butterflies erupt in my belly. It's easy to let Caleb hold my hand and pretend we're two nice people who happen to be dating.

We are the furthest thing from *nice*.

"Relax," he murmurs.

"This is very public. And you just dumped your girlfriend. Loudly."

He raises one shoulder, his eyes on the game. "You told me to."

"I told you to break up with Amelie?" I did not. I mean, I kind of did. Not in a direct way.

Not like this.

Jesus, she keeps craning around from her spot in the crowd of cheerleaders, squinting at us. It's one thing for Caleb to crucify her in front of the entire school—hell, Lion's Head's students, too—but now she's glaring daggers at *me*.

"You did. Now just relax, and then we'll go to the party after we win." He tosses me a quick smile.

I'm not used to his smiling. And I'm not used to his competitiveness showing. It wasn't this strong when I knew him before... he doesn't play football, and yet it's a *we*. Emery-Rose Elite as a whole. If one wins, we all do.

I cast a helpless glance back at Riley. Something happens on the field, because I'm jerked to my feet. Everyone around us cheers.

Caleb picks me up and swings me in a circle. "You're good luck. We just fucking won."

A joyous riot of Emery-Rose students flood the field,

surrounding the team, with Caleb and me at the center. This type of celebration—so very *male*—throws me off for a moment. They pound each other's backs, fist-bumping. No one touches me, though. It's like I've been encased in fire, and no one wants to get too close.

Caleb motions for me to get on his back, crouching. Suddenly, I'm a head above everyone else, my arms wrapped around his shoulders and my legs around his waist. Over the sea of black and gold, I can see the purple-and-black Lion's Head students. They're slower to filter out.

Caleb's body heat seeps into me, warming my chilled body. The sun set some time ago, dropping the temperature, and I've been shivering ever since. I slide my hands inside his jacket, and he chuckles.

"Ready?" Eli appears at our side.

Riley is tucked against him, watching me with wide eyes.

Caleb leads the way out of the crowd, toward the parking lot. He turns and walks backward, eyeing his friends. "We're taking a quick detour."

Eli snickers. "Oh, yeah?"

"You got a problem with that?" he goads.

"I think you're gonna go do dirty things to your new girl-friend." Eli laughs.

Riley elbows him, and I tuck my face into Caleb's neck. I don't have any desire to discuss sex—or lack thereof—with his friends.

Caleb spins back around, ignoring Eli, and stops at the passenger side of his car. He loosens his hold on the back of my thighs, letting me slip down. "Get in."

I'm grateful when he turns the car on and blasts the heat.

"So, where's the detour?"

"My house." There's something dangerous in his glance, hot and smoldering.

We drive toward his home, and my heartbeat picks up speed.

"I can't," I blurt out.

It isn't that I haven't had sex before—because *that's* what I'd imagine happening—but all I'll be able to think about in that house is our past.

My past.

His.

They collided in an epic explosion when we were ten, and I'm trying to put everything back together. Caleb seems to have healed... but inside, there are still jagged edges.

Am I afraid of those jagged edges? *Yes.* Get too close and they may cut.

He slows the car, pulling onto a shoulder and putting it in park.

"What are you afraid of?"

I stare out the window, as far as I can see. Only yards ahead of us, the headlights bounce against trees. The rest is darkness.

"Are you afraid of me?"

I dare to look at him. "Do you think I am?"

His eyes narrow. "I don't know, Margo. Sometimes I think yes. Sometimes I think... hmm, maybe she's grown a backbone after all."

"I have a backbone," I scoff. "You don't go through the system without developing one."

"You break too easily." He reaches out and grabs my face, forcing me to meet his eyes. "You cave. You *lose.*"

I jerk away from him. "Then why chase me if I'm so boring?"

He laughs. "Even if you're fragile, you're far from

boring." He watches me for a second, then exhales. "Okay. Let's go to the party."

An unexpected weight comes off my shoulders. I open my mouth, but he cuts me off with a hand on my thigh, squeezing.

"Don't thank me."

"Okay," I whisper.

It only means that something worse than his house is coming my way.

Chapter 25
Margo

UNKNOWN

You're in for a treat.

S omehow, I don't think they mean ice cream.
     I click over to my conversation with Riley.

RILEY

Where are you? Amelie is storming around
here like an angry bull.

We're on our way.

Caleb's driving like an ass

That was fast. ;)

Nothing happened. He wanted to go back
to his house but...

Can't do it.

Pro tip: less talking, more kissing. Makes
you forget about their bullying.

I frown.

> No chance of that.

> Psh. You might change your mind when you see what you're dealing with. Find me when you get here!

I put my hand over Caleb's, which has been slowly creeping higher up my thigh.

He grins. "You like it when I touch you. And you like it when I'm rough. So why stop a good thing?"

"Because we're about to go to a party."

"And those parties have dark rooms," he says. "It would be easier to keep everyone away from you if I kept you locked in a dark room... everyone could hear you scream, and they'd know I was staking my claim."

"I've had enough of your overprotective streak." I don't think I believe it, though.

He shrugs. "Easily avoided, baby. Just don't talk to anyone."

"In a house full of people."

He smirks as he parks. "Is that too hard for you?"

I release his hand as he turns off the engine. To my surprise, he leans into my space. His lips touch mine, the briefest kiss before he sits back.

More.

A smile curls his lips. Maybe I said it out loud, because he ducks back in and steals another one. His tongue swipes along the seam of my lips. I push into him, grabbing the back of his head.

Kisses like these make me feel electric.

Like I could be lost in a snow squall, but Caleb's lips would guide me back.

Once I'm properly breathless, he leans back. His smirk gets bigger. "I like you like this."

A confession for my ears only.

"Tussled. Horny. Did my kiss make you wet?"

I blush.

"That might be a yes. That's a mystery I look forward to solving." He gets out and circles around, opening my door for me.

I take the arm he offers, and we walk up toward Ian Fletcher's house.

Never mind that Ian and Amelie have been sleeping together, and that Ian is a dirt-bag bully, his house is *giant*.

"I thought *you* were rich."

Caleb laughs. "Yeah, but our wealth isn't in the house. You know it's been in the family since my grandparents bought it. Fletcher's house is purely new money. I'd rather just take you home and sneak into your room, but..."

Some football players rush past us, calling Caleb's name.

"That," I answer, "is why we have to make an appearance?"

He shrugs. "This is just football. Wait until hockey season really gets underway."

I shiver in my jacket. "It gets... bigger?"

Half the school must be here. Music and lights pour out of the house, and our classmates are everywhere. On the front lawn, around back, in the house. Through the window, couples are dancing in Ian's front room.

"Bigger?" Caleb snorts. "You haven't seen anything yet."

I swallow. And then we're inside the house, his fingers lacing through mine. We weave through the crowds, finding Eli and Ian talking in the kitchen. Riley is nowhere to be found.

"Sup, man," Ian slurs slightly. "Epic game, right? Listen,

S. Massery

I'm sorry about fucking around with Amelie. She's a real hot—"

"Better shut up, Ian," Eli warns.

Caleb watches Ian with a blank face.

"Oh shit." Ian laughs. He backs away, pointing at me. "You fucking downgraded, you know? To the coke-whore's—"

Caleb lunges forward, his fist snapping out faster than I can follow. Ian's head whips backward, and blood pours down his face.

"What the fuck?" Ian yells. He swipes his hand under his nose, then dives toward Caleb, swinging wildly.

Caleb uses one hand to push me up against the wall, and he ducks Ian's attempt to hit him. He keeps his body between us, and he rolls his shoulders back.

"Come on, Fletcher," he growls. "I've been wanting to hit someone all fucking semester."

He's amped-up energy and muscle.

"You're going to defend her?" Ian howls. "After she—" He jumps away from Caleb's attack.

The way Caleb moves is brutal. He's restricted by the jacket, but the fabric stretches across his back as he goes for Ian. Eventually, their little boxing match dissolves into something less human.

Eli's gaze goes to me, and he raises his eyebrows. "You having fun yet, Margo?"

I shake my head. Blood flies when Caleb gets another hit in on Ian's face. He suddenly has him pinned to the floor, his elbows coming up before his fist hammers down. I wince at the sound of his knuckles meeting flesh.

And Eli seems perfectly fine with letting it happen.

"Caleb," I step away from the wall.

We have an audience once again, but they're smart enough to stay the hell back. He doesn't hear me.

"Caleb!"

I put my hand on his arm, and suddenly *I'm* the one pinned. He jumps off Ian and leans into me faster than I can comprehend. His hot breath hits my cheek, and I realize I've turned my head away. He smells like blood.

"You're playing with fire, baby. I could've hit you." He bites my earlobe.

Heat floods through me.

"I don't know if I'm scared of you or impressed that you defended me," I mumble. "You won't hurt me."

His teeth are still in my skin. We have an *audience*.

"Be both." He picks me up, his hands on my ass lifting me higher.

I wrap my legs around his waist.

"I want to drag you into a room and fuck you senseless. I wanted that before we even came to this freaking party."

The way he's holding me, his erection brushes my core. We're in the perfect position—minus the crowd around us. My body is hot, and butterflies erupt through me.

He trails kisses along my jaw, and I tilt my head to give him better access.

"Tonight, you're fucking *mine*."

Chapter 26
Caleb

Someone drags Ian off to nurse his wounds.

Theo, Eli, and Liam threaten to kidnap Margo unless I go with them to clean the blood off my face. That gets me to relent, but barely. I keep an eye on her while Liam holds a bag of frozen peas to my knuckles, and Eli hands me a wet paper towel.

The music kicks back on, louder than it was before. It vibrates in my rib cage.

Ian got in a few punches, but I've suffered worse at the hands of my best friends. Or family.

That's a weird marker for me, perhaps, but I shrug it off. The paper towel comes away red. That damn cut on my lip keeps getting close to fully healing, then I do something to fuck it up. Meeting Eli's gaze, I silently dare him to say something.

He doesn't.

Theo finds me a cup and pours a healthy dose of vodka into it, topping it off with soda.

I take a sip and wince at the burn. Fire spreads through me, different than the sort I feel because of Margo. I take another swallow. It might rid me of the skin-crawling sensation that's come over me recently.

My family home. Margo. Plus the murderous rage that descends whenever someone looks at her.

"Ian's face could've passed for raw meat," Liam comments.

I shrug. "He deserved it."

"Not saying he didn't." He pauses. "We have a game tomorrow."

And Coach threatened to suspend me if I got in any more fights. I somehow got into not one—with Ian and *witnesses*—but also tussled with Theo at the farmers' market.

We move into the living room, close to the doors that lead out to the porch, so I can keep an eye on Margo. She's with Riley, and so far, most of the guys here are leaving her alone.

She's got a cup in her hand. While they sway to the music, she takes a sip. Then another.

I restrain myself from going to her.

Outside, boys are circled around a bonfire. The leaves are starting to drop, even if half of the trees in the county haven't changed colors yet. The damp leaves catch the fire, and it seems like the whole lawn is moving.

My cup is empty, and Theo refills it.

"We'll have to get the footage," I mutter. "Bribe some people. It might not get back to Coach."

Eli snickers. "He probably already knows."

"Margo is a lightweight," Theo says.

I jerk toward him. "What did you say?"

He points.

Margo's holding on to Riley's forearms, swaying, and

her legs suddenly fold under her. She drags Riley down, and they both end up on the floor.

Shit.

I shove my cup into Eli's chest and stalk across the party. I detangle her from Riley and lift her. Eli is right there with me, helping Riley up.

"You want some water?" I ask her.

She sighs. "No."

I clench my jaw. "It'll make you feel better."

"I don't think anything can make me feel better."

"We call this self-destructing." When her legs give out again, I scoop her up.

She latches on to my neck and peers into my eyes. Her tongue darts out, wetting her lips.

"I'm not," she slurs. "Just..."

She got fucked up fast.

"Just what?"

"Washing away today." She puts her cheek on my shoulder.

For fuck's sake. "I'm taking you home."

Riley lurches forward. "She can't—"

"Yeah, yeah." I carry her out of the party.

Hoots and hollers follow us.

"People are mean." She twists in my arms, gazing first at the onlookers, then at the arm curled under her knees. "Your knuckles are bruised."

I frown. "I've been hurt worse."

"This is self-inflicted," she argues. "Maybe *you're* the self-destructing one."

The truth of it cuts deep. Except she seems new to the self-destruction phase, and I've lived here for a while. Hockey holds me together, but that's about it.

I thought I was better at hiding it.

Luckily, we arrive at my vehicle. The matte black Audi stands out, even in the dark. It doesn't glint in the garish overhead streetlight.

"Are you going to puke in my car?" I set her on her feet.

"No." She crosses her arms, the picture of indignant, but uncrosses them a minute later so she doesn't topple over. Her balance is *gone*.

I stifle a laugh. "No puking allowed. If you do…"

She leans on my car door. "You'll what? Spank me?" Her expression is… mischievous?

I frame her in and smirk at her, while she seems to consider her own scenario.

"Earth to Margo."

Her gaze finds mine.

"You'd like that, wouldn't you?" I trace up her sides, taking the hem of her shirt up, too. I've been dying to touch her, and these sparks between us aren't enough to satiate me. "A little pain with your pleasure? Does it turn you on?"

"I—"

I slide my hand into her pants, cupping her pussy. My fingers find her hot and wet, and my dick leaps to attention. It wants to be inside her. My own alcohol consumption doesn't help my self-control.

"Soaked," I tell her. "How drunk are you?"

She makes a face. "There are two of you."

Well, fuck. I might get off on her fear, but I can't take full advantage of a drunk girl. That feels… wrong. I pull my hand out, making sure her pants are buttoned, then shift her aside to open the door for her. "Get in. Before I do something I shouldn't."

She just lifts her chin and smiles.

Turns out… doing something I shouldn't means kissing her in the driveway. I don't know how it happens, but one minute we're staring at each other, and the next, our lips are sealed together. My body begs for more of her. I lift her and slip my hand into her pants again. Doing something I shouldn't means thrusting my fingers inside her until she moans against my lips.

I need more. Her mouth, hands, pussy—I'm hot with the urge to fuck her. In public. Against my car, where anyone can see.

That would be the ultimate claiming, wouldn't it?

Finally, I pull back. "You're drunk, baby. I'm not a good enough guy to tell you no."

"Then don't."

Outside of our bubble, the world could be exploding for all I care.

I nip her throat.

"Caleb." She wraps her arms around my neck and draws me closer.

No. I really can't.

I practically toss her into her seat while she glares at me.

A thrill chases under my skin. "Don't worry, Margo. This is the only time I'll tell you no."

A dose of reality seems to come back for a second, and she slouches. "Maybe you should take me home."

"That's the plan." I exhale.

Her foster parents are going to kill me. I don't think I can afford to drive around until she sobers up. I'm not drunk, but I've been drinking. And I can only imagine what my uncle would do if I got pulled over in this state.

There's somewhere else I can go.

I drive carefully, one hand tracing invisible patterns on her leg. Her expression is blank, and it seems like her mind is very far away. She doesn't even register arriving at our destination. Or when I kill the engine and come around to the passenger side. I pick her up out of the car. She rests her cheek on my shoulder, but her fingers dig into the front of my shirt.

"They're gonna see," she sniffles. "They're going to send me back."

"It'll be okay." I stride up the wide front walkway and into Eli's family's home.

Her eyes crack open, taking in the unfamiliar location.

"Where are we?"

"Shh," I whisper. "If I bring you back to the Bryans like this, they'll crucify me."

"So this is a self-preservation thing."

I scoff. Of course she'd think that. She was just worried about them sending her back—whatever the fuck that means. And now she thinks this motive is purely my own?

If her foster parents turn against me, my job becomes significantly harder.

Eli's home is where I spend most of my time. I carry her down to the basement, where my converted room awaits.

It's not much, but it's better than any other option. And I am infinitely grateful to Eli's family for taking me in.

I set her on the bed. She's like a doll, all floppy and putting up zero resistance. I tug her sweatshirt off, then her shoes.

"Caleb Asher, are you trying to get me naked?" Her eyes are closed.

I roll my eyes. "You're so fucking drunk. On one drink?"

"In my defense, it was mostly vodka."

Ah, so Theo must've made her drink, too.

"That must've tasted great." I sit beside her and brush her hair off her face. She seems younger like this, without the worry lines between her brows or the scowl that so often appears when I do something unsavory.

S. Massery

"Stop." She knocks my hand away, and her tone stays rigid when she snaps, "Don't get soft on me."

Interesting.

"Sleep, then." I kick off my shoes.

"I have a curfew."

I climb onto the bed beside her, scooting her toward the wall, and stroke her hair again. Because it's soft and nice, and also because it seems to piss her off.

"You have two hours before curfew," I tell her. "And let me be fucking nice to you."

She doesn't relax.

"What's the issue? You're more tense now than..."

"I don't want to talk about it." She curls away from me.

"Didn't think I'd ever have a girl fully dressed in my bed." I laugh to myself. I didn't think I'd ever take a girl back here. Certainly none from Emery-Rose Elite.

After a long minute, her breathing evens out and her body releases its tension.

I lie beside her, fully awake, until my watch buzzes with the alarm I set.

I wish I could keep Margo with me here. I wish I could sleep. These days, sleep comes infrequently, or in small chunks of time. I content myself with watching her slow, deep breaths for another minute, then sit up.

I put my shoes back on and roll her onto her back.

She doesn't wake up.

Even when I pick her up and carry her back to the car, setting her in the passenger seat. I lean over her, buckling her in, and gently close her car door.

She stays asleep even after we reach the Bryans' house. I park at the curb and watch the lit windows on the first floor.

They're waiting up for her.

I give it another minute, then two. Then ten. If we want to be on time, she has to be inside in four minutes.

Four minutes isn't going to miraculously sober her up.

I lift her out of the car, and she wakes with a start.

I almost drop her, but she latches on to my neck.

"Where am I?" Her head swings around.

"You were sleeping. And we can't wait any longer, unless you want to be grounded for an eternity."

I put her feet on the ground, and her knees buckle. I don't let her fall, my grip sure. Still, she's clearly more drunk than anticipated. Even after her nap...

I release a long sigh. "Can you pretend to be more sober?"

"Aren't I?"

We make our way to the front door, her arm slung around my neck, mine around her waist. I've got most of her weight supported, but it would be nice if she could open her eyes the rest of the way.

"Aren't you what?" I ask.

"Sober."

I grunt and glance down at her. "Your eyes are closed."

"I'm just resting them."

"How about you open them until I can get you up to your room?"

Jesus.

She does, barely, and we make it up the front steps. I open the door and guide her in, pausing when I spot Robert.

He sits in a chair in the living room, a book in his lap.

Margo spots him, too, and cringes. "Uh-oh."

She might've got away with it if she didn't immediately break character. I'm left holding her up, while her grip tightens on my shirt.

"Are you drunk, Margo?" Robert asks.

I wince.

"Not *drunk* per se," she mumbles. "I mean, it was just—"

"I'm going to get her upstairs," I interrupt her. "Sorry, Mr. Bryan."

Her foster father's expression is severe when focusing on Margo—but shocked when he looks at me. "Caleb—your lip. What happened?"

I frown, tensing so I don't automatically touch it. "Just a little disagreement, Mr. Bryan. Nothing to worry about."

He stares at me for an extra beat. Then, to Margo, "We'll discuss this in the morning."

She'll have fun with that one. I lift her into my arms again and carry her up the stairs. Into her familiar bedroom. I set her feet down to free up my arm, and I drag the blankets back. Then guide her into it and pull everything back into place.

"You're gonna have a hell of a hangover," I warn.

She pouts. "Rescue me from the Bryans tomorrow. I'm gonna need it."

"You got it." I lean down and kiss her cheek. Her skin is warm under my lips.

And she's snoring before I make it out of the room.

But when I get back to the Blacks' house, Amelie waits on my bed.

"What are you doing here?" I raise an eyebrow. Things are finally smoothing out with Margo, and I'd be lying if I said I wasn't thrilled to gain her trust. If I wasn't positive Margo was passed out in her bed—the bed I just put her in —I'd be more inclined to drag Amelie out by her elbow immediately.

"You're not happy I'm here?" Her voice is husky.

I don't know what the fuck she's wearing, but it isn't

much. A cropped shirt exposes her abdomen, and a flared skirt covers her underwear.

Barely.

"I was looking forward to an empty bed." I cross my arms and lean against my doorframe, making it clear that I'll be venturing no further.

Her fingers play with the bottom of her shirt. "Quite the scene you made tonight."

"Which is why I'm particularly surprised at your visit."

She shrugs. "Thought you might want to know someone from our past found you."

I narrow my eyes. "Let's cut to the chase, Amelie. You want something for this mysterious information?"

She gets up and comes closer. "Of course I want something. I want *you*."

I laugh. I can't help it. Even if I wasn't all-consumed with thoughts of Margo, Amelie leaves a bad taste in my mouth.

"Not gonna happen."

She's close enough to touch. When she arches her back, her breasts brush my chest. She winds her fingers into my hair, and she pulls me down to her. I indulge her kiss for a second, watching her closed eyes. She makes some noises in the back of her throat, and it comes off more like something in porn than a real kiss.

I don't feel anything.

Which makes it pointless. Before, I felt... a glimmer of prospect, I guess. But now there's nothing. Just pressure on my lips and the sick feeling that it isn't Margo.

I shove her away.

She stumbles and falls on her ass. She bursts into tears. "You were my last chance."

I have no idea what that means. Maybe she's about to be

married off to some stranger? I heard rumors that the Page family was in deep with the Italian Mafia in New York City. I wouldn't put it past her dad to pull some stunt and solidify that partnership.

Just a theory, though. Amelie is seventeen and on the cusp of graduating high school. Surely her parents wouldn't do anything before the end of the school year.

Either way, it's not my fucking problem. I crouch and meet her tear-filled gaze. "Who found me?"

Amelie pushes to her feet, glaring at me. "Who do you think?"

I shake my head. There's only one person who Amelie would know about... one person with whom Amelie would know I don't want involvement.

"Get out," I snap.

"But—"

"No buts, Amelie." Anger floods through me, and I shift to make sure I'm not blocking her exit. I don't want her to touch me when she rushes out of here. "If you don't leave right now, you're going to wish you never set foot in here."

Ever the high-society princess, she turns up her nose at me. "Don't worry, Caleb. I already wish that."

She stomps past me, up the stairs, and slams the front door shut behind her. It resounds through the house, and I pinch the bridge of my nose.

What the fuck is her problem?

Eli comes down a split second later, whistling. "Wow. You doing Amelie behind Margo's back?"

I grunt. "Fuck, no."

"Then what did she want?"

I shake out my limbs. I need to go to the gym, work off some of this sudden anxious energy. *She could ruin everything.*

"Caleb." Eli waves his hand in front of my face. "What did Amelie want?"

"To warn me," I reply dryly. "Pretty sure she was looking for any excuse to come down here."

Eli laughs. "Yeah, man. Sure. Warn you about what?"

I heave a sigh. May as well tell him. After all, I pretty much owe him for the rest of my life. Oh, but he's going to freak out.

"If you say a word of this to anyone, I'll kill you."

He nods. He's used to my threats—takes them in stride and thinks something is off when I don't threaten him.

"Margo's mom is back in town," I say.

She's been gone for so long... Almost as long as her daughter.

Eli pales. He knows the history. He got the story from me, in bits and pieces as I learned it over time. I never keep anything from him.

"She's going to get in the way." I shake out my hand to keep from punching the wall. "I told her—"

"Doesn't matter what you told her, man," he interrupts. "You're going to find out what she wants and escort her the fuck back out of Rose Hill."

Yeah. Because it's *that* easy.

If she finds out about Margo...

Game over.

Chapter 27
Margo

Ms. McCaw is in the kitchen when I come down the stairs.

I hesitate for a second, then force myself to keep moving. My head hurts, my stomach is rolling. And now my social worker sits at the table with a mug of coffee, and no foster parent in sight.

"Good morning," she greets me.

I force a smile. "I hope you haven't been waiting long."

She cocks a brow. "I heard you had a late night. Stumbling in with a boy, drunk..."

The blood rushes away from my face. Why didn't I put that together immediately? She comes to visit right after I seriously fuck up—of course they don't want me anymore.

Tears burn my eyes. "I'm sorry," I choke out. "If I could just talk to them—ask them for a second chance—"

"No one is taking you away." She circles the table to stand in front of me. "This visit was scheduled with them since last week. Okay? Calm down."

I exhale.

"But..."

"Ms. McCaw—"

"To put it plainly: I'm concerned. What's up with this behavior, Margo? Does it have to do with your fath—"

"No!" I hurry past her and grab myself a mug. Once I've poured and doctored a cup of coffee, I take a seat at the table.

She joins me, watching me with concerned eyes.

"Where are the Bryans?" I ask.

"They elected to give us some privacy, so it's just you and me. You can be honest. How are you doing?"

I heave a sigh. "Good, I think. It's weird being back at school, with people I used to know..." I shake my head. Now's not the time to get sidetracked by thoughts of Caleb. "I'm still getting used to the Bryans being so *nice*."

Angela laughs. "From what I've heard, they think the world of you."

"Probably not after last night." I focus my gaze out the window.

"They know teenagers make mistakes. That includes getting drunk at a party." She touches my wrist. "Apologize, and things will be fine. Don't slip again."

"I won't." I sip my coffee. "I do have a question for you."

"Shoot."

"Claire's phone disconnected, and I haven't been able to reach her. Could you give her my number if I wrote it down?"

Claire is sixteen, and Hanna is twelve. They're real siblings, which means... well, there was a higher chance that they wouldn't get separated. The foster system *wants* them to stay together whenever possible. I don't know what happened to them, though.

I knew, at the very least, that I would not be going to the same new home as either of them. There was no way. Two teenage girls are one thing—three are nearly impossible to place together.

Ms. McCaw's lips flatten. She's not their case worker, to the best of my knowledge. But she works with her, so... maybe it's possible.

"I can't make any promises, Margo. But yes, if you write down how to get in touch with you, I can try to pass it along."

I smile. "Thank you. Seriously."

"No promises," she repeats. "But I'll do my best."

We stand, and she hugs me. We're usually a limited-contact type of relationship, and the moment surprises me. It takes me a second to hug her back.

She's been the only stable person in my life for seven years, and I think this is the first time she's hugged me. Besides one-armed side squeezes anyway.

"Take care," she says. "And no more drinking. This is your only warning. Got it?"

"Yes, ma'am." I hold back the urge to salute her.

I lock the door after she leaves. I lean against it, letting my head fall forward. I'm an *idiot*. Letting Caleb get me drunk—okay, well, that's not really fair. Theo put the cup in my hand. I was with Riley as I downed it faster than I should've.

The mistake was going to the party in the first place. That will *not* happen again.

When Lenora and Robert get back, I'm on the couch watching some mindless reality competition. They're armed with groceries, and once the bags are put on the kitchen island, they come in and sit with me.

"You saw your social worker?" Lenora asks.

I nod and bite my lip. Uncertainty wars inside me. Do I just blurt out an apology? Ease into it?

"Did you have any concerns? With us?" Robert's eyebrows crinkle.

"No! I just—I'm so sorry." *Blurting out an apology, it is.* "I've never drank. I've never been drunk—"

"Margo." Lenora frowns and reaches toward me.

"I don't want to put you in that position."

"It's okay," Lenora says. "We started fostering to be parents. It might not seem like it, but this is part of that."

Robert shoots her a look. "Well, it's not *okay* like you can do it again. But you're owning up to a mistake, and we appreciate that."

I nod quickly.

"But we can't let it go unpunished," he adds. "So until further notice: school and home. No exceptions."

I swallow. It's fair. Some other foster homes would've locked their kid in a room for a week with limited rations. "I understand. Thank you."

We all stand, and I retreat to my room. They could've slapped me with chores... cut the Wi-Fi... a lot of things. I set my coffee down and glance around, marveling—*again*—at the luxury of this house.

My phone vibrates.

I reach for it, half hoping it's Riley or Caleb.

My heart sinks.

UNKNOWN

Made a big enough fool of yourself?

[video attachment]

I click on the video and hold my breath. It's me...
Oh God.
Someone saw Caleb and me leave the party last night.

There's a clear view of me falling backward against his car. His hand going into my pants. And...

I drop the phone, covering my mouth with both hands. It lands on the bed facedown, but the video keeps playing. Over the music from the house, and people talking, there's breathing.

That noise will haunt me for a while.

My phone rings, cutting off the video. I jump a foot and slowly flip it over. If it's Unknown, suddenly *calling*, I may lose it.

It's a number I'm not familiar with, so I ignore the call and go back to Unknown's conversation. They've sent me another text.

UNKNOWN

Now... what to do with that? So many options.

What do you want?

That would be too easy.

Keep your phone on you. I'll be in touch.

My stomach heaves. I rush to the bathroom, falling to my knees in front of the toilet. When I'm done, I stand on shaky legs. My mouth and throat burn from the acid.

Lenora is in the doorway, her expression sympathetic. "As if you needed another reason to not overdo the alcohol."

I cup my hands under the faucet and rinse out my mouth. I spit and clear my throat, then straighten. "I'm sorry." *Again.*

She hands me a towel. "There are consequences you'll learn on your own. It's part of becoming an adult, unfortunately. Are you feeling hungover?"

"I was okay up until now."

A little white lie never hurt anyone.

She pats my shoulder and leaves me alone. I close the door and fall onto my bed, burying my face in the pillows.

I should delete the video and any evidence of Unknown.

They could ruin everything—my life at school. Staying with the Bryans.

What if my foster parents saw that? It'd be icing on the poisoned cake. One mistake is just that: a mistake. But two? Or more? Someone has a video of Caleb putting his hand down my pants, and that isn't an accident.

The funny thing is—it wouldn't even blow back on him. He'd be lauded as the guy who got some action from the drunk outcast. Oh, she was his girlfriend for a night? Weird.

Just to be clear, I'm the drunk outcast in that scenario.

I contemplate begging Unknown to delete it. But the more I think about it, the more I know it's a bad idea. They've been out for blood before I even started going to Emery-Rose. And now they finally have a blade sharp enough to cut.

My phone rings, and I flinch. The sound goes straight through my throbbing brain.

I check, and it's the same unfamiliar number. This time, I answer it.

"Margo?"

I sit up straight. "Oh my God, Claire! I just asked Ms. McCaw—"

"She dropped it off," she interrupts. "Things have been crazy here. I wanted to reach out, but I had to get a new number. My phone smashed; it was tragic—"

"Awful," I murmur. "How's Hanna?"

"As well as can be expected." *Pause.* "We were able to

stay together, thank God. But it's been a hard transition. We loved—well, you know."

I do. It's hard to get attached to a family. But once you do, something usually comes along to fuck it up. That's why I want to keep the Bryans at arm's length. I like them. But if I were to be ripped away, right this moment, I wouldn't be *that* devastated.

Okay, maybe I would.

It's the grief of losing families—over and over and *over*— that kills your spirit and hardens your heart to that kind of relationship. I've seen it happen too many times to let it happen to me. I've only got a few months left, and I need to emerge intact.

"Are you near Rose Hill?" I ask her.

"We're in the next town over. They put me in the fancy-as-hell high school. It's been a trip." She chuckles.

"That's good."

"Yeah. I'm ready to get the fuck out of here, though."

I sag on the bed. "Maybe since you're close, we can meet up one day. I'd love to see Hanna, too."

"We'd love that," Claire answers, her voice noticeably lighter. "We've missed you, Wolfe. Maybe we can swing it this week."

"Oh, shoot." I smack my forehead. "I can't for the fore-seeable future. I'm grounded."

"What on earth did you do to get grounded?"

"Came home drunk," I say in a low voice.

She bursts into laughter. "Priceless. Got any videos of that? I'd love to see you drunk—"

"No." It comes out a bit harsher than I intended. "Sorry. Little touchy about it, seeing as how it didn't end well."

"What's going on with you, Margo? Are the new foster parents that bad?"

"They're great." I flop sideways, my head hitting the pillow. "I just... I'm worried, okay? There are a lot of moving pieces, and I'm almost done..."

"Listen." Claire has never been a rational one. Her ideas are half-crazed most of the time. Of the two of us, she's been the instigator. The troublemaker. "Sneak out and meet me on Friday. At lunchtime. We can find somewhere to go."

Yep. She's crazy.

"I have to be back for last period. My foster dad is my teacher."

"Brutal." She clears her throat. "Oh! Let's meet at the mall! Friday at noon, and you'll be back before anyone notices. Pinky promise."

There's no use arguing with her. Claire with an idea is a girl on the warpath.

"I don't have a ride."

"Get one of your friends to drive you," she says. "Or the guy who got you drunk."

I groan. "I don't know. I'll let you know. Okay?"

"You'll figure it out! Love ya, sis." Claire makes a kissy noise into the phone.

The line goes dead before I can respond.

Chapter 28
Margo

I n the Emery-Rose Elite courtyard Monday morning, I spot Riley immediately.

She has a bubble of space around her, which is unusual. I mean, she has more space than normal. The royalty get their breathing room, and the rest of us rub elbows.

As I make my way closer, the courtyard slowly drains of noise.

It's so quiet you could hear a pin drop.

Riley's eyebrows crease, and Savannah is suddenly in my path.

"Following in Mommy dearest's footsteps, are you?" She laughs. "It only took a few weeks for your true colors to come out."

What the hell?

I push past her. Stares follow me. My skin crawls, but Riley meets me halfway and tows me back in the direction I came. I follow along, flustered and confused, but a terrible feeling kicks up inside me.

"Oh my God, Margo!" She stops and faces me. Her expression is horrified.

I flinch. "Why is everyone acting so weird?"

Her brows furrow. "Um, everyone got an email this morning..."

"I didn't."

"It's..."

My stomach drops.

"Spit it out. Please."

She opens her email and passes me her phone.

It's a picture, probably either taken at the same time as the video Unknown sent or a screenshot from it. I'm against his car. His lips are on mine, and his hand is clearly down my pants.

There's no more air in my lungs.

She grabs my shoulder, and suddenly I'm sitting on the ground.

"Breathe." She rubs my back. "It's okay. It's not even..."

"I can't," I choke out. "I can't do this. I can't go in there."

How could Unknown do this to me? Especially since I did nothing to them. *Nothing*. And with a single email, my life just got ten times worse.

"Given the circumstances, I think they'd understand if we skipped... oh no."

I lift my head.

Caleb storms toward us. He's impossibly angry.

He doesn't stop until he's right in front of us. He pulls me to my feet by my wrists, although I'm not sure I can stay standing. My knees wobble.

"She's hyperventilating," Riley says.

He touches my cheek.

I can't stop gasping. Something heavy has planted itself on my chest. I grab at his shirt, my eyes wide.

267

"Panic attack," Riley says. "Honestly, I don't even blame her. But it's going to be okay, Margo. It's just a picture."

It's so much more than a picture.

"Give us a minute," Caleb growls, not tearing his attention away from my face.

I may as well be in a vacuum for all the air I can drag into my lungs. I think Riley backs away, but all I can focus on is Caleb's startlingly blue eyes. I know they're blue, but today, with the morning sun angled just right, they're light and clear and dazzling.

And he's worried.

I'm worried, too.

"Margo."

My head shake is frantic. "I can't—"

He slams his lips to mine, cutting off my words. His tongue forces my lips apart, taking ownership of my mouth.

I shudder against him, finally sucking in a deep breath through my nose. Then another. He's not kissing me—he's resuscitating me. He doesn't stop until I've relaxed in his hold and my heart isn't hammering so viciously against my ribcage.

He finally rocks back on his heels, and his eyes search mine.

He's still holding my wrists.

"Wow," Riley mutters, a few feet away. "That was hot."

"I'll find out who sent that picture." A mask slips over his features.

"Mr. Asher!" The principal comes toward us. "Mr. *Asher*, you are suspended!"

What?

When did that happen?

He drops my wrists and faces her. "I know."

"So what on earth are you doing here?"

He shrugs, keeping me mostly behind him. Maybe he thinks she'll turn her wrath on me, next. Or maybe...

Oh my God. Did she get the picture, too?

"I'm on my way out," he informs her. "See ya Wednesday."

Even when he doesn't have the upper hand, he sounds arrogant enough to send the *principal* away. After a moment of consideration, she marches back into the school.

Caleb taps under my chin until I meet his gaze. "You'll be fine. Just ignore them."

"Right. You got suspended?"

He rolls his eyes. "Perk of Ian being a loudmouth. I'm also not playing the next few hockey games."

Oh, jeez.

Actually, didn't they have a game on Saturday? I spent it recovering from my hangover from hell... He didn't ask me to go, which I would've thought was weird if I was in any state to truly consider it. He heads back to his car, and I slowly rotate toward Riley.

"That bodes well," she says.

"He didn't fight Ian on school grounds. Why did they suspend him?"

She links her arm with mine. The bell rings, which means we've successfully avoided the courtyard.

"Ian's parents complained," she says in a low voice. "Threatened to sue if they didn't do something to curb Caleb's reaction."

"He's been getting in a lot of fights. Did Ian get suspended, too?"

"No, because they alleged that Caleb was the aggressor. He's got a little split lip, and Ian looks like he fought a cheese grater. I'm sure he's around here somewhere."

Lovely. Just what I need—for Caleb to be out and Ian to be potentially feeling vengeful.

All eyes are on me. I try to do what Caleb says—to ignore them—but it's hard when the hallway gets quiet again. Riley stays with me until we get to my homeroom, and she throws me a sympathetic look.

"I'll be okay." I think I'm lying.

She nods once.

I slide into my seat and keep my head down.

Someone kicks my bookbag as they pass, the contents scattering across the floor.

A cheerleader stops, one foot hovering over my fallen phone. She looks around, then laughs. "I expected more condoms, slut. Opening your legs to anyone who gets you drunk at a party."

I glare at her. "That's not—"

"Why else would Caleb go for you? You're an easy target."

She uses her toe to send my phone skidding out of reach. It stops a few rows away, under a desk. "Oops. My bad."

It continues like that throughout the day, only growing in intensity. I try to focus on the good: Caleb will be back on Wednesday, and I'll get to see Claire on Friday. Although, I need to figure out how I'm going to get to the mall and back... I'll have to both escape Caleb's clutches *and* get out of school undetected.

Should be interesting.

When I walk into my last class of the day, I'm defeated. Someone spilled chocolate milk on me after lunch, and my shirt smells sickly sweet. It sticks to my skin. Not to mention the brown stain on the white fabric.

Robert sees me and smiles, then does a double take.

Yeah, it's that bad.

He motions me aside.

The teachers haven't been acting any differently, which makes me believe it was just sent to the students. How *that* miracle happened, I'll never know.

"Are you okay?"

"I'm fine," I say.

"What happened...?"

I sigh. "It's been a long day."

He squints at me. "Are you being bullied?"

"It's nothing I can't handle."

The cheerleaders were the driving force today. Amelie and Savannah watched while their minions pinched me, ruined my things. The contents of my locker were coated in a fine layer of glitter. The back of my arms are bruised from fingers biting my flesh.

I've never been so tense.

And it's probably because Amelie and Savannah both want Caleb—and here's the proof that he wants *me*.

He's not even here to stop it. Won't be until Wednesday.

"Okay, take your seat." He does reach out now, putting his hand on my shoulder for a brief moment.

I tuck myself away in a corner for the rest of class, letting my mind wander. I thought I saw someone familiar at the party. It was just a brief moment, glancing out the window at someone by the bonfire. But I can't put my finger on who it was. Maybe they're the culprit.

Or it could be... literally anyone who went to the party and had their phone out. Someone smoking on the front porch or pausing their own make-out session in the shadows, or leaving the party at the same time as us.

I need to figure out who Unknown is. If I can uncover

their motive, maybe I can stop them or tell someone who can help me.

The bell rings, shattering my thoughts. Chairs scrape back, and my classmates perform a mass exodus.

I stay where I am, wondering if I can just wait everyone out.

Robert starts picking up, casting me a glance or two before setting down the canvases and approaching. "Something is wrong."

"It was just a tough day."

He sits on the stool next to me. The one Caleb usually takes. "Did something happen at that party on Friday?"

I flinch. "No, it's more complicated than that. It just needs to work itself out."

He exhales. "It hurts to see you like this, Margo. If you need anything, please don't hesitate to ask."

"Thanks, Robert."

He packs up his bag, and we head toward his car.

Unsurprisingly, Caleb is waiting for us.

The whole school emptied out fast. Besides cars belonging to students staying late for sports, the parking lot is deserted. He rises from where he was leaning against his car, parked next to Robert's, and shoots him a smile.

"Mind if I steal her?" he asks Robert.

My foster dad shrugs. "I think she could use some cheering up. Even though she's *technically* grounded."

I wince.

Robert chuckles. "Just be back before Len gets home around five, okay?"

"You got it, Mr. Bryan," Caleb says.

His gaze turns to me, and he takes in the chocolate milk stain on my shirt, then my bloodshot eyes. Is that from crying? I'll never tell.

He opens the passenger door for me and takes my backpack off my shoulder.

We sit in his car and wait until Robert drives away.

"Today was hell." Obviously.

He leans across the center console. "You're a fighter."

That might be the first time he's ever paid me a compliment.

"I'm sure it wasn't anything you couldn't handle." His fingers undo the buttons of my blouse, and fuck it, I let him.

"I don't want to handle it," I say quietly. "I just want—"

He finishes with the buttons and pushes the soiled fabric off my shoulders. His gaze rises to mine, his eyebrow up with a silent question.

What do you want, Margo?

"I have to do this again tomorrow?" I ask, my voice weak.

He reaches into the back and produces a sweatshirt. I'm collecting them now, I think. I shrug it on over my bra, settling the warm fabric around me. It smells more deeply like his cologne, and I lift the collar to inhale more of it.

"Maybe something more interesting will crop up tomorrow." He winks at me, then finally puts the car in drive.

We head in an unfamiliar direction. When he turns into a driveway and parks, I have no choice but to follow him up the front walkway.

"Whose house is this?"

"Eli's," he says. "He's busy. But since you only have a few hours, I figured I could make your day a little better."

The house feels oddly familiar. Like I came here in a dream.

We go into Eli's living room, and Caleb throws himself onto the couch. He pats the space next to him. "Sit."

"You just let yourself into his house?"

He nods. "Yeah. His parents are pretty cool. They travel a lot, though."

"Gotta love absentee parents," I answer.

His face shutters for a second.

"Why did you attack Ian?" I need to change the subject.

"Just protecting what's mine." His hand wraps around the back of my neck and pulls me to him.

Our lips touch softly at first, barely moving.

I open my eyes.

He's watching me. His free hand sneaks up the sweatshirt, dancing across my back. He unhooks my bra at the same time that he lowers me to the couch.

"Wha..."

"One choice," he says, his lips moving to my jaw. He palms my breast. His fingers find my nipple, rolling it and pinching. "If you want this—if you want *me*—just say the word."

One choice.

It's not just *one*. It's a series of choices that could lead to catastrophe... But certainly not happiness.

God, that seems like a possibility right now, with Caleb's breath in my ear and his hands on my skin. He could play me like an instrument, make me sing. I've never felt this way about anyone else. No one has ever bothered to try to touch me.

And then it comes back to me that we're in his best friend's living room.

I push his face away, staring up at him. "I do, but not here."

He laughs, and the walls that he let down for a split second are resurrected. "If not here, where?"

If not now, when?

He picks himself up off me and leaves the room. My silence must've spoken for itself.

With shaky fingers, I re-clasp my bra and straighten the hoodie.

He comes back with his jacket on. There's a new set to his jaw and a smirk on his lips. "My place. If you don't want to here... and you're not going to tell me where, then I'll choose."

I shiver.

But I can't say I'm against it. A distraction is sorely needed.

The drive to his house is quick.

As we pass the front room, I point at the covered furniture. "Why is this place so..."

"Haunted?"

I walk into Caleb.

He catches me by my upper arms. "A lot of ghosts in this house, little lamb."

I meet his gaze.

"Let's banish a few." He leans down and kisses me.

It's more ruthless than the kiss in Eli's house. Something has shifted. He's released the monster inside him.

I shudder at the infiltration. My heart cracks open as he backs me against the wall, taking my wrists and holding them above my head with one of his hands. His other continues his exploration of my body like we never stopped.

His tongue slides into my mouth.

I push his tongue out with my own. He tastes like honey and cinnamon. He growls, the sound resonating deep in his throat, and tears his lips from mine. He latches on to my neck, biting and sucking.

Tingling pleasure flows under my skin. I lift my leg,

wrapping it around his hip and pulling him flush against me. I tilt my head to the side to give him access.

He draws back only long enough to get the hoodie up and over my head. He unhooks my bra again, and it falls to the floor between us. I kick it away and go for his clothes. His t-shirt, jeans. My fingers drag over his abdomen.

His lips move down, off my neck. He draws one of my nipples into his mouth, teeth grazing it. Stars burst in front of my eyelids. I wind my fingers through his hair, holding him to me as every muscle tenses. The pain feels good. He could do this to me for an eternity, and I don't think I'd ever get sick of his touch.

He was made for me.

Pain and pleasure. Isn't that always how he does it?

He carries me deeper into the house. I'm so drunk on him. He sets me on the counter in the kitchen, dragging my lips back to his before I can register where we are. He kisses me like he's been starving and I'm his favorite dessert.

Completely.

Savagely.

He pushes my skirt up and tugs on my panties. I flinch at the sudden *rip*.

"Did you just—"

He raises my torn panties and grins.

"Caleb—"

"Don't worry. I have a feeling you'll like what's coming next."

He plunges a finger into me without warning.

My abdomen clenches. My lips part. His body wedges between my knees, forcing me open wider, and I lean back on the counter.

He taps my chin with his free hand. "Watch me."

I shudder when he lowers himself, his head going

between my thighs. He puts my legs on his shoulders. And then he pauses, staring at me with an odd expression.

"Caleb—"

He bites my inner thigh. I yelp, trying to close my legs, but his shoulders block the movement.

His tongue swipes up my center, swirling on my clit. His finger is still inside me, picking up a brutal pace while his tongue pays attention to my bud of nerves.

I groan. It feels too good. Unbearable, even. I try to shove him away, but he doesn't budge.

His teeth graze my clit.

I cry out and try to squirm away.

He grips my ass, dragging me to the edge of the counter. "Make as much noise as you want, baby."

His tongue plunges into me again.

Something animalistic claws out of me. I roll my hips into it. His finger takes over where his tongue left off, and he sucks hard on my clit.

I shatter. The orgasm explodes through me, my vision going white and fuzzy. I grab his head as he sucks and sucks. My body trembles in the aftershock.

But instead of stopping... he keeps going. His finger pushes in and out, a steady, quick rhythm.

"I can't do that again." My arms are jelly. I let myself fall back on the counter.

"No." He hauls me upright.

He undoes the button of his pants, and we both look down at his erection. There's a bead of liquid glistening on the head of his cock.

He rolls on a condom, then notches at my entrance. There's a pressure there, the beginning of a stretch, and fear bleeds through my lust.

Is this going to hurt?

He grips the back of my neck, drawing my face down to his. He kisses me at the same time that he thrusts into me.

The pain of it is... *shocking*. Eye-opening.

I gasp into his mouth, and he only pauses for a fraction of a second. Surely, he felt that. The deep pressure, a ripping away of innocence.

"You've always been mine," he says against my lips. "This just fucking confirms it."

I wrap my legs around his hips. We're at the perfect angle. The perfect height.

And the fact that he didn't just freak out on me lifts a weight off my chest. I never said...

Well, it doesn't matter. After a few seconds of discomfort—an alien feeling, something being *inside*—he moves. And then no thought in my head matters.

"I don't want gentle," I tell him.

"Good thing, because my self-control is about to go out the window." He slams into me, filling me completely.

In the back of my mind, I knew we wouldn't be able to do *easy*. Just like we wouldn't do *slow*.

We're fast and reckless and wild.

I dig my nails into his skin. He relentlessly hammers into me. A tingling feeling picks up in my lower abdomen, and my teeth tear his lower lip. My heart is beating so fast, it might take flight.

"Scream," he orders. He flicks my clit.

This orgasm is violent, a tsunami force. Better—or worse —than the first one. I open my mouth, but no sound comes out. It's made better by the way my muscles have something to squeeze around.

He presses on my clit, but he never stops moving. The slide of him in and out creates a new feeling... I let my head fall back and I do what he wants. *I scream.*

I yell his name, my thighs tensing around him, until my voice disappears. Until the pleasure finally releases me, one hot finger at a time.

He quickens, then abruptly stops. He groans, spilling inside me. His lips track along the top of my shoulder. We stay like that for a long moment, wrapped around each other.

His pulse hammers through our connection.

He pulls out slowly, and I wince.

There's blood on the condom, on my thighs, on the counter.

He touches my cheek, and his finger swipes under my eye. "You're beautiful."

I slip off the counter. My muscles quake. "I need a minute," I say in a low voice.

He inclines his head, and I slink away to the bathroom. It takes longer than I would expect to put my pieces back together. My resolve goes here, my dignity goes there. Inch by inch, I rebuild who I was.

Who knew sex would destroy me?

I clean myself. When I come out of the bathroom, Caleb holds out my bra and the sweatshirt he gave me earlier.

I stare at the kitchen island.

"I'm going to fuck you on that counter," he had promised. *"You're going to enjoy it, even knowing what happened here. Because all you'll be able to think about is my dick in your pussy, spreading you wide. Hitting every. Fucking. Nerve."*

Horror washes through me.

He spoke the truth.

I forgot.

I let myself fall into his madness, and now...

"Caleb," I choke out, grabbing his sweatshirt and hugging it to my chest. "How—"

"How could I?" His eyes are dark. Glittering. He leans down until we're face to face. "It's like you don't know me at all."

Tears build up and spill down my cheeks.

He yanks the hoodie out of my grip and puts it on me. Forces my arms through the sleeves and straightens it. He takes my bra, my panties from where he dropped them, and slides both into his pocket.

"Let's go." He puts his hand between my shoulder blades and guides me out.

"You got what you wanted," I say once we're in the car. There's a chill in the air, and my nipples pebble. I want to dive out of the car and walk home rather than let him see.

"Yeah, well, it's not all sunshine and fucking roses up here." He taps his temple.

We ride back to the Bryans' house in silence. I get out and jog to the front door without looking back, my backpack thumping against my shoulder blades. Lenora's car isn't in the driveway, and I slip up to my room undetected.

I go to my window in time to watch Caleb's car pull back out into traffic, slipping away like he was never there.

The haunted feeling I got when I walked into his house is still surrounding me, thicker than smog. He wanted to banish a few ghosts.

I guess that includes me.

Chapter 29
Margo

I loop my arm through Riley's as we walk toward the library. "I need a favor."

She tilts her head. "Like 'bury a body' type of favor, or 'want to stop and get coffee before school' type thing?"

I snort. She unlocks the door, and we slip inside.

It's been an exhausting week, but the good news is: it's Friday.

Once Caleb returned to school, he made a show of being extra nice to me. He glared at anyone he saw making rude comments. That alone seemed to quell most of the bullying. It was a weird turn of events, considering how we left things Monday afternoon. Half of me expected him to pretend I didn't exist and throw me to the wolves, as cliché as that sounds.

"Like a... 'drive me to the mall' type of favor."

She drops into her chair. "Oh, that's easy enough."

I don't sit.

"Wait... do you mean now?"

Riley got her license not too long ago. Technically, she's

not allowed to drive anyone. Her parents only just said she could take the car to school. That's not to say she doesn't do it occasionally, but we keep it under the radar.

"Just... miss lunch and maybe the next class? Please?"

She appraises me. "Why do you need to go to the mall?"

I give in and sink down into the chair next to her. I should've asked her yesterday, but I was nervous she'd say no outright.

"My foster sister, Claire, asked to meet me. She knows I'm grounded..."

"Of course," Riley groans. "And I'm the friend with a car."

"You know it's not like that. I haven't seen her or her sister since we were taken out of our last home. I miss her terribly." I don't have to fake the tears that spring into my eyes. "I should've asked you yesterday, or—"

"You haven't talked much about them."

"It hurt too much." I sniffle.

She finally stands. "Okay, fine. Don't cry or you'll make me cry, and then my makeup will be ruined. I can give you one hour, and I want to meet your foster sisters. And then we come back before seventh period, so Mr. Bryan doesn't fry both of our asses."

I nod. "Yes. Perfect. Thank you."

"Okay, follow my lead."

We walk over to the librarian's office. Riley taps on the door, and the woman inside jumps. I have never talked to her or seen her out of her office.

"Amy," Riley says. "Margo is feeling super sick. Can you write us a pass to the nurse?"

Amy looks at me. "You're sick?"

I put my hand over my stomach. "Yeah."

"Are you pregnant?"

I pale.

She giggles. "Just kidding, of course. Humor. I can write you a pass..."

Riley makes a noise in the back of her throat.

I bite my lip to hold back a frown. This isn't going to work.

"Oh, and can you write us a pass *back* from the nurse, too? I'll bring you Mom's cookies on Monday."

Amy's eyes light up. "Her homemade chocolate chip?"

"Yes," Riley agrees, nodding emphatically. "So..."

Amy sighs. "Okay, fine. One second."

"Leave the time blank," I cut in.

Amy glances at me, rolling her eyes. She hands us the slips, and Riley hugs her.

"I feel like I missed something," I say.

"Amy is my cousin." She laughs. "She's such an introvert... Before you came along, I'd eat lunch in her office."

We sneak out a side door and crouch-run to her car. It's probably more suspicious that way, but this is the first real time we've skipped a class. As soon as we're on the road, we burst into giggles.

"Tell me about Claire," Riley orders.

I smile. "She's sixteen. Smarter than me, for sure. Her sister, Hanna, is twelve. They both came to my foster family a few months after I got there. We became thick as thieves."

She glances at me. "Sounds nice."

"Claire's a wild child," I say. "Always coming up with these crazy ideas. Hanna and I were more similar. Quiet... grounded."

Riley snorts. "Shy."

"Yeah, that."

We get to the mall in record time, which is perfect. The

faster we get here, the more time I have to spend with Claire.

At the food court, I look around eagerly while Riley goes to buy us lunch.

The last time I was here, Caleb made a fool out of me.

Shoving that thought away, I spot her on the escalator. I wave frantically to catch her attention and rush toward her. We crash into each other, hugging and laughing.

I pull away first. "It's been, what, a month? You're grown up."

Her blonde hair, long when I first saw it, is short and curled. She has cat-eye sunglasses perched on her head, light eye makeup, and dark-red lipstick.

She manages to seem more adult than I feel.

"I missed you, Wolfe." She hugs me again. She's petite enough that she can tuck her head under my chin. "We have so much to catch up on!"

"How's Hanna?" I ask.

"Brilliant," Claire says. "Foster family loves her, of course. There's a brother in this one. I'm thinking they might be keepers."

My eyes widen. "That's amazing."

She shrugs. "If they keep *me* is a whole other issue. They're infatuated with Hanna—not her adventurous older sister."

"You two are a package deal."

"I'd rather her secure a home that loves her. I'll be fine."

Riley approaches with a tray of food, and Claire's head shoots up.

"Who's this?"

"Claire, this is Riley. She's my friend at school. Riley, Claire, my foster sister."

They shake hands, and we lapse into silence. Riley passes me a carton of food.

"So, how's things been back at Emery-Rose?" Claire asks. "Run into Caleb?"

I've managed to keep our sex a secret from everyone—Riley, even. I survived Tuesday without skipping, and he arrived back on Wednesday, as promised.

A stolen kiss or two before class, his hand on my thigh at lunch... other than that, nothing.

"Ooh, Riley, she's turning red. What is happening?" Claire leans forward.

"They're dating," Riley tells her. "After a tumultuous start."

Claire grabs my wrist. "Really? Margo, that's great!" She squeezes hard enough to bruise. "After all, you never shut up about him. It's like you willed this to happen against the odds."

I smile, pulling my wrist away. I put my hands under the table. She knows about my history with him, but her reaction isn't quite what I thought.

"What about you?" I ask. "Any cute boys at your new school?"

"Where do you go?" Riley asks.

"Lion's Head." She grins. "There're some cute guys there, Wolfe. They're deliciously rich."

"Is that all you care about?" I laugh.

"No, I also care about the size of their—"

"Claire!" I squeal.

Riley chuckles. "I suppose that's an important factor."

"Our girl wouldn't know," Claire confides, leaning across the table toward Riley. "She's never had sex."

Riley is unfazed. "That's not a bad thing."

"It is if the guy you want is the hottest piece of ass in

school..." Claire raises her eyebrows. "Isn't that right, Margo?"

I pause. "What do you mean?"

"Just that... you know, I'd imagine he would be quite demanding in bed and all. And I know you aren't really comfortable..." Claire pops a piece of gum in her mouth.

Great. That's so nice.

"We should go." Riley flashes me the time on her phone.

I latch on to that. "Oh, shoot."

We stand, and Claire rises a beat later.

"It was good to see you, Claire. My foster parents mentioned I would be ungrounded soon. Hopefully that means we can get together on a weekend with Hanna."

Claire grimaces. "My weekends are pretty packed. But Hanna would love to meet up! I'm sure you two can arrange something." She darts around the table and wraps her arms around my waist. "Good to see you, sis."

Riley and I leave her there. As soon as we're out of sight, she elbows me.

She says, "You didn't tell her about any of the bad stuff."

"Why worry her?"

"The girl didn't seem worried about you."

"Because I didn't tell her that Caleb was an epic bully?" I roll my eyes. "Some stuff is better left unsaid. Like how he and I had sex on Monday."

She gasps so hard, she chokes. I pat her back while she coughs, and her eyes are wide when she straightens.

"Holy shit. Tell me everything."

I do. The good, bad, and ugly. Because Riley's the sort of friend who can handle it.

She parks, and we hurry back to the side door that we had left propped open. We end up back in the women's locker room. It was a weird way out, I'll admit. But it's one of the only doors that isn't monitored, since the gym classes usually go in and out through the gymnasium entrance.

I grab our bags from my gym locker and pass Riley's back to her. We walk out, and I grind to a halt when I register who's waiting for us.

Caleb.

"Skipping class, baby?" He pouts. "Without me?"

Riley edges around us, shooting me an apologetic look. "Talk to you later."

Leaving me alone with the devil.

"I had somewhere to be." I dig my pass out of my pocket. "It's fine anyway."

"Ooh, a pass. Riley's librarian cousin, no doubt."

I blink at him. He appears relaxed, but I feel the tension between us.

He's *pissed*, but he's hiding it well. After days of nothing, this is what I get?

"How do you know Amy is her—"

"Cousin?" He lifts one shoulder. "It's no secret."

I glare at him. He doesn't impede me from continuing down the hall toward Robert's art class, however. He keeps pace with me, his hands in his pockets and bag slung over one shoulder.

"Where'd you go?" he asks.

"You really want to know?"

"Well, I'm not asking just to hear my own voice." At the door to the spiral staircase, he holds me back. "Are you still getting picked on?"

"Are you asking because you're concerned?" I scoff. "Yes, I'm still getting picked on. It's every day."

He slides his hand through my hair. "I've decided that the only person who can be cruel to you is *me*."

"Lovely."

How can he be so callous and turn me on at the same time? My body reacts to him like a tightly wound wire. One touch and I come alive.

"I'll see you tonight," he murmurs. "Wear something sexy under your clothes."

"What's tonight?" I follow him up the stairs. "Caleb."

He winks. "You don't want to tell me where you went? Two can play that game, love."

Getting answers from him is like trying to squeeze blood from a stone. Pointless and impossible. He ignores the questions I pepper him with when Robert is preoccupied, and we fall silent when Robert peers over our shoulders at our progress on our end-of-the-semester project.

Caleb approaches Robert near the end of class. They talk in hushed tones, but I can't make out Caleb's question. Only the reply, which seems to come with apprehension.

"I'll need to speak with my wife," Robert tells him.

Caleb returns to his seat and smirks at me.

"What was that about?" I whisper.

"Nothing to worry about," he says. "You'll find out soon enough."

The bell cuts off any further interrogation. Caleb slides off his stool and strides out the door, leaving me behind. No backward glance, no hovering like the last week. He's just... *poof*. Gone.

Robert clears his throat. "Ready?"

"What did Caleb ask you?"

He gives me a too-innocent look. "He just had a personal question."

He's not going to tell me. I try not to let that sting too much.

Once we're home, I retreat to my room. My phone has been unusually silent. No Caleb, no Riley... no Unknown.

I do have a text from Claire, though.

CLAIRE

So great to see you, Margo!! Really missed you. Hanna sends a kissy face. Want to meet up next weekend??

I grin at my phone.

ME

I'll double-check, but I think I'll be ungrounded by then! Yay!

I set my phone down to change out of my uniform. My phone chimes again, and I grab it, already smiling. The smile fades when I see who this new text is from.

UNKNOWN

Do you ever get tired of being fake?

My good mood plummets like a stone in the ocean. Down, down, down.

UNKNOWN

How does it feel to lose your virginity to a monster?

I choke on my gasp. How do they know?
I certainly didn't tell anyone...
Which means Caleb did.

Chapter 30
Margo

Lenora knocks on my door. "Hey, honey. We're going out. Will you be okay on your own?"

I sit up and look at her. I've been struggling through homework for the last hour. Math used to be my favorite subject, but I haven't been able to concentrate this semester.

Too many other things pulling my attention, I guess.

"Where are you going?"

She grins. "Robert got a reservation to a nice restaurant. He surprised me, and since it's a Friday..."

I mirror her smile. "That's awesome! Date night?"

"Exactly. And as of tomorrow, we're lifting your grounding."

"Really?"

"Yeah. You've been good, and we didn't want to make this a drawn-out thing. Besides, it's your senior year. You should have fun with your friends."

No mention of my impending eighteenth birthday. Will I even be in the county to *have* friends—or, more accurately, one friend—in three months?

"Thank you," I answer.

She ventures deeper into my room and sits beside me. "We need to talk tomorrow. Robert and I wanted to check in with you after your social worker's visit, but things just got a little crazy..."

"It's okay." I fiddle with the blanket on my lap.

Between Lenora working late and my inability to do anything except for homework, I've had a few movie nights with Robert and some nights of crashing early. In reality, I've barely seen Lenora this week.

"We'll do a brunch tomorrow. I found a new French toast recipe that I've been eager to try. Will you help me?"

I grin. "I love French toast."

"It's a date."

Robert calls Lenora's name from downstairs, and she pats my wrist.

"I'm being summoned," she says. "Have a nice quiet evening."

"See you tomorrow."

She tentatively leans forward, wrapping her arms around me. "Is this okay?"

"Yeah." I hug her back, resting my chin on her shoulder.

It feels... nice.

She releases me when I drop my arms, and then she's gone. I listen for the front door to close, then shove my homework off my bed. I flop backward and close my eyes.

My mother flashes in front of my closed eyelids.

"What did you do, Margo?" She looms giant in my memory, gripping my shoulders.

I don't answer, and she shakes me back and forth.

"Mom," I cry.

"Margo."

I thrash, trying to break her bruising grip.

"Margo!"

"Stop," I moan.

"Wake up!"

My eyes snap open, focusing on Caleb.

His eyebrows are creased.

I try to remember what I was dreaming about. It seems impossible that I fell asleep, but the clock tells me an hour has passed.

"You were crying for your mom," he murmurs.

The scene zooms back to the forefront of my mind.

I throw my arms around his neck and burst into tears.

"I-I-I can't remember what I did to make her hate me," I hiccup. "Why did she leave me?"

I know the answer. She loved drugs more than her daughter. She was declared unfit to parent—that's what Ms. McCaw told me. I don't remember much of the hearing with the judge, except that Mom never showed.

Dad was already gone at that point.

There was no one left to take care of me... so into the foster system I went.

Caleb rubs my back. "It's okay."

It isn't. It won't be until I find the answers I need.

I don't know which questions to ask, though. I don't know where to begin to look for Amber Wolfe.

"Will you help me?"

After Dad was arrested, I didn't see Caleb for seven years. He wouldn't know where my mother is, and he sure as hell wouldn't *care*.

"No."

His answer stings, but I get it.

Time to change the subject. "What are you doing here?"

"I told you I'd see you tonight."

His face is blurry through my unshed tears. The dots click into place, though. His cryptic words in class, the whispered conversation with Robert. My foster dad needing to check with Lenora...

"Did you get them the reservation?"

He brushes away some of the tears. "I might've been planning it for us, but you're still grounded. So... yeah, I offered it up to get them out of the house."

"You're an ass," I mutter. "And arrogant."

"And ruthless," he adds, kissing my cheek.

"And wicked." I turn my head slightly, catching his lips on mine.

"What are you going to do about it?"

"I'll beg you to make me forget about it." I kiss him again, harder.

Losing my virginity to Caleb has been confusing to say the least. My attraction to him in general makes little sense. My body likes him—almost too much—and I don't know what to make of it. I don't know what to make of *him*. They say that you forge connections when you lose that piece of yourself.

I didn't believe it. I still don't, to a certain extent. Caleb and I have been connected by an invisible string forever. The sex just made it better. *Or worse.* Any chance of escaping him has gone out the window, because now I don't want to run.

He said only he was allowed to be cruel to me.

The sick part is, I'm looking forward to it.

His fingers on the waistband of my shorts brings me back to the present. I raise my hips for him to tug the fabric down.

I unbutton his pants, freeing his erection. He pauses undressing me only long enough to toss a condom on my stomach. I tear it open and roll it on him carefully, half remembering past health class lessons. He groans into my neck.

My shirt is gone, and he stares down at me for a second before dropping more weight on me. I feel him at my entrance as he kisses my collarbone.

"This is going to hurt," he warns me. He rocks his hips forward, pushing into me.

I didn't realize how sore I was from Monday until right this instant.

I whimper, and he freezes.

"Relax." His tongue flicks out against the shell of my ear.

I loosen my muscles, one at a time, and he slides in deeper. I lift my hips to meet his thrusts, marveling at the feel of him hitting a deep spot inside me. Down there is more sensitive than I could've imagined.

He nips my earlobe, following it with his tongue. Who knew ears could be so... hot?

I dig my nails into his back.

This feels different.

And then the front door opens. It's easy to hear—the hinges squeal.

We both freeze. "Um, Caleb? Did you invite—"

"Margo, we're home!" Lenora calls. "Want to watch a movie?"

Her footsteps pound on the stairs.

"Caleb," I whisper. "You need to move."

He pulls out of me, grimacing, and hops up. "Where?"

"Um..."

"Margo?" Lenora calls. "You awake?"

"Closet!" I jump up, grabbing my shorts and yanking them back into place. I manage to get my shirt on, and I push him toward my walk-in at the same time, closing the door behind him just as Lenora cracks my door open.

"Oh, you're awake!"

I spin toward her. "Sorry, Lenora! I called back but I don't think I was loud enough."

She smiles.

I lean against my closet door, crossing my arms. "You're home early."

"Well, the restaurant was lovely. Service was a little too fast." She shrugs. "We're naturally homebodies, Robert and I. Decided we could go out to see a movie... or come home and snuggle on the couch."

I force a laugh. Sweat is trickling down my spine—and I don't think it's from the sex that she just interrupted. "That makes sense to me."

She grins. "I'm going to change. Come down and join us if you'd like. Robert is making popcorn!"

She closes my door, and I sag against it. A second later, my body moves as Caleb forces it open.

"That was close." He's fully dressed again, and he holds up my bra. "Figured you might want this back."

I double take. "That's the one you took on Monday."

He shrugs. "I've got a replacement."

"You also kept my torn panties. You like to keep trophies of your conquests?"

He chuckles. "No. But I do like help remembering your scent when I'm jacking off at night. And no offense, Wolfe, but bras don't really do the trick in that department."

I gape at him, my face getting hot. "You're not—"

"Serious?" He smirks. "Deadly."

Lenora taps on my door, and he ducks back into the closet. She doesn't open it, though. Just asks, "Coming?"

"Be there in a minute!" My voice is an octave too high.

Caleb cracks the door, silently laughing at me. "I'll just show myself out... via the window." He winks.

He opens it and climbs out. And then he's gone; the only trace of him is the scent of sex in the air.

Oh my God. I'll just have to pray that Lenora didn't notice.

I leave the window open to air it out and put on a sweatshirt, then go downstairs. I could use a distraction—and a movie sounds like the perfect one.

Chapter 31
Caleb

I pull up outside the only motel in Hillshire County. The neon No Vacancy sign flickers sporadically. There are lights on in half the rooms at this time of night. Any one of them could hold *her*. It took only a few calls to figure out where she'd booked a room. She had limited options, given her history. It was either here or the upscale place in Beacon.

I'm pretty sure that's beyond her means.

Margo almost erased the pressing need to come here... but then her foster parents got home early.

And the compulsion returned.

I force myself to relax, blowing air out through my mouth and sucking it in through my nose. I have time, but patience is another issue.

None of this would be a problem if Coach hadn't followed through on his threat to suspend me from six games. *Six.* I sat out for one, and there's a game tonight that I'm skipping for *this*.

My phone buzzes. A second later, my passenger door opens, and Amelie slides into the car. For fuck's sake. I glance over long enough to take in her dress: red, leather, tight. Her breasts are pushed up to her throat. Her lips are coated in bright-red gloss.

I have a flash of Margo wearing the same color as a kid, chasing me through the house and threatening to kiss me.

"What are you doing here?" I can't hide my utter loathing.

ELI

You need backup? I'll skip if you need me.

The thought of him missing a game because of me—and subsequently taking Coach's wrath—raises my hackles. I appreciate his offer, but I can't let him do that.

No. I'm handling it.

"I thought you could use some help," Amelie says. "Especially since your expression means you probably don't know which room she's in."

Amelie and I were a brief moment in time, and yet she still seems to reap the rewards of our past. Like knowing I probably wouldn't hurt her for getting in my way.

I could change that.

It's about damn time Amelie felt something toward me besides lust. Fear would look much better on her face than this hungry, desperate wanting. My skin crawls at the way she's staring at me.

I grit my teeth. "And you do?"

She smiles at me. "I wouldn't be *useful* if I didn't."

"And what do you want in exchange?" I only ask because... well, I don't want to make any more phone calls, and bribing the motel front desk would leave a trace.

I'm not going to like this. Amelie is slipperier than a snake in oil.

She puts her elbow on the center console, moving into my space. "Just give me a... secret."

I sigh. "What kind of secret?"

"What happened to Margo's dad? Where's *your* mom? You've been bottled up about all of it for so long—"

I grab her by the throat and shove her against the passenger window. She makes a gurgling noise, fingers scrambling on my hand.

"You're going to cut the fucking shit, Amelie, and then you're going to leave." I lean in, trying to curb the urge to squeeze until she turns purple. "And if you don't, I'll tell everyone *your* dirty little secret."

Her eyes widen.

The fear I've been craving flashes across her face.

Honestly... it doesn't do as much as I thought it would. Margo's fear has ruined me.

"Okay," Amelie wheezes. "Jesus. Room thirty-one."

"See how easy that was?" I release her, then lean around her and open the door.

She falls out of my car, landing on her ass with her feet in the air. She glares at me for a long minute, seeming to want to say something.

Now's not the time, and I'm not the person.

I make a shooing motion. "Run along, Page."

She climbs to her feet and purses her lips. Without a word, she storms off.

I head to the second floor, where room thirty-one awaits.

The lights are off, but I bang on the door anyway. It's late. Maybe she's sleeping. I wait a minute, then try again.

"Caleb?"

I turn. Amber Wolfe stands at the top of the stairs. Her

dark hair is in a high bun, and there's dirt smudged on her forehead. She wears an absurd number of layers. A hoodie under another sweatshirt with a jacket on top, and a scarf wrapped around her throat. There's probably another shirt underneath, too.

"Thought that was you." She comes closer, shuffling her feet.

I step back and let her unlock the door.

Her fingers tremble on the painted wood. She's frailer than I would've thought. Her eyes are sunken. Her cheeks are sucked in.

We enter the room, and she unwinds her scarf.

I bite the inside of my cheek. There's a ring of bruises around her neck.

Handprints.

It strikes me that I should be concerned. And yet, I can't muster any sympathy for the train wreck of a woman in front of me.

Disgust travels up my throat.

Even through the addiction, the similarities between her and Margo are obvious. They have the same hair, the same smile. Same face shape, even though Margo's still has traces of her childhood in her cheeks, and her mother's is extreme in the opposite direction.

"What brings you here?" She goes to the mini fridge, kneeling and pulling out a bottle. She offers me one. "Come to steer me right, son?"

"Don't call me that," I snap. "And no, I'm not."

She giggles. She removes her jacket, revealing a sweater that she probably got from a thrift store. It's two sizes too big and hangs on her frame, even with the hoodie under it. She starts taking off the sweater, too. The stream of noise coming out of her seems uncontrolled. Her movements around the room are jerky.

Nausea turns my stomach.

"You're high."

I should've anticipated it.

This isn't how I learned to play chess—I'm not normally reckless.

She takes a seat on one of the two beds, now only in her leggings and long-sleeved shirt. She twists the bottle in her hand.

Slowly, I mirror her movements. After sitting for a few seconds, I cross to the fridge and help myself to a beer. May as well. I'll need the drink while trying to reason with Margo's mother.

"Why are you back?" I ask, twisting the cap off. I hand it to her and pull the one from her hand, doing the same thing.

She lifts the bottle to her lips and doesn't lower it until half the beer is gone.

"I asked you that," she says.

I shrug. "I came to ask you why you're here. Are you going to answer?"

She's irritating. Infuriating. The woman who used to be my family's chef, and Margo's kind and warm mother, has disintegrated into *this*.

There's a reason the kids at school call her a coke whore. It's not just because she's addicted to drugs—it's because she'll do anything, sell anything, to get them.

"You look so much like your father," she says on a sigh. "I miss him."

My father. I grit my teeth. I can't do anything rash, not even when she goads me.

"What about your own husband? He's rotting away—"

"Please don't," she cries.

She folds over and rocks back and forth, winding her scarf around her hands. She makes keening noises, like this is the worst thing she's ever thought about.

I've had worse.

Finally, she sets the scarf down and straightens. Her cheeks are wet, but she doesn't dash away the tears. She grabs her beer and switches beds, sitting right next to me.

I hold perfectly still as she stares into my face.

There's kindness buried in my bones.

But... not for her.

She finally wipes the tears on her cheek with the back of her hand, running her arm under her nose. It's hard to be around her and not feel anger.

"I just want things to go back to normal." She latches on to my arm and lets out a sob. "Why did you come here?"

"You need to leave Rose Hill. Tonight."

"My money is gone. I have nowhere to go—"

"I don't fucking care, Amber."

She flinches.

"You promised you wouldn't come back," I remind her. "That you wouldn't..."

"Interfere," she mumbles. "But—"

I shove her off me. She tumbles to the floor, landing in a curled position.

"There's no fucking *but!*" I roar. "You're endangering everything by being here."

Way more than she fucking realizes.

I'm sick of this. Sick of being in the same room with a drug-addicted whore and family ruiner. I dig my toe into her ribs, flipping her flat on her back. She's so weak, she flops right over.

Her gaze locks on mine. Her mouth opens and closes.

She's in shock—or succumbing to whatever she probably shot into her veins. Her tears spill out again, flooding down her temples and into her hair.

"I'm sorry, Caleb."

I shove her sweater sleeve up, just to prove to myself that she's still the drug addict I remember. The track marks are dark, angry red. Infected, probably from dirty needles.

My skin crawls, and I release her just as fast.

The kids at school call Margo a coke whore's daughter. And they're right: Amber Wolfe has taken another lover. And there's nothing more alluring to her than her drug of choice.

"Here's what's going to happen." I thumb through the cash that I brought and make a show of dropping the bills onto her chest. "You're going to go anywhere but here. Upstate. Down south. West, even. You could be a happy homeless slut in the eternal sunshine. Who the fuck cares? But if I hear that you step back in Rose Hill, you're done. I'll kill you myself."

She shudders.

I promised Margo I would kill anyone who hurt her.

The biggest threat is her mother.

"Leave tonight, Amber."

She grabs my boot as I walk past her. "Please. I got a call—"

I shake her loose, my lip curling. I pause with my hand on the knob and drain my beer, then drop the empty bottle on the floor. It tastes like piss water.

Figures.

I slam the door behind me, hoping that Amber gets my message. I really don't want to have to resort to murdering Margo's mom.

Chapter 32
Margo

Intervention time.

Or... something like that. Maybe it isn't an intervention, but the way Lenora and Robert are staring at me, it sure feels like something momentous—and catastrophic—is going to happen.

The only sound is the clock ticking on the wall behind Robert's head.

We chose to sit at the dining room table, Robert at the head and Lenora and me on either side of him. And they're just... waiting for something.

Finally, Robert clears his throat. "How are you doing, honey?"

"Doing? Like..."

"In general," Lenora supplies. "Or specifically, if you want."

"I'm good." I shrug, forcing a smile at both of them. "I mean, I'm sorry for the other night. When I got drunk."

The late-morning sun streams in through the window behind me, warming my back. Caleb successfully snuck out through the window, and I made an appearance for movie night. It was nice. No talking. Just sword fights and British accents.

When I woke up, I was filled with inexplicable trepidation. I could barely move.

My body hurt. I discovered a trail of hickies and bruises on my neck, down my chest. I pressed my thumb into one, and pain hit deep. But it wasn't bad. It was the kind of pain that made me want to keep pushing on it.

And then I remembered the chat we're supposed to have.

So here we are, food in front of us that I'm too nervous to eat.

My mouth waters at the smell of bacon, but my flipping stomach prevents me from reaching out and taking a slice.

"We understand that these things happen," Lenora says. "Kids drink. Next time, please call us to come get you. We'd rather you be safe and in trouble than seriously hurt."

I wrap my arms around my stomach. The guilt of something terrible happening, and them not knowing about it, hits hard.

"Your social worker mentioned that your dad is in jail," Robert says. "He's actually quite close—"

"No." I want to crawl out of my skin at the thought of my dad in an orange jumpsuit.

"Are you angry with him?" Robert asks. "I can't imagine how you must feel, and we just want to understand—"

"I can't do this right now," I whisper. "Did Ms. McCaw suggest I see him?"

They trade a look. It's not a no, but it's not quite a yes either.

Lenora presses on. "We know your mother is—"

—*my head snaps back*—

"I'm doing okay, aren't I? Going to school, making

friends. My grades are good." *Ish*. "You're letting me be a normal teen with... not a lot of worries, really." I manage to smile at them. "Thank you for that."

Somehow this turned into a heart-to-heart.

"We love having you here," Lenora says.

I meet her gaze. "I love being here."

She sniffles. "Okay, enough of this. As long as you're content, and we're doing a good job... let's eat."

"And you're officially ungrounded," Robert adds.

I beam.

"How's your painting coming along?" he asks.

I start loading my plate. My anxiety has eased, and suddenly I'm ravenous. They've prepared a feast of breakfast foods.

And then I register his question and slowly set down my fork. "Oh, um..."

The answer? Not great.

Not only have I pushed it so far to the bottom of my to-do list that I'd forgotten about it, but I'm pretty sure it's going to come out awful.

"Do you need help?"

I squint at him. "Are you allowed to help me? Being the teacher and all?"

Lenora laughs. "Probably not, but that won't stop him."

"I can give feedback," he allows. "And maybe point you in the right direction. Just like I would do for every other student who asked for help."

"I just need to put the time in. I've been preoccupied."

He nods. "I've noticed."

Guilt crawls over me. "I'm sorry. I don't mean—"

He waves. "Stop. You're allowed. But if you want to work on it, I'm around today."

Once we're done eating, I run upstairs and change into

clothes I don't mind getting paint on. I need to figure out exactly how I'm going to capture Caleb. He's a riddle I haven't found the answer to yet, always shifting pieces and parts. A mirage.

I cart down my canvas, my box of paints, and brushes under my arm. Robert has already laid out newspaper in the dining room, along with an easel sized to stand on the table.

He comes in as I'm setting up.

"Do you know why I picked oil paints for this assignment?" he asks.

I shrug, staring at the vague outline of Caleb. "Because it's a difficult medium, and you wanted to challenge us?"

He nudges me, shaking his head. "It is difficult, but it's also forgiving."

I tilt my head. We've been working with a bunch of different paints—watercolor, acrylic, oil. I haven't picked a favorite. Maybe we haven't worked with oil enough.

"You make a mistake? Go over it. Erase it. Hell, do a painting and then repaint it the next day. You can't do that with watercolors."

"Ah."

"You've barely touched the surface here, Margo," he says. "You've painted an interesting background... and that's it."

That's all I had the nerve to do last time Caleb and I faced each other in class.

Robert leans on the table. "You don't need him in front of you to paint him. In fact, I think you'd capture his essence better when you're *not* looking at him. Go with how he makes you feel."

He leaves me alone while I stare at the canvas. The space where his head and shoulders should be, filled in only by the shadows and highlights from a few weeks ago, and the boring background texture I tried out on Friday.

Sooner or later, I just have to start. Take a chance.

I take my time putting the paints on my palette, preparing my brushes, lining up the charcoal and turpentine. I mix a few different colors together, experimenting until I find the right shade to match Caleb's skin.

But nothing is perfect, so I just...

Put a stroke on the page.

So what if it isn't beautiful? He's not beautiful—not on the inside. He's broken, just like me. It comes out in the way the colors clash on the page. I take Robert's advice and redo the background. The blues and purples I had originally painted, trying to go for a *nice* look, don't work.

His jaw comes to life with dark slashes.

I leave his eyes blank for now. I'm tempted to paint them completely black, honestly. Yet, that wouldn't quite do.

"Wow," Robert says over my shoulder.

I twist around. "How am I doing?"

"Fantastic emotion." He leans closer. "Once this dries, you can go back with an artist's eye and clean up some of the lines. Make every stroke purposeful."

I nod and glance at the clock. I've been sitting here for two hours.

"What do you have planned for his eyes? And lips?"

"I haven't decided." Because I can't see it yet.

He chuckles. "That boy is in trouble."

"I think I'm the one in trouble." I stare at Caleb's face. It isn't exactly in his likeness—it's a little too abstract for that. Plus, there are the blank gaps: his eyes, his lips, his eyebrows. To capture the scowl or make him smile...

"Speaking of," Robert says, going to the window. "He just pulled up."

"Distract him!" I grab the canvas. "I need to hide this!"

He chuckles as I dash around, but he keeps Caleb engaged in conversation just inside the door long enough for me to put it away. Caleb walks into the dining room to me drying my brushes.

"Hey, baby. Were you working on our project?"

I grin. "Yep."

He makes a show of looking around the room. "Where is it?"

"Hiding from your nosiness." I brush my hair off my face and sigh. "What's up?"

"Didn't you say you were ungrounded today?"

"Did I say that?"

He lifts one shoulder, smirking at me. "Not sure where else I could've heard it."

"Maybe that's true."

I try to slip past him, but he moves too fast. He frames me in against the wall, just out of sight of Robert. My foster dad is almost definitely eavesdropping on the other side of the wall.

"You running from me?"

"No," I breathe.

He hums. "I think you are. Let's change that."

"How?"

His fingers dig into my hip. "Come to the Fall Ball with me."

I pause, then remember what the hell that is. Which is a *dance*. I don't dance. Going to a school function, surrounded by students who may or may not hate my guts, sounds like the definition of Hell.

"I don't dance," I tell him.

His eyes glitter, and he leans closer. His lips are right above mine.

Not fair, I want to complain. He knows how to make my body react. Always has.

"The theme is masquerade."

Masks...

"We'd be anonymous enough. Come with me."

"I... okay."

His lips brush mine, but then he's gone. Straightening and stepping back.

"That was easy." His grin is devious.

Shit. Did I seriously just fold?

"Caleb—"

He goes into the kitchen. He mentions the Fall Ball to Robert, confirming that I'm going with him.

"That's great, Margo," Robert says when I suck it up and join them. "It's hard to go to the dances alone, but from my time as a chaperone, the kids always have a lot of fun."

"Are you chaperoning this year?" *Please say no, please say no.*

He shakes his head. "I didn't volunteer this time. Lenora gets a little pissy if I'm out partying with the high schoolers past our bedtime. Besides, she doesn't like to give candy out alone."

Caleb laughs. "I'm sure you're a reckless partier, Mr. Bryan."

"That I am, my boy."

My boy. Jesus.

"Wait, give out candy?"

Caleb eyes me. "It's on Halloween night. Don't worry, you have plenty of time to find a dress."

Bastard.

"Right..."

"Lenora would love to help," Robert offers. "We never got to go dress shopping with..."

I look at my shoes. With their dead child, he means.

Robert clears his throat. "I don't mean to bring up the past."

Caleb goes over and pats his shoulder. "It's okay, Mr. Bryan. I understand."

I glance at Caleb.

My foster dad nods and pats his shoulder. "I know you do. But anyway, I'm sure you two have better things to do. It's Margo's first day of freedom, after all."

"It's only been a week of being grounded," I point out.

"Just go with it," Caleb murmurs. "I was actually going to go run an errand in the city. You don't mind if I take her, do you, Mr. Bryan?"

New York City is about an hour and a half away. By a stroke of pure luck, I didn't end up in the NYC foster system. That would've been... significantly harder.

Because I lived in Rose Hill, which is part of Hillshire County, I got looped into that foster system. There are enough homes and group housing around here to keep me within an hour radius.

And that meant I avoided New York City.

"What errand?" I ask, perking up. "I haven't been—"

"Since you were a kid?" Caleb finishes with a nod.

Robert tuts. "We could plan a day trip, Margo. I didn't realize it was something you might want to do."

"I used to watch all the holiday events on TV. The tree lighting and the parades..."

"I was hoping you would come with me," Caleb says. "It's still too early for the Christmas vibe, but..."

"Can I go?" I ask Robert.

"After that spiel?" He chuckles. "How can I say no?"

Yes.

I run upstairs and change into nicer clothes. We're going to the *city*. Manhattan, maybe? I didn't ask the borough. Either way, it all seems luxurious and daunting. I've heard horror stories about people getting mugged, pickpockets, insane taxis. But over all of that is the shiny appeal of Times Square. Central Park. Horse-drawn carriages and huge, floppy slices of pizza.

Caleb comes upstairs before I start on my makeup.

He takes my makeup bag out of my hand. "You don't need this. Not today."

I frown. "But I want to feel pretty."

"You can feel pretty without it."

I try to snatch it back, but he raises it over his head.

"Caleb," I snap.

"Stop."

I jump for it.

"Goddamn it, Margo," he snarls, shoving me back against the wall. "Just—*stop*. You don't need it, okay?"

His hand stays on my chest. His fingers are dangerously close to my throat, splayed over my collarbone, and his thumb brushes my nipple.

I suck in a breath. I'm an idiot. My face gets hot.

"Go to the car."

I stare at him, then lift my chin. If he wants to bare me to the world without a speck of makeup, *fine*. He's the one who will hate it as soon as he realizes how out of place I am. Caleb follows me down the stairs, and it's absolutely intentional.

Because if he didn't, I would've rushed back up and locked myself in the bathroom to swipe on some mascara and eyeliner in peace.

I wave goodbye to Robert, and Lenora, who returned home just in time to see us leave.

Robert stops me, handing me a few folded bills. "Have fun."

"Thank you!" I wasn't planning on spending more than I could afford—which wouldn't have been much at all. I tuck the money in my wallet, and Caleb follows me out.

He beats me to his car and opens the door. I smile and climb in, and we're on the road in a flash. There's a mischievous look in his eye that I can't place. I bite my lip instead of asking about it, and soon enough we're on the highway.

Up, up, and away.

"Why is makeup so important to you?" he asks. "You don't think you're pretty?"

"It's hard to have self-confidence when everyone is trying to bring you down." I rub my hands together.

"Of course."

"Of course?" I echo. "Great."

He shoots me a glance. "It makes sense. It doesn't mean it's true, though. You're beautiful."

There are skyscrapers in the distance. I focus on those instead of the compliment I'm not ready to swallow.

"I don't really like Halloween," I comment.

He keeps glancing over at me. "Why?"

I tick off the instances on my fingers. "Getting chased by a foster brother with a machete. He threatened to cut off my hair. Being locked in a closet for trying to take a piece of candy meant for the other kids. Having my costume ripped the morning of Halloween by a foster family's kid. She didn't like that I got to be a unicorn."

"How old were you?" His voice is dark.

"It was every year."

"And the last two? With your supposed good family?"

I shrug. "Hanna ate a Snickers, and her throat swelled shut. We spent the night in the ER. And then the next year, our foster mom let us all go out, but she took our candy when we came back. Said she didn't trust us not to eat it all in one night."

"I thought you liked her."

"They were strict. Everyone is strict at first. It's how they manage expectations. Start with strong ones and ease them over time."

"But...?"

"The Bryans are different," I admit.

I hope they keep me.

I almost say it out loud, but wishes and hopes are dangerous. They inflate us, make us buoyant. And in the end, they just make a harder fall.

I know better.

"We can find complementary masks," he says. "Something fit for a king and queen."

He can't be serious.

"We aren't *royalty*," I sputter. "This isn't—"

"You know as well as I do that hockey is king. And I'm the fucking king of hockey."

My face warms. "Arrogant, much?"

He cracks a smile. "I am aware of my value."

"The school... people really love hockey that much? They'd bend rules for you, or bend over and kiss your ass?"

"We remind the students why we're the best in the league." He drums his fingers on the steering wheel. "There's a good costume shop off of Times Square."

"What's the errand you have to run?"

He makes a face. "Just have to sign some papers nearby. Won't take long."

"And you decided to take me with you?"

"You haven't been to the city. Besides, this type of conversation can't be had with just myself."

I roll my eyes. "Right."

He glances over. "You don't believe me."

Not really.

"The teachers don't ever yell at me, give me detention, call me out for being late or skipping." He puts his hand on my thigh.

Hate to say I like it, but...

"You got suspended. And you can't play hockey for a while."

"For fighting Ian, whose dad is a massive dick." He winks. "I don't blame the principal for suspending me. Easier to do that than get on Fletcher Senior's bad side."

I harrumph.

"You'll see," he promises.

His words from my first day of school come back to me.

Margo Wolfe. Haven't you heard? I'm king now.

What does that make me? Queen—or joker?

Chapter 33
Margo

"**A** fair lace mask for the pretty girl?"

I glance up at the shop owner. He's been hovering, pointing at various costumes and accessories. None have been quite right. Although, I'm not quite sure what I'm looking for. I don't have a dress, and Caleb, who seemed to have a plan, has disappeared.

The shop owner holds out a delicate, pale-pink mask. It's meant to cover half the face, not both eyes.

"No." Caleb comes up behind him. "I found it."

I raise my eyebrows. "Where is it?"

"You have to wait outside." He grins. "I'm going to buy it either way, but I think it'll be better if it's a surprise."

"Seriously?"

The shop owner appraises us.

Caleb narrows his eyes at me. "Out."

I raise my hands in surrender. "Fine. I'm going to get coffee."

I leave the shop, contemplating circling back and trying to get a glimpse of whatever Caleb is buying. Instead, I resist the urge and cross the street. There's a cute little coffee shop directly across from the costume shop.

Playing nice, I order myself a latte and Caleb a black coffee.

We were both obsessed with tasting coffee when we were young. It never failed to wrinkle our noses. But at the time, coffee was synonymous with caffeine. And what better way to help two ten-year-olds stay up past their bedtimes than caffeine? It never affected me much, but it didn't fail to make Caleb bounce off the walls.

I shake the memory out of my head. Caleb enters the shop, and a paper bag dangles from his fingertips.

"I got you a coffee," I tell him.

"Is this bribery?"

"No." I roll my eyes. "Not everything has a string attached."

He shrugs. "You'd be surprised."

The barista calls my name. I grab both cups, and we find a table. We sit and drink it, and I try my hardest not to even look in the direction of the bag. It's tempting, though. My curiosity burns bright.

He glances at his watch and straightens. "We have to go. My appointment is soon."

"You said you had to sign papers? For what?"

"Just boring business stuff."

"For your dad—?"

He rubs his eye. "Can we go ten minutes without questions?"

He doesn't say please, but I imagine the plea chasing his request.

"Fine," I murmur.

I'll just have to observe and see if I can figure out what Caleb Asher is hiding.

We take a taxi. It drops us off in front of a tall building, and Caleb winds his hand through mine. He leads me into the lobby and points to a group of armchairs in the corner.

"Sit."

Since I promised no questions, I shut my mouth and take a seat.

Caleb approaches the front desk and leans toward the receptionist. They chat for a minute, and she types something on her computer. Finally, she gestures to a bank of elevators to her right. He pushes through a turnstile, goes down a hallway to the elevators, and waits. When he glances back at me, I pretend I wasn't watching.

He steps onto the elevator a second later, and I shoot to my feet.

"Hi," I say to the receptionist. "Can you tell me where he was going?"

She raises her eyebrow. "Excuse me?"

"I just—"

"We can't give out that information." She lifts her chin. "Are we going to have a problem?"

I narrow my eyes. "No problems on my end."

As I slink back toward my seat, I scan the placard of companies and the levels. Where would Caleb go to sign paperwork?

There aren't too many names listed. Half of them take up several floors. There's a public relations firm and a real estate office that might be promising. Besides that, there's a law firm, a plastic surgeon, and an investment firm. Oh, and insurance.

I shake my head and sit.

Caleb reappears twenty minutes later. He comes over to me and offers his hand.

"That took longer than expected," he says.

I allow him to pull me to my feet. "It's okay."

"Do you want to do anything else? Or should we call it a day?"

We'd already walked around Times Square, took a selfie together under the glowing screens, and found masks. The day catches up to me, and I yawn. "Food, then home?"

He nods. We round the corner, almost smashing into a man walking toward us. He freezes, staring at Caleb. His face goes pale.

"Mr. A-Asher," the man says.

"Tobias." Caleb's voice is cold. Except for his hand in mine, his body is stiffer than a board. He's practically transformed into someone else.

"I wasn't aware you were in the city," Tobias continues. His voice wobbles.

"I wasn't aware I had to notify you when I wanted to get away from Rose Hill for an afternoon." Caleb's brow rises. It's more like a tick, up and then smoothed out an instant later.

Tobias shakes his head. Once he's started, he doesn't stop. His body trembles, like a strong wind is rushing through him.

My curiosity is officially piqued.

Caleb glances down at me, and Tobias follows his eyes. He flinches when he registers me.

I tilt my head. "Do I—"

"No." He switches the hand holding mine, and his free hand lands on the small of my back. He propels me around the frozen man.

"We'll talk soon," Tobias calls.

Once we're half a block away, I force us to slow down. "Who was that?"

Caleb shakes his head. "I thought we were still not asking questions."

"You can't just—"

His eyes flash. His hand slides around my neck, threading through my hair. He yanks my head back, exposing my throat.

"I can," he murmurs.

There are still bite marks under my shirt, speckled along my breasts. There were a few that ventured too high up my neck that required concealer.

He tugs the collar down, eyes heating. "You covered them up."

He wets his thumb in his mouth and rubs at my skin. His touch is delicious and dangerous, and I find myself enraptured by his expression.

"There." He releases me. "Now the world will know you're mine. Don't hide it."

We'd managed the day without him going all dark on me. And here we are...

I press my thighs together, but the impact of his words on my body is a strong one. Especially because we're in the middle of the freaking sidewalk in Times Square.

People move past us like we're rocks in the middle of a river.

He's hungry, and I can't help but feel the same. Like we've unwittingly been starving ourselves.

He touches my neck again, and then he straightens. He smirks at me.

He *knows* what he does to me.

My phone buzzes.

How's it feel to be so small in such a large city?

I choke on my gasp, shoving my phone back in my pocket.

Caleb raises an eyebrow. "What on earth was that?"

"Riley trying to be funny." I clear my throat. *Please don't call me out on that lie.*

He narrows his eyes but doesn't question it.

We eat pizza at a diner on the second floor of a building. It overlooks the busy street in the theater district, which hosts some colorful characters. When the sky opens up, every single person on the sidewalk seems to have a black umbrella at the ready.

Caleb frowns. "I'll call the car."

We had left his at the edge of the city, then took a black car into Manhattan. The driver didn't say a word to either of us, although I caught Caleb slipping him cash.

We wait at our table until a car pulls up to the curb and Caleb's phone chirps.

"Ready?" he asks.

The pizza was delicious. The diner was cute. The city is impossibly big and daunting and everything I could've imagined as an almost-adult. It's a lot different to how I experienced our neighborhood as a small child in Brooklyn.

I can see how people would come here to chase their dreams. And I can see how the city would chew up anyone not one hundred percent committed.

I take his offered hand. "Let's go home."

Caleb opens the car door for me, letting me slide into the backseat first. He follows, closing us in, and scoots close to me. God, he's a giant in this small space. I didn't realize it before—no, I was *ignoring* it before—but his presence sucks up all the air in the car.

The driver glances back at us in the rearview mirror. "Have fun?"

Caleb smiles. "It was refreshing."

The driver navigates back toward the outskirts of the city, and Caleb traces patterns on my leg. I try not to look at him, but soon, my body aches. One touch has me burning up.

We park next to Caleb's Audi, and the driver climbs out, opening my door for me. He even offers his hand. I take it, letting him help me to my feet. Caleb scowls at him over the top of the car, and the driver releases me.

"Mr. Asher," the driver says, inclining his head.

"I'll call you," Caleb answers. "Can you do that errand we discussed?"

The driver smiles. "Of course, sir."

I look back and forth between them, but Caleb turns away before I can dissect the conversation further.

We get into Caleb's car. Without warning, he reaches over and grabs the back of my neck, yanking me toward him. We slam together, lips parting. His tongue slides into my mouth, invading my senses. I groan and press against him, forcing his tongue out of my mouth and into his. We've spontaneously combusted, igniting more heat than I could've imagined.

He tugs me over the center console and onto his lap.

I run my hands up and down his chest, then venture lower. I palm his dick through his pants, and he growls.

He's hard.

I unzip his fly and reach in, fully grabbing him and pulling it out. It jerks in my hand.

I lean back a fraction. Our mouths are a hair's breadth apart when I whisper, "Who's Tobias?"

He glares at me. "You want to do this now?"

I stroke him, meeting his glare.

"You're not going to like the answer," he warns, exhaling sharply. "Fuck, Margo."

He likes my hand on him.

"Tell me." I lick my lips. We're still close enough that my tongue touches his lips, too.

He tries to scowl but shudders at my nails raking up and down him.

"Tobias was..." He shakes his head. "I can't believe I'm fucking telling you this. Tobias was your father's attorney."

I freeze.

"What?"

He grabs my face, holding me in place. If he didn't, I probably would've bolted. Away from him, out of the car.

I've been filled with ice.

I pull my hand away from his erection, but he just watches me.

Tobias was my dad's attorney.

The one who couldn't stop him from going to jail.

The one who is on a first-name basis with Caleb Asher.

My dad's attorney, who is going to call Caleb Asher later.

Why?

This is what self-destruction looks like. I fell for a monster.

I try to retreat, but his fingers just dig into my skin. He has me trapped against his body and the steering wheel, his hands on my face. His thumb caresses my cheek, just below my eye. Once, then twice.

He's blurry.

Am I crying?

"Why?" I manage. "Caleb—"

"Do not ask me," he warns. He leans forward and steals a kiss.

Steals my breath.

I can't breathe.

"I need to know *why*—"

"You don't." His voice is deadly. He's deadly. He kisses me again, biting my lip.

I hate that he's using this to distract me. To revive me.

I'm so fucking cold.

"Come back, Margo," he says against my lips. He presses kisses along the edge of my mouth, my jaw, my throat.

"Did you put my father in jail?" I close my eyes, letting my head fall back. I already know the answer is *yes*. Deep down, I've always known. I just didn't want to believe it.

His teeth nip my throat. His lips chase away the pain, back up, up, up. My jaw. The spot just below my ear. My earlobe. My temple.

How can he destroy me and make me feel better at the same time?

We're fucked up.

I'm fucked up for enjoying this. For letting him melt me down to liquid again and again.

His lips touch my eyelid. His tongue flicks out and tastes my tears.

This is more than just... him trying to ease the pain. Him trying to erase what happened in our past.

My heart is splintering.

His lips find mine again, but everything is soft. His touch. His tongue, sweeping along the seam of my lips.

I exhale a long, shuddering breath.

When I open my eyes, he's watching me. Maybe he's trying to figure me out. If I'm stable, or if, once he releases me, I'll run.

I would if my legs didn't feel like jelly.

"How could you?" I whisper. "Was it your idea?"

He shakes his head. "We're not doing this right now."

I move back into my own seat, clicking my seat belt into place. My desire for answers chews at me, but he's right. We can't do this now. Not after that.

He starts the car. I close my eyes. Whether I actually fall asleep or just doze, I couldn't say. But what feels like minutes later, he's lifting me out of the car.

I keep my head tucked under his chin. Everything hurts, but what stings the most is my pride. I let myself be swept away by him, *enamored* by him, and I forgot the most important part.

He carries his own share of fault in our families' destruction.

"Is she okay?" Robert asks.

"She just fell asleep in the car," Caleb's voice is soft. "I didn't want to wake her. I'll just put her in bed..."

I snake my arms around his neck as he's laying me down. He chuckles in my ear, his hands sliding along my forearms.

"I hate you," I mumble, "but I still want you to stay."

He exhales. "Your foster parents wouldn't be happy with me."

I adjust my grip, plastering him to me. It isn't really fair for him—I have the leverage.

He lies next to me, petting my hair. "Okay, Margo. For just a minute."

I sigh and inch closer. I still feel broken.

It's unexpected. It's sharp. If I move the wrong way, my

heart may start bleeding. Best to stay completely still and hope that I heal overnight, and then I can wish away all the bad pieces of Caleb—and me.

I fall asleep with his hand in my hair and my nose against his throat.

Chapter 34
Margo

A melie and Savannah have pulled a disappearing
act.

It's not surprising, Riley informs me. They
like to take trips, and the school is resigned to accept their
halfhearted attendance. After all, their parents make consid-
erable donations each year. Moreso Amelie's family, but
still.

Rumors fly that they've jetted off to Paris to find the
best dresses and masks for the Fall Ball. Always a step above
us little people, I suppose.

"Do they have dates?" I ask Riley.

May as well ask, since both would've been vying for
Caleb if I wasn't here.

She makes a face. "Last I heard, Amelie and Ian were
going together. Not sure about Savannah."

Ian Fletcher has been keeping his distance, but his stare
burns like a hot coal against my skin. Why he's taken such
an interest is anyone's guess.

"We need to pick out dresses," Riley continues. "I was
thinking we should have a shopping day this weekend."

We're in the library, which has remained our safe haven. So far, Caleb and Eli haven't come searching for us. A few times Caleb has shot me questioning glances as I slipped into the class right after lunch. But he never asked, and I never mentioned it.

It's been three days since Caleb and I went to New York City. He kept his distance on Sunday—letting me sort my emotions, I guess—and on Monday we were back to normal. As normal as we can be anyway. And unsurprisingly, people have stopped making so many remarks. The picture drew attention at first, but they've all but forgotten it now.

"Lenora mentioned dress shopping this weekend, too," I tell her. "Want to come?"

Riley grins. "Absolutely."

The door to the library creaks open. We can't see it from where we sit in the back, so both of us automatically slink down. Students aren't supposed to be in here—let alone with food. It's only because of Riley's familial relationship with Amy that this is even possible.

A few times, we've had to hide in the stacks because the principal came in to speak with Amy.

"I thought you locked it," I whisper to her.

She cringes.

Caleb appears with Eli right behind him.

I groan. "There goes our safe haven."

Caleb looks down at me. "Are you hiding?"

"No."

"We just like the quiet," Riley says.

Eli scowls. "Save it, Applebottom."

"Let's go." Caleb offers his hand.

I shake my head. "The last time we went with you, bad things happened."

He raises his eyebrow. "And if you don't come with me now, *worse* things will happen."

I lean back and cross my arms. "No."

He sighs, but I can tell he's enjoying this. It's not my fault I want to push all his buttons, and then some. His mind is working, coming up with the best punishment, and I wait with trepidation.

I started it, though. Too late to stop.

Caleb exchanges a glance with Eli. He seems to come to some decision.

He leans down and hauls me over his shoulder. I squeal when he straightens and I'm upside down, my ass in the air. I stare at his lower back and grab on to his waist.

"Oh my God." Riley laughs.

"Are you going to come quietly?" Eli asks her.

"Yep." She rises. "Sorry, Margo."

Caleb's arms are banded around my thighs, keeping me in place while he walks. The four of us pass Amy's office. She glances up but quickly buries her head back in her book.

Traitor.

"Is my ass on display?" I hiss at Riley.

Caleb swears and shifts his hold. He pins my skirt down, although that's not much better. He walks right into the cafeteria with me over his shoulder. My face is hot, but I know begging won't stop him. Things have to be done his way. Always.

Without Amelie and Savannah here, the cheerleader table is quiet. No one wants to step up and own the bullying or their hatred of me. Still, they all whisper when Caleb and I pass. Eli and Riley follow us, and the whispers double.

Caleb pats my ass, then lowers me back to my feet. He's

careful about the skirt, and his burning gaze takes in my slightly rumpled shirt and hair.

I can only imagine what he's thinking.

I glare at him and try to fix myself. Finger combing my hair, straightening my shirt and skirt. "Not cool."

He shrugs. "I gave you a choice."

"Not really," I argue. "It's not a choice if the end result is the same."

His grin turns sly. "You could've walked here on your own two feet. Instead... I enjoyed the show."

Theo and Liam are already at the table. Eli and Riley sit next to Liam, and I slide onto the bench next to Theo. Caleb comes over with two trays of food, setting one next to me. He shoots a glare at Theo, then sits on my other side.

Theo grins at me. "Thanks for bringing my girlfriend out of hiding, Asher."

I snort and grab Caleb's arm before he can do anything crazy—like punch his best friend. *Again.* I don't think Emery-Rose would survive if Caleb had to sit out any more hockey games.

"Watch it, Alistair," Caleb growls.

"Calm down." I stroke his arm. "He was joking. Right, Theo?"

Theo appraises me with dark eyes. "Right."

"See?" I turn to Caleb, triumphant.

Caleb's face is still shuttered. He puts his hand on the back of my neck and leaves it there for the rest of lunch. The others joke around. Eli and Riley share a few looks and smiles. It's weird being part of their table—at the center of it, really—but so separate. Is it Caleb's doing or mine? I've never fit in. And I suspect, even though Caleb could charm a snake, he doesn't try it on his friends.

They accept him as the monster he is. And me, I guess

I'm just the possession he's been trying to acquire. They ignore it, or they're comfortable in it. Comfortable with their own demons, with the thrones they sit on. The royalty of Emery-Rose Elite are cherished from afar... because no one wants to get close to them.

No one except those who don't know any better.

Amelie. Savannah. Who knows who else.

The bell rings, and Caleb takes his time getting up. His hand is still on my neck, holding me to him. I like the feel of his fingers on my skin. The way his short nails scratch lightly.

My heart beats faster.

I skip going to my locker to make it to class on time—not that he cares. We're in it together, and he makes sure I'm seated right in front of him.

Our two afternoon classes should be quiet. Mr. McGuire assigns homework, then lets us work on it for the last ten minutes.

"I'll meet you up there," I tell Caleb before our painting class.

He nods and brushes his lips to my temple, and I head to my locker. It's on the opposite side of the school, but I'm not too worried about being late. I'm halfway there when the hallway empties out and the bell rings.

It's silent for a beat. Two.

I should've said: I'm not too worried about getting in trouble for being late.

My heart pounds, and I quicken my steps. Will Robert give me detention for being late, or if he'll let it slide this time?

I just got ungrounded, after all. Who knows how far he can be pushed?

Does he separate home from school? I mean—I know he

does, technically. But will Mr. Bryan factor in my recent grounding as a prior offense?

Someone slams into me from behind.

I go flying forward, falling to my hands and knees. The impact rattles through my shoulders. My backpack slides away from me.

What the fuck?

Hands yank me up, pushing me face-first into the lockers. The cold metal kisses my cheek. The hands turn me around, keeping me pinned. They touch too much—my chest, the side of my breast.

My skin crawls.

"Wrong place, wrong time." Ian Fletcher's face is wild with excitement.

How long has he waited for a moment where I'm alone and unguarded?

Caleb should be in Robert's class by now. How long will he wait before coming to find me? Two minutes after the bell? Five? Fifteen?

I lick my lips. "Ian. What are you—"

My words are cut off when he pulls me forward and shoves me back again. My head cracks against the locker, and stars burst in my vision. Blood fills my mouth.

I never thought I'd actually see *stars*. They're more like white fireworks, really.

"No talking," he says in my ear. "You and me are going for a little walk."

His fingers dig into my arm. If I saw someone I knew, I'd yell out. But we don't pass a single filled classroom. He drags me down a narrow, lesser-used hall, and through a side door that leads out toward the soccer fields.

I don't make a sound. My chest is tight, my head throbs. We skirt the field and head toward the woods.

The path that the cross-country runners use. I ran into Theo out here once, but I doubt I'll be that lucky a second time.

I stumble, but he keeps me upright and moving fast.

Fear trickles through me.

It's darker in the forest. We're ten steps in, and suddenly the world is a whole lot more sinister. Muted sunlight flickers through the trees. It's cloudy today, so even the golden leaves of autumn don't make it a happier—or warmer—place. We could be standing in a graveyard for all the warmth I feel.

He releases me.

I don't know why that surprises me more than anything. Maybe I thought he'd reveal a knife and slice me open. Or hurt me in some other way. I put some distance between us, rubbing my arms.

"You managed to ensnare Caleb Asher," he barks. "How?"

This is about Caleb? "I don't know."

His face contorts into fury, and he lunges at me.

I stumble backward and hit a tree. It's the only thing that keeps me upright, and I grip it with both hands.

"You. Margo Wolfe. He *hated* you for how many years? Six?"

I glare at him. The best course of action is to hide my fear, right? Don't let him see how afraid I am. "Seven years."

"Seven." He laughs loudly. He's not afraid of being heard at all, is he?

Birds take off to our left in a great flurry of motion.

"He uses people," Ian warns. "Whatever you think you feel... it's a lie. A manipulation."

"Why are you telling me this?"

His hand coasts over my jaw, his fingers gripping my

chin and moving my face to the side. It's painful, but I don't make a peep.

His eyes latch on to the bite mark on my neck. It's mostly faded—enough that I only put a light layer of concealer on it—but the makeup must've worn off.

"We were friends," he says. "I play the same fucking sport as him, but it's not enough. I'm on the outskirts of his friend group."

"You showed him," I reply weakly. "You stole his girl-friend. She cheated on him—"

"Fat lot of fucking good that did."

"Your problem isn't with me." My voice is low. The fear is strangling me the closer he gets.

He's too close. Heat pours off his body, radiating into mine. My stomach knots, and I swallow sharply against my nervous nausea. He releases my chin, and I duck my head. I don't want to see whatever madness is on his face.

"My problem is most certainly with you." He wraps his hand around my throat.

When I just stare at him, he slams me back against the tree, and his grip tightens. Not enough to suffocate me, though. I can get in the smallest gasps of air. I keep my hands at my sides. If his goal is to make me beg, he has another thing coming.

"You're the key to getting back at Caleb," Ian muses. "I think he may even love you."

It's hard to breathe. Swallow. Panic claws at me.

Caleb Asher does not love me.

"It's a game to him," I wheeze.

Ian frowns.

If he wasn't a maniac, he might even be handsome. He sure got Amelie's attention.

"Please," I mumble, finally bringing my hands up to his wrist.

He grunts, releasing me, and I slide to the ground. I cough and gulp in air. My fingers dig into the pine-needle-covered ground.

This seems familiar.

Déjà vu?

Ian squats next to me, grabbing my arm. He yanks it toward him, shoving my sleeve up. "Something to remember me by."

He pulls out a permanent marker, biting the cap off, and writes a word across my forearm.

I watch in horror as he puts his teeth to my skin. He bites hard, and I cry out. The pain travels up my arm. It's nothing like what Caleb has done to me. This is fear and disgust wrapped in one. The pain keeps coming, though, the harder he bites. Until he breaks the skin and blood drops past his lips.

He finally releases my arm, and I bring it in to my chest. My breathing is ragged, and I can't seem to calm down.

His bite, the word he wrote, is more violating than I would've imagined.

"Who do you hate worse?" I can't look at my arm, which has a pulse of its own, but I have the burning need to know what this is really about. "Me or Caleb?"

Ian sighs. "I don't like you. But I think I really do hate Caleb Asher. With this... you're the easier target. The button to push to make Caleb feel something other than self-righteous." He lifts one shoulder. "Pity he wasn't there to protect you this time."

He stands, and something cold slides over his features. A mask that foretells something bad.

I have an instant to prepare before his foot snaps forward. He slams it into my stomach.

Pain and helplessness explode through me. I can't describe how it feels. He kicks me twice more, and each time the air leaves my lungs without warning.

I cry out again and fall to the side. I wrap my arms around my middle, just trying to protect myself. I didn't see this coming. Should I have? Did he give me warning signs?

Ian pushes me flat onto my back with that same foot. He leans over me, a scowl marring his face.

"I meant what I said before." He raises his eyebrow, daring me to remember.

I don't. There are so many awful things he's said that I've pushed out of my mind.

"You're nothing to anyone here. You're a girl from a trash family, and you're so fucking out of place. You should leave before someone worse comes along."

I watch him walk away from my fetal position on the ground. I blink rapidly as the tears come once more.

I'm so fucking sick of crying.

I spit on my arm, scrubbing at it furiously, but it's permanent marker. It holds fast. I can't even see the word anymore, my vision is so blurry.

My throat burns. My arm throbs. My stomach is on fire.

I curl further into a ball, giving in to the misery rattling around my chest. A sob bursts out of me, the tears falling faster. They puddle in the crook of my eye and spill over, dripping to the dirt and pine needles my face is pressed to.

I can't face Caleb now, or even Robert. I can't walk into school like this.

Can I stay here?

I pant and lie there and contemplate screaming.

How long I'm here, I don't know. My eyes close, and I just try to make myself breathe normally. In through my nose. Out through my mouth. Spit out the dirt. Inhale, exhale.

A branch snaps, and suddenly Caleb is there.

"Oh my God, Margo." His voice is pure worry.

I can't move. My muscles are locked, stiff. My stomach is agony, and so is my throat. I couldn't even pull down my sleeve to cover the evidence of Ian's more noticeable cruelty.

Caleb gently moves my wrists away from my body.

He takes in the tears on my cheeks, and God knows what else. I stare into his eyes. Maybe he'll take the pain away for good. Set me free.

In one motion, I'm lifted into the air. I cry out but wrap my arms around his neck so he doesn't put me down. Ever perceptive, he pauses.

"Who did this to you, baby?" His tone promises violence, and my heart sings with the need for vengeance.

No matter what I've done, I didn't deserve *this*.

I try to inch closer to him. My face in his neck, my arms locked around his shoulders. He walks carefully, mindful that every step jostles me.

"Ian," I whisper in his ear.

His exhale is loud and sharp.

"I'm going to kill him." He presses a kiss to my temple. "He'll pay for this, baby."

There's something to be said about having my own personal monster. I know he'll avenge me.

He puts me in his car. Tells me to stay. Locks me in and disappears back into the school.

Maybe he'll go hunt down Ian. Or maybe he's finding Robert?

My mouth still tastes like blood; the coppery taste never quite left.

I focus on my knees. They're a bit scraped up, but I don't know when that happened. There's dirt on my legs. The pantyhose we wear with our skirts, part of our uniform, are ripped on my calf. When I move, dirt falls from my shirt. My eyes keep filling with tears. I make fists out of my hands, my nails pinching my palms.

I blink furiously.

Caleb returns, tossing something into the backseat. He slides in behind the wheel and looks over at me, then jerks back to face forward. "Just hold on."

We go to Eli's house. Maybe it's because Caleb doesn't want me to see his parents and Eli's are away—I don't ask. I don't really want to see his parents or go back to that house either.

He comes around and opens my door, scooping me up. In silence, he carries me into the house and down to the basement. It's vaguely familiar down here. There's a couch and a television mounted to the wall, a bed in the far corner.

He sets me on the edge of the bed and kneels next to me.

"I'm thinking there's more to this than your arm," he whispers. "Am I right?"

I nod.

He unbuttons my shirt, slowly pushing it off my shoulders. It falls behind me, and he leans back slightly. He presses his lips together, rage flickering over his face like candlelight.

I follow his gaze down.

My stomach is already a map of bruises. I'm surprised they showed up so fast.

He traces one. "Did he kick you?"

I force myself to nod again.

"I'm going to kill him," he repeats. His eyes meet mine. "What else?"

I touch my throat.

"Fuck."

He lifts my arm.

Ian's teeth left a red, angry mark. And right above it, the word I couldn't bring myself to read: *whore*.

"I'm sorry," I say over the lump in my throat. "I'm so s—"

Caleb leans forward and kisses me.

It's infinitely sweeter than the emotions I know he's feeling. I taste his guilt, and I want to cry again.

"Do not apologize." His voice is low. "You're staying here tonight."

My eyes widen. *It's against the rules*, I almost say. The lump in my throat blocks all noise, but he reads my mind.

"Fuck the rules, Margo. You're staying."

He storms off. The door to the basement slams closed, and then I'm left alone with my silence.

My breath hitches. It hurts to inhale; it hurts to move… I examine my arm.

We need to clean the bite. Get the marker off.

Whore.

It mocks me. My mother. My past.

I scratch at it. There's dirt under my nails, too.

I notice it with vague detachment. In fact, I'm feeling rather removed from it all. I mindlessly scratch at the writing, trying to get the ink out of my skin.

Caleb comes back. He tucks his phone into his pocket and rushes over, grabbing my wrists. "Margo."

He hauls me up, ever so gently, and carries me into the bathroom. He sets me on the counter, flicking on the light.

I wince when he takes my wrist and pulls my arm straight. I've managed to gouge my arm. Blood trickles down my hand, dripping off my finger.

"We'll get it off," he mutters. "I told Robert something bad happened. I ran out of his class when you didn't show up."

There's guilt in his eyes.

I felt it on his lips. That was one thing, but seeing it?

Not ready for that.

I quickly look away, focusing on his shoulder.

"He said the way to get to you was through me." My voice is raspy. I don't have to tell him I'm not talking about Robert. "I'm your soft spot."

He doesn't react.

I keep my attention on his face. He soaks a washcloth in warm, soapy water, and runs it over my arm. I let him care for me. God knows I can't do it myself.

He takes his time cleaning my arm. And then he runs the washcloth over my shoulders, up my neck. Down my chest. He unclips my bra, tossing it over his shoulder. Re-soaks the washcloth.

Water runs down my body, and I shiver.

He washes away Ian's harshness. His hand on my arm, around my throat. His Italian fucking leather loafer in my stomach.

And when Caleb's done, he steps between my legs and kisses me softer than I could've imagined.

But... we're not meant to be soft.

I lean into him, stifling my moan of pain. He holds me back, hands featherlight on my shoulders.

"Kiss me like you mean it," I demand.

He hesitates. "You're hurt. The responsible thing would be to take you to the hospital."

"Tomorrow. Tonight, you can make me forget. Please."

Caleb's lips part. I press forward, catching his lower lip in my teeth.

And.

I.

Tug.

He lets out a groan.

But... he doesn't give in like I hoped. Instead, he pulls back, shooting me a look.

"You're trouble." He shakes his head and motions for me to stand. His gaze goes to my chest.

I forgot I was shirtless.

Slowly, I bring my arm up and cover my breasts.

He frowns, but for once, he doesn't argue. He goes to his dresser, fishing around in a drawer for half a second before he's back with a t-shirt and a pair of shorts. His dresser because he lives here... in Eli Black's home.

I've been down here before. Drunk, delirious, half-unconscious.

I take the clothes he offers and bring the shirt up to my nose. I don't know why I do it with him watching me. Maybe I secretly like keeping him off guard.

Maybe it isn't a secret.

His lips twitch when I inhale.

It smells like him. His cologne. I slip the shirt on, the fabric concealing my face as I raise my arms. It hides my wince. He leans against the doorframe. I drop my skirt and slide his shorts on. If I wasn't hurt, I'd be enjoying this more.

As it is, Lenora and Robert are probably going to kill me.

"Did you tell Robert after you found me?"

We both sit on the couch. There's light coming in through the narrow windows toward the top of the basement walls. The windows are ground level. The curtains are open. I forgot, momentarily, that it's still daytime.

He grimaces. "I actually called Eli. He's going to have Riley talk to Lenora. But I told Robert in school that something was wrong, and I was going to track you down."

"I should get my phone. Make sure Riley's okay with... lying."

"I think you need rest," he murmurs.

He puts his arm around me, and I lean my head on his shoulder. He turns on the television, some mindless show about an international race, and we both kind of zone out. Every once in a while, he leans over and wipes a tear from my cheek.

I don't know why I'm still crying.

"Painkillers." He jumps up minutes or hours later. "I should've thought of that. Are you hungry?"

It feels like my internal organs went through a meat grinder.

I shake my head, and he frowns.

"Soup?" he asks.

"I'll try." The truth is, I might throw up. It could go either way.

He returns with ibuprofen and a bowl of chicken noodle soup for me, and a sandwich for him. I sip the broth so he'll stop staring at me.

Boys eat a lot. I knew that in the back of my mind from the past. Temporary foster brothers, boys at other schools I went to. But seeing Caleb inhale a sandwich, while I can barely keep down broth? With his physique, it just isn't fair.

He's got abs. The V that girls rave about. A trim waist and *muscles*. Hell, his face is gorgeous, too, but it's the body that sells the whole package.

And he's sitting next to *me*. How'd that happen?

"When's the other shoe going to drop?" I ask.

He blinks. "What?"

"This is nice. Like, you're being *nice*. Something is bound to go wrong."

He rolls his eyes. "It doesn't have to go wrong."

I straighten as much as I can. "So, what? We'll live happily ever after and get married and have babies—"

"Whoa," he says, taking the bowl from my hands. A little had sloshed over the edge onto my fingers. "I think you're afraid."

I jerk back. "Afraid of what?"

"Happiness?"

"Do you even *like* me?"

I think he may even love you. Except, Ian's voice in my head is the last thing I want to hear.

I hit my temple with the heel of my palm. Once. Twice. It's automatic. The urge to get him out of my memory is startlingly strong.

He may even love you.

It's on fucking repeat. I smack my head, my ears. Anything to forget Ian Fletcher's voice.

"Margo," Caleb says. "Stop."

He grabs my wrists, but it isn't enough.

One meltdown just became two.

I wrench myself away, almost falling off the couch, and then...

Caleb moves too fast. Faster than my mind can comprehend.

He stretches himself out on top of me, pinning me to the couch. He catches both of my wrists, yanking them up over my head.

It pulls on my stomach, my abs, and I cry out.

He doesn't relent, though. This is the Caleb I know—

the Caleb I deserve. His face is angry. Hell, furious. He leans down, his hips digging into mine.

"You don't get to beat yourself up," he whispers. "You don't get to be cruel to yourself."

"I can't—"

"I don't know what you think you can't fucking do," he growls.

His face is right over mine. Our legs are tangled together. His hands hold my wrists, but I can barely feel it.

Even when he's angry, he's gentle.

I meet his gaze.

"Face it, Margo. You're a lot stronger than you think."

I shift my hips.

He smirks. "You trying to proposition me?"

"It would be a good distraction." I sigh.

"Is that what you want? Just a distraction?"

I ponder that. *No*, I don't think I want just a distraction.

The answer must be written on my face, because his expression clears. He releases me and hops up. "What you need is sleep."

I glance out the window. Sometime between us sitting and now, the sun set. "Is it even eight o'clock yet?"

He scoffs. "Does it matter? You're hurt. Sleep will help you heal."

I push myself up and walk toward the bed. There's a picture on the dresser of Caleb and Eli. It occurs to me that I've accepted his living situation far too easily. Questions bubble up—the why and when most urgent.

I face him. "How long have you lived here?"

He pauses.

Him being here full time would explain the sheets covering the furniture at his house. But then... what about his parents?

He touches his throat. "The basement is mine, yes. If and when I ever need it."

"You took me here when I was drunk."

"Well, I hate to break it to you, baby, but you kind of have a bad reaction to my house."

I shudder. *I do.*

"Bed." He looks pointedly at the mattress.

I climb in and lie down, pulling the blanket up to my chin. It smells like him, the same as the shirt. I almost bring it up again—why he's living here, why he's being nice—but I can't do it.

He crawls in beside me, lying flat on his back. His eyes close.

"Sleep," he says.

If I close my eyes, I might see *him.*

Caleb exhales and tucks me into his side. I cling to him and force my eyes shut.

"I've got you," he whispers into my hair.

I relax. And eventually, I sleep.

Chapter 35
Margo

Lenora rushes out of the house, down the steps. She throws her arms around me, holding me close. The scent I've come to associate with her—orange blossom from her shampoo—envelops me.

Tears prick my eyes. *Again.*

She pulls back and looks at me. "Robert said something bad happened, and then you didn't want to come home?"

Caleb didn't let me out of his sight until I was safely tucked in Riley's car. Now, Riley stands awkwardly behind me, fidgeting.

"I'm sorry. I didn't want to worry you..."

Today, there are new bruises. My stomach looks terrible—worse than yesterday, even—and my neck... there's no hiding the handprints. Caleb got the marker off my arm, but the bite is going to stay for a while.

I showered this morning, moving slowly. I almost vomited at the thought of reaching up to wash my hair. But then Caleb came in, eyed me, and took over.

The memory of his hands massaging my scalp will keep me warm tonight, that's for sure.

"My dear girl." Lenora cups my cheek. "I understand that sometimes it's better to have a friend's comfort. Especially since you two have become so close." She gestures for Riley to come closer and loops her arm around Riley's shoulders. "Thank you for taking care of her."

Riley shifts from side to side.

I widen my eyes at her. *We've been over this.*

I'm not sure how Robert and Lenora would react to knowing I was at Caleb's house overnight. Well, Eli's.

Does Riley know Caleb stays at Eli's house? Has she been there?

When I tried to question Caleb about it again this morning, he wouldn't answer me. I've abandoned the topic for now.

"I already called Emery-Rose to report a sick day," Lenora says. "And I think you should see a doctor. At least to make sure..." Her gaze falls to my stomach. It's hidden under Caleb's t-shirt, but it's like she can see right through it.

I swallow.

"My best friend is a trauma doctor," Lenora says. "I asked her to stop by on her way in today."

"So it's already decided," I mumble.

Lenora nods. "Better safe than sorry, honey. Riley, you should head to school."

"Yes, ma'am." Riley gives me a quick hug, then retreats.

Lenora and I walk into the house. I go to my room and shrug off my jacket, quickly switching Caleb's shirt for one of mine. I stuff his under my pillow.

I exchange my skirt—couldn't exactly wear his shorts home—for comfortable pants.

Lenora closes the front door as I come back down. She has my backpack in her hand. "Riley forgot she had this."

I manage a smile. "Thank you."

"Couch? Soup?"

I nod and collapse on the couch, grabbing the remote. A day to do nothing but recover? I'm okay with that.

It's early in the morning. There's the rest of the day ahead of me.

Once Lenora is done hovering—she brings me water and a creamy wild rice soup—I dig into my backpack. I can't just sit here and do nothing, as peaceful as that sounds.

I find my phone at the bottom of my bag. Reaching in, I scroll through missed calls and texts from Caleb and Riley. My attention settles on one text from my mystery texter. The timestamp shows that they sent it yesterday afternoon. My hands tremble.

I click on the text before I wimp out.

UNKNOWN

This is the only time I help you.

[image attached]

It's a photo of Ian towing me across the field. Did Unknown send it to someone to help me? Caleb?

I shudder. I didn't even think to ask how he found me.

There are too many people pulling strings in my life. It makes me angrier than I could expect.

Lenora's doctor friend comes over, a portable ultrasound machine in hand, to inspect my stomach. Both women gasp when I raise my shirt. There's a lot of gentle probing—*ow*—and she finally rocks back on her heels. She fires up the ultrasound machine and squirts gel on my stomach, like they do for pregnant women.

I cringe at the idea of being pregnant.

"The ultrasound is clear," she finally says. "It seems like deep bruising. Have you been nauseated? Vomited at all?"

I shake my head.

"If you do, or if the pain travels into your back, call me. If there's blood in your urine—call me." She raises her eyebrows and holds out a card with her number written on it. "Do you understand?"

I jerk my head up and down. "Pain in my back, blood in my urine, call you. Got it."

"Ice on and off. Stay away from strenuous activity." She cleans the gel from my stomach and packs up her machine.

"Okay." I force a smile. "Thank you for checking on me."

They both rise, and I lower my shirt. I cover myself with the blanket again and close my eyes. Still, I hear Lenora's friend say, "I'd keep her activity down for at least a week. I'll write a note for you to send into the school."

I push myself upright. "Wait," I blurt out. "The dance—"

"Halloween is still ten days away," Lenora says gently. "I'm sure you'll be recovered enough by then." She raises her eyebrow at her friend.

The doctor smiles. "I'll come back on Sunday and check on you."

For the rest of the day, I drift between consciousness and sleep and try to forget Ian Fletcher.

When I wake up, it's completely dark. The television rolls through end credits of a movie I completely missed, and I'm impossibly groggy. I feel around for my phone, and my hand lands on... skin.

I snap my hand back. Caleb is reclined in the chair adjacent to the couch, his eyes closed.

My heart does this awful thing: it softens.

I must've touched his hand, dangling off the chair's arm.

Slowly, I sit up and readjust. I smooth down my hair, ensuring my shirt is in place. And by the time I look up, Caleb's gaze is on me.

"Feeling better?"

"Not really." The melted bag of ice slides off the couch. "Did you...?"

Caleb frowns. "Find Ian? Do anything? No. I've been warned not to cause any more waves at school."

I grunt.

He leans toward me, tucking a chunk of hair behind my ear. "Lenora said you should be good to go for the dance, though."

I manage a smile. "I hope so."

"I know it."

He turns on the lamp. I squint, blocking the light with my hand as he switches seats and slides in behind me. I lean on him while he inspects my throat.

"He's not going to touch you again. Even if I need to get the whole fucking hockey team to keep him away from you—"

"Isn't Ian on the team?"

Caleb rolls his eyes. "Yeah. But not for very much longer. There's a code of ethics to stand by. Plus, he's a twat."

Clearly.

The idea of him being kicked off the team is oddly satisfying.

"Where are Robert and Lenora?"

"They went out. They've been hovering, making sure you were still breathing. Or snoring, like you were when I came in."

I elbow him.

"You'll be back to school next week," he promises. "And then the dance. And after..."

He wiggles his eyebrows.

I break into laughter. "What are you going to do, rent a hotel room?"

He grins.

My heart skips. "Did you?"

"Where's the surprise in that?"

"Haven't I mentioned that I don't like surprises?"

He laughs. "No."

A new movie comes on, and Caleb and I fall back into silence. I actually stay awake this time, getting through most of it before the front door opens. Lenora and Robert enter in a flurry, dropping their bags and shedding coats. They come over to me, feel my forehead, pat the top of my head.

It's nice to be cared about. Suffocating and completely unfamiliar... but nice.

Caleb rises. "That's my cue. I'll see you later."

Robert and Caleb shake hands.

When Caleb's gone, the place feels a bit colder. I try not to let it show, though, because Lenora takes his seat almost immediately.

She puts the back of her hand on my forehead again. "How do you feel?"

I shrug. "The same."

Everything hurts.

She shakes her head. "If you want to tell us who did this, we can go to the school."

"What?" I would've guessed Riley told her. Hell, the whole school probably knows already. The big bully, Ian Fletcher, takes out his anger on Margo. Again.

"We know Caleb found you, but no one will tell us anything." She wraps her hands in mine. "Please, honey, tell us so we can put an *end* to this. I don't want you to feel scared—"

"I don't. I'm not scared." It's a bald-faced lie. I'm terrified.

She seems to analyze my face. Eventually, she nods. Whether she's going along with my lie or unable to tell is anyone's guess.

I carefully stand. "I'm going to go to bed. I'll see you tomorrow."

"Feel free to sleep in," she tells me. "I'm leaving pretty early for work."

"Okay. Goodnight."

I hobble up the stairs—at this point, walking doesn't totally hurt, but I'm indulging my melodramatic side—and slip into my bedroom.

"'Bout time," Caleb whispers from the shadowy depths.

I jump, and my body greatly protests. Covering my groan with a rough exhale, I flick on the light. He's sitting at my chair, fingers drumming on the edge of my desk.

"What?" he questions.

I shrug and glance back at the window. It's cracked, letting in a biting chill. All the better to cuddle, I guess...

"Thought I locked it, is all."

He smirks. "I unlocked it when I was here on a sanctioned visit."

I sigh. The idea of not sleeping alone seems pretty damn good right about now. I was going to suffer my nightmares solo, but now I don't have to.

He already has his shoes off.

I take a step toward the bed and freeze when he reaches under my pillow. "Planning on keeping this?" he asks, holding up his t-shirt.

I snatch it back and cradle it to my chest.

He just chuckles.

I lock my door and drop his shirt on my dresser, then venture closer. Somewhere between the beginning of the school year and now—only two months, shockingly—I stopped being afraid of him. I step between his legs, putting my hands on his shoulders. His eyes are level with my breasts, and he looks at them before tipping his head back and meeting my stare.

"Take my shirt off," I whisper.

His hands are cold against my skin, lifting the hem of my shirt. He pulls it off me in one fluid motion, ruffling my hair. He tosses it to the floor beside him.

My bra goes, too. My nipples stiffen under his hot stare. His hand hovers between my shoulder blades, keeps me from jerking back as his thumb skates over my nipple. He focuses on the other one, leaning forward and flicking it with his tongue.

I groan.

"Does that hurt?" His thumb is still making lazy circles on my skin.

"I like it when it hurts." The words slip out before I can stop them. I'd be mortified if I wasn't enthralled with the way Caleb is touching me.

His eyes narrow. "Be specific."

A shiver racks up my body.

His palm flattens against my stomach.

It's a light touch, but my breath catches.

"This?"

I shake my head.

His hand goes down, slipping into my panties. He presses on my clit, and my lips part. His lips tip up in a smirk at my reaction. One finger slides inside me.

"This?"

I put my hands back on his shoulders, if only to make sure I remain upright.

"Caleb—"

"I asked you a question, baby." His finger pushes in and out of me.

I can't do much standing in front of him. One of his hands is on my back; one causes chaos inside me. His nail scrapes along my clit.

I shudder.

If I admit it, he might stop. This is just to prove a point, after all.

Three fingers.

His fingers curl inside me. I groan at the new feeling, widening my stance. I close my eyes.

Mistake.

His teeth are on my skin, biting my breast. He doesn't do anything to soothe me. It's just a trail along my chest, little spikes of pain. It's maddening.

"You're fucking soaked." His eyes are impossibly dark. "You get wetter each time I do something to your body. So I guess that answers my question."

I whimper when he pulls out.

"The doctor said no strenuous activities." He smirks at me.

Bastard.

I grip his shoulders tighter and lower myself onto his lap. His erection brushes my thigh.

"Do you care what the doctor said?" Need and desire overrule common sense.

"I care about you being well enough to fuck you all night long after the ball," he replies.

My core tightens.

"Like that idea, do you?"

"I—"

"Lie down."

I do, shimmying off his lap and stretching flat on my mattress behind him. He twists on the bed and sprawls out next to me, so we're arm to arm. He draws the blanket up over us and rolls onto his side.

He watches me, then reaches down between us. I narrow my gaze, but it isn't until he lifts my leg and positions himself at my entrance do I release a breathy sigh.

He tips my hips back and slowly enters me. The stretch makes me ache, and I squirm. He holds me still until he's fully inside me.

But he doesn't move.

Instead, he exhales and whispers, "Sleep."

"With you...?"

"I like a little torture, too." He chuckles. "Just try."

I could be petulant and throw a fit. Reach down and finish off the job myself—a scary proposition with Caleb wrapped up in me. I could beg him some more.

Yet, I doubt any of that would work.

Still. I close my eyes, and there's no doubting that he's right behind me. There's no space at all between us. He shifts his hips slightly, sliding deeper, and I groan.

"Thank you," I mumble.

"For what?"

"Chasing away my nightmares."

He leans forward and kisses my forehead. "Anytime. Sleep now, love."

Chapter 36
Caleb

No one talks to me in the courtyard. Going to school when Margo is lying at home, *hurt*, just sets my teeth on edge. Theo, Liam, and Eli create a buffer. The doors open, and we walk down the hall, and they run impeccable defense.

I'm not sure what it is about us that attracts girls like bees to honey. The metaphor should be the other way around: we're the ones who sting, not them.

Eli heads off Amelie, grabbing her shoulders and spinning her away.

If I find Ian, I'm going to beat his fucking head in. I've already done it once this semester, but clearly the lesson didn't stick. I already got in trouble for it, too. The principal gave me a stern talking-to about how I couldn't touch a hair on his pretty little head... but I'm not against ulterior strategies.

Like circumventing his head and cutting off his dick.

Theo glances at me out of the corner of his eye. He's the darkest fucker I know. It isn't a surprise that he can tell I'm boiling on the inside. It's why we're friends—there's a madness in him, too.

We file into homeroom, and I nod at him. Ian is leaning against Amelie's desk. I grit my teeth, and Theo steps in front of me.

Ian doesn't so much as look up as we enter.

Waiting for homeroom to end is torture. Each tick of the second hand buries itself in my eardrums.

Finally, it's over.

Liam grins at Eli. "Race you."

They bolt toward the door, and Liam's foot catches Ian's bag. He flicks his toe, sending the bag flying. How many times did they do that to Margo? Not Ian, but Amelie and her cheerleaders?

Ian scowls, then collects his things. Theo and I linger and exit the room just after of him. We follow him toward his next class, and I look over at Theo.

"You ready?" he asks.

I roll my shoulders.

Liam and Eli are coming back toward us.

The bell rings, making the five of us officially late.

Ian raises his hand toward my friends, and they stop in front of him.

"Thanks for making me late, dick," Ian says to Liam.

Liam shrugs. "All part of the plan."

Ian shakes his head. "What?"

"Our plan," I say.

Ian spins around. His eyes widen. "You so much as touch me—"

"We won't touch you. But you're coming with us," Theo says. He crowds Ian's space. They're friendly on a good day, but today... today isn't a good day.

For any of us.

As much as it pains me to admit it, my friends have gotten attached to Margo. And that means they're in this with me.

Ian holds up his hands in defeat.

Eli leads us to one of the empty classrooms in the science wing. The walls here are thicker due to the extra venting. Liam and Theo follow right behind Ian, and I slow my pace until I'm trailing them all.

This isn't about violence—this is about scaring the shit out of him so he never so much as thinks about Margo the wrong way.

By the time I enter, Liam and Eli have Ian pinned to the whiteboard.

Theo paces in front of him.

"Just fucking hit me already, Alistair," Ian taunts. "We all know you're smitten with the Page girl—"

Theo slams his fist into Ian's stomach. Ian grunts, lurching forward. Eli and Liam hold him upright.

I sigh.

"Fuck—"

Theo punches him in the jaw. There's a *pop* as something breaks or dislocates.

"Shut. Up," Theo growls.

Apparently, I'm not the only one Ian's pissed off.

"No faces," I tell him. I stand back and let Theo get his anger out. After all, the principal only told *me* not to hit him.

Theo readjusts, but as soon as Ian coughs up blood, I stride forward and grab Theo's arm.

Liam and Eli release Ian, letting him fall to the floor.

"How does that feel?" I ask, crouching next to him. "Kind of like a kick in the stomach?"

He glares up at me.

I wrap my hand around his throat, pinning him flat to the floor. I see red at the idea of Margo in this position, him hovering over her.

I squeeze until Ian grabs at my wrists. He can't pry me loose.

He grins. His teeth are tinted red.

"Caleb," Eli warns.

"You don't touch her," I say to Ian. "You don't look at her. You don't—"

"This isn't really about her," he wheezes. "She's just your soft spot, Asher."

I dig my fingers into his neck.

"By the way," I say, leaning down. "You're off the hockey team."

His eyes bug out.

I'm not myself.

His face turns red, and I still don't let go.

I can't, when he's staring at me with a fucking challenge in his eyes.

He'll have bruises around his neck... much worse than Margo's, I'd reckon.

His eyes flutter shut. Theo and Eli grab my arms, pulling me away from him.

I struggle for a second.

"Any more and you'll kill him," Liam admonishes, shoving me away. He kneels next to a now unconscious Ian.

Theo drags me to the door, shoving me against it. "That wasn't part of the plan."

I try to clear my head. "I know."

"You lost it."

"I *know*."

He grunts. "Go. We'll take care of the rest of this."

I roll my eyes. "You lost it, too."

"Nah, he had it coming."

I shake my head. Yeah, Ian has a lot coming. *Had.* A broken team won't bring championships, and we were screwed the moment Ian went against me. There's still time to bring up one of the backups into his position.

I go to my car and slide in. Skipping isn't something that I push often, but no one ever says anything. A few other students indulge in the same luxuries. Theo could mail in his final and still get straight A's.

Lenora is at work, and Robert is at school, which means Margo is alone.

My phone rings halfway to her house. One glance at the caller ID, and I frown.

"Yes?"

"What a lovely greeting, nephew. Are you not in school?"

I shake my head. "Had to run an errand."

My uncle is silent. "We heard about your old friend's unfortunate incident."

Now I'm quiet. How the hell did my uncle hear about Margo? I've taken care not to mention her.

He chuckles. "Relax. We're not doing anything... yet."

"Aunt called Amber, didn't she?" It all snaps together. Loose pieces that suddenly make sense. "Which means she didn't leave town."

"I really don't appreciate you threatening people, Caleb. I thought you learned to be better than that."

To maneuver better.

Yes, I thought I had, too.

Margo and her family have me all twisted around.

"What can I do for you, Uncle?"

"Stop by the house after your... *errand.* And keep it between us."

"Got it." I hang up on him. He's not the most sociable person. I'm surprised he didn't hang up on me first.

I sit in the driveway for a second, then get out and walk into Margo's house.

It's interesting how the Bryans have made her feel so at home, but she's unwilling to call it that. She's gotten used to moving around so much, she seems to have forgot what stability looks like.

Maybe she never had it to begin with.

She's asleep on the couch, curled on her side. I close the door quietly and kick off my shoes, then go and kneel next to her.

There's a furrow in her brow. Her lips are pinched.

Even though she's sleeping—I can tell she isn't having a good dream.

I smooth back her hair and smile as she exhales.

"I'll keep you safe," I tell her.

I don't know if I'm telling the truth or not.

My feelings are all mixed up.

When I look at her, I see... *her*. But I see our past, too. Every fucking moment reminds me of the day she ruined our lives. One confession.

I begged her not to, but she did it anyway.

She whimpers in her sleep.

I loosen my grip in her dark hair, smoothing it out again. I should go, but I can't stop touching her.

She blinks and focuses on my face. The smile that spreads across her lips rips my heart out. Even so, tears spill down her cheeks.

"Why are you crying?" I swipe the tears away, but they keep falling.

I almost tell her that Ian's been taken care of, but I don't want her to stress about it. As he said: it was never about her. It was me.

"How did you know to search for me?" she asks.

"Someone sent me a text."

"A picture," she says.

I meet her gaze again. "Yes."

"Who?"

I shake my head. "Don't, Margo."

"Who texted you, Caleb?" She reaches out and grabs my wrists.

"A blocked number," I finally say. It's not the truth, per se. I have an idea of who sent it. Why they'd block their number to send it to me... It makes sense.

There are traitors at Emery-Rose.

Her face falls. She collects herself in record time, pushing up onto her elbow. "Shouldn't you be in school?"

I grunt. "Maybe I just wanted to see you."

She pats the space next to her, but I shake my head. I stand and pick her up—her and the blankets draped over her. I sit and balance her on my lap. She runs her hand over my chest, tucking her face into my neck.

I kiss the top of her head.

It's sappy. I feel impossibly guilty, even as my abs tighten and my dick hardens in my pants.

Margo and I aren't destined for a happy ending, even if we both want to pretend otherwise. Our destiny is to crash and burn.

Chapter 37
Margo

Wednesday afternoon is my first outing.

It's been a whole boring week of nothing but staying home, trying not to move. Riley and Caleb visit, but they have other obligations. School, for one. I've been doing my due diligence on the homework, keeping up with my classmates even while I'm away. It staves off some of the boredom.

Now, I'm *free*.

Tomorrow I'll return to school—a daunting idea that I refuse to think about.

Riley and Lenora frame me in as we walk toward the dress shop in the mall. This particular store carries special, one-of-a-kind dresses. Some are unusual, but there are diamonds in the rough.

That's what Lenora said anyway.

We walk in, and I immediately doubt her. The first six dresses that catch my attention are horrible: bright colors and ruffles, gaping holes in the sides, velvet and shoulder pads.

"Don't judge," Lenora admonishes, touching my shoulder. "We'll find a gem."

I told them that Caleb had picked out a mask for me, but I didn't know what sort of dress I wanted. Lenora had swooned at that—*literally*, she thought it was adorable and charming of him. I'm not sure how he got on her good side so easily.

And Riley... she got a mischievous gleam in her eyes. When I questioned her in the car, she merely shrugged. "I've been sworn to secrecy. But I'll let you know if you're going in the wrong direction."

I grit my teeth and go with it.

Dress shopping is weird. We spread out around the store. I run my hands across fabrics I have no right to be touching. Some are soft, some are shimmery.

When I was a kid, at the age where my parents could've dressed me in whatever cute outfits they wanted, it was overalls and sneakers. I ran, skinned my knees, played pee-wee baseball with the boys at eight. Minus the time I forced Caleb to play dress-up with me...

I pause in the corner of the room, my hand on my chest. It's overwhelming. If only my parents could see me now: Shopping to go to a *ball* with a *boy*. And not just any boy— Caleb Asher.

"Find anything?" Lenora asks behind me.

I turn around, blinking rapidly.

She must see my expression, something like panic and dread, because her smile drops. She steps closer. "What's wrong?"

"I just..." I swallow. "I never saw myself doing this."

She nods. "You didn't have much opportunity before this?"

"No boys paid attention to me," I say. "It was like they

were all afraid to touch the foster kid." I tried not to let it bother me. But sometimes, your only friends are the ones you're in the trenches with.

Riley comes over, oblivious to our conversation. She has a few dresses draped over her arms and a wide smile. "Listen, I grabbed a few for you and some for me because half the fun is trying them... Are you okay?"

I wipe at my face. "Yeah, I'm good."

Lenora smiles. "Let's see the dresses!"

Riley holds up the first one. It's pale blue, tight-fitting past the hips, and then it flares. Silk with lace covering it. It's pretty but absolutely not my style.

"You could try it on," Lenora says, nudging me.

"What else did you find?"

"This one is my favorite." Riley doesn't lift it up, though. She shoves the dark, gray-blue fabric into my arms and propels me toward the dressing room. "Trust me."

I exhale. "Fine."

There are no mirrors in this dressing room. I manage to close it and let my hair fall over my shoulders. I take a moment to look down at the dress, the color of thunderclouds.

Here goes nothing.

I step out, and they immediately jump up. Riley bounces, a wide smile splitting her face.

"That good?" I ask.

Lenora steers me to the three-sided mirror, and I'll admit, even my heart skips.

It's... perfect.

The top is fitted, with mini glass beads sewn in spirals around the waist. It flares out gracefully and stops at my knees. The neckline is high enough that I feel secure, but the fact that it's backless is sexy. I spin, giggling, because the dress floats around me.

"Beautiful," Lenora tells me. "Do you like it?"

I stop and stare at myself in the mirror. I try to imagine what sort of mask Caleb picked to make Riley suggest this dress. But honestly, I don't know. I couldn't guess.

I feel beautiful. Maybe with my hair up in a braid...

The tag dangles under my armpit. I glance at the price, and my eyes nearly pop out. Anger floods through me, followed quickly by embarrassment.

There's no way I could afford this.

"No," I chirp.

"You... don't?"

I glare at Riley. "Why would you pick such an expensive dress? I can't—"

Lenora comes over and leans down, reading the price.

Tears prick my eyes. If figures—I feel pretty for once in my freaking life, and it's so far out of my budget it's not funny. And yeah, maybe I shouldn't have fallen in love with a few yards of fabric, but...

"I'm buying," Lenora says in a low voice.

"What?" I whisper. I can barely see.

"I'm buying it. I should've said earlier that this was my treat, and I'm sorry for putting you through such distress." She tucks a strand of hair behind my ear. "Wipe those tears, honey. You're getting the dress."

I stare at myself in the mirror. Teary eyed, red-faced, but the dress is brilliant.

My mother would've swatted me away from this store. We wouldn't have gone to the mall in the first place. She was a personal chef, but money was always tight. I got new-to-me jeans and shirts at thrift stores. Shoes on clearance. Toys that had been donated.

We lived in one of the wealthiest neighborhoods, yet we struggled to fill our small, retro fridge.

And Lenora tells me she'll buy a five-hundred-dollar dress that I'll wear once. She does it without batting an eye.

Riley pulls me back into the changing room. I step out of the dress, still in a state of shock. I blink and blink and can't think of anything to say.

"This is how they operate," she whispers. "She's trying. Money is nothing to them."

I twitch. "Where does their money even come from? How much could they possibly make on her salary and Robert's?"

Riley grins. "Clearly, you don't know your foster parents."

I raise my eyebrow, but Riley just shoves my clothes at me and slips out the door.

By the time I'm in my clothes, she's in another changing room. Lenora has my dress bagged and over her arm.

Lenora grins at me, tapping my nose. "I wouldn't take no for an answer."

"Thank you," I murmur. "I really, *really* appreciate it."

Riley's door cracks open, and she slips out.

We both *ooh* at the same time.

The fabric is slinky, hugging her body like a glove. She's as thin as the popular girls, even if she hides it most of the time. The black dress has a deep, plunging neckline and widens below her hips.

She does a little shimmy. "What do you think?"

"It's beautiful." Lenora winks. "And spicy."

Riley tosses her hair back. "I think I'll knock Eli's socks off."

He officially asked her while I was home recovering, apparently. And she said yes, amongst a sea of jealous

367

onlookers. It was quite the spectacle. Singing, a marching band, the hockey team surrounding Riley and lifting her in a chair that they carried around the football field.

Still, she tries on two more dresses before she declares herself satisfied with the first. We walk out of the store with our arms linked—the three of us, me at the center. Bags dangle from Lenora's wrist and Riley's. There's a warm feeling in my chest, and it's easy to ignore the pain in my stomach.

We get pretzels and browse around a few stores. I hesitate picking out jewelry. There are some things of my mom's I could get. I'm sure they're in her room in our old house. Going in to get them would probably give me a panic attack, but...

It would be nice to wear her earrings or necklace. Feel closer to her.

Riley holds up a stunning necklace dripping in crystals. "I'm getting this," she announces. She tries it on, lifting her hair up and turning every which way.

"I love it," I tell her.

She grins at me.

As we're leaving the store, someone shouts my name.

A blur shoots past Riley and knocks into me.

Someone latches on to me, their arms around my waist. All the breath is expelled from my lungs. It takes me a few seconds to comprehend that the small person isn't a stranger —it's Hanna.

I laugh and wrap my arms around her, rocking back and forth. Screw the searing pain in my stomach. It's *Hanna*. My expectation of seeing her again was lower than low.

Claire jogs up, panting.

"Jesus, Hanna," she admonishes. To me, she says, "She saw you and took off."

Hanna makes a face, and I brush back her hair. She's only a few years younger than us, but I babied her more than Claire ever did. Probably because I never had a permanent kid sister, and it felt like we were going to be together for a while.

I remember my manners suddenly and turn to Lenora. "Claire, Hanna, this is my foster mom. Lenora, these are my old foster siblings, Claire and Hanna."

Lenora's nostrils flare—or maybe it's my imagination. She smiles at the girls, reaching out to shake their hands.

Claire stares at her outstretched hand and doesn't move.

Embarrassment creeps up my neck in the form of a blush. I've been telling Lenora and Robert about my foster siblings, how much I missed them, and here Claire is, shoving that all out the window.

Hanna steps forward and takes Lenora's hand, shaking it up and down enthusiastically. It makes up for the iciness of her sister.

"Can we steal Margo?" Claire glances at Riley, then averts her gaze. "We were hoping to see her this weekend."

After Lenora bought me a dress, and Riley and I are spending time together? I automatically feel guilty for even thinking that I could break away and go with Claire and Hanna.

I start to turn her down. "Claire—"

"It's okay." Lenora shares a look with Riley.

Riley shrugs.

"You go spend some time with them. I'm going to put our stuff in the car, and we'll meet you in the food court? In an hour?"

Guilt.

It's all I feel.

I start to say no again, but Hanna grabs my hand.

"Come see this shirt Claire's gonna buy me!" she says, hopping from one foot to the other. At my nod, she drags me down the hallway.

Claire, Riley, and I end up in a kids' clothing store, chasing Hanna around. She excitedly tears clothes off the racks to try on. I glance at Claire, who now smiles openly.

"We get an allowance," she tells me. "And we've been saving up for a shopping spree."

And my foster mom bought a five-hundred-dollar dress without flinching.

Now *I'm* the one trying not to flinch.

Claire follows Hanna toward the dressing room, making her come out after each shirt. They end up selecting three, all from the clearance rack, and a pair of jeans.

I try not to let it bother me.

Money, friends, love.

It's all luck of the draw for us.

"Ice cream?" Hanna asks.

Claire frowns. "We can split a cone."

Lenora had given me a twenty-dollar bill earlier. I feel it in my pocket and smile. "My treat."

Hanna screams. It's high-pitched and intense. Even after she's stopped, it bangs around my head.

But Claire just chuckles, rubbing Hanna's head. "She got into this excited squealing in school. All her friends do it."

"Right."

My own screams echo in my ears. *Not* the happy kind.

I shake my head.

We go toward the food court, and Claire grips my arm.

She bites her lip. "Remember how you used to talk about Caleb all the time?"

I blush. I didn't talk about him *all* the time. But if we

Wicked Dreams

were talking about our pasts, which we did often—trading war stories, as it was—then... yeah, I mentioned him.

She gives me a knowing look, and then she's right back to watching me with an odd expression. It takes a minute to place the emotion on her face, because she so rarely shows worry or concern. But now both are flashing across her features.

We watch Hanna skip ahead of us, then circle back.

"I didn't realize..."

I glance at her. "What?"

"I recognized him."

Her words aren't computing. "Huh? Who?"

"Caleb. I... I don't know. I'll keep trying to remember, but it's weird. I saw a picture of you and him on Instagram, and he just seems so familiar."

"There's a picture on Instagram? Of us?"

She rolls her eyes. "Yeah. Some girls at Lion's Head are obsessed with the Emery-Rose hockey team. They have a fan page for them because our hockey team apparently isn't good enough. Anyway, they reposted that photo..."

My mouth drops open. First, that he'd post a picture of us. Second, that he has a *fan page*. What?

"That's... weird."

She shrugs. "He has some pretty rabid fans, if you ask me. Just search his hashtag."

Caleb has a hashtag?

Hanna slams into me again. I failed to mention my stomach, so maybe it's my fault that I suddenly can't breathe. But then Riley is there, gently prying Hanna off. Claire shoots Riley a dirty look but otherwise stays silent.

I take a shaky breath.

Lenora is slower to come up, her brows furrowed with concern. "You okay?"

371

"Yep." I straighten.

"We've got to get going." Claire takes Hanna's hand, tugging her backward a few steps. No hug goodbye for us, then. "I'll talk to you later."

They make a beeline for the closest exit. They're pushing out the door, and it occurs to me that I didn't get to ask her more.

Hashtags? Rabid fans? Where have you seen Caleb before?

We pile in Lenora's car. I let Riley take the front seat so I can stare out the window the whole way home. It starts raining halfway there, and I remember to check Instagram. I pull up his profile, biting my lip until it loads.

He posted a photo of us that someone else took a couple of weeks ago. His arm is around my shoulder at that football game, and we're both... we seem happy. That's probably the most shocking part. I'm grinning, leaning into him, and his gaze is on me.

His attention is always on me.

I stare at it like it'll give me the answers I need.

Where has Claire seen you before, Caleb?

Chapter 38
Margo

Friday.

Halloween.

The masquerade ball starts at seven o'clock, which means...

Six hours to go.

Only four hours before kids start trick-or-treating, but I refuse to think more about that. I'll be upstairs getting ready with Riley, suppressing the anxiety spikes every time the doorbell rings.

Lenora picks us up from school after lunch. Most of the girls in the junior and senior classes leave early to get ready for the Fall Ball. It's actually kind of fun to follow Lenora up to Robert's classroom. There's a goofy smile on her lips, and she admits that she wishes she could visit Robert in his 'natural habitat' more.

His whole face lights up when she knocks on his door.

A quick peek into his room, a kiss, and then we're off.

"I booked you a hair appointment," Lenora tells me in the car. "It's at the same time as Riley's."

S. Massery

My lips part. "What? You didn't have to—"

"I want tonight to be great." She pats my thigh. "So just let me pamper you, dang it."

"Thank you, Lenora."

It's a whirlwind from there. I quickly sift through pictures for the hairstylist and point to something a little more extravagant than I would've been able to do myself. When in Rome, right?

The stylist is a master, making a braided crown intertwined with ropes of gold and pearls. Curled ringlets frame my face.

I'm the same, yet different.

Once we're back at the house, Riley and I lay out our makeup in my bathroom. Our dresses are hanging on the door. I wipe off the day's makeup and think about a plan. It's setting in that this is real. This is happening.

The doorbell rings, and luckily, I'm still removing my makeup, because I almost jump out of my skin.

Riley throws me a curious glance, then crosses the hall into my bedroom. She returns and says, "The trick-or-treaters are starting to show up."

I shudder.

"Do you not like it? Halloween?"

"Just some bad experiences." After a while, even the association with terrible things was enough to make me want to hide. "No pity, please."

"Got it. So, music?" She pulls out her phone and opens the music app. "Some fun pop, coming right up!"

Justin Bieber starts playing, and I laugh. "How'd you know I had a crush on him when I was twelve?"

She smirks. "Didn't every girl?"

We do our makeup in silence, occasionally belting out

lyrics. Robert or Lenora must be sitting on the porch, since the doorbell has stopped ringing. In fact, the house is almost *too* quiet for a while.

I decide to take Caleb's words to heart, and I don't pack on the eyeliner like I'm inclined to do. Instead, I fish out my palette of eyeshadows and create a muted, gray-blue smoky eye. It pairs nicely with my amber-brown eye color.

I coat my skin with a light layer of foundation, contour the hell out of my cheeks, and add shimmer to my cheekbones and eyelids.

Riley is done at nearly the same time as me. She gets close to my face and swipes lightly just under my left eye. "Perfect. Want to see my mask?" She puts the finishing touches on her lipstick, which is so dark red it's almost purple.

"Of course! I can't believe you didn't show me before."

She laughs. "Sometimes surprises are good!"

We go into my room, and she rifles through her bag. She takes out a white box. She lifts the mask to her face, and I grin. It's *perfect.*

It's delicate black lace, patterned like flowers. One side is bigger, sweeping high over her head with black feathers. The other side angles down, ending in dainty lace curls.

I love it.

I tell her as much, and she bursts into giggles.

"Thank you. I think Eli got the white half-mask from *Phantom of the Opera.*" She pouts behind the mask. "We'll make a great pair."

"I know you will," I say.

Lenora knocks on the door, pushing it open. "Ah, you girls are so pretty! Riley, that mask is gorgeous. We've got about fifteen minutes before the boys show up."

Riley jerks. "Fifteen minutes? Shoot. Len, we didn't even get to eat anything!" She rushes out the door, down the stairs.

I chuckle. I hate to admit it, but as soon as she mentions food, my stomach growls. The week has been an ongoing saga against food. Or for it, depending on the day.

Lenora's doctor friend came back with her ultrasound machine after I threw up one morning, but she couldn't find any internal bleeding. Everything else seemed okay.

Riley returns with a plate of crackers and cheese. "Robert said this was for us?"

Lenora nods. "I bought that yesterday just in case."

"You're the best." I hug her.

Because I'm in a hugging mood? Because I'm overstimulated on emotions? Either way, she hugs me back tightly.

We demolish the plate, then rush into the bathroom to brush our teeth. Riley reapplies her lipstick. When we return to my bedroom, Lenora is in the hallway.

"Anticipation is half of any romance," Lenora says in a low voice. "The guys are here, but take your time. Come down when you're ready."

We're not even dressed! Makeup and hair, yes. Crackers and cheese, obviously.

Riley and I exchange a look. She's the first to crack, covering her mouth as laughter sneaks out.

"I have a feeling they'd come up and drag us to the ball..." She clutches her stomach, laughing harder. "Imagine showing up half-dressed!"

"No shoes." I snort.

"Let's get dressed." Riley closes and locks my door, then unwraps her dress from the plastic. "We're going to dance our butts off."

"And where did Caleb say we're going after?"

She rolls her eyes. "The school hosts an after-party. They lock us all in a building with games and stuff. It's very... well, lame. No alcohol or anything."

"When do we get let out?"

"Hypothetically, seven in the morning."

My lips part. "They'd keep us there until seven? A full, what, eight hours?"

She laughs. "Yeah. It's ridiculous. Hence why we're not going..."

She turns away from me and strips, quickly sliding her dress on. "Zip me up?"

I venture closer. She has a tattoo on her shoulder blade. It's the outline of a bird.

I tap it, not bothering to ask, because she immediately sighs.

"Long story."

"Okay." I zip her dress and finagle the eyehook clasp at the top.

She smooths the fabric and spins around.

I love it just as much as when she tried it in the store.

"Your turn."

What I didn't think of—that I definitely should've—is that this dress is backless. Backless means no bra. My breasts are pretty small, so that isn't a concern. What *is* a concern is the fact that Riley brought sticky circles for my nipples.

It's embarrassing, but I guess I'd prefer them to showing everyone how cold I am...

I roll my eyes. "I'm gonna need to figure this out in private."

She tosses me the pack. "Have fun."

I take my dress and the stickies into the bathroom, staring at myself for a minute. I still don't know what my mask looks like. The anticipation of finding out is almost unbearable.

Once the stickies are on and everything is situated, I slide my dress up over my hips. It has a higher neckline, like a shallow crew neck, and the straps over my shoulders are wide. The whole thing dips low in the back, cutting just inches above my tailbone.

It's dangerous, but I secretly love it. And the *beading*. I run my fingers over the intricate swirls along my waist. They curl up toward my breasts and down lower, onto the skirt. The dress is seriously perfect.

"Ready?" I ask Riley.

Time is picking up speed, hurtling us toward... *Social anxiety*.

"We got this." She hands me a matte red lipstick from my tiny collection. "Put this lipstick on, and let's dazzle them."

I smile. I swore Riley to secrecy about my dress, just in case Caleb decided to interrogate her while I wasn't around. I'm not too worried about matching him. Something tells me he'll have that handled. But something tells me she's seen my mask.

After my lipstick is in place, Riley and I strap on our heels. She picks up her mask. And... off we go.

"I'm suddenly nervous," I admit.

She nods. "Want me to go first?"

"Please."

At the top of the stairs, I lean against the wall and take a few deep breaths. Riley heads down, and the conversation below screeches to a halt.

"Wow." Eli's voice has a way of carrying. "You... that's beautiful."

I imagine her raising the mask, pouting like she did in my room.

"Where's Margo?" Caleb asks.

"Oh, she's coming," Riley answers.

He grunts.

"Okay, Margo." I shake out my arms and remind myself to keep breathing.

The heels—gold—aren't tall enough that I'm going to have trouble. But I still feel off balance as I grip the banister and walk down the stairs.

I hit the landing, round the corner, and my eyes lock onto Caleb.

I go closer, and he holds out his hand to me. There's fire in his eyes, and I break out in goosebumps. I can't focus on anyone else—just him and the sudden tension between us.

I slip my hand into his.

His typical smirk is in place. He squeezes my fingers, and I get the chance to really examine him.

His suit is dark, dark blue. And his tie? Spun through with muted gold and royal blue. It's subtle enough to escape attention at first glance. But I have a feeling that the two of us together will bring the color out.

It'll send a message that we're a pair, him and me.

Someone gasps, and his spell is broken.

I blink and realize he and I have crept closer and closer. My chest almost brushes his. I take a step back, but his hand tightens on mine, keeping me from retreating too far.

Fair enough.

Lenora and Robert are by the kitchen, arms wrapped around each other. And Riley and Eli are staring at us like we're crazy.

"You're stunning," Caleb says in my ear.

I blush.

"And later," he continues, his voice lowering, "I'm going to fuck you senseless in your dress."

I shake my head. He's so inappropriate. Yet, my whole body hurts from the way my muscles clench.

"Would you like to see your mask now?" He grins.

Anticipation floods through me. "Yes."

He presents a familiar box.

Carefully, I undo the tape on each side and lift the lid.

Damn.

The mask is shining gold, with negative space cut in a similar pattern to the beads on my dress. It's inlaid with pearls, highlighting the eye space. There are tiny gold chains that loop along the bottom of the mask, made to drip down my cheeks.

It's stunning—the same word Caleb used to describe me. A word that is *much* better suited to this accessory than me.

"And yours?" I ask.

He opens his own box and shows me a matching gold mask. It's masculine, though: the cutout spaces are smaller, more of a honeycomb pattern, with a single crystal between the brows. It covers the entire upper half of his face.

"Pictures," Lenora says, stepping forward. "We'll do a few with and without the masks."

I don't have time to react to his mask—to *him*—other than a smile. Lenora ushers us over to the fireplace, and the four of us strike a pose. And then another. She gets a few of just Riley and Eli, who matches her in his all-black attire.

"Masks on," Robert suggests.

Caleb gestures for me to turn around, and he ties the mask's ribbons behind my head. He secures his own, and then his finger trails up my spine. It's quick, probably unnoticed by anyone else.

It's weird only seeing his eyes, the quirk of his lips.

We pose for pictures, and I'm too aware of him at my back.

"We should go," Caleb finally says.

Lenora lowers her camera. "I'm sorry, I think I got carried away."

Robert wraps his arms around her shoulders.

"It's just, our daughter would've loved this." Tears fill Lenora's eyes.

My heart skips. I feel the urge to go over and hug her, but I don't dare move.

She waves in front of her face.

"I'm so sorry." She rushes away.

Robert rubs his hands together. "Sorry about that. She's happy for you, Margo. It's just a little overwhelming."

I nod.

Caleb frowns. "We're going to head to the dance."

"Have a great time," my foster dad tells us. "Text me when you get to the after-party. And then we'll see you home in the morning."

"Will do!"

On our way out, Riley loops her arm in mine. "Do you think he's going to check the log? For who signed in?"

I pause. "Oh God."

"Already taken care of," Caleb says. "I've got someone who will add our names to the list."

We pile into Eli's truck. Riley starts to get in the backseat with me, but Caleb stops her. He slides in next to me, his hand on my thigh. We have a whole bench, but we're pressed close together. Our legs touch, hip to knee, and I lean into him.

"I have something for you," he says.

I raise my head. Our masks are on our laps. My phone

381

and ID are in a clutch that I totally plan on leaving in the car, because it doesn't match anything. But being maskless means he sees my eyes widen.

"Nothing bad," he promises.

I grimace. "I hope not."

"Just close your eyes."

I watch him for a moment, but he doesn't move. Slowly, I close my eyes. He shifts, then takes my hand and turns it so my palm is up. He puts something hard and flat on it, supporting my hand with his underneath it.

"Open."

I do. My gaze falls to the kind of box you'd put a neck-lace in. About the size of my palm, square, shallow. At least it isn't a ring.

"Buying me jewelry already?" I quip.

"Open it."

Eli pulls into the hotel parking lot. The dance is in one of their ballrooms—and I'd bet our room is in the same building. He hasn't said as much, though.

"Dude," Eli says. "Quit staring at your girl. We're here."

Caleb doesn't tear his gaze away from me. "Leave us. We'll be there in a minute."

Riley and Eli get out. I'm not sure why I'm nervous, but my heart rate has spiked.

I flip it open, and it feels like Ian's kicking me in the stomach all over again.

There's no oxygen in here.

Sitting on a bed of foam is a bracelet. The hand-woven strip is encased in a cage of sterling silver. I lean closer to get a better look at the work, because it's familiar. Like a dream or a long-lost memory.

It's blue with a single thread of gold. In the fading light, it's hard to make it out, but the gold glitters.

"I... I made this," I whisper. "A version of it anyway."

"You did." He lifts the bracelet. It's been lengthened by chain. Altered. There's no way it'll fall off now, not unless the metal clasp breaks. "Do you remember when?"

"I made two." It *is* a memory. One I've dreamed about recently. Still, it seems to be coming at me from a long way off.

We're married until these fall off.

He shows me his wrist. There's the other one, also fortified with metal. Half gold and half blue. I remember—I remember making those. Presenting them.

Kissing him in a flower girl dress, while he wore his father's suit jacket.

I wasn't wrong when I said he was my first kiss... but I was wrong about when. It wasn't this year; it was when we were eight.

"I remember." His eyes are dark. "Do you?"

God, I used to hate him. And now—I'm pretty sure I just fell in love with him.

Again.

I nod. There's a lump in my throat I can't swallow around.

"You fixed them?" My voice trembles.

He fastens it to my wrist. Surprisingly—or maybe not, since this seemed to be his color scheme all along—it matches everything. The dress, the masks, my shoes.

He meets my gaze. "I didn't want them to fall off."

There goes my heart.

"Let's have fun, yeah?"

I exhale. "And then sneak away early?"

His eyes dance. "If you're persuasive enough."

"Oh, I see how it is."

He opens the door, taking my thin clutch from my

S. Massery

hands and tucking it into a pocket in his jacket. He helps me down and carefully ties on my mask. He lets me do the same for him.

Once we're ready, he offers his arm.

I take a deep breath. The bracelet is all I can concentrate on. That, and what it might mean.

Does Caleb love me, too?

Chapter 39
Margo

W e're dancing. I don't think we've *stopped* dancing.

It's an excuse to touch Caleb. And to feel his hands on my bare back. Each tiny stroke of his thumb under the edge of my dress, inching closer to my ass, sends sparks through me. It's dangerous and dirty, and I desperately want him to take me upstairs already.

Tonight has been an exercise in ignoring Amelie and Ian, who always seem to be in the corner of my eye. She came in with a gorgeous black mask that has feathers and jewels, and a tight, *tight* red dress. Ian matches her: red mask, black-and-red suit.

I wonder if anyone's compared her to the Queen of Hearts. *Off with their heads!*

Luckily, Amelie doesn't have that much power.

Savannah brought a new boy to the dance. His mask obscures too much of his face, but people are whispering. This student body loves to gossip about anyone and everyone.

The slow song ends, and I step away from Caleb.

"Thirsty?" he asks.

I nod, searching for Riley. After a moment, I find her and point. "I'll be over there."

He grins. There's a spot of red lipstick on his lip, and I start to rub it off for him.

He stops me. "Leave it. I like your mark on me."

Of course he does.

Halfway to Riley's table, a girl approaches. She grabs my arm and pulls me out of a side door, into a brightly lit hallway. It's quite the change from the dark ballroom.

"Hey! Let go of me."

She lifts her mask.

Claire.

"What are you doing here?" I gasp.

She huffs. "Nice seeing you, too, sis."

"Sorry. I just wasn't expecting you to crash the party."

"Yeah, well, I wasn't expecting you to ignore my phone calls."

"I'm not. I haven't got any from you."

She scowls.

"Seriously. I'd prove it, but my phone is in Caleb's jacket..."

"I have something important to tell you, Margo." She takes both of my hands in hers. "I need you to listen to me."

I focus. "Okay, okay."

It must be bad if Claire is willing to travel all the way to Rose Hill to tell me something. Bad or good, but my bet is on the former. And as I think that, that Halloween-induced anxiety flutters in my chest.

"I was worried about you," she said. "And you know how we met your foster mom the other day?"

Last week, at the mall. How could I forget?

My face answers for me.

Claire sighs. "She was familiar—but like, in an 'I have a bad feeling about this' kind of way. You know those moments where you just want to follow your gut?"

"I... guess." I don't like where this is going.

"Remember when we lived together, and you found my stash?"

Of newspaper clippings. Yes.

Her parents died in a car accident, and for a while, she was obsessed with other kids who lost parents in accidents. If there was a newspaper write-up about it, you could bet that Claire had it cut out and pressed into a notebook.

"Some of them had pictures, you know? Like of the family mourning or raising awareness.

"Okay, and?"

"Your foster mom seemed familiar."

I don't love where this is going. "You said the same freaking thing about Caleb," I point out.

"He still is familiar," she mutters. "But that's not what we're talking about right now. The point is: I figured out your foster mom!"

I squint at her. It takes a moment to dislodge her grip, and I untie my mask. I take it off. "You recognize her from... your newspaper clippings?"

"Yes! Her daughter died in a crash like, five years ago. There was a picture of her and her husband at the grave site."

"That's awful, Claire. And, for the record, I knew she died."

"No, but look." She pulls a paper from her pocket, shoving it into my hand. "Just read that!"

"Margo?"

I spin around, crumpling the paper in my fist. Caleb

S. Massery

walks toward us, gaze bouncing back and forth between Claire and me.

"Are you a friend of Margo's?" he asks Claire.

I glance back at her, but her mask is back in place. She takes a few steps backward, shrugging. "See ya later, Wolfe."

Weird. She's always been kind of skittish around people, though.

"You good?" he asks.

"Yep." My dress has small pockets. They aren't big enough for a phone, but definitely for a scrap of paper. I tuck it in and retie my mask.

Caleb hands me a cup of punch, and we go join Riley and Eli.

Claire's warning is swept away in the excitement of the rest of the evening. Eventually, Caleb's hand on my back is too much for me to bear. The room is slowly emptying out, and I find myself leaning on him more and more.

We've done our part. We showed up, we danced, we were seen and admired. The last two things were just what I figured Caleb wanted. We talked with Theo and Liam, who both opted to come alone.

At one point, Theo stole Amelie away from Ian and whisked her around in a proper waltz. The fact that they both knew more than how to just sway was impressive. I didn't figure him as the type to fall for her charm, though.

Caleb chuckled at my expression. "He's using Amelie."

"For what?"

He just shakes his head.

Now, I lean against Caleb and try to telepathically tell him that it's okay to leave.

"Tired?" he asks.

I nod, emphatic.

He tuts and leans down. "Poor thing. I thought our night was just getting started..."

His words undo me.

I press my thighs together, turning so my lips brush his ear. "Tired of being surrounded by people," I clarify.

He smirks. "If you insist."

He takes my hand, lacing our fingers, and tugs me up. I come closer to his height in my heels, but he still manages to feel... bigger. Infinitely more imposing.

"We're out," Caleb says, slapping Eli's hand. "See you tomorrow."

We say goodbye to Theo and Liam, too. The latter has found a girl, and he keeps her in his lap as we walk by.

The music is much fainter in the lobby. He hands me my clutch and withdraws a keycard.

Our bags should already be in the room. This morning, Riley and I tossed our overnight bags in Caleb's trunk. We all figured it was easier to explain it away than have Lenora and Robert ask me a million questions.

The elevator ride is quick, shared with another couple, and Caleb and I keep eyeing each other. Once we're in the hallway, he takes my hand. We stop in front of a door, which he unlocks, and he quickly scoops me up. I throw my arms around his neck, suppressing a yelp, and he carries me over the threshold.

"Cute," I say.

He just smiles.

He doesn't set me down. He walks down the hall and into the room. But it isn't just a room. It's a whole freaking suite. There's a living and dining room, complete with a giant oak table. A door with locks on it on the right, which I assume means it can connect with another suite, and the bedroom and bathroom on the left.

There's a giant vase filled with flowers on the table.

"Wow."

He shifts, lifting me higher. "It's worth it."

"Bedroom?"

"As you wish." He strides toward the bedroom and places me on my feet.

I have a second to get my balance before he's on me, pushing me against the wall. I arch into him as his lips meet mine. He teases me with the barest brush.

"Remember what I said?" he asks.

"Yes," I breathe. He's going to fuck me senseless.

His hands slide up my legs, inching up the hem my dress. Slowly, he drags my panties down. He kneels, keeping a hand on my hip while I step out of them. He grasps one of my ankles and puts it over his shoulder.

God, I'm wet from just thinking about what he's going to do to me.

"Hold on tight," he warns, then he leans forward and puts his lips on me. He sucks on my clit, hard.

I buck, trying to get away.

It—it *hurts*.

My hands grip the skirt of my dress. I wriggle at the feel of his teeth on me, but he just bites my inner thigh.

I moan. The back of my head hits the wall.

He pulls away, groaning, and suddenly I'm in the air. I hold on to his shoulders while he carries me to the bed, tossing me on it and following.

I swallow, moving backward.

"You like it when I hurt you." He pushes my dress up again. "You're going to come with my tongue inside you."

My shoulder blades hit the headboard.

He goes back down on me, his tongue sliding through my folds. My back comes off the bed, pleasure spreading through me. The bite on my thigh pulses. He thrusts his tongue into me.

"You're wicked," I whimper.

He trades his tongue for fingers, and his mouth goes back to my clit, biting and sucking.

It doesn't take long for the sensation to build and build and build.

He thrusts into me with his tongue again, fucking me with his mouth just like he said he would.

I shatter, moaning his name. It's unbearable.

There's a gleam in his eye.

He's not finished.

I collapse back as two fingers slide into me, hitting my G-spot with deadly accuracy. I can't control my hips, which begin to rock into him. My eyes close, and I lose track of where he is.

That's my mistake.

He thrusts in another finger, spreading me wider, and licks my clit. It's so fucking slow, every stroke makes me tremble.

"Caleb," I groan, trying to push his head away. It's too much. My legs tingle.

"Give it to me," he growls.

His finger, wet from being inside me, slips back, teasing my asshole. He enters at the same time that he slides his tongue into me.

The sensation is overwhelming. Another orgasm crashes over me, and my legs shake. I keep coming.

"Oh my God."

He just stuck his finger in my...

He smirks. "You can call me that, if you want."

"Ass." I'm panting. I'm pretty sure I can't move.

"Wasn't that worth waiting for?"

Who would've thought two weeks was a long time to go without sex? And not just sex—any orgasms. My stomach is still bruised, but it doesn't hurt much anymore. The limited activity order did wonders.

"Yes," I manage.

He gets up and hauls me up, too. "Keep your dress on... lose everything else."

I gulp.

More?

While he's out of the room, I unbuckle my heels, more than happy to be rid of them.

Caleb comes out of the bathroom.

I go in and pee, then contemplate taking down my hair. It's a little messy from the dancing and what just happened. Still, it's not a bad look. I analyze the rest of my body, lifting the dress to examine my skin. My stomach's bruises are yellow and green, with some spots still light purple or red.

I've had Ian's bite mark on my wrist covered with makeup. The scratches on my arm have healed, except for a few deeper gouges that scabbed over.

In another few weeks, I'll be whole again.

Caleb opens the door, meeting my eyes in the mirror. He's naked. I drop my dress, letting it fall back down around my thighs.

He comes and stands behind me, touching his mark on my breast. It's covered by the dress, but he knows exactly where it is. His hand glides down my arm, closing over my bracelet. He wears his on the same arm.

"I'm really fucking glad you decided to wear your own version of a crown." He kisses my neck.

I tip my head to the side. I guess I didn't think about that implication. But the more I think about it, the more... *I like it.*

He peppers kisses down my shoulder, lifting my arm. His lips hover over the bracelet.

"Did you mean it?"

I shake my head. "Did I mean what?"

"That you wanted to marry me. When we were nine."

"We were eight," I murmur. "And yes, I did mean it. As much as I could've at eight years old."

Our eyes collide in the mirror again, and this time...

I avoid it. I scoot past him and grab a bottle of water from the mini fridge in the living room. My dress swishes around my legs, and I focus on that when I cross to the windows. We're high enough that there's no chance of anyone spying us.

Top floor.

Caleb's reflection appears behind me again. He takes the water bottle and sets it aside, then uses his foot to widen my stance. Slowly, he bends me forward. I automatically put my hands on the window to keep my balance.

He flips the skirt of my dress up and pushes into me without a word.

I bite my lip, trapping my whimper behind my teeth.

Two can play that game.

There's always a game between us.

He thrusts faster, stoking something hot between us. His hand reaches around me, and his fingers find my clit again.

It's sore. Everything is sore.

I bite my lip harder. He can't win this, too.

I push back to meet his pace. His finger on my clit, rubbing fast little circles, is insistent.

His other hand slides into my hair, keeping my head up. I see us in the reflection, my whole body moving with every

393

slam. And beyond us, a city that couldn't give a damn. Students filter out below us.

He changes angles, rolling his hips, and I can't take it anymore. I let out a whimper.

His hand moves from my hair to around my neck. He pulls me so I'm almost upright, then growls and picks up the pace. "So. Fucking. Perfect."

"I can't," I pant.

"Fuck," he growls, biting my shoulder. "Scream, Margo."

I do. I tip my head back and scream his name, abandoning all self-control. My legs tremble while the orgasm rolls through me. I squeeze my eyes shut.

He slams into me at a whole new angle, grunting into my neck. He jerks forward, burying himself all the way inside me, and comes with a hiss of breath.

We stand like that for a long moment. Eyes closed.

I'm so tired I can barely move.

He pulls out and takes off a condom I didn't notice him put on.

Slowly, I sink to my knees.

Caleb returns and comes over to me. He undoes the zipper of my dress, and it puddles on the floor around my legs. He lifts me out of it and pauses, staring at my breasts. "You have stickers on your nipples."

Oh, shit.

A laugh bursts out of me, as tired as I am, and peel them off. They hurt like a bitch, and Caleb can't hide his fascination.

When they're off, crumpled in a ball and tossed in the trash, he hooks his arm around my waist.

"A nap, then maybe we'll try this again," he says.

"Great," I mumble. "I can barely keep my eyes open."

He tucks us into bed and turns off the light. We're still naked—a fact he takes advantage of with his wandering hand. I press closer to him, raising my head.

"Kiss me," I say.

He places a soft kiss on my lips. It's exactly what I need.

I exhale, wrapping my arms around him, and within seconds, I'm out.

Chapter 40
Margo

Our alarm goes off at six-thirty.

Caleb rolls over me, smacking the 'off' button, and blinks down at me.

He's adorable when he's sleepy.

I don't dare tell him that, but I take a mental snapshot and file it away.

And then he shifts, and his erection brushes my leg. I stare at him, spreading my legs. It's too early for chitchat, but it isn't too early for this.

He looks over at the nightstand. I don't know why he does—we both already know there aren't any condoms left.

We woke up after a short nap and had sex. Then again, a little while later. That time, he stayed inside me until he got hard, and the whole thing repeated. We didn't sleep for long. I went down on him, but that... that turned into him fucking my mouth.

"Just pull out," I whisper.

He hesitates a split second, his gaze darting around my face, then slides into me.

We both groan.

It's quick and dirty. He flicks my clit until I fall apart. Once my spasms start, he pounds into me with fervor. He stills for a split second, then jerks back and comes on my stomach.

I reach down and stroke him, eliciting a groan from him. His cum is hot liquid on my skin, and it smears between us when he drops down on top of me.

"You felt fucking amazing." He kisses the hell out of me, his tongue invading my mouth.

We kiss until a pounding at the door interrupts us.

He scowls in that direction. To me, he says, "Get dressed."

He tugs on a pair of shorts and closes the door behind him.

I pause for a second, then rush for my clothes. Underwear, leggings, sports bra, t-shirt. It's all on in a matter of seconds, and I make sure my hair isn't crazy before I step out. The strands of pearls were yanked out sometime during our second fuck. I twist my hair up into a high bun, frowning at my reflection.

After brushing my teeth, I walk into the living room.

Riley sits on the couch, biting her nail. "Oh my God, Margo! First, amazing room. Second, this is an emergency—"

"Slow down," I mumble.

"Where's your phone?"

It was in the clutch. Where said clutch ended up, I don't know. "I'd have to look around."

She huffs, then whirls on Caleb. "I need to take her."

He raises his eyebrows. "You can keep the room, Ri. I've got an errand to run anyway." He comes over and kisses the top of my head. "I'll check out, so don't worry about it. Eli can give you a ride."

"Okay."

He grabs his bag and goes into the bathroom. When he reappears moments later, he's fully dressed. *Ugh.* I need at least a half hour to get my act together. He leaves, and Riley follows me into the bedroom.

She immediately starts laughing. "Jesus."

"What?"

"Smells like you had a *lot* of sex."

"Gross. But... true."

I collect my stuff, throwing it in my bag while Riley watches. I save the dress for last, smoothing it as I fold it over my arm. My fingers touch something that crinkles, and I suddenly remember the paper Claire had given me. I never even thought to mention it to Riley.

I pull it out and slip it into my leggings pocket, vowing to read it later.

Finally, I place the dress in my bag and zip it shut.

"Okay, I think that's everything."

"Except your phone." She's still gnawing at her finger.

"Did you try to reach me last night? Did something happen with you and Eli?"

"What? No. No, he's waiting for us in the lobby."

I shrug. "It was in the clutch with my ID. Maybe in the living room?"

We scour the place, and I finally find it under the dining table. How it got there, I'll never know. I'm about to get my phone, but Riley lays her hand on top of mine.

"Stop," she blurts out.

I stare at her. "You're acting *weird.*"

She shifts. "Remember that picture that got emailed around?"

Oh no.

"Um... there was a video."

Oh no.

I don't tell her I know there's a video. That would open up a whole different can of worms—particularly because, while she knew I got a strange text when I first started, I haven't told her about any of the following texts.

"It's bad," Riley whispers. "It'll be okay, though. I just... your phone might be blowing up, and I don't want you to freak out. In fact, you should probably just turn it off."

I shake my head. "I don't understand."

It's more for myself, directed at who I now consider my stalker, than Riley.

What did I do to push them over the edge?

"Who got the video?"

She hesitates.

I have to physically stop myself from getting angry at her. She's just being a good friend.

"Everyone," she blurts out. "Like, the school. And someone posted it on social media. And—"

I'm going to be sick.

The noises from that video—noises *I* made—play on repeat in my mind.

I rush to the bathroom, falling to my knees in front of the toilet. I throw up. The acid burns on my tongue, but my stomach doesn't settle for a few long moments.

Finally, I'm able to straighten. Riley hands me a glass of water, giving me a sympathetic look.

"Don't do that," I plead. "Don't pity me."

She grabs my toothbrush and toothpaste from my bag, placing it on the counter. "I'm not trying to pity you, Margo. You know I love you. I just hate that this is happening. *Again.*"

I nod. "Yeah. I just—"

"I've already reported the video. Eli did, too—"

"He saw it?" I drop the toothpaste and cover my eyes. I don't want to know how many people are watching me get finger-fucked by Caleb Asher. But if people I'm close with are seeing it? I can't show my face. I can't go back to Emery-Rose after that.

"He didn't," she says. "Once we realized what it was... No, we didn't."

I let out a shuddering breath.

She wraps her arms around me. "Let's get you home. There's no need to worry. The Bryans will probably let you take a few more days off, and the school board can get it removed..."

"Yeah." I find myself nodding along with her plan. "Good idea."

She smiles. "I'm full of good ideas."

We leave, and I lift my hood, just in case there are more students in the lobby. I'm not ready to deal with anyone's comments.

The backlash from the photo was bad, and the video will be even worse.

Eli's truck is out front, and I practically dive into his backseat. He throws me a glance, eyebrows raised.

"You okay?" he asks.

I force myself to smile, although I think it's more like a grimace. "Yes."

I wonder if Caleb knows yet. I doubt he had a chance to check his phone before he ran out of the hotel room. He would've told me.

Right?

I spot Caleb's car in the Bryans' driveway as we come up the street.

"Keep going," I tell Eli. Shock and dread twist through me.

He glances back at me. "What—"

"Keep. Going." I can't breathe. I automatically expect the worst. I shouldn't, because it's *Caleb*. The man who reminded me that we were fake married, who reminded me that I loved him as a kid. Who...

Riley twists around. "Is that—"

"Yes. Eli, drop me at the corner."

He groans. "What are you planning?"

"Nothing."

He pulls over, and I grab my bag, hopping out before they can advise against it.

"Keep your phone close, Riley. I'll call you later."

She nods, and I slam the door.

Eli drives away.

I cut through the neighbor's lawn and creep into the Bryans' backyard. I slip into the mudroom, holding the screen door to keep it from slamming. There's another door that leads into the kitchen, but I'm betting Caleb might be in there.

Sure enough, as soon as I press my ear to the door, I can hear what they're saying.

"We appreciate you trying to be candid, Caleb," Robert says. "But you haven't quite told us *why* you're trying to warn us about Margo."

"And forgive us for thinking so, but we thought you enjoyed Margo's company," Lenora adds.

Warn them about me?

My heart hammers.

"I'm sorry for not being direct," Caleb says. "It's just that... I thought her and I were it. And then earlier today, she put out a private video trying to destroy my credibility."

I cover my mouth with both hands. He thinks *I* leaked

that video? Like the picture, I'm sure he's going to be lauded for it.

No—he said he had to go on an errand. He didn't seem upset at all.

"So, this is revenge?" Robert asks.

"Not at all. Honestly, I was going to let sleeping dogs lie. This just proves that she isn't the girl I thought she was."

Silence.

"Your daughter..." Caleb pauses. "She died in a car accident, right?"

"That's right," Robert answers. His voice is faint.

"My aunt liked to gossip," Caleb says. "She said the car accident was caused by a drug overdose."

"We've never hid that fact," Lenora says. "Our daughter was troubled. I'd like to think we can spot the warning signs. That's why we foster teenagers, because sometimes they just need more guidance—"

"Was it cocaine?"

I wish I could see the expression on Caleb's face. If he regrets what he's saying. But I'd bet his face is the picture of innocence, because that's who he is: a good fucking liar.

"The fact of the matter is... your daughter's death is Margo's fault."

My heart stops.

"What? How?" Lenora demands. "Margo would've been *twelve* when Isabella died—"

"Margo was the cause of her mother's drug use," Caleb says.

Each word is a dagger in my heart.

"And because of her parents' split, Amber Wolfe had no choice but to resort to selling drugs. Cocaine, specifically. She sold it to anyone who had cash. College kids, high schoolers. She preyed on innocent lives because Margo—"

Lenora wails.

It's a haunting sound. Chills break out across my body, and I really, *really* wish that I couldn't hear it. I'd love nothing more than to scrub that noise from my brain.

"Margo's mom was responsible for your daughter's death, but everything circles back to your foster daughter," Caleb finishes. "I thought you'd want to know who was sleeping in your home every night."

I've heard enough.

I lift my bag and creep back outside. Hidden on the side of the porch, I pull out the newspaper clipping Claire had shoved at me.

The headline reads: Isabella Bryan in Fatal Car Crash

Late Saturday night, Isabella Bryan of Rose Hill, New York, was found in her flipped vehicle. Firefighters and EMTs pulled her out and brought her to a local hospital, but she was dead on arrival. Isabella has had problems with substance abuse, and doctors confirm that this was the cause of her accident. Her parents, Lenora and Robert Bryan, request privacy during this difficult time.

That's it.

A paragraph and a picture of the three of them. Farther down, there's one of just Robert and Lenora in a cemetery. My mother was the one who put them there.

They're never going to want me back now, because what Caleb said has to be true: my mom sold drugs to a teenager, and that teenager *died*. What're the odds that I'm placed with their family?

It's a sucker punch straight to my gut.

I hoist my bag higher and run through the neighbor's backyard. I don't have anywhere to go, but I sure as hell don't want them to find me snooping around their yard.

Not after that.

I get to the corner and grab my phone. It's the first time I've looked at it since before the dance.

Riley was right: it's blowing up. There are too many numbers texting me crude things.

I'm too far into shock to consider crying.

Caleb just...

My heart isn't working right.

I sink to my knees at the curb as his words replay.

It hurts like a knife burrowing into my chest. I can't stop it. I can't fight him.

Let's play a game, he told me. *First to give in loses.*

I lost, Caleb. My heart folded first. I thought it might be the kiss, but that... that was just the beginning.

I find a text from Claire from the middle of the night.

CLAIRE

Call me.

And when I didn't respond, she sent another.

I realized where I recognized Caleb from. He was talking to our foster parents before they got rid of us.

I shudder. The betrayal digs deeper. This isn't a new thing for Caleb... he's done this before. He's unwound my life, piece by piece.

Has Caleb ever let me out of his memory? Or is he responsible for every single transition, every bully, every fucking family that's passed me along?

His fucked-up games didn't start when I got back to Emery-Rose.

No, they started the minute I left.

I get a new text—this one from Unknown. I almost drop my phone. Even they couldn't have predicted Caleb's tricks. His betrayal. He's single-handedly ruined the best home I've ever known.

UNKNOWN

Run away, drug princess.

Way ahead of you, Unknown.

TO BE CONTINUED
in *Wicked Games*
Pre-order: http://mybook.to/fallenroyals2

Acknowledgments

Thank you so much for coming along on this wild ride! We're just getting started with Caleb and Margo.

I want to give a special big thank you to my friends, who didn't quite call me crazy for wanting to re-release this series. My editor and proofreader for going over the book again, some early readers for doing a reread (and even going so far as to read the original and the new one back-to-back!). I'm forever grateful to Najla Qamber & her team for doing such a wonderful job on my covers.

This series was the start of dark romance for me, and I was so thrilled to get to revisit it.

Thanks for reading!

xoxo,
    Sara

About the Author

S. Massery is a dark romance author who loves injecting a good dose of suspense into her stories. Originally from Massachusetts, she now lives in Southern California with her dog, Alice.

Before adventuring into the world of writing, she went to college in Boston and held a wide variety of jobs—including working on a dude ranch in Wyoming (a personal highlight). She has a love affair with coffee and chocolate. When S. Massery isn't writing, she can be found devouring books, playing outside with her dog, or trying to make people smile.

Join her newsletter to stay up to date on new releases: http://smassery.com/newsletter

Also by S. Massery

Hockey Gods

Brutal Obsession

Devious Obsession

Secret Obsession

Twisted Obsession

Fierce Obsession

Shadow Valley U (co-written with SJ Sylvis)

Sticks and Stones

SVU Book 2

Sterling Falls

#0 THRILL

#1 THIEF

#2 FIGHTER

#3 REBEL

#4 QUEEN

Sterling Falls Rogues

#0 TERROR

DeSantis Mafia

#1 Ruthless Saint

#2 Savage Prince

#3 Stolen Crown

More at http://smassery.com

Where to Find Sara

Thank you so much for coming along on these crazy boys' journeys with me.

If you like my stories, I'd highly encourage you to come join my Facebook group, S. Massery Squad. There's a lot of fun stuff happening in there, and they're who I go to for polls about future books (fun fact: some key details in this series is decided by their votes!), where I share teasers, etc!

My Patreon is also an awesome place to connect and get exclusive content! On release months, I do signed paperbacks. Plus, get ARCs, audiobooks, and artwork before the rest of the world. Find me here: http://patreon.com/smassery

And last but not least, here are some social media links for ya:

Facebook: Author S Massery

Where to Find Sara

Instagram: @authorsmassery
Tiktok: @smassery
Goodreads: S. Massery
Bookbub: S. Massery